A DARK AND HOLLOW STAR

ASHLEY SHUTTLEWORTH

Margaret K. McElderry Books

NEW YORK · LONDON · TORONTO · SYDNEY · NEW DELHI

MARGARET K. McELDERRY BOOKS

An imprint of Simon & Schuster Children's Publishing Division

1230 Avenue of the Americas, New York, New York 10020

This book is a work of fiction. Any references to historical events, real people, or real places are used fictitiously. Other names, characters, places, and events are products of the author's imagination, and any resemblance to actual events or places or persons, living or dead, is entirely coincidental.

Text copyright © 2021 by Ashley Shuttleworth

Jacket illustration copyright © 2021 by Christophe Young

All rights reserved, including the right of reproduction in whole or in part in any form.

MARGARET K. McELDERRY BOOKS is a trademark of Simon & Schuster, Inc.

For information about special discounts for bulk purchases, please contact Simon & Schuster Special Sales at 1-866-506-1949 or business@simonandschuster.com.

The Simon & Schuster Speakers Bureau can bring authors to your live event. For more information or to book an event contact the Simon & Schuster Speakers Bureau at 1-866-248-3049 or visit our website at www.simonspeakers.com.

Jacket designed by Laura Eckes

Interior designed by Hilary Zarycky

The text of this book was set in Adobe Garamond Pro.

Manufactured in the United States of America

First Edition

2 4 6 8 10 9 7 5 3 1

Library of Congress Cataloging-in-Publication Data

Names: Shuttleworth, Ashley, author.

Title: A dark and hollow star / by Ashley Shuttleworth.

Description: New York : Margaret K. McElderry Books, 2021. | Series: A dark and hollow star ; [1] | Summary: "A queer cast of characters—a half-fae teenager, a temperamental ex-Fury, a fae prince, and his brooding guardian—must track down a serial killer whose disturbing murders are threatening to expose the hidden faerie courts to the human world"—Provided by publisher.

Identifiers: LCCN 2020011475 (print) | LCCN 2020011476 (ebook) | ISBN 9781534453678 (hardcover) | ISBN 9781534453692 (ebook) |

Subjects: CYAC: Fairies—Fiction. | Alchemy—Fiction. | Serial murders—Fiction. | Murder—Fiction. | Lesbians—Fiction. | Fantasy.

Classification: LCC PZ7.1.S51834 Dar 2021 (print) | LCC PZ7.1.S51834 (ebook) | DDC [Fic]—dc23

LC record available at https://lccn.loc.gov/2020011475

LC ebook record available at https://lccn.loc.gov/2020011476

For Juli, who's been there for every adventure

AUTHOR'S NOTE

This book is a work that comes from an incredibly personal place; it is also a work that features fairly heavy subject matter that may be difficult/potentially triggering for some readers. It is vitally important that we destigmatize the discussion of mental health, depression, and suicide, especially among our youth. While books are one of the safest spaces we have in which to talk about these very real and serious issues that affect so many of us, it is also crucial that you—the reader—be fully aware of and consenting to that exploration. As such, please be advised of the content warnings listed below, provided for your discretion.

Content warnings: anger, arson, blood/gore, body horror (minor), death of a child, depression, disownment, divorce, drug use/addiction, grief/grieving, human trafficking, poverty, psychopathy, stalking, suicide (past, off-page), suicidal ideation, toxic relationship/manipulation, trauma/PTSD, racism, violence/gun violence

PROLOGUE

Alecto

~⌒~

The Immortal Realm of Chaos—Infernal Palace

THE FLOOR ALECTO KNELT on was a glittering sea of black marble flecked with diamond white. Such a perfect mockery of the night sky, this was the closest she'd felt to the heavens in some time. Admittedly, Alecto couldn't remember when she'd last found comfort in such a place, but it was strangely reassuring now to imagine she could sink into the starry stone beneath her and vanish altogether.

How wonderful it would be to vanish—to simply cease existing, and disappear.

Now that her revenge was complete, there was nothing left to tether her here, or anywhere else for that matter. She felt no guilt for what she'd done and no fear of whatever came next. Not even pain could rouse her from her apathy.

To ensure the safety of those who'd gathered for her trial, enormous iron stakes had been driven through the sleek membrane of her unfurled wings, pinning her to the floor. The touch of such a poisonous metal should have been excruciating, but Alecto felt it no more in her wings than she felt that same corrosive iron eating away at her shackled wrists—which was to say, not at all.

Alecto was facing death for her actions. She could still taste ashen bone in her mouth and smell burning flesh in the air. She could even hear the echoes of her rage reverberating from the yawning pit her soul had become. Yet for all of this, Alecto was at peace. She was *relieved*.

She hadn't been expecting that—not to this degree, at least.

She hadn't been hoping for it either.

She'd taken revenge, straightforward and simple, and hadn't acted with the fool's belief that vengeance would change anything. Tisiphone—her beloved sister, her dearest friend—would still be dead, and that was a truth Alecto could never recover from.

"Do you have anything to say for yourself, Erinys Alecto?"

Alecto raised her head.

An emotion clawed its way out of the darkness of her heart and shaped itself into the razor-wire parody of a smile.

"To say for myself?"

She laughed.

It was a hollow sound, an ugly sound, but it was hers. The laugh was fury of a different sort, and Alecto would make sure that it would be a sound these gathered powers would never forget.

Alecto slid her gaze to the throne—a throne that writhed with living tongues of flame and twists of billowing wind—and locked eyes with the goddess who sat there: Urielle, Goddess of the Elements, Lady of Chaos. Urielle was queen of the largest Infernal domain of the Immortal Realm. Urielle, Alecto's mother.

"Well," Alecto replied as her rasping laughter died off. "I think it's safe to say the title of Erinys is no longer mine."

Unease rippled through the guards, who lined the room like pillars. Murmurs rolled like waves from the rest of the crowd—so many people Alecto had once considered friends, now craning their necks to bear witness to her humiliation. Everyone liked a show. Loyalty meant surprisingly little to Alecto's people.

Beside the goddess stood Erinys Megaera, the only sister Alecto now had left—however much they disliked each other. As Alecto expected, there was no love for her in Megaera's gaze. No pity. Alecto would be replaced when this was over—so, too, would Tisiphone. The realm's respect for Alecto's grief would no longer delay what was inevitable. Other immortals would be trained to fill Alecto's and Tisiphone's roles, and the Furies would be three once again.

Perhaps Alecto should have cherished her eldest sister a little better, but there was no altering the past—she knew that well. Megaera might once have loved her, but that had been some time ago, and now all that shone in her steely glare was disgust.

Out of everyone, only Urielle remained impassive, though Alecto could see a torrent of emotions deep within her infinite black eyes.

"There is no humor in what you've brought before me," said Urielle, her voice as smooth as undisturbed water but hard and cutting as jagged stone. "You stand accused of murder, Erinys Alecto. You took eleven mortal lives without permission—lives unmarked for death. Your actions this night in the name of vengeance have not only violated the laws that govern our realms but also the very oaths you swore when you became a Fury. To these accusations, how do you plead?"

"To the crimes?" Alecto took no time for thought. "I plead not guilty."

Megaera snarled. "I *saw* you."

In the flare of her temper, her wings burst wide. The gathered crowd shrank back in a scattered shower of gasps. Beautiful things, those wings. Gossamer soft, neither leather nor feather, and black as beetle shells. They were great enough to span the room behind the throne. Alecto's wings had once been just as glorious. Now they were pierced and tattered and singed down to smoldering rags, like the sails of the gutted ship she'd left to haunt the waters.

"*I* was the one who dragged you from that ship you set ablaze— with Starfire, no less!" Megaera was trembling with rage. "Your tantrum tethered eleven souls to the ocean floor and to a flame even eternity cannot extinguish. *I* was the one who pulled you from the devastation you unleashed upon the Mortal Realm, and *I* was the one to witness your unrepentant delight in your victims' suffering. Do not deny the truth!"

"You mistake my meaning," Alecto drawled. "I freely admit to all crimes you accuse me of. I did it, yes. I simply don't feel guilty about any of it."

Megaera opened her mouth to retort, but Urielle silenced her with the wave of her hand. "The punishment for these violations is Destruction," Urielle continued.

Destruction, not death.

Immortals didn't die, they were Destroyed. Unmade. Their souls were ground down to dust and thrown back to the stars to be woven into something else—someone else—but not reborn, as mortals were.

For what she'd done, Alecto would be erased from existence altogether. It was almost a blessing.

"I'm happy enough with the destruction *I* caused to accept your gracious offer," she countered.

"Erinys Alecto!" At last, the goddess's emotionless mask broke. She rose from her violent throne and descended the dais, fiery sparks igniting at her heels with every step. In Urielle's anger, she filled the chamber entirely. The space around her flared lightning bright. Alecto winced, but she refused to drop her gaze. "I have made thee. I can unmake thee just as easily," the goddess declared. "Do you truly show no remorse for your crimes against *me*? You have no regret about seeing *my* Law—a Law that you swore to uphold—now broken at your feet?"

My daughter, you were meant for so much more than this.

Her mother's words were gentler in Alecto's head than how they were spoken, but they were no more welcome.

I am meant for whatever I choose, Alecto scathed in return. Aloud, she added, "Goddess Mother, I can unmake myself, and have."

For a moment, Urielle stood frozen. Then she sighed. "So be it."

The goddess raised a hand, and the shadows in the room began to twist away from the walls. "Erinys Alecto, you are hereby stripped of your name."

The shadows lashed out like angered cobras. Launching themselves at Alecto, they wound tightly around her body.

"You are stripped of your rank."

The shadows began to constrict. Alecto struggled. She grunted and groaned and gnashed her teeth. Her satisfaction with her revenge had placed her in the eye of her own storm—in a calm that had belied her rage—but she was sailing out of it now, back into the dark and thunderous tempest of her ever-simmering anger.

"You are stripped of the privilege of your office. You see fit to dole out punishment to mortals at your own choosing, and so your own punishment will be to live forever among them." Alecto blinked up at her in surprise, but Urielle wasn't done. "You are expelled from the Immortal Realm. You are expelled from the Sisterhood, and from my favor, and from my heart. I banish thee to the Realm of Mortals and tether your eternity to its soil."

At last, Alecto's storm broke free. *"No!"*

This wasn't what she'd wanted. She'd been counting on Destruction— on release from the torment inside her own head—not this *banishment* her mother was inflicting, this eternal torture, trapping Alecto forever in her anger and grief . . .

"I have never needed your name!" Alecto seethed. The shadows coiled around her throat, but she ignored them. "I have never needed *you*, you coward. You have failed, Goddess Mother!"

The tighter the shadows squeezed, the harder Alecto struggled. She threw her all into this fight, pitching forward with every ounce of might she could muster. In the process, her wings tore further around the spikes that kept them pinned down, but still she continued to rage. "You've *failed*. You've failed Tisiphone! You've failed *me*. I will *never* forgive what you allowed to take place—what you allowed to go unacknowledged and unpunished. You are no mother of mine, no goddess of mine!"

Alecto could only see in slivers now, but it was too late for the sorrow beginning at last to soften Urielle's expression.

When this sympathy was needed most—when Tisiphone had needed this understanding, and after, when Alecto had first come to the mother she'd once adored so fiercely, in grief so profound she'd hardly been able to speak—it had been withheld in favor of Law.

Alecto's actions were her own, she knew that full well, but if Urielle didn't see the hand she'd had in her daughter's fall from grace, Alecto didn't care to make her see it now.

It was done.

She was done.

Urielle bowed her head. "I did fail you, my daughter."

"Nausicaä," said Alecto.

Nausicaä. A beautiful, mortal name. "Burner of ships," it meant, and she couldn't think of a more fitting title. Her revenge had altered her in a way that could never be undone, and if they weren't going to Destroy her, Alecto—*Nausicaä*—would not preserve what she no longer was. She would wear her crimes like a badge of honor.

"Nausicaä," the goddess amended.

The brief glimmer of sadness in Urielle's gaze was the last thing Nausicaä saw before the shadows sealed themselves around her fully, but the storm inside her raged on. "I EXPEL YOU!" she bellowed. Though she had no way of knowing whether the goddess heard her, she continued to shout until stars burst behind her eyes and her consciousness began to fade. "I EXPEL YOU FROM *MY* FAVOR! I EXPEL YOU FROM *MY* HEART! I EXPEL YOU, AND I WILL NEVER LOVE YOU AGAIN FOR WHAT YOU'VE DONE TO ME!"

Forget that you loved me, if you must, but please . . . do not forget you loved at all, and do not forget you loved so fiercely it made you the best of your name.

Oh, Nausicaä wouldn't forget she'd loved her goddess mother.

She wouldn't forget she'd loved Tisiphone.

She would remember both, and in remembering, she would never allow herself to feel that love again. Much like that whaler and its disgusting crew—and among them the mortal who thought he could make fools out of Furies—all of them burning forevermore at the bottom of the North Atlantic Ocean, Nausicaä's rage would survive the ages, and it was all that she would be.

It wasn't until she found herself on her back, blinking up at the too-cheerful blue of the Mortal Realm's sky, that she realized she'd succumbed at last to the shadows.

She was no longer in the throne room of the Infernal Palace.

Her family, her former *friends*, the freezing starry marble . . . All were gone, but her mother's final words still echoed in her ears.

You still have it in you to be what the stars design, my daughter.

"Tch," she scoffed. Fisting the grass that carpeted the rolling plains of wherever in the Mortal Realm she'd been discarded, she ignored the tears that clung to her lashes like the dew around her.

It was no longer up to the stars to decide Nausicaä's fate—they'd lost that privilege in their treatment of Tisiphone. Her fate was now up to her, and if the oh-so-powerful deities weren't brave enough to Destroy her, she was going to make them regret letting her discover just how satisfying it was to watch things *burn*.

All was quiet at NevaLife Pharmaceuticals, and that was how Hero preferred it. He didn't like the bustle of day: the coming-and-going couriers with their jokes that weren't funny at all, but mean; the numerous doctors and research assistants who—with their college degrees and their salaried pay—lorded over the place like they were better than everyone else, particularly Hero; the general staff, who seemed to delight in making Hero's job more difficult, the way they treated the spaces he cleaned.

Hero was a janitor.

It wasn't considered a glorious job to many, but it was money he desperately needed.

He was twenty-eight years old with no family or partner to help make ends meet, and certainly no savings to allow him to pursue higher education in hope of finding a better career. When he wasn't unclogging toilets and mopping up spills, he worked at a local tech-support call center. He delivered flyers. He bagged groceries and retrieved wayward carts and cleaned up yet more spills at the grocery store closest to his one-bedroom apartment in a neighborhood that shouldn't cost as much to live in as it did. And still it wasn't enough. Still Hero struggled to pay all his bills and afford the little luxuries of life like food and clothing and deeply necessary medication.

The world was rough, but it was better when it was quiet . . . even if it was also a little lonely.

"And don't forget to lock the door when you leave this time, dumbass."

Hero nodded vigorously. Darren, his supervisor, was a short middle-aged man with an even shorter temper, brown hair, watery eyes, and the build of a high-school football star slightly gone to seed. Darren didn't like Hero, who was a little bit mousy, a lot a bit skinny, with wide eyes ringed by dark fatigue and black hair that made him seem sickly pale in contrast. Then again, no one liked Hero. Odd, they called him. Awkward. But he couldn't afford to get fired from another job because of this. And he couldn't let his increasing forgetfulness cost him so dearly again, not when he was already behind on last month's rent.

He was keen to keep Darren happy even if he'd much rather do something else—the bottle of bleach on his cart, for instance . . . Hero allowed himself a moment to fantasize the sound of Darren's scream if some of that chemical somehow found its way onto his face.

"What are you, a bobblehead? Stop nodding like that. You'll shake what's left of your brains loose, and I'll *really* have my hands full with you, then."

"S-sorry, sir," Hero stuttered.

Darren barked a laugh. "S-s-s-sorry, s-s-sir," he mocked. "Stuttering like some damn girl at every little thing. Man up, kid."

"Yes s-sir." Hero winced.

Darren shook his head. "Hopeless." He reached out to flick Hero's name tag and chuckled again. "*Hero*—what a joke. Remember, lock the fucking door, Superman."

And finally, he was gone.

Releasing a sigh, Hero sagged against his supply cart, taking a moment to collect himself.

It hadn't always been this way. Once upon a time, he'd had ambitions beyond finding a repellent that would actually keep cockroaches out of his apartment. Once upon a time, he hadn't had this stutter, his memory hadn't been so poor, and his sleep hadn't been plagued by nightmares and terrors, leaving him constantly tired. It wasn't until recently that any of this had started, that his already bad situation had taken an alarming turn for the worse, with random voices in his head and flashes of memories that couldn't be his . . .

9

and that's what the medications were for—those criminally expensive medications that forced him to choose between mental health and things like electricity.

Hero kicked a wheel of his cleaning cart hard enough to topple several of its contents. There was no use getting upset about things when nobody cared, and he figured it could always be worse. "But it could be better," he muttered.

"Significantly so, I imagine."

Hero startled so violently he almost collided with his cart.

A man stood behind him where there hadn't been a man before— hadn't been *anyone*, just a dimly lit hallway. Hero's first impression of him was that he was tall. It wasn't the ordinary tall that belonged to the other tall people. It was a tall that, if Hero had ever thought about it before, he would have attributed to gods.

His face was . . . beautiful. Splattered with unusual, silvery freckles, like specks of starlight, and his eyes were so bright a green they gleamed like acid. Half of his wild gunmetal hair hung all the way to his waist, while the other half had been shaved to the skull. He was willow lean but strong, and his long-fingered left hand was capped with lethal claws. Hero had never seen anything like this man with all the presence of a shadow in his tight black pants and an elaborate black jacket, studded and gilded with yet more silver and buckles and elegant chains. It was possible he *was* a god, all this considered—even more likely, though, was that he wasn't real at all.

Hero closed his eyes.

It wasn't the first time he'd seen something that wasn't there at second glance—bizarre creatures with wings and horns and blue-tinted skin or bustling shop fronts that were actually just abandoned buildings—and usually these sights vanished within a blink. But when Hero opened his eyes again, the beautiful man was still there, and he was grinning.

"Hello," Hero greeted. He didn't know what else to say. "Can I . . . help you? I don't th-think you're supposed to be here."

The man laughed. It was a sound like creaking floorboards. "Oh no, you're absolutely right, I really am not! But then . . . you aren't supposed to be here either."

Hero bristled. "Of course I am. I'm the janitor."

"Mmmm, yes, you are, aren't you." The way this man looked him over made Hero shiver, despite the heat. To be *seen* in such a way by someone Hero would never expect to notice someone like *him* . . . "The janitor—one who turned down full scholarships to very impressive schools because it suited your negligent mother better to have you at home taking care of your siblings, and you were oh so desperate to please her. The janitor—one who understands much more of what goes on here than he lets on, who devours whole textbooks on scientific theory and likes to put to *experiment* the things he learns from them."

Oh hell, was this man some sort of undercover cop? Hero paled. He thought of the storage unit that served as his makeshift lab in the next neighborhood over, where nobody asked any questions so long as his payments were timely. "Listen, those animals were already dead," he lied. "I found them on the side of the road! I didn't do anything wrong, I was just—"

"You've been having some trouble lately, yes?" The man cut him off, his grin growing sharper. "Headaches . . . sleeplessness . . . lapses in memory . . . hallucinations and vivid dreams and things that feel familiar, but shouldn't?" He sighed then, but the action lacked sympathy. It only seemed to fuel his amusement. "The stutter—an uncommon side effect, I admit, but there have been other ironborn like you who've responded similarly to having their magic suppressed . . . to being Weighed by the Fae High Council and found wanting, power locked away, only for it to grow stronger just a little bit later than expected and *rebel* against its confines."

The Fae High Council?

Weighed?

Hero had a lot of questions.

Who was this man? How did he know so much about him? What

was he even talking about? He didn't look like a police officer, but what else could he be, if not that? What Hero said aloud, though—and very carefully—was, "What do you mean by 'magic'?"

A warm and pleasant tingling washed through him at the mere mention of the word—a memory, barely there, only just out of reach.

The man's grin had spread across the whole of his face now, and it was terrible. *He* was terrible. He was beautiful in a way that was difficult to look at, but at the same time horrifyingly wraithlike in a way that disfigured that beauty entirely. By all means, he was the very sort of person who should make Hero's anxiety shoot through the roof, and yet . . . Hero was nothing but calm.

"You know, I think I'd rather show you," the man said, and took a step toward Hero. He reached out a claw-tipped finger and tilted Hero's name tag.

"Hero. Your life has been so hard. Cast out by your family, adrift in a world you were never meant for, your cunning and brains and *passion* wasted on tending to other people. Tired . . . hungry . . . *poor* . . . I took your magic, those ten years ago, by order of those I'm bound to serve. But what if, like you, I've grown tired of service? What if I could give that magic back? What if I could restore you to your proper role, make you that *hero* you were clearly born to be? What, then, would you do for me?"

If this was anyone else, Hero would have laughed and brushed them off as insane.

This talk of magic? It was something a therapist would prescribe him more medication to cure, were he actually able to afford either. But there was a look in the man's eyes, a gravity in his air, a tone in his voice—he wasn't leading Hero on. Despite his teasing, this wasn't a joke; he was serious, and above all else, for the first time in far too long, Hero felt like someone was actually *listening*. Everyone Hero talked to about his problems seemed to think it was all in Hero's head, but here was someone who not only acknowledged them as real but could possibly explain their cause, and that was . . . well, it was very tempting. Hero would readily accept the wild improbability that magic existed if it meant getting to the root of *why* his health was so rapidly deteriorating.

Besides, this was the very thing countless others like him dreamed of, finding out they were meant for greater things, that the world possessed *magic*, and they themselves did too. It should be impossible, but this man . . . the way he'd so suddenly *appeared* out of nowhere . . .

What if . . .

Hero eyed his mysterious intruder.

He took a breath and released it slowly.

"I'm listening," he said, and for the first time in years, he stood tall; his voice didn't tremble; his hands didn't shake; his head was clear and his focus sharp.

The mysterious man swept an arm toward the door.

This time, when Hero left through it, he left it unlocked on purpose.

CHAPTER 1

Arlo

~⌇~

Present Day
The Mortal Realm—Toronto Fae Academy, Canada

THE FLOOR THAT ARLO stood on was a glittering sea of white marble flecked with charcoal black. So heavily polished, every flaw and feature had been scrubbed from its surface, and left behind was an icy gloss that nothing—not even the dying sunlight streaming through the glass-dome ceiling—could ever warm.

Unfortunately, the same could be said for the Fae High Council.

Eight proud fae from the Four Courts of Folk made up this panel of judges. One each from the factions of Seelie Winter, Summer, Autumn, and Spring—those folk who drew power from day and most valued the qualities of grace and responsibility in their people. One each from the factions of UnSeelie Winter, Summer, Autumn, and Spring—those folk who drew power from night and were known for their indulgence and their cunning.

And all were staring down at Arlo as if she were a bug beneath their boot.

In Arlo's opinion, there was no real difference between the Seelie and UnSeelie fae, no matter what each group liked to think. The stony faces before her, for instance, were all the same—as cold and hard as the marble under her feet.

All eight of these representatives had been chosen to uphold the High King's laws. Not one of them was known for displays of compassion. Facing them now for their judgment drove home that this meeting was little better than a formality: all eight minds had already made their unanimous decision on the matter of Arlo's "suitability" for the magical world long before she'd come to plead her case.

It was safe to say that her Weighing was not going very well.

"It isn't a matter of lineage," said Councillor Sylvain, the Seelie representative of Spring.

Tall and lithe, his numerous years were yet unable to conquer his sinewy strength. His voluminous emerald and turquoise robes, fastened by gleaming gold, did little to soften the severe cut of his glamoured ivory face.

"No one is questioning your bloodline, Miss Jarsdel," he continued dismissively. "You are Thalo Viridian-Verdell's daughter; of that there is no dispute. What we question here today is whether or not it matters."

Arlo already knew the answer to that question.

In the eyes of the High Council, the only thing that mattered was that half of Arlo's heritage was human. The fact that the other half had come directly from a royal fae family—*the* royal family, the family that currently sat as head of the magical community above even the heads of all the other Courts—was actually a mark against her. The fae were quite proud of their undiluted bloodlines, and the very long line of the Viridian family comprised only that—fae. There were no faerie relatives—those folk who possessed some animal or natural trait like bark for skin or leaves for hair. The Viridians certainly had no human relatives either, not until Arlo's mother had married one, and then shortly after had given birth to Arlo. At least Arlo herself looked *similar* to the fae; she shuddered to think how much worse she'd be treated right now if her magical heritage came from anything else.

Arlo was the first ironborn royal in a family whose "purity" predated the Magical Reform, when the Courts hadn't even been thought of, let alone formed, and all that had existed were the warring Seelie and UnSeelie factions. Unfortunately, she'd inherited very little of her mother's side of the family. She was about as magical as a box of lemons and had been so overwhelmed trying to keep up with the others at her local faerie elementary that her mother had taken pity on her and moved her to a human school. The Council cared an awful lot about Arlo's background—the problem was, it wasn't in the way that would help her.

Working to conceal her wince, Arlo forced her gaze level with the Council's collective stare. Her eyes—as bright and hard as jade—were one of the few things about Arlo that made it impossible for anyone to refute her ties to the Viridian family. But in moments like these, she wished she'd inherited her mother's skill for cutting those green eyes into a glare.

"It . . . it *should* matter that I'm a Viridian," Arlo heard herself say, in a voice made small by nausea and nerves. "My magic might not be very strong, I might have much more of my father's iron blood than you'd like, but I can still alter and conceal my appearance with a glamour just fine, and I possess enough of the Sight to see through the glamours of other folk as well . . ."

The speech was something her mother and cousin had helped her prepare. But Arlo knew that it would do no good to try to pretend that she was anything other than terribly unremarkable. The only exception to this was the strength of her ability to sense the magic around her. But this trick was something all fae could do, and however stronger Arlo suspected *her* command of this ability was, it wasn't going to win her many points today. Her overall power was woefully weak, but she *did* have the bare minimum needed to qualify for common magical status in their community. If she kept the Council on the facts, they had to grant her this, at least.

"You possess less talent on the cusp of adulthood than what a goblin infant can perform by instinct," Councillor Siegel—Seelie representative of Autumn—interposed. Her eyes were hard as amber as they fixed on Arlo, her tone eviscerating. "Furthermore, you have reached eighteen years with only minimal grasp on the rudiments of magic, having spent your education thus far under human tutelage.

Tell me, Miss Jarsdel, what is there for you to miss should the Council rule against you?"

Arlo's throat dried up like the colorful leaves woven into the Councillor's robes.

They were going to reject her status even though she had enough magic and very much wanted to remain a member of the magical community.

"Councillor Siegel," she pleaded. "Please, you . . . you can't! If you rule against me, if you lock away my powers and erase my memories . . . my family . . . my mother, and my cousins . . . I'd forget them! If you rule against me, I'll be missing the largest part that makes me *me*."

There was so much for Arlo to miss if the Council not only denied her fae citizenship but also inclusion in the magical community as a whole. Fae citizenship, with its isolationist rules and responsibilities, was not something she was sure she even wanted, but she knew without a doubt that she didn't want to be expelled from magic altogether. She didn't want to forget the truth about her family any more than she wanted to forget that magic had ever survived the collapse of human memory that it had existed.

Councillor Siegel raised a fine chestnut brow. "Quiet your theatrics, Miss Jarsdel. You would still be you, and you would not forget your family. You'd forget only what is unnecessary for you to remember. Your father remembers you still, does he not?"

Her father.

Marriages between fae and humans had to be approved by the Courts, but in this approval was a caveat: if the marriage ended, the human party had to forfeit what they'd learned of the magical community. It had been Arlo's father's decision to file for divorce. He'd given up his memories freely because, as far as Arlo understood, he'd grown a vast contempt for magic and those who had anything to do with it.

Her father remembered who she was, yes.

Arlo wouldn't say they had a good relationship, though—not with

18

the constant, nagging fear in the back of her head that her own father would hate her too, if he ever remembered why he should. And on top of that was the exhaustion that came with ensuring she never let anything about the magical community slip in front of him or any other human. Arlo didn't want anyone else in her family to know what that felt like any more than she wanted to give up something that had been a part of her life for a full eighteen years.

And she had to believe the Council couldn't be that unnecessarily cruel.

"Yes, My Lady, he does *remember* me, but—"

An air of finality bled from the stands. Arlo's desperate attempt to explain herself failed with her courage.

"If you have nothing else to say in your defense, Miss Jarsdel, perhaps the Council may now move on with this hearing?" Councillor Siegel said.

Arlo could only stand and stare, distress spreading through her like an anesthetic.

Councillor Sylvain opened his mouth to reclaim the floor and announce his verdict—when the door behind Arlo suddenly burst open. She jumped, spinning around to face the source of this disturbance as the Council rustled in irritation behind her.

"Can you *believe* Sunday traffic?" the intruder said by way of greeting.

Arlo's relief was so profound that it nearly dragged her to the floor.

Celadon Cornelius Fleur-Viridian—Arlo's first cousin, once removed, and youngest of her great-uncle the High King's three children—was brilliance and mischief in equal measures. In many ways, he was also the worst role model a freshly turned eighteen-year-old girl could find, but he was the closest thing Arlo had to a brother, and even though he was a couple of years older than her, the molasses rate that fae aged meant there was little difference in their maturity.

"High Prince Celadon!" Councillor Sylvain spluttered, both indignant and begrudgingly deferential to his much younger superior.

"This hearing is a closed affair, restricted to the Council and Miss Jarsdel only. You are out of line, Your Highness. I must insist, with all due reverence, that you take your leave at once."

Arlo continued to watch as Celadon crossed the marble sea, striding purposefully toward her.

For all that the High Prince delighted in ruffling the feathers of aristocracy, there wasn't anyone she knew who could turn more heads.

Of all the races of folk, the fae were the ones who most closely resembled humans in their appearance (though they insisted it was the humans who resembled *them*). This likeness was exaggerated into absurdity by their overwhelming beauty, but even among the fair folk, Celadon was exceptionally striking. As a full-blooded member of the Court of Spring, he was tall and lean, with fair white skin and features sharp as new-cut glass. As a Viridian, he was recognized by the bowlike curve of his lips, his jade eyes, and russet hair, which curled around his nape and ears almost exactly as his father's did.

Like all fae of royal blood, there was a glow beneath his skin. Even through his glamour, it shone greenish soft as setting twilight, a color that marked him UnSeelie. If Arlo's inheritance had been stronger, she'd wear that same glow, but as it were, only their eyes marked their relation.

This was better than nothing, and despite the things Arlo had inherited from her father—her burnt-red hair, her underwhelming height, and the sturdy width of her build—Celadon had never once treated her as anything less than a true Viridian. It filled Arlo with teary relief to see Celadon, blithe as ever, wafting into the room in his tight jeans and crisp sage button-down, as usual looking like he'd just walked off the set of some glamorous photo shoot.

Sylvain was right, though. Even a prince was no exception to the rules.

Turning back to face the Council, Arlo could tell they were deeply unimpressed.

"Of course, I would be happy to remove myself from your affairs,"

Celadon chimed, congenial down to the gentle smile that spread across his face. "I'm sure you'd all prefer to get back to discussing more important matters like this"—he raised his wrist and tapped the screen of his Apple Watch—"especially since you've already had plenty of time with my cousin's Weighing."

From his watch, a sound clip began to play from a video that had gone viral in their community only days ago.

"—*Do something, or we* will. *You will not stamp us out. You will not silence our voice. If the Courts continue to ignore this issue for what it really is, the Assistance will only grow bolder in our attempt to reveal your corruption! Your power comes from your people. I advise you to start showing some care for them instead of just yourselves.*"

Arlo stared, hardly daring to breathe as she watched the Council's reaction to Celadon's audacity.

The Assistance . . .

The magical community had invented all sorts of ways to bend human technology to suit their needs, but the Assistance—a growing underground group of vigilantes devoted to the protection of the common folk—was bold in how they used it. In light of growing rumors about a series of ironborn murders throughout the magical world—and the fact that the High King didn't seem to be doing much about them—the Assistance had taken to posting guerrilla broadcasts about the murders on human sites like YouTube. The UnSeelie Spring Court now had an entire division dedicated to searching out and removing these videos before humans started growing suspicious that they were more than some hoax.

Unnecessary, many in the faerie community whispering behind their hands, and Arlo had to agree. *The High King cares more about rooting out the Assistance than he cares about finding who's killing his folk . . .*

"An ironborn boy was found dead in British Columbia," said Celadon, with far less amiability than moments prior. "And even though this is still far from Toronto, the situation has now moved right into the High King's own backyard. I'm certain the Assistance is wrong. Surely you're as concerned about these murders as the rest of us."

The Council shifted uncomfortably, both at Celadon's implication of negligence with the murders and at the reminder that the Assistance wasn't as easily rooted out as they'd originally hoped when the group first started attracting wider attention. In response, Arlo's own unease ratcheted higher, fearing what this not-so-subtle accusation would do to her chances of a favorable outcome in this Weighing.

When rumblings of the murders started, the Courts insisted that the victims were human, not ironborn, and therefore not their concern. But when it became clear that the dead had, in fact, been ironborn and the Courts still did nothing, tensions between the ironborn, faerie, and fae communities grew to an all-time high.

If the most recent case had indeed occurred right here in Canada—in territory that belonged to UnSeelie Spring—their government could no longer afford to do nothing. The Fae High Council would be forced into searching out possible culprits; they had enough to keep them occupied without grilling Arlo for what was now twice as long as her Weighing should have taken, but throwing their failures in their faces and rushing them along probably wasn't the best way to force their meeting's conclusion—certainly not, given the look on most of the Councillors' faces.

"No," Celadon continued on, "I only came to collect my cousin. It *is* her birthday, after all, and her family would like to spend what little time you've left her now to celebrate this fact." He lifted his watch higher to exaggerate this point, then shook his head despairingly. "Apologies for the interruption, Councillors. I wish every one of you a wonderful night."

It would never be that simple, even if Celadon hadn't just scolded them all like children. The High King himself could come to Arlo's aid right now and she doubted it would make a difference. But Celadon reached for her wrist anyway and started pulling her toward the door.

Councillor Sylvain shot up from his seat, a blue flush bleeding through his glamour to heat his face. "High Prince Celadon!" The Councillor's words were more like thunder.

Celadon kept Arlo's wrist in his grasp but angled around once again to face the stands. "Councillor Sylvain," he returned, the reply spoken light as air, yet somehow just as gravid as the mood of the room.

"You seem to be laboring under the delusion that our business here is concluded."

"It's not? Forgive me, Councillor, but your inspection of my cousin has worn out the hour it was meant to take and now runs dangerously close to an interrogation."

Councillor Chandra rose from her seat, displeasure etched into her stunning sand-brown face at the thinly veiled accusation in Celadon's statement. "Weighing the worth of an ironborn child is no trivial matter, Your Highness."

"I beg your pardon—the *worth*?"

Chandra was unflinching.

"The laws to which we must adhere may seem harsh, but they're our laws for a reason. Arlo Jarsdel's case is not simple. An ironborn girl with little to no magic will find our world difficult at its kindest. It's better, no, to set them on the path that will help them best flourish? To trim away the excess knowledge that would do them no good anyway? We've made these laws to keep our people safe, Your Highness. You know this."

Celadon allowed silence to infuse the room a moment longer than what was comfortable for anyone. Even Arlo shifted at his side, her heart beginning again to flutter in panic.

They hadn't said it outright, but this was the closest they'd come in this entire meeting to announcing their verdict—to condemning Arlo to a fate she'd never choose if her life were actually up to her.

"Safe?" Celadon glanced at Arlo, incredulous. When he turned back to the Council, he was frowning. "You confuse me, Councillor

Chandra. You speak as though you're set to rule Arlo expelled."

The umber in Chandra's eyes flashed at the unspoken challenge. "She is too human."

"I'm sure it hasn't escaped your omniscience that her mother is niece to my father, the High King? Arlo *is* human. She is also *fae.*"

"Be that as it may, this counts for very little where Miss Jarsdel's power is concerned." Arlo's stomach took a dive for the floor. Gaining momentum, Chandra continued, "Her father's blood dilutes too much. She has magic, yes, but so little of it that she may as well not have it at all. While our deliberation might seem like prejudice to you, Your Highness, you must understand that there is much more for Miss Jarsdel to gain in pursuing her humanity than there is for her in chasing the formidable shadows of her mother's family."

"*Enough,*" Celadon commanded.

More often than not, the world looked at Celadon Viridian as though he were a pampered princeling barely out of the throes of adolescent dramatics. And at times he was, especially when in the mood to be difficult, but on the whole, this image was something he'd purposefully cultivated. This image meant that people (unwisely, and often to their own detriment) assumed he was more than a little vapid. It felt a bit like winning when he shed it now to pin the Fae High Council with a look that made them visibly falter.

"What Arlo chooses to chase is her prerogative—and is, in fact, the law you seem to set your store so firmly by. You've already stripped her of one avenue by forbidding alchemy, the talent that would have come most naturally to her as a child of both magic and iron. No doubt she's demonstrated the minimum requirement of aptitude in *other* areas to satisfy the lofty standards of our government? And you may dismiss it as common, but I would stake my life on her ability to sense another's magical signature as far beyond what you, the Council, are collectively able. However scant, everyone in possession of magic must be granted the protection and guidance of the Courts should they choose to submit themselves to our rule. It's her *choice,*

Councillors, not yours—something you all seem to have forgotten."

He paused a moment to fix his glare on each of the Councillors in turn, and Arlo felt her breath catch painfully again in her chest. Celadon was steering the conversation back to the argument he'd helped her form, and was doing so with much more conviction than Arlo's nerves would ever have allowed. Not for the first time, she found herself wishing she had a little more of this brand of bravery for herself.

"If that isn't enough to satisfy your misgivings, let me remind you of something else: it counts a great deal that your suppliant today is the blood of House Viridian. I, myself, as an example, was a late bloomer. *Me*, the faeborn son of High King Azurean. I didn't begin to demonstrate *any* affinity for air—that element of *my* Court—until Maturity hit nearly two years ago, when I turned nineteen. And it was only months ago that I discovered I possessed a Gift in addition to that affinity."

Shifting broke out in the stands as the Council no doubt realized where Celadon's argument was leading. Arlo was just as uncomfortable.

"As you know," Celadon continued, "we base the ironborn Maturity timeline on the human standards of puberty. It's expected that their magic will develop before the age of eighteen, but that isn't the way for the folk, is it? That isn't the way for fae, many of whom can only play around with bursts of breezes or electric sparks or puffs of flame before our own coming-of-age, which can happen any time between eighteen and twenty-five."

Arlo wanted to beg him to stop—to remind him she was *just Arlo*, and while Celadon might have been so clear an exception, she clearly wasn't—but her growing discomfort had rendered her speechless.

Celadon ignored her obvious embarrassment. "For most fae, this tiny elemental magic is all they're ever able to do, on top of the basic Sight and glamour all folk should be able to wield. Not every fae even comes into a true elemental Gift, correct? We don't all possess the required strength to do things like manipulate others by the water in their bodies, or make weapons out of elements, or pull secrets from the air. Has it not occurred to any of you that it isn't Arlo Jarsdel's humanity keeping her from her inheritance, but proper fae biology?"

Finally, Arlo broke her silence. *"Cel!"* she whispered urgently, tugging on her cousin's arm. This topic was nothing they hadn't already gone over ad nauseam, but Arlo wasn't entirely sold on Celadon's vehement insistence that she could yet be fully fae. It was a point he wouldn't budge on when it came up in conversation. "Cel, I don't think now is the time to bring this up. We really don't have anything to back this claim. I'm not—"

"Now is the *perfect* time to bring this up," Celadon countered under his breath. "Anything we can use, Arlo. Remember?"

Anything they could use to win a pass from the Council, they would. That had been their determination going into this hearing. But playing a card Arlo wasn't even sure she held seemed a lot like making a promise she'd never be able to deliver on. With people like the fae, a bad promise was tantamount to a lie, and that was one more thing that would make her stand out as unsuitable, because while the folk *could* tell lies, they avoided doing so with every bit of distaste as they avoided iron.

"Okay, but just . . . please don't start shouting at the people currently considering kicking me out of the 'family business,'" she breathed, trying to inject some levity into the moment on the chance it would trick her panic into receding.

It didn't.

Tension churned in the room following Celadon's speech. Councillor Sylvain waved a hand through the air. "Look at her!" Sylvain seethed. "The blood in her veins is red, not blue—not *fae*—and she possesses none of the traits that would make her one of us. She is *human*, High Prince Celadon, and we cannot make exception for this simply because you enjoy throwing your favor around for attention."

A gasp erupted from the stands.

Several Councillors turned in horror on Sylvain.

Arlo gaped at him, his face drained down to silvery white in realization of the extreme disrespect he'd let slip for someone so important as his High Prince. "Thank you, Briar Sylvain," said Celadon, his tone as bland as his smile, but the threat in both was unmistakable. His green eyes flashed. "I was starting to think you weren't *brave* enough to say to my face the things you whisper behind my back."

His unfortunate comment aside, Arlo wasn't surprised by the content of Sylvain's outburst. The ironborn had earned their name in reference to the oxidization of iron that turned a human's blood red once met with open air. Fae and faerie blood didn't possess iron. It ran blue even when spilled. And enough fae still regarded it as a deep betrayal that their blood should blend with humans' at all, let alone to the point that it changed its hue, that this prejudice persisted even now—Sylvain a clear example.

But many more had stopped putting such importance on the color of blood, and it was considered abhorrent behavior on anyone's part to do so anymore, but especially a member of the Fae High Council. It was also the very *worst* thing to say in front of a powerful prince he'd just insulted, whose personal time had long been devoted to advocating for ironborn rights. And not only that, but in this current climate of unease, if word got out that one of the Council's own had displayed such elitist behavior . . . Arlo didn't know what would happen.

Nayani Larsen rose from her seat at long last, taking the floor away from the disgraced Councillor Sylvain in an attempt to contain the situation. As Larsen was Minister of the Council, it was odd to Arlo that the UnSeelie representative of Spring seemed to be the kindest of the group—if only because she wore a genuine expression of indignation on Arlo's behalf in her deep hazel eyes and warm tawny face. "The Council apologizes for Lord Sylvain's remark and assures you it will *not* go unpunished." Her nostrils flared, as though she'd dearly like to expand on her obvious contempt for her fellow Spring representative's wording and was only just managing to hold herself back. "We mean no disrespect to you *or* Miss Jarsdel, and you are, of course, correct,

Your Highness. This *is* Miss Jarsdel's decision. She has demonstrated enough inherited magic to have earned her place in the Courts. You must agree, however, that she has not given us cause to grant her higher status—it would be abuse of our power to cede her the right to fae standing when she has met none of those requirements."

"Save, of course, that she *is* fae, and born of one of the Eight Founding Houses," Celadon replied irritably.

Councillor Larsen nodded. "Save that she is fae, and born of one of the Eight Founding Houses. This the Council will not ignore."

Only her husband, the man at Councillor Larsen's side—short by fae standards, golden-tanned and very blond—showed no surprise at her words. The rest looked up at their Headship in confusion.

"Arlo Jarsdel."

Arlo felt the moment all eyes in the room transferred their focus to her.

If she'd found it difficult to breathe before, it was nothing compared to her dizziness now, being thrust back into the Council's spotlight.

"Y-yes, Minister?"

"You have, as our law dictates, a choice: You may submit to your human heritage and surrender your knowledge of the Courts' existence. Should you wish it, however, your sufficient inheritance of magic affords you the option of keeping this knowledge and retaining your citizenship in the UnSeelie Court of Spring. Your fae status will not be recognized, but you will be permitted a place in the magical community."

Relief flooded Arlo, filling her up with a tingling sensation a bit like needles prickling her skin, feeling trying to return to her limbs. She couldn't really believe what she was hearing, that after everything she'd gone through tonight, this was actually ending in something other than her expulsion.

Arlo's decision hovered on her tongue. She already knew what she wanted to choose, and she was moments from blurting it out, but Councillor Larsen was not yet finished.

"*However*, we present to you a third option. A compromise, as it were. In light of the family from which your magical inheritance comes, the Council shall recognize the possibility of—to use the High Prince's term—'proper fae biology.' You are not the first ironborn child of royal fae parentage, and none yet have followed the standard cycle of fae Maturity. But in deference to our High King's House, we shall extend to you the option of deferring this decision to a later date."

Shock painted itself even clearer across the Council.

Arlo felt more dazed than she had all evening.

They would put this hearing off until a later date? They were actually going to humor Celadon's desperate scramble for Arlo to be granted full fae status and a place in the Viridian line?

"I . . . *really?* Until when, Your Headship?"

"Should you choose it, the Council will reconvene this hearing on the day that marks the start of your twenty-sixth year. At that time, you will resubmit for Weighing, and if your fae inheritance has manifested as it should, you will be allowed the full privilege and status of the royal blood that runs within your veins. However, if Maturity has not found you by this time, your choices shall revert to what they are now: human, or common magical citizen."

"And what does she do until then?" a new voice at the back of the room inquired.

Unable to help herself, Arlo turned around.

There, in the doorway still left open after Celadon's entrance, was Arlo's mother, Thalo.

Thalo and Celadon looked eerily alike, despite the fact they were only first cousins. Her mother looked so much younger than her forty-two years, and with the same twilight-glow complexion, willowy height, russet hair, and lovely features as Celadon, it was a fair assumption to make that they were siblings, when in fact it was the High King and Thalo's mother—the princess Cyanine—who were brother and sister.

Three other fae, sharply dressed and equally curious about these unusual proceedings, were gathered around the edges of the threshold, peering into the room. They quickly pulled up straight when they realized Thalo had drawn attention to their spying—most likely, they were the staff tasked with keeping this hearing private.

Councillor Larsen raised a brow.

No one thought twice about *Celadon* deciding rules were meant for other people, but from Thalo, who was the High King's Sword—General of his Royal Guard—and Head of the Falchion Police Force, they expected a little better. "Until then," Larsen continued gracefully, "we shall withhold her adult status in the Courts and allow her to continue as she has lived these past eighteen years—a probationary member of the folk and a spectator only in our affairs until her next Weighing."

Thalo turned her focus back to Arlo, hope beaming through her otherwise guarded expression. "It's Arlo's decision," she said. Her breathlessness spoke volumes.

"Yes," said Gavin Larsen, Nayani's husband and Seelie representative of Summer, looking nothing but amused by the proceedings. "And what *is* Arlo's decision?"

What *was* Arlo's decision?

The Council could erase her memories and she would walk out of this room as good as human for the rest of her unnaturally long life. That was the very opposite of what she wanted.

She could take the boon of common citizenship and allow her life to get on with itself as originally planned. She wouldn't hold the glorious rank of fae, or be allowed to study at fae universities, or take a position in the palace any higher than general help. But she'd at least have a place in both her parents' worlds, and with all her memories intact.

Or, this new third option: deferment.

Deferment meant she would have to prolong her adolescent purgatory, kept out of everything that was Court-related until the Council reconvened in eight years' time, all for the *prospect* of full fae citizenship. And even if she did turn out to be fae, it would mean more secrets in her life and less contact with a world she didn't want to lose entirely, but she would be *accepted*. She would no longer be a disappointment to the majority of the people she loved. She would be a recognized royal, allowed to live in the palace, and the full privilege of fae life would be hers to enjoy—the parties, the studies, the decadence, the *respect* . . .

But in Arlo's opinion, there were only two paths her future could conceivably take. The Council was surely humoring Celadon and the possibility that he could make their lives miserable for what Sylvain had said. It was highly unlikely that Arlo was *too fae* to possess any magic right now. No matter how or what she and her family had tried over the years to coax it out of her, she'd simply never shown a hint of promise in that area.

But *what if*, her heart seemed to whisper.

What if . . .

"I choose to defer the Weighing."

The decision burst from her mouth in the first firm declaration she'd made all day, speaking to a hope she'd long kept boxed away.

Councillor Larsen nodded her head, and the matter was so abruptly concluded it left Arlo reeling. "Deferment granted. The case for Arlo Jarsdel's fae citizenship shall be heard again in eight years' time, on this fifth day of May, by Arlo Jarsdel and *only* Arlo Jarsdel." She paused to flash her gaze first at Celadon, then at the crowd by the door. "The Council dismisses the room. You are *all* free to go."

CHAPTER 2

Aurelian

～～

THE LUMINOUS PALACE OF Summer was a spectacle of
radiance. It was glittering stone and polished glass; it was
elaborate, lifelike friezes and vaulted ceilings, many of them
magicked to look instead like sunny sky; it was tremendous halls,
gilded in gold and encrusted with so many pale jewels the palace was
never truly dark, even at night, for the way their facets refracted light.
But for all this splendor, never had Aurelian forgotten his first impression of this place . . . or the people who called it home.

The brighter the light, the darker its shadows . . .

"Forty-seven days—that's all there is between now and the Summer
Solstice, a celebration that falls to *us*, this year, to host. Every Head
of every Court, including the High King Azurean himself, will be in
attendance, and the Dark Star has set a *bull troll* loose in the foyer."
Riadne Lysterne, queen of the Seelie Court of Summer, spoke in a
voice that was quiet as still water. There was no need to shout—every
person in the room could hear her perfectly and was petrified by the
stare she fixed on each of them in turn. "The staircase—destroyed. The
chandelier—in pieces. The pillars, the fixtures, the floor, the *ceiling*—
this *entire* place is in ruins, and so I repeat: who *laughed?* Who thought
this was funny? I will not ask again."

Aurelian seethed internally. Most of the queen's servants were
sidhe fae, but she also had several lesidhe fae in her employment. Of
course, there was no real visible difference between sidhe and lesidhe
save for the fact that lesidhe all had varying shades and intensity of
golden eyes. What set them most apart from each other was magic.
Sidhe fae were tied to the elements of ice, water, fire, electricity, earth,

stone, wind, and wood, but lesidhe magic was tied to aether, the force that held the entire universe together. Their power was most like what humans imagined of faeries. A lesidhe could wave their hand like a wand and command magic to all sorts of things like levitating objects, and weaving greater illusions, and wiping away messes in the blink of an eye.

Which meant that, even as she stood here terrorizing her staff, her disaster of a foyer was nothing that couldn't be fixed by morning.

Pointing this out right now would be a grave mistake, though. Riadne was upset—she was fairly incandescent with it, the light she commanded as queen of Summer glowing in a visible halo around her—and in this mood, she could go from bad to worse with little instigation.

"Ah, sorry, Mother—that was me."

If it weren't for the fact that Riadne rounded immediately on her son, Vehan, and Aurelian standing behind him, he could have groaned. It had *not* been the prince who'd snorted and set off the Seelie queen's temper, but Vehan Lysterne knew better than anyone else what this could turn into if left to spiral out of control, and was a noble fool, besides.

"*Vehan.*"

"Sorry!" Vehan raised his hands in immediate surrender. "Sorry, it's just . . . it was *you* who told the other Courts that it was possible the Dark Star had something to do with all the ironborn dying lately, so you're not actually surprised she retaliated, are you?"

They were nearing a dozen cases of ironborn turning up dead here in Seelie Summer territory alone. *Murdered* was putting it kindly. Mauled beyond visible recognition was a better description . . . scattered in pieces in various locations . . . no hint as to who could be the next target save that every victim was an ironborn *child*. The oldest they'd discovered had only been nineteen. Aurelian didn't blame the ironborn community for their anger over the Courts' lack of action. He didn't blame them for turning to the only group of people who seemed to care, an illegal operation known as the Assistance. The faeries and fae and even other humans who comprised its ranks worked diligently to ensure every new case was made public knowledge and couldn't be forgotten or covered up. It was the Assistance's involvement that necessitated the recent meeting between the Fae High Council and the Heads of the Courts. In an effort to appease the community, the Council had gone with the High King's unusually hasty decision to name the infamous Dark Star a possible culprit, as suggested by Riadne—but Aurelian suspected even the queen didn't truly believe the Dark Star was involved.

It was funny how good the fae had become at finding their way around lies.

"You admire her." If Riadne's tone was any flatter, it would be concave.

"No! I don't. It's just that I don't think she actually did what she's been accused of, and if it were me, I wouldn't be happy either. I mean, she *is* a menace. The Dark Star has been terrorizing the magical community for over a century now. . . . She does stupid things, reckless things, things that cost an awful lot to fix and, yes, things that have even led to others' injury, but no one has ever *died* because of her. I don't believe she's the culprit. This wasn't her. *But—*"

Once again, Aurelian suppressed his desire to groan. He knew where the prince was going with this conversation—what he was about to say next. Judging by the look on the queen's face, she already knew as well.

"Vehan . . . ," Riadne warned.

"Listen to me!" Vehan begged. "There's more going on than we're seeing. This is bigger than handfuls of ironborn dying. You've heard the rumors, just like I have. Even the *human* police have started noticing that an awful lot of their street workers and homeless have gone missing. Someone is going around practically harvesting humans off the streets right here in Nevada—in Seelie Summer territory—and it's *connected*. I *know* it's connected. I just don't know how yet. If you could just . . . talk to the High King, or let *me*. I know he's forbidden our involvement, which is . . . really questionable, if you ask me. Why aren't we allowed to investigate this? He's always been so understanding, always been fair to his people. Maybe if he knew—"

"Vehan."

The queen's hand, viper-quick, darted to grab her son firmly by the jaw.

Aurelian twitched and almost stepped forward, which would have been a fatal mistake, a challenge the queen would be all too happy to meet; he caught himself just in time.

The relation between Vehan and his mother was subtle in appearance. Vehan looked much more like his late father, Vadrien, with his beauty and his suntanned golden complexion and stronger-than-standard build. Vehan's hair, however—black as the holes that devoured space—and his eyes—so bright a blue they seemed to spark like the electric element he and his mother wielded, that magic that was native to the fae of Seelie Summer—both came from the queen, an ethereal fae of sharp angles and radiant yet forbidding beauty.

It was only in moments like this—standing opposite each other, locked in a minor battle of wills—that Aurelian ever saw such startling resemblance between the prince and his mother.

"That's enough," the queen continued. "I've had it to here with your conspiracies and your theories and your looking for trouble where *trouble can't be found.*" Riadne drew to full height, glaring down her nose at her much shorter son. It was an expression so stern that most people couldn't help but look away, and it was packed with all the intensity of the sun the Seelie worshipped. Vehan always lasted longer under that stare than Aurelian expected him to, but even his gaze drifted downward eventually. When it did so now, the queen continued, only a touch more gracefully, "I am proud of your bravery. I'm proud of your sense of duty to your people. It's very rewarding, as a sidhe fae of Seelie blood, to see my son embody so much of what our people prize, but your obsession with following in the footsteps of our Founders—your endless desire to play the hero, to mimic their acts of chivalry and valor . . . I fear one day your noble intentions will get you hurt, my love."

Riadne's hand relaxed to glide beneath Vehan's chin. She tilted his face up to meet her gaze and smiled down at him. "You don't want to make your mother worry, do you?"

Vehan sighed, and Aurelian—relieved—knew Vehan wouldn't press the issue further tonight. "No, I don't."

"Good. Put all this nasty business of human disappearances and ironborn murders from your mind. You're just a child, Vehan. This isn't your concern. We have so many other pressing matters to give our attention, besides—like my foyer." She turned back to her servants, and however soft her tone had grown for Vehan, the look in her eyes was still lightning fierce. "Clean this up."

She needed no threat to incentivize her staff.

"Yes, Your Majesty," the room echoed back at her.

With one last glance at each of them, the queen turned and made her way back up the battered staircase she'd had installed upon her coronation—a feature famous throughout the Courts for being made entirely of pure, gleaming iron. Aurelian suspected Riadne enjoyed watching each of her visitors and staff pretend it didn't sting a little just to walk them. "Don't stay up much longer, Vehan," she added over her shoulder. "You have school in the morning. If your grades fall for these antics, I will not be happy—with you, or your *retainer*."

Years ago, Aurelian might have flinched at this comment. Not anymore.

"They won't, Mother, I promise! I'll go right to bed, don't worry. Good night."

Aurelian regarded Vehan as he watched his mother leave, the prince absently rubbing where she'd gripped his jaw.

"Do you know why I brought you here, Aurelian?"

No, Aurelian could never forget his first impression of the palace—nor the queen herself.

There were times he forgot how young the crown prince was—

how young they *both* were. There were times Aurelian looked at Vehan and longed to take him away from this life—from the danger constantly around him. It pressed in from every angle: from the Radiant Council of Seelie Summer, hoping to turn their future king into their puppet; from the conniving aunts and uncles and cousins just waiting for him to give them a single opportunity to narrow down the Seelie Summer's line of succession by one; from the other Seelie Summer royal families, looking for any way to knock the Lysternes off the throne altogether and claim it for their own.

There were times Aurelian longed to go back to the way things were between him and Vehan, to when they'd been younger and closer and so innocently intertwined—best friends who loved each other fiercely; to when Aurelian hadn't yet known the worst threat to Vehan was anyone the prince was fond of, hadn't yet known that Vehan's own mother would take those people and turn them into knives against her son's throat.

"I'll give you a hint—it had nothing to do with your parents."

As the queen was out of sight, tension drained out of the room, but the silence lasted a few moments longer. Then, "Thank you, Your Highness."

It was Teron, a young pixie girl not much older than Aurelian but who'd only been here a year. She was shorter than Vehan, incredibly small-boned and slim, and while many faeries didn't feel the need to flaunt their power by keeping glamours up inside human-free spaces as the fae did, Teron had gone to great lengths to keep her features human, her hair mouse-brown, wide eyes muted blue. Her pastel-pink skin and her wings, thin as spun sugar and lovely as stained glass, were the only evidence that she'd relented a little on a glamour that would take too much energy to fully maintain as long as the fae did.

Vehan turned around with a smile Aurelian didn't have to see to know it packed more feeling than Riadne's own had shown—a smile Aurelian missed being able to return. "No, no, you don't have to thank me, Teron. I'm sorry. Mother's in a bad mood lately. . . . There's a lot of heat on her, what with the majority of the murders and disappearances happening here in our territory, and she really wants this year's Solstice celebration to stand apart from all the others. The Dark Star better keep her head down for the next little while if she doesn't want it mounted on the ballroom wall." He laughed. Aurelian knew him too well to miss the awkwardness in it.

"I shouldn't have laughed," Teron replied miserably.

No, she really shouldn't have.

Aurelian had seen the queen pin faeries to those iron steps of hers for lesser insults—had seen Vehan wear punishment for standing against kinder moods.

Teron owed the prince much more than her thanks, but Vehan wasn't the sort of fae to capitalize on such debts—and that was the prince all over, much to Aurelian's frustration. He was too damn *good*, too damn eager to take care of others, no matter the cost to himself.

No matter that Riadne saw this just as clearly as Aurelian did and used it *constantly* to her advantage.

"Ah, well, next time, try to save it for when she's gone, okay?"

With a nod of her head and a bow that made her wings clip Vehan in the nose, Teron scrambled back to the others to help them repair the foyer.

Silence stretched once more between Aurelian and Vehan. Sighing deeply, Aurelian stepped up beside Vehan and nodded after the pixie girl now darting glances Vehan's way. "That's another you'll be seeing in line to dance with you at the Solstice."

"There are worse things in life than having pretty people think you're charming." He positively beamed at Aurelian. It was false cheer—something Aurelian didn't buy for a moment—but even so, it was only thanks to years of practice that Aurelian was able to keep his show of indifference from cracking. He'd always been weak to the way a smile tugged at the prince's full mouth. Something of his frustration must have leaked through, though, because next Vehan added, "What? Why are you looking at me like that?"

Aurelian shook his head.

It wasn't uncommon for fae to Mature at eighteen—for them to come into their full power, for their aging to slow to a crawl, and their youthful human softness to start sharpening into true fae beauty once the initial weeklong phase of illness, mood swings, and temperamental magic passed—but Vehan's had hit the very day of his birthday a little over a month ago. It had been more or less the same for Aurelian, whose own eighteenth birthday had passed back in January, with Maturity following a few weeks after. But Aurelian wasn't the prince of a Court. He wouldn't be walking into this year's Solstice with marriage painted like a target on his back. There was no doubt in him that part of Riadne's game this year was trying to use the Solstice to arrange the best union possible, and who didn't want to play significant other to someone like Vehan Lysterne, already well-known for his looks and his kindness and princely demeanor?

A true prince of light, his people called him.

Aurelian wished he didn't agree.

"Fine. Judge me in silence—I'm used to it." Vehan sighed. A bit of his fake cheer melted away. There was clearly something on his mind.

"What?" Aurelian said before he could stop himself.

He was going to regret asking, but as Vehan's retainer and steward in training, it was better to learn what was going on in the prince's head now rather than later.

Vehan grinned.

He looked at Aurelian in that odd way of his, as different from the way everyone else here looked at him as he had from their very first meeting.

Aurelian Bessel was tall and lanky, a lesidhe fae born to Seelie Autumn parents, who'd moved here to Nevada from Germany when he'd been all of eleven. He was quiet, aloof, and exceedingly intelligent—a genius both in fae and human standards, all modesty aside, though his parents had tried very hard to dissuade him from the latter.

In his human glamour he was lightly tanned, with a delicate jaw, strong features, and dark brown hair shaved to stubble around his neck and ears. It was left longer on the top of his head and dyed a smoky lavender, and his current favored style was to sweep it toward his thick brows. Recent years had added piercings up the outer shell of his ears and an entire sleeve of tattoos, black and brown foliage etched in ink, the colors of his native Court. They covered his right hand like a glove and stretched all the way up from his fingers to his shoulder blade. It hadn't been hard to find a faerie willing to do this, despite his being sixteen when he'd gone to them, but it had certainly earned him no small amount of grief from nearly every adult in his life and many of their peers, much the way the rest of him did . . . from everyone except Vehan.

When Vehan looked at Aurelian—looked *at* him, not simply turned attention his way—it was the only time Aurelian was ever caught off guard enough to let himself wonder what things might be like if he were . . . different; if he were a little less observant, a little less rebellious, a little more like what Riadne and her underlings wanted as partner for her son—pliable.

If only being that partner wouldn't turn him into one more tool for control over Vehan.

"Oh . . . it's nothing, really . . ." Vehan trailed off slyly.

Aurelian frowned. "Cut the wordplay or let me go to bed."

"Well, you heard my mother, didn't you?"

"Yes. She's going to skin you and wear you as her dress for the Solstice if you distract any more of her staff. Are we done here?"

"Okay."

Vehan said this too brightly. It had been too simple, and Aurelian felt a headache bloom in his temples. *"What."*

"It's just, we've been looking for trouble in all the wrong places . . ."

Aurelian didn't require an explanation. "The Courts can track you now, you remember that, right? You've Matured. We *both* have. If you're thinking of going somewhere we're not supposed to be—"

"Aurelian."

Aurelian glared at him.

"I *am* the Courts. And I agree. We've been looking for trouble where 'trouble can't be found.' It's time to start looking in places it can be."

That grin of Vehan's unspooled even wider, and Aurelian felt all hope of getting any proper sleep tonight unravel with it.

CHAPTER 3

Nausicaä

~⌐~

IF THERE WAS ANYTHING Nausicaä had learned in the past 116 years on earth—and the almost 300 she'd been alive—it was that revenge was not a cure for pain, but exacting it did make her smile.

However irritated she still was that her name had been dragged into this "bunch of dead ironborn" business—she didn't kill innocent people, thank you very much; there was already enough blood on her hands, even if she'd never regret certain stains—taking time out of her busy schedule to remind the Courts what she was about had been worth Queen Riadne's expression when she tore into her precious palace foyer to discover a bull troll knocking around.

"The Iron Queen and the infamous Dark Star." Nausicaä sighed, tilting her head to the starry sky. "Now, *there* would be a fight. Sucks we had to leave—I'm almost feeling an emotion about it."

More than a century into her banishment and still Nausicaä had yet to satisfy her anger with her immortal family. She'd done numerous things to make them regret sending her here, to make them wish they'd sentenced her to Destruction instead.

She had her morals, the whole one or two of them that stubbornly clung to existence. Apart from her refusal to be the cause of any more unwarranted death, she also tried to keep out of dark magic if only because no one had done anything about her previous attempts. For zero reward, it wasn't worth the hassle. But when she wasn't trying to trick the magical community into revealing themselves to the humans they lived alongside or poke the Heads of the Courts to watch them buzz in agitation, she was baiting hothead deities by torching their already neglected shrines, defacing their once-glorious temples (now little better than curious tourist attractions), and stirring up trouble among their followers in an attempt to weave doubt in mortal belief—the one thing that sustained the deities and the one thing that the treaty of peace between the Immortal and Mortal Realms hinged on.

Her brand of chaos was exactly that: chaos; it *wasn't* picking off the magical community's children.

"But maybe it fucking should be," she mumbled to herself, kicking a stone on the path where she stood, which led from the town behind her and into a vast, dense forest ahead.

They were already terrified of her, the mortals. In the rare instances she allowed them to capture her—less and less, as time wore on—just for a change of pace, it had been with the hope that *someone* would prove interesting. That someone would brave the violence and rot in her magical aura—a reflection of her mental state she didn't care to examine—to look her in the eye and do something other than tremble, or cower, or declare her not worth the effort to reprimand.

A lost cause.

Maybe she should embrace what *both* the realms now thought of her . . . but that was a depressing line of thought she didn't feel like venturing down, not at the moment, not with the happy memory of Riadne's rage still fresh in her mind.

Turning to her partner in tonight's crime, Nausicaä allowed her grin to spread wider. "You weren't half-bad, you know? For a troll. Maybe I should team up with others more often . . ." She tapped her chin in a show of thought.

The troll standing across from her, looking around in confusion, had been the first exception to her lone-wolf rule in well over fifty years. She didn't like working with other people—other people were complicated, and everything seemed to be about *feelings* with them. Nausicaä didn't have room in her life for that nonsense. Besides, she'd *had* friends—many of them, once upon a time. She'd been well-liked by her immortal people before everything that had happened after

Tisiphone's death. A lot of good that had done her in the end, and good riddance, really.

But trolls were stupid—bull trolls especially.

This one in particular clearly valued brawn over brains, towering over her own six-foot-two height somewhere off into eight feet tall. He was squash-faced, with skin the color of old, gray porridge, and every bit as lumpy. His yellowing tusks protruded from his mouth. Pointed black horns grew from his temples. He was big as he was strong, all too ready to take a swing at her when she'd arrived in his forest to forge their temporary union. No, Gar—at least, that's what she made of the sound *he'd* made when she'd asked for his name— wasn't going to try to make this anything other than what it was, and all it had taken to win his cooperation had been three cows and the promise he could smash a pretty building.

"Wrong."

Nausicaä dropped her hand from her chin. "Say what now?"

"Wrong. Forest . . . wrong!"

The troll's confusion had morphed into agitation. It wasn't surprising; while Gar was leaps and bounds more intelligent than many of his brethren (the fact that he cared enough to learn words in human English was proof of that fact), popping him out of his home in the tucked-away town of Darrington, Washington, and whisking him all the way to Paradise, Nevada, then all the way home again, was definitely too much for so little brain power to process . . . and trolls had a tendency to lash out at things that overwhelmed them.

"Excuse you, it is *not*."

The troll made a grumbling noise that sounded a lot like grating rock.

"Listen, this is the right forest. And before you get any big ideas there, pal, I'll have you know your first shot was free, but if you take another fucking swing at me, I'll—"

"No. Not wrong forest. Forest! Forest is wrong."

Nausicaä paused, then looked around.

Darrington sat in a cradle of snow-capped mountains and emerald forest wrapped around the city's limits. It boasted no more than a handful of homes and necessary buildings. The air was rich and clean and fragrant with moss and wood, and the late hour meant there was very little movement apart from the rustle of leaves and the breeze that stirred them.

Nausicaä hadn't been paying attention—she'd missed the signs of magic altogether, so naturally whimsical was this place under night's veil. Plus, when she'd been banished to the Mortal Realm, the majority of her immortal powers had been stripped of her, as was the case for all who dared to come here uninvited. Her ability to sense magic was woefully diminished. But so concentrated was it in the air here that she now wondered how she had missed it.

Magic . . . It was there in that telltale tinkling, soft as glass chimes. It was there in that spark she tasted on her tongue and in the vibrancy of her surroundings. It was there in the deities-damned fog spilling over the cusp of the woods to swirl around her boots. The narrow strip of trampled dirt that stretched between a row of slumbering houses and Darrington High's football field was barely wide enough to accommodate them, but it was about to get even more crowded if the tendrils of mist curling around her legs were what she thought they were.

"Changelings . . . What are *they* doing here?"

Most wrote these particular faeries off as tricksters too preoccupied with games to be of much use. The belief had once been that faeries would grow more resilient to iron if they were raised by human hands, and so some parents had disguised and swapped their offspring at birth for human children. In theory, when the faerie was grown, their parents would reverse the trade and neither would be the worse for wear. Except in practice, it all went to shit. Most of the children, both faerie and human, ended up dying. The ones who survived . . .

Magic had its rules, and woe betide anyone who tried to sidestep them.

The children, both faerie and human, were never returned to their families. In retribution for trying to outsmart magic itself, both were, instead, stolen away by it. Claimed and trapped forever in their youth and raised by the wild, nobody and nothing else were quite so connected to magic—pure magic—as these wayward wraiths of the woods.

If changelings were here in Darrington and mucking about, it was because something else had attracted magic's notice. Something dark . . . something unnatural . . . something with great potential for upheaval. Nausicaä thought quite highly of her own proficiency in these areas, but she knew it wasn't *her* they were swarming to tonight.

"But if it isn't me . . ."

She looked back at the troll. Gar had shrunken a few steps back, and she couldn't have that—as fun as it would be to set him loose a second time and prod the Seelie Summer hive again, a confused troll was dangerous. A *scared* one was deadly.

"To me, Gar," she commanded, employing a bit of her former Furious tone.

Gar shuffled forward. "Forest . . . is wrong."

"Yeah, I can feel that now. Don't worry, handsome, I'll walk you home."

She flicked open her hand. In her palm, a ball of fire sparked to life. The flame was small—as weak as Nausicaä was herself, these days—but it was fire unlike anything this realm could conjure. Livid red and seething orange and boiling, furious gold, it was the element from which she'd been created by Urielle so many years ago.

She watched this ball of fire burn for all of a minute before returning her gaze to her forest.

Wrong, indeed. She might not be able to sense magical auras as profoundly as she once had, but regular odors she could smell just fine, and what currently lurked in the air's undercurrent was one that even a human couldn't miss—something heavy, rancid, like gore and sewage and dead fish left to bake in briny air.

It was disgusting . . . and familiar, now that she'd had some time to think. And if that thinking was correct, she hadn't encountered an odor like this in . . . hells, since she'd been Alecto—too long.

But a *Reaper* . . .

The scant few left of their kind were long forbidden to come anywhere near Court territory, but here one was, skulking around smack-dab in the middle of it.

Interesting.

A former Fury and a Reaper—what if *they* could join forces? Reapers weren't known for their temperance, and neither was Nausicaä, but the chaos they could inflict with each other's aid . . . Would it finally be enough for the Courts to demand immortal interference? Would it finally be the deed that made her mother admit there was no reforming Nausicaä's ways?

It was dangerous. It was dark. It was a path Nausicaä had been avoiding to get her way—the one that ended in significant, innocent casualties—but if this realm was so determined to already smear her with that evil . . .

"I think this Reaper and I need to have a chat."

She lowered her hand.

The flame in her palm lingered a moment in the air, then took on a life of its own. It floated to the space above her shoulder, swirling and churning and spitting out sparks like a miniature sun. The pool of light it spilled at her feet made the fog there flinch back.

Fog was the best indication of the presence of changelings; it was their favorite place to hide and execute their trickeries. The thicker the fog, the bigger the gathering, as went the general rule. Right now, the opaque mist swirling through the forest was dense enough to white out all but the first row of trees. Anyone foolish enough to wander into that mess deserved what they got—even the humans they often went against Court law to toy with would take one look at it and turn right back around.

Nausicaä plunged forward, stepping off the path at last and advancing into the forest. Gar followed behind, however reluctantly.

The fog retreated, parting around her light. Visibility was still limited, though, and trees kept popping at her out of nowhere, forcing Nausicaä to be way more careful than she usually was.

One step.

Two.

The first leg of her journey seemed to wear on forever and began to feel almost suffocating, with all that white pressing in on her from every side. There was no telling how far this fog stretched, nor indeed if it would let up at all or continue until she stumbled across what she was after. Her ball of fire and innate sense of direction could only take her so far, and while a bit of determination often saw her through to the other side of the changelings' little games, this particular prank seemed to want to keep her.

"All right, listen." She came to a halt—Gar and the fireball, too—and the fog inched closer. "What's going on? I'm all for throwing around dramatic effect, but there's an uber dark creature of terrifying death running around this forest, not to mention a Reaper, and *I* don't get in the way of *your* fun, so what gives?"

For a moment, the fog remained unmoved. It sat around, swirling in place, very clearly listening but showing no sign of offering answers. Then, just as Nausicaä began to contemplate conjuring a few more fireballs, the fog began to thin. Little by little it drained from the air until, finally, all that was left of it was a vaguely damp, translucent haze.

She could only stare at what was revealed.

"Huh," she breathed when speech at last overcame her surprise. "This is . . . new."

It wasn't just the changelings that had gathered. They were present, of course—one a mere step away. Nausicaä briefly took in the unmistakable pale green tint of his fawn-brown skin and the snaking twists of ivy that grew from the sharp flares of his little shoulders.

But there were others.

There were so *many* others. In all of Nausicaä's very long life, she had never encountered so many of magic's children in one place.

The crowd of them stretched far in almost every direction, faces of all shapes and sizes peeking out of and around the foliage and trees. There were centaurs, goblins, brownies, imps, and sprites. There were redcaps, with their crimson-stained hats and vicious scythes, which glinted in flecks of moonlight. There were kelpies dripping sodden weeds, lilies strangled in their manes. Littered throughout the branches above were crows that weren't really crows at all, but sluagh—wandering souls of violent dead who preyed on those soon to die.

There were larger things too. Unnamable things. Things that had undoubtedly been calling this forest their home long before Nausicaä had even been born. She narrowed her eyes at the distance—something massive as a mobile hill stood still as silence too far away for mortal eyes to see. Their form was not unlike an overlarge, poisonous tree frog, all vibrant blues and yellows and greens, a crown of velvet antlers on their head and hundreds of glittering black eyes on their face. A freaking *Forest Guardian*, she would hazard as a guess, not that she'd ever before seen one to say for sure.

"Uh . . . okay, well, weird time to have a company meeting, but you do you, I guess. I'm going to . . . go. Gar, maybe it's best you stick with these guys until I square things up with my Reaper. Thanks for lifting the fog, forest brats! Good luck with . . . whatever this is. May the force be with you." She turned back around. There weren't any faeries in front of her, no movement, either—just trees and misty gloom and a darkness unnatural even for this time of night.

And, of course, the glass-chime tinkling of magic, which now sounded to her a bit distressed.

One step.

Two.

Nausicaä didn't have to look behind her to know the entirety of the forest's occupants followed, however cautiously.

Another step.

Four.

She halted. Rolling her eyes, she whirled on her heels with every intention of snapping at her unwelcome entourage. But just as her gaze locked with the ivy-bound changeling from before, she realized at last what she'd missed.

Something else hung in the air, familiar and as tart to the taste as battery acid.

She almost couldn't believe it.

"You're *afraid*!"

This wasn't some clandestine meeting of powers, some odd-sorts troupe of faeries drawn by curiosity and sport. This was *fear*. This was huddling together and *hiding*. She hadn't noticed—fear was something Nausicaä inspired, it wasn't something she felt. This wasn't the first time she'd dared to wander into the depths of horror. It wouldn't be the last. But everything here . . . this all against some measly *one* . . . Nausicaä wrapped her arms around her middle and doubled over in laughter. "Holy crap, you're all afraid? Seriously? Of what? You can't tell me none of you have ever met a Reaper before."

It had to be what the Reaper was up to that made these faeries so uneasy, but that only made Nausicaä even more intrigued, even more excited to talk with it.

A shriek from deep in the forest rent the air—sudden, loud, and suspiciously delighted.

Nausicaä's laughter died abruptly. This was wasting her time. If she spent any longer with these terrified faeries, she wouldn't be able to capitalize on their misfortune. Reapers had the ability to camouflage completely with their surroundings, almost to the point of turning invisible. And they were wicked fast, able to cross impossible distances in impossibly short bits of time—she didn't want her hopeful business partner to get away before she could speak with it.

"Gotta go," she clipped. "FYI: you're all a bunch of cowards."

A hand snagged her own.

She looked at the tiny green fingers that stopped her, then up at the face of the changeling to whom they belonged. The one with the ivy—Haru, he was called, if memory served her correctly. She knew several of these tiny disasters by name for how often she encountered them bouncing around the world. "I don't have time for this."

It's dangerous, Nausicaä. Haru's voice was a quiet, steady presence in her mind, incongruous with the mood around them.

"Yeah? Story of my life. I'll live."

Haru's hand gripped tighter to hers.

I'll come with you.

Nausicaä bit her lip against a swell of something that felt, again, too much like emotion, evoked by a memory she quickly repressed. Stupid forest kids . . . Tisiphone had always been fond of them, the way she'd been fond of anything she saw to be abandoned and alone. "Oh my gods, *fine*, but can we actually go now?"

The changeling nodded. Dirt streaked his green-tinged skin. His clothing was little better than tattered rags—dated now; it was rare that faeries left children to become changelings anymore, and Haru was one of the last from the time no one knew that's what they'd become. The deep black nest of hair on his head was tangled with leaves, twigs, and carcasses of insects. Haru looked every inch a ten-year-old boy claimed by Nature, but Nausicaä knew better than to argue with a changeling's conviction.

They set off at a run.

The fireball followed, and so did the faeries, a little more eagerly now.

It was much easier to traverse the darkness with the fog gone, and Haru seemed to know his way around better than she did. They moved at unnatural speed, weaving through trees, and in no time at all reached a clearing. Nausicaä would have barreled on in if it weren't for Haru digging his heels into the dirt. The sudden stop wrenched her arm painfully behind her, drawing a snarl from her chest. She rounded on him, but all Haru did in response was stare over her shoulder.

They were too late.

The clearing was empty—of the living, at least. The Reaper was gone, leaving behind only carnage. Extracting herself from Haru's hold, Nausicaä stepped through the trees. The scene was oddly beautiful (as much as it was also grotesque). The discarded limbs . . . the drape of lifeless bodies . . . the splashes of claret across a shadow-swallowed canvas of muted brown and green . . . It all made this into some romanticized painting of death.

The strewn little corpses were easily recognizable as changelings either foolish enough to intervene in what had happened here tonight or too slow to get away, but the epicenter of this terrible tableau was something else. Carving her way between the gore, Nausicaä crouched by the remains of a brown-haired teenage boy.

She doubted very much he'd come into the woods of his own accord. More likely he was chased by the very thing that had torn his limbs from his torso and cracked open the cage of his ribs, spreading them like a parody of wings. Reapers . . . They didn't tend to go after humans. Their preferred prey were the folk—particularly folk who practiced dark magic. In Nausicaä's previous life, when she'd been a Fury and it had been up to her to police the use of such things, Reapers had been a signal they looked out for.

And perhaps that was why the mortals had been so keen to chase them away—less Reapers, less chance a Fury would catch you doing something you shouldn't. Plus, Reapers were notorious in the community as faerie cannibals that had once been faeries themselves, now devoured and twisted by the same dark magic they'd dared to once use.

"Hang on . . ." Nausicaä examined the body closer. She couldn't sense this boy's magical aura by smell anymore, but it still had a taste on the back of her tongue—bitter and slightly metallic. "Are you . . . ironborn?"

She hadn't been following the crimes she'd been accused of too closely—all that stuff about the ironborn murders. There was always something going on in the Mortal Realm—always some war, some disagreement, some atrocious act that only reinforced her decision to keep from getting too involved with humans *or* the magical community. What little she knew was thanks to the Assistance and their tireless efforts to keep this in circulation. And the state of the body before her? It looked an awful lot like every single case they'd reported so far.

"W-T-fuck?"

There was something on the boy's chest, revealed under tattered clothing. Broken bones . . . coagulating blood . . . It was difficult to piece together the shreds of the body's skin to make out what this symbol was, but *something* was stamped on his chest as though branded. Something that—in the back of Nausicaä's considerably large collection of random knowledge—struck her an awful lot like an alchemic array.

It wasn't unheard of—she'd encountered many ironborn who still practiced alchemy in secret despite the laws that forbade that—but this array in particular . . . the bits she was able to match together . . .

Blowing out her cheeks, she reached over to close the too-young boy's open, glassy eyes. Then, using her teeth to pull an elastic off her wrist, she tied back her shoulder-length, white-sand hair and plunged her hand unceremoniously into the young man's chest.

What are you doing?

Haru was suddenly at her side, watching her rummage through organs with no small amount of curiosity.

Nausicaä angled a grin at him—the sort that would have made anyone else shrink warily back, but Haru merely cocked his head. "Spelunking." With a sickening squelch, she pulled her hand back out, something too hard and smooth and cold to be a heart in her grasp.

Yet a heart it had been.

Now it looked more like a polished hunk of gray stone, twisted up in tubes, but at its core it glowed red and bright as a candied apple. The glow faded quickly, but it was proof that Nausicaä had been right.

This boy *was* ironborn. Her Reaper was behind these attacks—but it wasn't the true culprit. Someone had to be using it, had teamed up with it as Nausicaä had intended herself, the trade of food for service too tempting for these starving creatures to ignore, because no solo Reaper would risk drawing as much attention as this, and holy effing shit. This stone in her hand . . . it wasn't just the work of *alchemy*, it was . . .

"Put it down."

Nausicaä froze. A few seconds ticked by. She took a steadying breath, clamped down on the immediate swell of fury that voice behind her ignited, then unfurled herself to full height. She turned around, petrified heart in her hand dripping blood, gore slathered up to her elbow. "Hello, Meg."

How long had it been since she'd last spoken with her sister? Megaera stood before her, dressed in human glamour. Though not exactly blood-related—it was Urielle who gave them life, yes, but only by way of her magic—they were incredibly similar in appearance, with their matching gray-metal eyes, shapely, strong builds, and features sharp as knives. But Nausicaä was blond and suntanned gold, and wore combat boots, tight jeans, and a leather jacket, all of which was black. Megaera's hair was long, the blue-black color of ink, and in her favored glamour of silver-ice skin, pale as a corpse, her only covering a purple slip of silk that highlighted every curve.

"Put it down and step away. You have no business here."

There was nothing soft about Megaera's imperious tone, however quiet it was. Even Haru had retracted a step from them, wary of the being who was tasked with making sure that the two realms of this universe followed magic's laws.

Nausicaä grinned, tossing the heart she held in the air and catching it as it fell. "Why don't you make me?"

Megaera's face hardened ever further. "I am not here to play games, *Nausicaä*. Put down that heart and leave. I will not ask you again."

"Mmmm . . ." She considered the heart she continued to play with and the barely contained disapproval on Megaera's face. "Yeah, no. I think I'll keep it. Say, did you know there's been a *murder* in these woods?" She stepped aside, pulling a look of deep alarm, and pointed down at the heap of flesh and bone that had once been a boy. "It looks like a case of dark magic—isn't your job to, like, look into that?"

She cocked her head, glancing back at Megaera, her smile nothing but innocent.

"Yeah, let me think . . . I've read something about this somewhere. The three Furies: Alecto, Tisiphone . . . *Megaera*. They police the realms and punish anyone they catch breaking the Three Principles of Magic." She raised a hand to visibly count off the laws that had once been up to her to maintain. "One: thou shall not use magic to alter someone's destiny without permission of the Titans. Two: thou shall not use magic to completely strip away free will. And three: thou extra *super* shall not use magic to bring someone back from the grave . . . or put them in one." She paused to let a little of her ever-burning anger touch the edges of her mouth, curling it like the scorched ends of paper into something more resembling a smirk. "I'm feeling a bit of déjà vu here—you, me . . . a bunch of dead bodies. Hang on, let me light something on fire for old time's sake—"

"Nausicaä, that is *enough*!" Megaera surged forward and took hold of Nausicaä's arm. The heart she'd caught only moments before fell to the forest floor, and if Nausicaä were the mortal she was halfway to being, the strength in those bone-slim fingers would have crushed her wrist to dust.

There was nothing kind in the cold depths of Megaera's stare, no hint of warmth in her glacial expression . . . but then again, just as Nausicaä had been forged in flames, Megaera had been carved from ice. Even when they'd been close, there had never been much kindness or warmth between them.

"What is a philosopher's stone doing inside this mortal child?" Nausicaä held her ground but abandoned her teasing at last. Wholly serious for what was probably the first time since coming to this stupid forest, she matched her sister's glare with one of her own.

"I already told you."

"This is unbelievably dark magic—what's going on?"

"It's none of your business."

"We don't come to the Mortal Realm to keep mortals from making poor choices—that's part of the treaty, part of what allows us to keep our powers when we're here. We can't interfere, can't take away the choice to fall, can only act once the deed violates the Principles. But *this*"—Nausicaä waved her hand at the boy's body—"has happened before, and it almost cost this realm *everything* when just *one* of these things was created. And this time, even after several murdered ironborn, there was not a single word from the Immortal Realm to warn this one? The mortals are playing this off as the work of a human serial killer, Meg!"

Megaera's eyes narrowed. "You are not one of *us*. There is no *we* anymore, Nausicaä."

It was almost as though the entire forest stopped breathing—the critters, faeries, and trees alike. There was silence, and then there was *this*. . . . Nausicaä worked harder than she'd ever admit to keep her face from showing the pain and loss she felt just from seeing Megaera again.

Good riddance, she reminded herself. *You don't need any of them.*

"This is big, Meg. Please tell me you've at least told the High King."

The dreadful not-silence lasted a full minute longer; then Megaera released her hold. She said nothing. Only bent to fetch the iron-boy's heart and return it to his chest.

I can take you to find your answers.

Megaera stood. Nausicaä turned to Haru, but not before she caught a glimpse of what was almost curiosity in her sister's watchful gaze.

"You know what that is?"

She pointed to the ironborn—to the thing inside him that was now more stone than heart.

Haru nodded.

"You heard my sister—this isn't my business, and to be perfectly honest, I don't actually care. My field of fucks to give to the mortals and their problems? Barren, burned, and salted. But . . . let's say I was *really* curious to know where that Reaper might go. Let's say it might be interesting to know who's behind this bit of ambition. Eternity is a very long time, and a girl gets bored, so I'd be in your debt, if you could point me in the right direction. . . ."

Faeries were all about debt. There was no such thing as a gift or good deed where they were concerned. A favor done meant a favor in return. It was a foolish bargainer who left the particulars vague, because what faeries loved even more than racking up debts was warping them into a geas—those promises imbued with magic that would result in great torment if those particulars were not met.

Nausicaä didn't bind herself to debt for just anything. Haru would be one of an extremely rare few who could call in a favor with the former Fury.

He turned his head to look past her, obnoxiously insensible to the great honor he was about to receive.

Other changelings crept from the woods now that they saw it was safe to do so. They made for their fallen, to remove them from this scene before it was inevitably discovered.

"I'm . . . sorry about your friends," she said, a little awkwardly, noticing where his attention had drifted. It earned a snort from Megaera, probably unable to believe the comment was genuine.

My family.

Nausicaä swallowed around an infuriating emotion that was once again trying to be acknowledged. "Yeah. That."

If I take you where you need to go, will you help?

"Help? That's . . . not really what I do—help people. Not really my thing. And I was kind of after this Reaper to stir up trouble of my own, so . . ." This escalating situation wasn't something she wanted any part in.

You'll help. I'll take you.

"What?" Nausicaä looked up from the ground, where her thoughts had pulled her gaze. Changelings were smart—they were also prescient; she didn't like where this was heading.

I'll help you now, and you'll pass that help on. Those are the terms of my trade—I already know you'll accept.

"Oh yeah? And to whom am I providing this service, exactly?"

You'll know when you meet them.

Haru extended his hand, the ivy around it writhing.

It would be foolish to turn her nose up at this offer. Haru wasn't trapping her in anything too difficult to minimize—help was a broad term, doled out in various ways. Accepting his trade was very little skin off Nausicaä's back, and in return, she might just be able to learn something useful. The higher-ups were anxious, judging by Megaera's appearance here, and maybe hoping to keep Nausicaä from getting involved herself with how little her sister was willing to yield.

That was enough for her, and yet . . . she hesitated.

Haru seemed strangely convinced Nausicaä would *want* to help whoever it was needing her assistance, despite her insistence other-wise.

Even after 116 years, her rage was still as all-consuming as it had been that fateful night long ago. All those years and the pain of being torn in half—the ruthless agony of losing her sister, which rent and shredded and hacked apart her very soul—still plagued every step, every breath, and every beat of her heart.

She didn't want to get involved with anyone ever again. She would not *want* to help Haru's charity case, no matter who they were.

"Deal."

The abruptness of Megaera's response startled Nausicaä. She looked at her sister, whose arms were now folded across her chest, a haughty expression on her face that was so typically *her,* Nausicaä could have laughed. Instead, she groaned. "Oh my gods, Meg, he wasn't talking to *you.*"

"I'm coming too." Megaera's tone held no room for argument. "Nausicaä will pay your price, changeling, and I will permit you to escort the both of us to where the Reaper has gone. I would like to know that answer myself." She turned to Nausicaä. "Agreed?"

"Fine. Fine. Yes, agreed."

Nausicaä took Haru's hand. Megaera took the other. The fog returned, spilling from the forest like a flood. She felt it sweep her into its current and then watched as Darrington disappeared into the mist.

The fog receded.

The rushing in Nausicaä's ears softened to the tinkling of glass chimes.

When she was able to focus again, she realized she stood now in some street-corner park. The grass beneath her boots was dewy, the air heavy with the scent and taste of iron, rain, and damp stone. She looked up, past the crawl of cars on a surprisingly busy street to a mass of towering buildings. It was impossible to see how high they reached, devoured as they were by the low-hanging ceiling of clouds. What was visible of their metal-plated skeletons glinted dully in the fog-muted dawn. None of it looked familiar.

"And this is . . . ?" She turned to Haru, hoping he'd supply that answer, but already he'd begun to fade into the haze that lingered around him. "Hey! Wait, where the fuck did you take me, forest brat?"

Remember our deal.

"Haru, don't you dare!"

He vanished.

"If I find you poking any further into this, there will be consequences, Nausicaä." Megaera vanished almost as quickly, her glamour slipping just enough to reveal great wings unfurling behind her. They wrapped around her body and compressed her down to nothing, and she was gone just as abruptly as she'd come.

Nausicaä growled. Reaching into the inner pocket of her leather jacket, she fished out her phone. "Thank goodness for modern technology. Let's see . . . location, location . . ." Google Maps would obligingly answer the question. "Hold up, *Toronto?*"

What the hell?

Toronto—a bustling hub of human activity to the untrained eye, capital of UnSeelie Spring and the entire Courts of Folk to the magical community. It was a city that even a former Fury would be disinclined to mess with, what with the famed viciousness of the UnSeelie brand of faeries, the particularly powerful magic of the Spring Court, and the bloody *High King*. That a Reaper would venture here was unlikely—not without reinforcements, at least; not without something here to protect it. Haru wouldn't steer her wrong, which meant that someone else here had a very high opinion of themselves. Someone else here thought they were strong enough to make a mess in the High King's house and get away with it.

"Interesting." Nausicaä clicked off her phone. "Interesting, and *stupid*."

And very, very promising.

In the pit of her ravaged heart, Nausicaä thought she felt something a little bit like joy.

"So, you don't want me to get involved. Consequences, you say. I wonder, what am I going to find if I track down this Reaper before *you*, Megaera?"

What sort of chaos was brewing that needed an actual fucking *philosopher's stone* for fuel?

That ironborn's heart . . . It wasn't a full-fledged stone, hadn't been strong enough to survive the process of becoming one. She really didn't approve of all this killing, but how pissed would the deities be if she lent the many things she knew about this legend to the person attempting to make it real? Not that she particularly wanted to do that, but if her immortal jailers thought she could . . . Options, options, so many options to make them regret sending her here.

But why—*why*—was no one as properly panicked as they should be that this was going on?

One stone created, centuries ago, and the Courts of Folk had been so afraid that they'd shut down the practice of alchemy altogether.

This veritable silence on that magic's apparent return meant no one knew—they couldn't, not after last time, not after the fear that haunted them even now.

"Interesting," Nausicaä repeated. "All right, well, first things first: let's see what sort of person you are, my mysterious, murderous entre-preneur."

Shoving her hands into her pockets, she set off into the heart of Toronto; if she didn't know better, she could almost swear it was luck she had to thank for this exciting turn of affairs.

CHAPTER 4

Arlo

EVEN THE THREAT OF rain in the Monday morning sky failed to depress Arlo's spirits.

The worst of the previous night's Weighing was over.

She'd been allowed to keep her magic and her memories, and now no one would have to pretend with her (the way she had to pretend with her father) that they were just a normal human.

By the time she left her condo for school, the steel and glass behemoths that crowded Toronto's skyline appeared half-consumed by an opaque mist descending from the sky. The air was so hazy that traffic lights seemed to hang from nothing. The morning commute had slowed to a crawl, which meant that, once again, Arlo was late for first period—but still her happiness persisted.

It persisted through her homeroom teacher's comment of "Oh, I hadn't realized you were absent, Miss Jarsdel" when she finally dropped into her seat.

It persisted through her classmates' whispers of: "She only gets away with stuff because she's rich . . ." and "Guys, the teacher didn't even *notice* she wasn't here, what a loser!" and "Rach tried to invite her to her house party this weekend, because, like, we feel sort of bad for her—but she was all *Oh uh oh no, thanks, sorry, I have a family thing.*"

"Ha! What family thing? The only family I ever see is her hottie cousin. He must just feel sorry for her too."

Arlo stoutly refused to let the usual school gossip puncture her relief and joy. But as the day wore on and she watched that dreamlike white sky darken into dingy slate outside her classroom window, she felt herself start to deflate a little. The fog hadn't let up, and when she was released from her classes at the end of the day, the air was so dense that she could almost cup it in her hands like water.

This was typical for Toronto.

Ontario weather was such a fickle thing, and it changed as quickly as a thought. Springtime was the worst culprit for this mutable behavior—part of what had attracted the Viridian royal family to stake their claim here. A bit of rain shouldn't have been all that concerning. It *wouldn't* have been concerning, if Arlo had remembered to grab an umbrella before flying out the door this morning and didn't also have to traverse the city to meet her father. Now if she wanted to escape getting drenched by her poor life choices, she was going to have to race the heavens to the nearest subway station.

Resigned, Arlo wrapped her pastel-pink windbreaker tighter around her body and bent her chin closer to her chest, concentrating solely on her desperate flight down the school's front steps.

"Finally."

As soon as Arlo reached the iron gates of the school grounds, a familiar voice halted her in her tracks. She glanced up from the sidewalk to the young man standing just far enough from that gate to keep from burning his skin on the metal. In his dark, fitted jeans and emerald cable-knit sweater, Celadon might have passed for human if it weren't for the all-around general "otherness" in his high cheekbones and too-pointed ears, and it was a bit bewildering to Arlo that she'd failed to notice the telltale rain-and-cedar scent that clung to his magic.

The ability to sense auras—a magical signature unique to each individual—was one of the few talents Arlo possessed that not only met lofty fae standards but had recently surpassed them. Where most folk only ever sensed auras like a pressure in the air or a sparking through their nerves, *she* had been able to hone this particular talent with a fairly sophisticated amount of precision. Signatures now carried scents for her. If she focused deeply enough, she could track an aura directly to its source and discern well before that whether it belonged to a faerie, fae, or ironborn person.

Celadon's magic fluctuated depending on the reason for its use and his mood when he used it, but Arlo knew it so well it was almost as familiar to her as her own. She could usually pick it out from a considerable distance, too. That she'd completely failed to notice him now was a little damaging to her pride.

"Hi . . . ," she greeted her cousin in return, wondering what on earth had brought Celadon to her school. It wasn't exactly a stone's throw from the palace, where he lived and worked, and far beyond where he was allowed to venture without the High King's permission. "What are you doing here? Did you get kicked out of the house again?"

Quirking a hint of a Cheshire grin, Celadon made to reply, but whatever he'd been about to say was interrupted by a giggle—and what could only be described as a purr—of: "Hi, Celadon."

Arlo rolled her eyes at Celadon before turning around. "Hello, Rachael. Paige." She greeted them as brightly as she could manage. Rachael and Paige seemed to have some sort of innate Celadon-radar and could always be counted on to pop up whenever he came to the school campus.

Arlo stepped aside, looking warily between her cousin and her classmates. There was a glint of mischief in Celadon's eyes that said he was definitely about to do *something* that would prompt a whole new set of vindictive rumors about Arlo come tomorrow morning if she didn't keep control of this situation.

"You can call me Rach, Arlo. It's what all my friends call me." Arlo almost winced at the patronizing tone.

"Hence why she prefers 'Rachael,' I imagine," said Celadon.

Rachael stared. Her smile took on a brittle quality.

"Anyhow!" Arlo jumped in before Rachael decided that, yes, Celadon *was* attempting to insult her. "*Rach.*" She shot her an awkward double finger gun. Rachael merely blinked, unamused. "Sorry, can't talk now! We've got . . . things. Cel and I have to go and meet my dad. I'll see you tomorrow, though, and hey, hope you had a good weekend with your party and underage drinking and . . . stuff."

"And stuff." Rachael's eyes narrowed. She clicked her tongue, sharing a glance with Paige.

Perhaps they were just unused to being rebuffed. Arlo could count on one hand the amount of times they'd willingly sought her out. It was a number even less than the tally of people who'd turned them away, and perfectly equal to the number of times Celadon had met Arlo here.

School had never been her favorite place. She'd been terrified of letting something slip about magic and the Courts in case it hurt her chances with her Weighing. Eventually, it became default simply to keep her distance from the other students. By the time she realized how often she was doing this, she was halfway through her high school career. Friendships were already made. Groups were already formed. Nobody sought out Arlo's company without some ulterior motive. Rachael and Paige had made it clear from their very first invitation it wasn't Arlo they were out to befriend, and while Arlo didn't exactly like being a loner, she liked feeling used even less.

"No worries," Rachael allowed, sliding her cheerful mask back into place. She flipped her sheet of honey-brown hair over her shoulder and eyed Celadon like she was trying to decide if his handsome face could make up for his personality. It was a look Arlo saw him receive quite often. "If you have to go, that's fine. You're always welcome to hang with us, though, just so you know—and so is your cousin, of course."

"Great—thanks, Rach. Rachy." Arlo shot another finger gun. "Rach . . . ael, yeah, sorry, I'll stop. Okay, bye!"

She ushered Celadon away from the gates before she could embarrass herself any further. As they retreated down the sidewalk, identical snorts of laughter sounded from where they had left the two girls.

"Ah, the legendary teenage-human drama I've only ever seen on television," Celadon mused, wistfully fond. "Funnily enough, it's pretty much the same as what goes on at the Academy."

Sidhe fae attended Academies. There was one in every Court. They weren't allowed to attend human schools or have much to do with humans in general, though the lesidhe who chose to align themselves to the Courts were allowed to choose where they wished to learn. Something about pride, and maintaining a sidhe standard, Celadon had once explained.

There were public folk schools, of course, for everyone else—in fact, there were three right here in Toronto alone. Arlo had attended one for all of kindergarten to grade three. But her father had been far too curious about this place he'd never heard of, his memory of magic having been erased when Arlo was eight. And Arlo had worked herself up into such a state trying to keep up with her snickering peers and meet her exasperated teachers' impossible demands that Thalo had finally intervened. With the promise to homeschool Arlo on everything the Courts required she know about the magical community (as was the custom before the schools were built), she'd enrolled Arlo instead in human school . . . only for Arlo to discover she didn't fit in any better here.

"What. Are. You. *Doing?*" she snapped, punctuating her sentence with slaps to her cousin's shoulder. "Thanks, but I can insult my classmates well enough on my own—I don't need your help with that. Why are you here, Celadon?"

"First, please stop hitting me." Arlo scowled, but stopped all the same. "Thank you. Secondly, I barely said anything at all to your classmates. I wanted a walk, if you must know—and you would too if you'd spent your entire day listening to people at least five times your age argue over budget reports. Here." He thrust an umbrella between them. "You're going to meet with your father today, right? It looks like rain, and I've known you too long to believe you actually remembered to bring one of your own."

Highly suspicious of his motivations, Arlo took his lime-green offering. "You came all this way just to bring me *this?*"

"For you, there is nothing I wouldn't do, dearest cousin."

"Uh-huh. And what's the real reason?" As wonderful and sometimes overprotective as Celadon often was, she'd never known him to be *quite* so attentive, even when it came to her.

"What do you want me to say? That there's a mass murderer on the loose, picking off ironborn teens, and until they're caught, I'm going to be annoyingly present in your outdoor activities?"

Arlo rolled her eyes, threading her arm through Celadon's. "You're being silly. There has to be, what, a couple thousand ironborn in this city? A lot, sure, but there's like over two million humans. Double that, with the rest of the magical community heaped on top, so good luck trying to find *me*. Besides, it's Toronto, the capital of UnSeelie Spring. No one's going to do anything *here*." Celadon's continued silence was a clear refusal to see her sense, but that was sometimes his way—fae and their stubborn natures. "You know, I think you only come to meet me at school for the attention."

"Arlo." Celadon's tone bore something of a whine as he fell into place at Arlo's side, a little too eager to latch on to a different subject. "You really don't appreciate how exciting your life is. You get to go to high school—*human* high school! Most fae don't get to experience this total immersion in human life for themselves. *And*"—here he paused for dramatic effect—"you don't have to learn from Feng. You do realize you get to do absolutely nothing that resembles slacking off with a dragon for a teacher, yeah?"

He sighed theatrically. Arlo tugged him toward the subway station, still hoping to beat the rain. "You do realize you're one of the rare few in this world who get to *say* they had a dragon for a teacher, yeah?"

Feng was an impressive woman, and not only in her carefully manicured appearance. Nobody knew how many dragons were left in the world, not since the Courts had forced them into hiding long ago. Not even Feng could say for certain, because according to her, their human disguises had been made of more than simple glamour, and after so many years, most had forgotten how to shed it.

Some had forgotten they were dragons to begin with.

"Besides," Arlo continued, "I don't exactly get the full immersion experience. Nobody talks to me. I mean, they certainly talk *about* me, but I'm pretty sure that conversation back there with Rachael and Paige was the first thing someone's said *to* me since I got here this morning. They all think I'm some snobby rich kid, which, all right, there are tons of snobby rich kids to befriend at this school, but the snobby rich kids don't talk to me either. *They* think I'm *weird*. The only time anyone acknowledges my existence is to ask whether or not you're single and interested in going to some stupid party with them."

Celadon shot Arlo an overdramatic look of outrage. "Do you care to explain why I've never received any of these alleged invitations?"

Shaking her head, Arlo pressed her lips together in silent disapproval. She must have looked a great deal like her mother doing so, because the action earned her a particular peal of wind-chime laughter that Celadon reserved for what he liked to call her "Thalo moments."

Making their way down the gray-cast street, Arlo and Celadon curled through the mass of people who also hoped that a bit of luck and haste would help them beat the rain. Arlo's Sight was nowhere near as strong as it should be, especially through this haze, so she couldn't pierce through glamours well enough to actually *see* if the people they passed were the folk disguised as humans. But if she focused, she could scent their auras.

Some of the people around them were human. Others, however . . .

They passed a young man with bright blue hair and numerous tattoos crawling up his neck who smelled like seaweed and damp wood. There was also a little girl in rain boots and a dotted yellow jacket, smelling like decay and mossy soil, and a group of loud and laughing teens, who parted like fish around the people in their way and left a briny scent in their wake, which stuck in Arlo's nose long after they'd passed. Arlo watched as a tall man with a clean-shaven face and slicked-back hair—who smelled strongly of orange and tar—winced after he'd stumbled and grabbed for the iron stair-railing on his way down into the station.

There were so many folk in Toronto . . . so much *magic* hidden in this human city. Iron was no less toxic to them now than it had always been. Direct contact with this noxious metal could befuddle, sicken, and—in certain cases of prolonged contact—even kill, but hiding an entire Court away in some forest had become impossible quite some time ago. The gods were no longer here to help conceal whole islands and impressive caves carved deep into the mountains and pockets of forest the folk had once called home. The ever-spreading human population had grown to be a force with which they just couldn't contend on their own.

It fell to the Heads of the Courts to maintain the magical buffer that allowed folk to live among this poison with only muted effects—a little sting, with direct contact, and a little weakness if there was too long a gap between detoxifying wilderness vacations. Arlo had learned through lessons with her mother that part of the reason the Heads of the Courts had chosen to unite was for the boost to their power such unity awarded. Their magic had grown so strong because of it that the Courts themselves had become a sort of shield, and any who swore them allegiance would be able to enjoy its protection.

That shield became less effective the further one strayed from Court capitals.

When her great-uncle had won his crown from his father, when he'd become High King of all Courts, Toronto had become an epicenter of the magical community. Creatures of all walks of life had been drawn into its folds, and Arlo liked nothing better than to hone her talent on them all.

Today, however, she was too distracted by the conversation she knew she was about to have with her father to indulge in this. She was silent as she and Celadon crammed themselves into a subway car, and even as Celadon filled her ears with palace gossip. Thankfully, their ride was untroubled by delays, but by the time they reached their stop and exited the subway, the downpour had started in earnest.

"Just like you to remember to bring *me* an umbrella and not one for yourself," Arlo joked. She suspected Celadon only pretended not to hear her over the roar of the raindrops that hammered their now-communal umbrella.

"Is this where your father's meeting you?" he asked when they reached their destination—a pocket of sidewalk off College Street. A slab of gray stone engraved with the words UNIVERSITY OF TORONTO marked out the area as one of the enormous campus's many entrances. It was the spot where her father usually came to collect her whenever they decided to meet on the days he worked here at the school; no one liked driving around the city this time of day any more than they could help. "Where's he taking you?"

"I think he said it was called 'Good Vibes Only.'"

"Good Vibes Only?" Amusement was clear in Celadon's voice, which Arlo found slightly unsettling.

"What am I missing?"

Waving off the comment, Celadon smiled. "Are you sure I can't come with you? I wasn't kidding; being at home right now is a nightmare."

"Not that I don't love you and all, but if you're only here so you can shirk responsibility, you're going to have to deal. Everyone already thinks I'm too much of a distraction for you as is. Anyhow, I don't think today's a good day to tag along. I have a feeling we're going to have the Talk."

"Really?" Celadon waggled his brows, mood instantly recovered. "In the middle of a café? Scandalous. Please let me join you?"

"Wha—urgh, no, not *that* talk. I think I've worked out where babies come from by now, thank you. I've already had to live through that awkward discussion with *both* parental units. No, I mean the School Talk. The Talk where Dad wants to know what I've decided about university in the fall."

Celadon sighed, angling the umbrella to match a change in the rain's direction. "Fine. Call me when you get home?"

"So clingy. We need to find you a significant other. Or a cat."

"I do like cats. I'd also like you to call me."

"Oh, look, there's my dad," said Arlo with some exaggeration.

She waved at an oncoming car as it slowed to a stop beside them. "*Bye*, Cel. Thanks for walking me from school."

"Bye, Arlo! If you don't call me tonight, I'll just assume you've been murdered, shear off all my hair in mourning, and write lengthy poetry immortalizing that one time you beat me at Mario Kart." He beamed, holding the umbrella over them both as they approached her father's blue Ford Focus.

Arlo shook her head. Sometimes the only response for Celadon's antics was to say nothing.

She opened the door to her father's car and climbed inside, instantly greeted by an overloud radio broadcast.

". . . police have yet to confirm whether or not these human remains have any connection to the three identical cases uncovered in other areas of Washington State as well as Arizona, Nevada, and California."

Arlo's father reached to turn the volume down while Arlo gave one last absent wave farewell to her cousin, who shut the door behind her.

"There's my girl," he greeted, his English accent rounding his words. "Was that Celadon? I haven't seen him since Christmas. Is he all right? From here he looked a bit peaky."

Arlo glanced up from the radio. The sudden encounter with this gruesome report had momentarily distracted her. Another mutilated corpse—another dead ironborn. She hadn't been lying; she wasn't really concerned about becoming a target—it was just too unlikely that anything would happen here . . . but the more she heard about it, the longer it was in the news and circulating in conversation, the more she felt a prickle of unease with every mention.

Shaking her head, she tried to locate Celadon on the sidewalk and see if what her father said was true, but he'd already begun his way back to the subway. All she could see of him through the crowd was his obnoxiously bright umbrella.

Arlo frowned. *Had* he been looking unwell?

She hadn't noticed. He'd been looking tired, sure, but she'd written that off as the wear of dogging her every move and weathering the High King's accountants and their argument over budget reports, as he'd mentioned.

"I think he's just had a long day. I'll ask him about it later." She'd check on him after dinner. "Anyhow, hi, Dad. How are you?"

Rory Jarsdel was a man of exceptional intelligence and simple pleasures. He liked ridiculous woolen sweater-vests and floral printed china for his afternoon tea. One of his favorite pastimes was scouring bookstores for science-fiction novels to add to his already overflowing bookshelves. Not particularly tall, and handsome in a very modest way—at least, in comparison to the ethereal loveliness that was the Viridian family—Rory had his own peculiar charm. What Arlo liked best about him was the fact that he wore the signs of his age in the softening of his gut, in the smile lines etched around his eyes and mouth, and in the dimming fire of his hair, which had recently started turning an ashy silver.

Fae aged—they could even die of it if it wore on long enough—but for them the process was nowhere near as quick as it was for humans. The same held true (to varying degrees) for the ironborn and faeries. The folk developed at the same pace as humans from birth to Maturity, that time when folk came into their full power—their version of puberty. Once it kicked in, both physical and mental aging began to cement in many of their kind, slowing down so drastically that decades could pass without much noticeable change. Eventually, even if Arlo would always look far too young for her age (and what she'd do when her father noticed *that* was a whole other problem to worry about), she'd start looking older than her mother.

"Oh, I'm doing just fine. Much better now that I have my best girl with me! And how are *you* doing? How does it feel to be eighteen years old?"

"Like I'm going to be tired for the rest of my life, I think," she replied. "Yesterday was . . . kind of busy."

72

Not that she could tell him why.

"Tired?" Rory teased, pulling back into traffic. "Poor old girl, eighteen going on sixty."

"I'm not the one who phones his daughter every time David's Tea brings out a new flavor, you know."

"Simple joys, Arlo. We can't all live in Success Tower's seven-million-dollar condos."

Arlo brushed off the passive-aggressive comment with an awkward laugh.

Arlo liked her father. She often got on well with him too, when she could overlook the extreme aversion to magic he'd supposedly had—that, and the ball of resentment in her chest she felt for having to shoulder the responsibility of *his* choices to keep him in the dark about the magical world. But she found it hard to deal with Rory's not-at-all secret opinion of both Arlo's mother in general and the extravagance of her lifestyle. At this stage in the game, it was almost second nature to start tuning him out whenever he started in on either. The disparaging comments ended there, however, and soon they were both laughing over their favorite scenes from the Marvel movies Arlo had finally convinced him to watch.

Engrossed in the conversation, she almost didn't notice it.

As they pulled into a parking space outside the café, an odd and wriggling sensation—cool and clammy as death—ghosted over her skin. Through the open passenger-side window, a faint and sickly sweet scent like rotting flowers threatened to make her gag.

Whose aura was *that*?

Arlo stopped laughing and diverted her attention to the opposite side of the street, where that cool sweetness seemed to originate. It was disconcerting. She'd never felt an aura like *this* before—beyond a pressure in the air, beyond a shiver through her nerves . . . wrong and dead and *writhing* against her skin like worms in a grave. But even as she focused her Sight to locate the source of the aura, she knew it was too late. The feeling had faded, and its source was gone.

73

When she turned back to the café, Sight still active, the identity of what might have been roaming past them was chased fully from her mind. Arlo knew immediately why Celadon had found their destination so entertaining.

Good Vibes Only was a faerie café.

CHAPTER 5

Arlo

————— ⤳⤲ —————

TUCKED AWAY IN A crowded strip of office buildings, clothing boutiques, and numerous ethnic restaurants, Good Vibes Only was an innocuous slip of dark red brick and faded silver lettering, barely noticeable to human passersby. But judging by the obviously human couple who'd just left through the glass front door, it was not entirely concealed from detection.

Faerie cafés were an increasingly popular trend in the Courts. The common folk—faeries and ironborn—weren't quite as restricted in their relationships with humans as the fae were, but it was still the law that no one outside of the magical community could know about the Courts' existence without their Court's approval. This meant that sometimes, faeries needed somewhere they could go to unwind without fear of discovery, and rather than exhaust themselves on erasing such places altogether, the folk had come up with a trendy alternative.

When Arlo and her father entered Good Vibes Only, it had taken little effort to sense the many auras perfuming the air. It was far beyond Arlo's current ability to separate one from the other in this sort of setting, the effect a bit like stepping inside a scented candle shop, but not as overwhelming as she'd feared it would be.

For a human, Arlo's father had quite the ability to pick out magic around him, drawn like a moth to its beckoning flame. Coincidence, most likely, though she supposed it was possible he had a relative somewhere back in his line who was one of the folk, which would explain why he'd been initially drawn to Arlo's mother, and why Arlo's own ability to detect magic was stronger than so many other fae.

"So," Rory hedged when they were halfway through their meal.

He was partially absorbed in sopping up the innards of his burrito with a corner of its soft shell, but as he spoke, he shot a glance across the table at Arlo. "Have you made up your mind about school?"

And here it was—the Talk.

"Not really, no," Arlo sighed. "I know, I know, you were hoping for a better answer. We've already paid the university an acceptance deposit, and . . . I get it, but honestly, I just don't know if I want to go." She leaned back in her chair, dropping her fork to her plate. "I mean, I'm super grateful that U of T accepted me into their arts program, but . . . what am I even going to *do*? I don't have the brains for science, like you. I can't take your biochemistry classes, and *everyone* has an English degree . . ."

She'd only really applied to university because she'd wanted to make sure she had something going for her if the Fae High Council rejected her status altogether.

The Toronto Fae Academy—better known as the TFA (or Teefa, for short), where Arlo's Weighing had taken place—was emphatically *not* on the list of Arlo's options.

Once upon a time, simply *being* ironborn would have guaranteed Arlo's placement there. Their magic was different, was more than the illusions and command of the elements that the fae and faeries practiced. Witches, wizards, sorcerers, warlocks . . . Ironborn had been called many things over the ages, but what they *were* were alchemists. Their talent was that of blending the ancient runes of old magic and the chemical formulas of science into intricate arrays, which helped them to do all sorts of things like cast spells and enchant items and brew potions.

Arlo had no idea why only the ironborn could do this, why those chemical formulas refused to cooperate with magic unless iron blood was present to ground it. She would *never* know why, because all she was permitted to learn now about the art was that centuries ago, an ironborn had tried to use alchemy to make themselves greater than the Courts, and the price of such arrogance had been devastating.

Lives had been lost . . . their secrecy had nearly been blown. . . . After this, the High Council had determined alchemy too dangerous for continued practice and imposed tighter restrictions on the ironborn community as a whole in consequence.

Now the art was outright forbidden, and Arlo would have better luck applying to Starfleet Academy for an education, because the TFA taught *fae* and no one else.

"I was thinking that I could put off this decision for a year or so—travel, like some of the others at school are doing. Or maybe pick up more work here? Because going off someplace where I don't know anyone who could help me if something happened . . ." It was terrifying even to contemplate.

University seemed like the safest and most obvious solution, and the one both her parents wanted her to choose. But that had been before the Weighing, when Arlo had still been content with her faerie status. Ever since, in spite of all her lingering hesitancies and doubts, she'd started giving thought to the things that *she* wanted, neither safe nor practical.

The Council conceding that she could still become a full-fledged fae (however condescendingly) made it impossible for her to shake hoping for the same. It blossomed inside her, pushing her toward something *more*. . . . But it wasn't like she could explain the depth of her indecision to her father, as much as she wished she could.

Sighing, Rory placed his latte on the table. "It's fair, Arlo. It's a lot, I know, and in the end it's your decision. I just don't understand why you don't want to go. It's all right to be scared—nobody knows what they want in life when they're your age. The world's a confusing place, but that doesn't mean you just lay yourself down on the tracks and wait for inspiration to hit you."

"That's a really morbid metaphor—thanks, Dad."

"I know you're worried about doing the right thing, and for whatever reason, you feel like university might not be it? But sometimes you don't figure out what you want until you're right in the thick of it. Your tuition is free since I work at the school, so if you did change your mind, all you'd be owing is what you took out on loan for staying in residence—and even *that* you could avoid by staying with either myself or your mother," he added meaningfully.

"I know." Arlo sighed again. Some of her father's frustration was actually just his own hope that she'd come live with him during her undergraduate career.

She was grateful he seemed to realize there was something beyond teenage theatrics holding her back, but not for the first time, Arlo wondered what her life would be like if her father had never forfeited his knowledge of magic—if she could actually confide in him, play the role of the child she was instead of the parent she needed to be to protect *him*.

"I know. It's not that I don't want to go to school at *all* . . ."

Arlo going off to school was just about the only thing her parents agreed on anymore.

Thalo, enchanted by the human way of life, so much so that it was what had driven her to take one for her husband, wanted Arlo to go to university. Arlo had a feeling this insistence was her mother's regret that she'd never been able to go herself.

Rory wanted Arlo to get a higher education. Blissfully unaware of the life his daughter lived away from his human gaze, school to him meant a job and security and lifelong friendships that would help her discover what she wanted from what he saw as an uncomplicated future.

Flicking her eyes away from their table in an attempt to find a change of topic, Arlo surveyed the café and its patrons.

The quaint little space was crammed with cherry-stained tables, matching chairs upholstered in floral print, and scenic oil paintings hanging on the redbrick walls. On a counter laden with cake plates and fancy bell jars full of pastries was a stack of pamphlets enchanted for human senses to read about some upcoming festival on the Danforth, but were actually the latest in Assistance news—not exactly illegal (freedom of speech was just as much a right in the Courts as it was in this part of the human world) but a surprisingly bold move nonetheless.

The Good Vibes Only employees were going to be in for quite the interrogation once the Courts found out these were here and would be on very close watch here on out.

Beside their table sat a small family, mother and father both engrossed in a phone they held between them. The pair reminisced over photos while their preteen daughter chased ketchup around her plate with her fries. She was completely disinterested in the phone whenever her mother held it out for her inspection, and in Arlo's opinion, looked like she wasn't enjoying herself much at all.

Farther on and seated by the window at the front of the café were two young human men in a great deal of brightly colored spandex, helmets hanging off their chairs. At the table beside them was a group of women in expensive jogging gear, happily chatting away over their lattes. At least one of them was faerie, Arlo could tell by the concentration of aura around the group, but with Arlo's Sight not as strong as it should be, she'd never be able to tell which of them it was, or even what kind of faerie they were.

And that was the real draw of faerie cafés.

The folk didn't come to places like this for the energy found in caffeine; they came to recharge their glamours. With the café's well-trained staff suffusing the air with as much of their magic as possible, no human patron would notice folk around them easing up on their own disguise. Weary members of the magical community could pop into a café, rest without having to retreat to their homes, and absorb a bit of the magic that was freely given. Upon their leave, they'd feel as refreshed as they had at the start of the day, and the staff were paid extremely well for this service, funded by the Courts themselves.

Despite her curiosity regarding this faerie jogger, Arlo allowed her gaze to continue to drift around the room. She tried her best to divide her attention between her perusal and the story that had taken up their conversation now—her father's move to Canada—which she'd heard numerous times before.

". . . so I get why you feel that way. I mean, I moved all the way across the North Atlantic Ocean when I married your mother. It was frightening as all hell—I didn't know a single person here—but I was very taken with Thalo, and she was pregnant with you, and . . ."

It was the girl in the far corner who next snagged Arlo's attention, although at first Arlo couldn't say why.

Two seats down from the chatty joggers, this new source of interest was casually folded against the back of her chair, but her nonchalant posture was incongruous with the rapt attention she focused on the family next to Arlo. The girl was all alone with nothing but her latte and sandwich, and by the looks of things, somewhere around Arlo's age, if just a little older. The way she dressed wasn't anything unusual for city fashion, but it gave her the appearance of someone who kept rough company.

With the girl's black skinny jeans, black leather boots, and equally black leather jacket, thrown over a simple tank top in yet *more* black, part of Arlo wanted to write her off as the sort she went to school with—the ones who smoked in the drama-wing bathrooms and pierced their own ears with the backs of pins.

The cool girls.

Arlo had never fit in with them, even when the kids her age hadn't actively ignored her. Not that she'd ever really fit in with any crowd, but her spectacular inability to push boundaries made her woefully ill-suited to that one in particular. Instinct urged her to look away, but the intense way this girl stared at that family . . . Was she planning on mugging them or something?

It wasn't any of Arlo's business.

What could she do, besides? Give the family a heads-up? Tell them the girl in the corner looked like a "shady character" and they had better keep an eye on their possessions? Most likely she was completely harmless, and all Arlo would end up doing was cause problems where there were none before.

Really. She should just look away, but there was something so *off* about her.

". . . honestly, it felt a bit like waking from a dream and falling straight into cold, hard reality. But I had my job, and I had my friends, and I had you, and life was going to carry on whether I wanted it to or not. So I told myself, 'Ror, you can't just sit around feeling sorry for yourself. You either shit or get off the . . .'"

The longer Arlo looked, the harder it became to look *away*, and the more she was convinced that the girl in the corner was more than what she seemed.

Was she faerie?

Unlike the girls at her school, who'd done a good job at playing tough and dangerous, there was an air about this one that said she was no act. It was all in the way she held herself. That casual grace. She was pretty well-covered and obstructed by her table, but there was strength at rest in her long body, and all that black seemed like snakeskin stretched over pure muscle.

Most concerning were her eyes.

Her outward appearance was sun-bronzed skin and pale-sand hair gathered messily behind her head; her face was an armory of sharp features and deadly edges; her steel-gray eyes were bright as the glittering points of daggers.

Too bright.

Something flexed behind them, a shadow of something Arlo couldn't quite make out—but it was there.

Her magical signature was not.

This girl was strong, and she was beautiful, and most of all she was *frightening*, but Arlo could detect nothing about her to mark her as anything other than human. Was her magic simply too weak to stand out against everything else in the café?

Arlo began to focus her Sight once more, probing for even a trace of magic—or that had been the intention, until the girl finally realized *she* was now the subject of someone's attention.

Steel eyes slid to Arlo.

The glare the girl narrowed in Arlo's direction made Arlo recoil violently. Pressure exploded behind her eyes as deadly pain blossomed in her stomach, and her vision splintered momentarily into darkness.

"*Arlo?*" Rory gasped. "Hey, are you all right? What's wrong?" His hands flew out to steady the drink that Arlo's alarm had almost knocked over.

She stared at her father, blinking through her daze, trying to comprehend his simple question.

At the same time, her hand slid over her stomach, and she was genuinely surprised when it didn't come away red. She could almost swear she'd been stabbed through the gut, that she was hurt, and badly, yet . . . all was well.

The pain had faded as quickly as it had been inflicted.

A few red hairs were out of place, thanks to her inexplicable spasm of horror, and neither her jeans nor the white T-shirt under her cardigan showed any sign of a wound.

She was fine.

Had what Arlo felt been the girl's *aura*?

Impossible.

She had *never* felt an aura that fiercely. Arlo's mind was playing tricks on her. How much caffeine was in her drink? Frowning at her cup, she apologized with the lie, "Sorry, I'm fine. I spaced out there for a second. Something touched my leg and it startled me."

Rory allowed his daughter's weird behavior to slide with nothing more than a quirk of his brow. Before Arlo could stop herself, she shot another glance over her father's shoulder at the girl who might have just tried to murder her with a glare. If that hadn't been in Arlo's imagination, was that girl fixing the same strange power on the family she'd been watching?

That preteen girl at the table beside her . . . Was that the reason why she looked so distinctly uncomfortable?

The girl in the corner wasn't looking at Arlo now. She'd gone back to watching the family as they packed up their belongings. Her brow started to cave under what looked a lot like . . . concern? Curiosity? It was hard to tell.

"You don't seem too interested in your meal. Are you ready to go, then?"

"Huh?" Arlo turned her attention back to her father. "Sorry, not really hungry today, I guess. We can go, yeah."

"—told you, I'm not feeling well!" the preteen girl complained, stealing Arlo's focus once more.

Her words were an understatement.

She didn't look like she was feeling well at all. She'd begun to sweat and was now turning an alarming shade of white. Hunched in her seat, she'd abandoned her fries in favor of rubbing her chest and was much worse off than she'd been a moment ago, to the point where Arlo wondered if she was going to vomit on the floor between them.

"Cassandra, honey, *honestly*—"

"Carl, she really doesn't look well. Maybe we should go back to the hotel and just relax for the rest of the day?"

"She's been complaining this whole trip, Chloe. Just because this isn't Palm Springs doesn't mean she can't enjoy herself, God forbid! Listen, Cassie, you really need to stop this."

"You never *listen* to me!" Cassandra cried. Her words started to slur together, and genuine tears began to streak down her far-too-pale face. "M'not feeling well. My *chest* hurts! I w-want to go home." She groaned then, fisting the fabric of her shirt. "M'going to be sick."

"You're *making* yourself sick!"

"*Carl.*"

"Arlo, are you listening to me?"

"What the . . . ," Arlo gasped, shooting straight up in her seat as something *very strange* began happening with the girl—Cassandra.

At the same time, Cassandra doubled over. "I d-don't . . . ," she stammered through what sounded like a firmly clenched jaw, right until she threw up on the ground and proceeded to collapse. Her

83

mother's chair clattered to the floor as she flew to her daughter's aid.

"Cassandra!"

Arlo could only stare, eyes wide.

It wasn't Cassandra vomiting that had her so entranced—it was the way the blood in her veins had started to *glow* as bright and ruby red as a traffic light.

"What the hell is *that?*" Arlo marveled under her breath, rising slowly to her feet.

Cassandra's frantic parents were now both huddled around their daughter and calling for help. They were nowhere near as concerned as they should be about their daughter's unusual glowing . . . almost as though they couldn't see it at all.

Instinct kicked in once more.

Arlo's gaze drifted away from the family, away from the staff now rushing over, away from the stunned onlookers whose faces were slowly crumbling in horror as they picked up words like "not breathing" and "no pulse"—and over to the girl in the corner.

The girl sat statue-still, watching as one of the employees carefully stretched Cassandra out on the floor so they could administer CPR. She was watching like this was all to be expected . . . like this was just the next step in some horrendous plan, and everything was going accordingly.

"Hey!" Arlo growled, suddenly too angry to be surprised by her own boldness. "You—"

Oblivious to her shouting, Rory launched from his chair, deftly circumventing the table to pull Arlo aside. His focus was solely on clearing space for the family and those attempting to help the girl on the floor.

The faint call of sirens began to sound in the distance. Someone had summoned an ambulance, and it drew closer by the second. The faerie in the group of joggers was now identifiable, the only one looking on in something of bemused interest, more fascinated by the spectacle than horrified by some random human death, but one of her companions (a nurse, she declared herself) came out of her shock to join the staff on the floor with Cassandra.

There was already enough commotion without Arlo shouting across the room at callous strangers, and it wouldn't help anything besides, but she'd succeeded in drawing the girl's attention once again.

This time, Arlo was the one to wield a glare.

Already the glow in Cassandra's body began to dim. Arlo had never encountered magic like this before, but the girl in black . . . Arlo was willing to bet *everything* that she had something to do with this. In the very least, she knew more than anyone else here about what was going on, and that was enough to make Arlo suspicious.

Even if this girl wasn't the reason for this turn of events, she'd done nothing to try to prevent this. She'd known something was wrong—why else would she have been staring so hard at them—and now a mother was kneeling in hysterics on the floor, begging her too-still daughter to "open your eyes, sweetie, *please.*"

The paramedics finally arrived, bursting in through the front door and ushering everyone farther away. It was only because Arlo had been watching the possible culprit instead of Cassandra that she saw her try to slip away, to make for the café's entrance and use the commotion as cover for her flight.

"It's all right," Rory whispered, misreading Arlo's agitation and drawing her closer. He dropped a kiss against her hair without looking—his attention was fixed on Cassandra, now being lifted onto a stretcher. "It's all right, everything's okay."

A lie.

For Cassandra, everything wasn't going to be "okay." Arlo didn't need the shell-shocked mother and father or the grim-faced paramedics to tell her that little girl was dead. The glow that had started to dim in her veins had died off completely even before they could cover her body and hurry her out to the waiting ambulance. Arlo didn't need an official proclamation to know what that meant.

She pulled away and ran, without thinking—it was the only

explanation for the burst of bravery that set her off after the girl in black.

"Arlo!" her father called. "What are you doing?"

"Sir, I'm going to need you to stand back, please."

"But my daughter—Arlo!"

Arlo burst out of the Good Vibes Only café and looked around wildly. "Hey! You! *Stop!*"

The girl in black had made it far enough down the street that she could have pretended not to hear her. Already at the curb of the crosswalk that separated this block from the next, she could have escaped quite easily, even with Arlo rushing after her. But for some reason, she chose instead to freeze. Arlo didn't question it. Her outrage propelled her forward, distracting her from how terribly uncomfortable she usually was with confrontation.

"What did you do?" Arlo shouted the accusation whipping around like a storm inside her.

She'd caught up at last. With no real idea what to do next, Arlo did the first thing adrenaline suggested—she reached out and snatched the girl's arm, tugging the girl around to face her.

"*Excuse* me?"

Whatever tension had been in the girl relaxed into threatening poise. She glared down at Arlo, those gray eyes even sharper now that Arlo was close enough to count the barely-there freckles on her tanned face. She wasn't human—Arlo could finally say that for certain. What she *was* was a little more ambiguous, but there was just enough other-worldly keenness lurking beneath her human guise to give her away.

It infuriated Arlo that she couldn't help but note the girl was even more beautiful up close.

And that painful sensation she'd felt in the café . . . It *was* the girl's magic, she could feel it better now. Two auras in one day . . . Arlo didn't know what to make of this startling progression of her ability to physically *feel* magic, but this aura was different from the one she'd felt earlier before entering the café. This one was *violent*, angry and writhing and hot. It smelled like woodsmoke and metal—not rotting flowers—and lashed out at Arlo the very moment her own tried to brush against it.

She almost recoiled.

She would have, except . . . something in the girl's glare seemed to *want* that, and Arlo could be just as obstinate as the fae in her family when she was in a mood.

"I *said*, what did you do to that girl?"

"Bold assumption, Red. Listen, is this all you wanted? Because I'm a little busy at the moment. I don't have time to play another round of 'Pin the Blame on the Dark Star' today."

The Dark Star . . .

"What?"

The girl in black sneered. She allowed Arlo to keep her hold on her right arm, but with her left, reached up to tug aside the collar of her jacket.

Arlo's eyes widened.

There on the hollow of her neck was the tattoo of a great black star, and she immediately knew what it meant, even though she'd never seen it with her own eyes before this moment and all she had to base her conclusions on were rumors.

Arlo dropped her hand. There wasn't much known about the Dark Star—the infamous faerie who was more a plague than anything else to the magical community. It had been quite a while since anyone had caught her long enough to hold an actual conversation—in fact, some of the folk thought she wasn't even real, just the faerie version of a bogeyman, a scapegoat for things gone wrong that no one could explain.

The High King had issued a statement only days ago naming the Dark Star a suspect in the string of ironborn murders. It had raised a lot of doubt, both in the High King's sanity by placing the blame on some wild poltergeist of their imagination, and in his famed nerve. But Arlo had just witnessed with her own eyes a little girl *die* because of something this girl in front of her had done . . .

Was Cassandra ironborn? Arlo hadn't thought to check her aura. But if this was the Dark Star and she *was* responsible for all the other ironborn deaths . . .

"It's *you*." Arlo cringed away.

"It's *me*." Something a lot like triumph flickered across the girl's face, but it wasn't quick enough to mask the disappointment that showed there first. Arlo had no idea what that meant.

She didn't care.

"You're coming with me."

Wherever all this boldness came from, Arlo wasn't going to argue. Perhaps it was a side effect of her relief over her Weighing, perhaps it was the disconcertion of witnessing someone's *death*, but Arlo snatched up the Dark Star's arm once more and turned to march back down the street.

"What . . . what are you *doing*?"

Perhaps the Dark Star was just as shocked by Arlo's boldness. The girl stumbled along behind her, putting up no fight. "Hey, Red—what the shit?"

"I'm taking you back to the palace."

"Uh . . . no thanks?"

"I didn't ask if you *wanted* to."

"Okay, Miss Sassypants. Are we *walking* the whole way, then?"

This was . . . a very good question that only served to make Arlo more irritated. This girl, whether or not she was the genuine Dark Star, had no appreciation for the situation she was in or apparent remorse for what she'd potentially just done. "Yes," Arlo gritted out.

"Huh. You're . . . really not afraid of me, are you. You know, this is the first time I've ever been arrested by a pretty young maiden, and such *fury*—I like that. Want to get coffee after this? At a different café, of course. That last one was sort of a buzzkill—"

"Are you kidding me?" Arlo stopped and whirled around. "A little girl just *died*. She's dead. In front of us, in front of her parents . . . She's *gone*, and you're making *jokes*?" Arlo was shouting now. Pedestrians practically ran by them to avoid winding up a part of this scene. The girl in black looked back at Arlo in pure astonishment. Arlo had a hard time believing no one had ever yelled her down before, so that couldn't be the reason for it.

"It . . . wasn't *me*."

The words were spoken so softly, too much like the teen this girl looked to be underneath all her swagger—young and lost and, at the moment, slightly terrified—to be the monster everyone accused her of being. A bit of Arlo's anger relented, seeing this. "You can tell that to the High King, then."

"Yeah, no, hard pass on that."

The moment of sincerity was gone, swept away by returning bravado. The girl in black collected herself, and before Arlo could stop her, she tore her arm easily out of Arlo's hold.

"Wait—get back here!"

"*Arlo*, what the *hell* do you think you're doing, running off like that?"

Rory latched on to his daughter, spinning her to face him. It was all the distraction the girl in black needed to escape, to hurry back up the street and disappear into the crowd.

That was fine.

She could run.

Too bad for her that Arlo had something better than a description of her face to track her down.

The Dark Star . . .

The girl in black was gone, but she wasn't getting away. Whether or not she was who she claimed, that tattoo on her neck would only make her easier to find again. The girl had answers. Unfortunately for whatever devious plot this Dark Star made herself a part of, Arlo was going to ensure it wouldn't stay secret for long.

A year had passed since Hero had first met the acid-eyed Hunter. The seal on his magic had been lifted and his memory of the magical community restored—a feeling much like waking from a dream and stepping into cold reality—but regaining these had been . . . *unpleasant*.

It had taken months for Hero's illness to subside. His stutter, his forgetfulness, his headaches and sleepless nights and soul-weary fatigue . . . These things had only gotten worse before they got better. His body had needed time to adjust to the sudden reorganization in his brain. The reversal of the High Council's violation hit him like an angry storm, his power a living thing, extremely displeased with its confinement and intent on making this known.

And then . . . he was fine.

As though he'd never known this hardship at all, Hero felt like himself again.

Of course, there had come a toll. Without his knowledge, his leaving home had been nothing more to his memory than a dramatic affair of his mother tossing him out, and Hero had been all too happy to leave. The squalor they lived in, his six younger siblings who were often left to Hero's care, his mother rarely home and his alcoholic father only coming around between girlfriends . . . None of this had ever given him any joy.

His knowledge returned, he now remembered the event as his mother wanting him gone because letting him stay would mean too much work on her part. She would have had to keep her other children from showing their magic in front of him, as was the rule in these cases, not to mention she no longer received a child bonus check from the Courts now that he was eighteen and no longer of "magical status." Hero's use to his mother had completely run out, and remembering exactly why—that it all boiled down to *value*, that his own mother had deemed him *worthless* to her—had hurt.

But it was no matter.

Hero had now what was most important: all of the pieces that made him *him* . . . and no idea what the acid-eyed Hunter wanted for giving this back.

"Malachite—dear man, what on earth has brought you all the way out to *Nevada*?"

The voice that had spoken snapped Hero from his thoughts and struck something inside him . . . a memory he'd yet to reacquaint himself with. He looked up from his cappuccino and out across the small café where he worked and immediately pinned the source as a man—unquestionably fae, though glamoured—who'd just come through the door.

Tall and lithe but visibly strong, ivory fair and handsome, outfitted in an expensive suit so dark an emerald it verged on black. His magic only barely stretched to cover the points of his ears and the flush of blue beneath his skin, and he had a way of moving that said he thought incredibly well of himself—a *wealthy* fae, then, and one with power.

"Briar Sylvain," exclaimed another glamoured fae with a chuckle. "I could ask the same of you!" This was obviously "Malachite"—just as tall as Briar Sylvain and a little stronger, with skin tanned sunny brown and eyes a jade so bright they had to be the result of magic. Beautiful, poised, and a twilight glow about him . . . This one was royal, if Hero remembered correctly what that glowing actually meant.

They embraced, and Hero's head started to ache as he struggled to recall a memory. Briar Sylvain . . . He *knew* that name . . .

"Out here on business, then?"

Malachite grinned. "A Tracker never sleeps, you know that. You as well?"

Briar took a seat at his friend's table, smoothing out the creases the action put in his pants. "Yes, a Councillor doesn't sleep either. It's that time of year we make our rounds to the Academies and check on progress. You know, I'm surprised to find you all the way out here—didn't your sister just give birth to a baby girl? What was her name again?"

"Arlo." Malachite pulled a face. "Arlo Jarsdel—what an ugly name. An ugly iron name for ugly iron blood. She's no family of *mine*, so I don't see the cause for celebration."

"Yes, yes, I agree. Quite a sin, in my opinion, that the old families should start to *rust* at all—best to keep yourself removed from that sort of shame. At least she wasn't given the Viridian name." He shook his head, as though that would be the worst offense of all. "Not to worry, when her Weighing comes, I'll do everything in my power to ensure that stain is *removed*. The ironborn . . . They should all be cast out, in my opinion. Why, just the other day—"

The man's voice was drowned out by a ringing, which Hero realized belatedly only he could hear.

He remembered now . . . Briar Sylvain—the Seelie representative of Spring from their Court in England, whose *vote* had been against eighteen-year-old Hero at his Weighing when he'd stood before the High Council in control of his future.

Hero felt his lip curl over itself in the beginnings of a sneer. *Briar Sylvain*, who, much like his mother, had looked down on him and judged him—

"Revolting, aren't they?" a new voice said in his ear.

Hero nearly spilled coffee down his front. The acid-eyed Hunter had a way of appearing out of nowhere.

"How do you keep doing that?" he sputtered.

The Hunter's grin reminded Hero of a shark. "I've been here all this time. A Hunter's glamour is special—I can render myself completely invisible at will. In fact, at the moment, no one can see me or hear me but you."

"Wonderful," Hero muttered. "At least I'm used to people thinking I'm insane." His gaze wandered back to the Councillor and his friend. "They think they're so much better than everyone else."

"Hilarious, isn't it? If only they knew what little Arlo Jarsdel will someday be capable of . . ."

"What makes her so special?" Hero snapped, and then winced. He hadn't meant his words to sound so demanding of his savior and— more importantly—the first friend he'd had in some time.

But for some reason, this only made the Hunter's grin deepen. "I wonder which is greater in you—your avarice or your jealousy?"

"I didn't mean—"

"Forget the girl. I'd rather talk about what makes *you* so special, Hero. What makes you so much better than fae like Briar Sylvain and Malachite Viridian-Verdell . . ."

Yes, Hero would rather talk about that too.

"What sets them apart from you, do you think? What makes them think *they're* better?"

"Wealth."

Hero's reply was immediate—sour—almost before he could think what to say. It made the Hunter creak out a laugh. "Oh?"

"Power, favor, beauty—wealth is more than money, but they've certainly got that, too. They're *worth* more, and so they *are* more."

"Avarice it is, then."

Hero looked at the Hunter. This stunning individual . . . He was worth more too. What would it be like, to stand beside him as an equal—to be more than some charity case but a *partner*? What would it be like if Hero could become someone the Hunter found *attractive*, the way Hero found him? If he could become more like Briar Sylvain, well-dressed and well-liked, wealthy in both appearance and air?

As if reading his mind, the Hunter smiled fondly. "If only there was a way for you to be more too—to give you all the riches in the world, to fund your intelligence, your experiments, your *legend*, my Hero . . ."

My Hero . . . He shivered. He liked when the Hunter called him this.

And he knew the Hunter well enough by now to read the proposition in this statement.

Hero looked at Briar Sylvain. He looked at Malachite. Then he looked back at the Hunter, whose name he hadn't earned yet but was determined he one day would, and repeated what he'd told him upon their first meeting: "I'm listening."

CHAPTER 6

Nausicaä

$\longrightarrow\!\!\!\!\sim\!\!\!\!\longleftarrow$

ALL NAUSICAÄ HAD WANTED was a deities-damned
coffee.

It had been a long day of poking random faeries for
gossip, hoping to learn as much about the area as possible. She hadn't
been in UnSeelie Spring territory for quite some time—not since it
had been in Europe, under the previous sovereign's rule—but the
Viridians had done an impressive job of maintaining their claim on
the Season. There were quite a few royal fae families, after all, none
of which got on all that well, and it wasn't uncommon for Courts to
change hands as well as geographical locations.

Though the Viridians had only settled in this portion of the world
a little over a century ago, that they'd managed to keep UnSeelie
Spring under their control since its founding was no small feat. No
other family could boast such an impressive accomplishment, and as
a result, the magic that followed UnSeelie Spring was uncommonly
powerful . . . but so, too, were its folk, and it was this that Nausicaä
was currently stuck on.

"She shouldn't *exist*. What the *shit* is going on in this Court?"

Nausicaä stopped in her tracks, ignoring the disgruntled cries of
the people behind her on the sidewalk.

Red . . . When Nausicaä had first spotted her in that café, she'd
thought for a moment she was staring at Tisiphone. It was all that
red hair, though Tisiphone's had been the color of precious coral, not
fire. It was those bright green eyes, though Tisiphone's had been like
the sea, not jade. It was the power at her core, though Tisiphone's had
been shaped from Water, not Wind, as what billowed inside Red. All

that power was building like a storm that would one day break free of its confines, and if Red survived that, the Mortal Realm would never know what hit it, because *that girl* . . . Nausicaä had sensed it immediately.

Fate had gone and assembled a mortal with *immortal* magic.

When immortals were Destroyed, they didn't go back into the same Starpool that Fate used to mold her mortal children. Their pool was kept separate, because the stuff that made immortals was much too strong and wreaked havoc on the mortal mind, body, and soul alike that wasn't born of divine parentage.

Did Red have an immortal parent? Unlikely—the immortals were no longer permitted here to make that possible. The Furies and the Wild Hunt and a handful of similar others in various parts of the world were allowed to perform their jobs in this realm, and the Heads of the Courts could extend temporary invitation to any immortal who consented to such a meeting, but that immortal couldn't go farther than the designated meeting grounds.

Besides, Red was very distinctly ironborn; Nausicaä had sensed that in her magic too.

The Titan Fate had been known to do this once in a while—though she hadn't since the immortals' banishment from this realm. She'd take a mortal, "spruce them up" with a bit of otherworldly magic, and throw them into the mix, for the other deities to fight over like a cruel game of capture the flag.

So much of the deities' powers depended on worship. Once upon a time, they'd lain with mortals to produce offspring—demigods, as both folk and humans called them—to help spread word of their grandeur and superiority over other deities and garner favor. Now, though, humans had forgotten the old gods completely. With the folk only worshipping a select few—and only when convenient for them—immortal powers had waned considerably in the passing centuries. People like Red were wild cards, up for anyone to grab for their own. Once Red Matured, once she came into her powers, the deities would *swarm*, clawing at one another to figure out how to win her to their side. And they'd find a way to circumvent the treaty holding them back to do so. No one in the Mortal Realm truly appreciated just how starved the immortals were for their powers to be restored— for the worship that would make them strong again and allow them to break the bonds of the treaty altogether and *return*.

Red would give them an advantage they desperately craved.

So Fate had to be behind this, but *why*? Nausicaä could make all kinds of guesses, but she really couldn't say. She'd never really understood the minds of her elders and hadn't been privy to their plans for some time. The Titans of the West: Fate, Luck, Hope, Ruin, Chaos, Nature, and Time . . . These beings played by their own set of rules. All the best of luck to Red, if she was one of their pawns too.

It wasn't any of Nausicaä's business.

She'd tried to ignore her.

Easily done, at first—the focus of her original curiosity had gone and died, and *she* was definitely ironborn too, judging by that glow inside her veins and the faint magical aura clinging to her mother. The Reaper had to have been nearby. It had clearly been sent to clean up the tracks behind whoever was really responsible here. Nausicaä hadn't been able to sense it, but she knew if she did a bit of poking around, she might be able to find what waited in the offing, biding its time to strike.

Then once again, there was Red, chasing Nausicaä down, all blustering fury, and Nausicaä couldn't help but pause—couldn't help but interact—any more than fire could help the wind that blew it hotter.

Remember our deal.

You'll know when you meet them.

You'll help. I'll take you.

"Fuck that." Nausicaä blew out her cheeks and propelled herself forward once more. Red wasn't who she was meant to help. Nausicaä refused—just as she refused to linger any longer on what had happened. "Now, if I was a giant ass death monster, where would I be hiding . . ."

More and more of late, Nausicaä wondered if the Titan Luck was growing bored with peace just the same as Fate apparently had, because almost in answer to this question, a chorus of screaming grabbed her attention. She stopped once more, eyes grown wide, head whipping to her left.

Toronto's iconic CN Tower loomed directly above her, and at its base sat Ripley's Aquarium of Canada—currently echoing with the terrified cries of humans.

"Huh," Nausicaä said, an important connection clicking into place.

The Courts had driven the Reapers so far from their territories that these creatures had taken to hiding in the world's deepest cracks and caverns. They'd been gone so long from society that a city like this— with all its people and cars and contraptions, lights, and sounds—had to be overwhelming to it.

The Reaper that Nausicaä hunted . . . It was very possible it had been found in some lonely grotto or cave by the sea, where everything was calm and damp and cool. And now that it was so far from where it lived, it was also very possibly homesick . . . and coming across an aquarium would be like finding a desert oasis.

Nausicaä didn't even get the chance to decide if she was going to stop the Reaper or help it.

A monstrous shriek rent the air, much less triumphant than it had sounded back in Darrington, and the aquarium's front doors burst open, spewing out a horde of people. Moments later came a shattering of windows—followed by a *tidal wave* of water and fish and sea creatures.

Nausicaä threw her arms in front of her face and turned to brace herself against the sudden surge . . . but just as it hit, she was whisked away—away from the wave, away from the Reaper, away from the aquarium.

As quickly as she realized someone had teleported her, it was over. When Nausicaä opened her eyes, she found herself, drenched, in the middle of . . . "A cemetery?"

St. James Cemetery, to be exact, the oldest still in operation in Toronto. It was a stone's throw away from the Spring Palace and consisted of the usual things one might find in a graveyard: old and drooping oak trees, mossy headstones, crumbling monuments, weathered marble mausoleums, and a handful of sluagh masquerading as crows, all contained within a flaking, rusted, wrought-iron fence—a superstition developed by humans (back when belief in such things was stronger) to protect them from restless spirits. The day allowed for human traffic, but once night fell, it turned into a thriving faerie hotspot, despite the metal that should have deterred them. At the moment, it was empty of both, save the sluagh.

"Hello, Nausicaä."

Airy, lilting words spilled damp and cool down Nausicaä's neck.

She shuddered and darted instantly away. Her katana assembled itself from a burst of soot-black smoke in her hand. When enough space existed between her and the person who'd brought her here, she whipped around. There were very few in this realm who could successfully sneak up on her, and it was her very worst luck that across from her stood the one she could honestly say she wished *least* to encounter.

"Lethe."

The tall, slip-thin immortal was built a bit like driftwood—a little warped and oddly angled. Everything about him seemed too long and far too narrow. His pale skin possessed a silvery quality that gleamed pearlescent at certain angles, and the freckles splashed across his nose were as white as pricks of starlight. Together with his antifreeze-green eyes and the dark metallic gray of his hair, shaved to stubble on one side of his head and wildly tangled around braids and bits of forest debris on the other, he was the very image of "dangerous magic."

Unfortunately, that image was correct.

Even by Nausicaä's standards, and despite the strict laws that governed his stay in this realm—stay, not banishment, as what kept Nausicaä here herself—Lethe was easily the most dangerous thing this realm possessed; should she spark his mercurial temper, there was very little love between them she could call on for protection.

"It is still Nausicaä, right? It's been so long since we've seen each other that you might have changed it without me knowing." Lethe's owl-wide eyes looked her over in a flick. "Stars, but you make an ugly mortal."

"What do you want, Lethe?" She'd been intentionally avoiding Lethe and the three others who kept his company. All this time, she'd managed to get by without running into him, and he'd clearly not wanted to seek her out himself, so she doubted this decision offended him. But it was better to keep this conversation moving. There was no telling what would set Lethe off, and Nausicaä wasn't exactly known for keeping her cool either.

"What do I want?" He lifted a leather boot to the stone bench between them and leaned against his knee. Neither his boots nor his tight-fitted trousers were all that exciting—as black as the ones Nausicaä wore—but his obsidian, high-collared tunic boasted an elaborate, lethal web of silver fastenings, buckles, and chains that was much more his usual style when out of uniform. "We're family, are we not, *dear* cousin? You come all this way after so long absent, and I don't even get a hug."

"I would rather hug a Reaper. No offense."

Lethe chuckled, a sound like splintering wood. The long fingers of his left hand drummed against his knee, causing the deadly adamantine claws that capped them to glint in shards of light. "Interesting choice of words. A Reaper, hmm? Funny you should bring that up . . ."

Nausicaä stiffened. "You know something."

"Ah, Nausicaä, I know many somethings. I'm very old, and the stars are privy to so many secrets. You'll have to be a little more specific."

"Fine, asshole—you know that there's a Reaper here. In this city. In your keeper's *Court*. In that aquarium you so rudely stole me away from before I could check it out, so thanks for that, *by the way*. You know there's a Reaper out there either cleaning up after some other asshole or capitalizing on their extra-level villainy, using alchemy and ironborn children to whip up their very own—"

"Stars, I know all that?" Lethe raised his right hand—free of the claws on his left—to trace a finger down the acute edge of his jaw. "What a wild imagination you have. But then . . . you've always been this way."

The stiffness in Nausicaä's voice had nothing to do with her wariness now, or unease. "Excuse me?"

Lethe grinned deeply for a taunting second, revealing a mouth crammed full of shark-sharp teeth. Then, abruptly, his face rearranged into exaggerated sincerity. "Yes, you've always been quite good at spinning tales—at thinking with your passions instead of your head. I almost envy that."

"I invite you to shut the fuck up." She knew where this was going. It was nothing she hadn't heard before, numerous times, in numerous versions, but invariably it was the same story.

Tisiphone . . . She'd suffered for so long from chronic depression. It wasn't . . . surprising, given their line of work, being the ones to deal with the very worst that the very worst people could inflict. It wasn't surprising, given how competitive and vicious immortals could be to one another. Tisiphone had been a gentle soul, had never been able to look at suffering with indifference, and this way of life had eaten at her mental health. But immortals were proud. They didn't talk about things like this because they liked to believe "things like this" just didn't happen to them. Nausicaä had had no idea how to relate to this part of her sister, how to keep from making things worse instead of better—hells, what her sister's illness was even *called*—and Tisiphone, desperate for help, had fallen in with an abhorrent mortal fae. Heulfryn . . . He'd pretended to be so sympathetic to her problems, so in love with her, so *loyal* . . . only to make her into the latest of his "conquests," to use her and discard her when he'd gotten what he'd wanted, and it had been the last of what Tisiphone could bear.

Always, the stories that spread about them were Alecto, painted like some tragic hero, driven to madness by grief and convinced of blame where blame wasn't due because immortals never liked admitting a mortal could ever affect them at all, let alone so deeply. In their opinion, it was really Tisiphone to blame for the way things "turned out." *Her* they painted as the victim of her own "dramatics," as though her self-inflicted Destruction—her death by suicide—was some shameful failing on her own part. Always these stories attributed Alecto's rage to overreaction, and *always* it made her stomach turn.

"Like I said, I *almost* envy you, but then I remember how dreadfully pathetic it was to watch Megaera pull you from that burning ship. Pathetic, to see something so magnificent fall to something as petty as grief. And after everything Eris did for you . . ."

Nausicaä shivered.

She tried to focus on her breathing, the way she'd learned in the few therapy sessions she'd managed to talk herself into attending: inhale deeply, hold; exhale deeply, hold; in and hold again. Lethe's words were only that; she couldn't let their sparks catch on the tinder sitting in place of her heart.

"And look at you now."

In and hold; out and hold.

"Your fire's gone dim. You're threadbare rags of your former glory. You *reek* of iron—if I can be completely honest, it embarrasses me to call you family."

"So don't," she growled.

In and hold; out and hold; in and hold again.

It wasn't working.

Her shivering grew into tremors. Her hands began to shake with the fury Lethe knew full well he stirred. Already thrown off by the events in the café, by Red, by the aquarium, it wouldn't take much for Nausicaä to lose herself to the rage now yawning in her chest, lifting its head to scent the air.

She angled the point of her katana at Lethe's heart—a gorgeous assembly of glittering black glass and steel as dark as a void—and curled her lip in a silent snarl. "I'm not going to tell you to shut up again."

"It's your fault too, you know? Tisiphone's death. You torched some insignificant mortal all because he dared to be the latest in your sister's oh so many woes, and you got all hot and bothered at the other immortals for spurning the idea that one of their own could suffer human illnesses. But remind me again, what did *you* do to help where the others didn't? In fact, I distinctly recall you—"

Nausicaä's rage *exploded*.

She lunged and struck . . . and struck . . . and struck at the gleefully laughing immortal, as he dodged, and dodged, and dodged every blow. Darkness ate away at her vision the way heat ate away at film.

Every failed swing built strength for the next. Though none of them landed, they forced Lethe back, step by step, until he was pinned against a tall burgundy headstone.

Nausicaä lifted her katana high above her head. With all the savage might she could muster, she brought it down—

He caught it without a flinch.

The black glass blade wedged firmly into his claw-tipped hand, and sapphire blue welled up around it to trickle down his arm, but he was otherwise unharmed.

He was also, apparently, tired of this game.

His laughter fell flat. With a strength only few could manage, he took advantage of Nausicaä's frustration to wrest her katana clean from her grip and toss it aside. The sword burst back into the same black smoke that called it into this realm, and disappeared. At the very same instant, he gripped her by the back of her neck and hurled her into the headstone he'd been pinned against.

"*Urgh!*" she cried, the wind knocked from her chest.

Lethe held her, bent over the granite stone with all his weight on her back. No matter how she struggled, or screamed, or snarled at him, she couldn't break free—his strength was greater than her own, backed by the full force of his undiminished magic. Her body still trembled with residual anger and adrenaline. Even her teeth chattered with it. When she aimed a kick back at his shin, he blocked it too easily, and kicked back at her just as hard. "Enough," he hissed into her ear.

"Up . . . yours," Nausicaä gritted out, but despite herself, began to settle.

Lethe chuckled another round of splintering wood. "It's nice to see you still have some fight. You're going to need that, cousin. Whatever I do or don't know about what's going on, my hands are tied . . . but others' are not. I hear you're looking for the Faerie Ring."

Known far and wide as the Court of Exiles—a tongue-in-cheek name for the sort of clientele it served—the Faerie Ring would be the perfect place to harvest information about rogue Reapers and nefarious plots. Yes, Nausicaä had been looking for it. The problem was, no one could agree on where it was, if they even had a guess at all. She'd followed directions to multiple locations, none of them correct, and after several hours of trekking her way around Toronto, all she'd wanted from the rest of her day had been to sit in the Good Vibes Only café and eat her sandwich and drink her coffee in peace.

"I despise you," Nausicaä said with great vehemence. "We could have had a normal fucking conversation about this. You didn't have to fucking *bait* me like—"

"How boring."

She ground her teeth. "You're an asshole. You haven't changed a bit. Yes, I'm looking for the Faerie Ring. You know where I can find it, then?"

In response to this question, Lethe released his grip from her neck. He eased his weight off her back, and slid far enough away for her to straighten and gingerly work the kinks from her muscles. "Well?" She glared at him.

Lethe's grin blew uncomfortably wide.

CHAPTER 7

Arlo

T HE SOFT KNOCK AT Arlo's door pulled her from her mired thoughts. She watched it creak open, and through the gap peeked a familiar blond head.

It had taken nearly an hour of adamant reassurance for her father to make peace with dropping her off at home that evening. As far as Rory knew, Thalo worked as security detail for some fancy government official, and when he called her personal cell to learn she wouldn't be back home until much later (something about an incident at the Ripley's Aquarium of Canada), this together with Arlo's inability to explain why she had fled the café so quickly had made it difficult to convince her father she would be okay on her own.

But all Arlo had wanted was to go back home and surround herself with the familiar comforts of her bedroom. Apparently, Thalo was just as concerned about Arlo being alone as her father had been. The blond head poking into her room belonged to none other than her second cousin, Elyas Viridian, and if *he* was here, Arlo suspected Celadon was as well. Elyas and Celadon were the only Viridians, apart from her mother, who cared enough to check on her, and Elyas was too young to travel all this way on his own.

"Arlo?"

"Hey, El."

Arlo slid off the edge of her bed. It was all the permission High Prince Serulian's eleven-year-old son needed to throw the door wide open and hurl himself inside her room of pastel pinks, cream-colored carpeting, and dollhouse-inspired furniture.

Remnants of her childhood.

Arlo's tastes hadn't exactly outgrown things like the princess canopy above her bed, but her teenage years had added an abundance of video games and manga to her now-overflowing bookcases, a plastering of different anime posters to her pink walls, and a veritable mob of collectible figures from all her beloved fandoms to her overcrowded shelves.

"Are you okay?" Elyas asked, immediately wrapping his arms around Arlo. "Uncle Cel said something happened today and you might be upset."

Elyas's sensitivity was something she hoped he'd never outgrow.

He was an absolute brat when he wanted to be, and so much like Celadon in so many ways (not least of all in his delight in causing mischief). His capacity for kindness, though—for compassion, and sympathy, and love—was so great that it often took even those who knew him best by surprise.

But that was Elyas.

Tall and boyish-skinny, Elyas looked a great deal like his grandfather, with his jade-green eyes and the way his hair curled around his ears. But there was his father, High Prince Serulian, in the beginnings of his sharpening cheekbones and jaw, and his mother in his starlight-blond hair.

Arlo could remember being all of seven and holding the newborn prince for the very first time.

They'd grown up together. Arlo had taught Elyas everything she'd known about coloring, and swinging across monkey bars, and playing make-believe, and hosting tea parties for their numerous stuffed animals. She'd been there at every birthday party and every family holiday, and there was so much more left in their lives she wanted to be there for. It hadn't occurred to her until now how easily lost all that could be.

It wasn't until today that she appreciated how *final* death really was.

There was so much she would miss out on if she died now, and that girl . . . Cassandra, barely older than Elyas . . . It was unfathomable to think of *him* in Cassandra's place, his future as cruelly torn from him as hers had been.

"Um . . . Arlo?"

"Yeah?"

"You're squeezing kind of tight."

"I'm sorry," Arlo muttered, unable to ease her hold in the slightest.

Elyas breathed a laugh, and in response, only hugged her tighter. "That's okay. You can hug as tight as you need to. I'm sorry you had such a bad day. Uncle Cel said . . . He said someone died? That's . . . I'm sorry."

"Yeah, me too."

It wasn't until Elyas started rubbing her back that she realized she was crying, now of all times, when she hadn't shed a tear all day. "What do you need?" he asked her softly. It was funny, somewhere in the back of her head, that he was the one allowing Arlo to break down on his shoulder, as though their roles were reversed and she was the little kid and Elyas the newly minted young adult.

She cried, and the more tears that fell, the louder her grief became. Celadon appeared in the doorway.

Still dressed as he'd been when she'd seen him after school, he'd most likely spent the rest of his day avoiding his father's advisors. When Arlo lifted her head, she saw through her tears his pale look of heart-wrenching relief mixed with profound concern. For some strange reason, this only made it harder for her to contain her grief.

"I-I'm sorry!" she wailed, pushing out of Elyas's hug to draw her arms around her middle. She felt distinctly childish, crying in the middle of her bedroom, and it frustrated her that she couldn't stop. "I d-don't know why I'm c-c-crying."

"Yes you do," Celadon soothed. He sounded fairly distressed himself, though whether that was because of Arlo's tears or emotions of his own, Arlo couldn't say. Regardless, he pushed his way into the room, and Elyas moved aside so Celadon could collect Arlo into a hug of his own. Walking her to her bed, they sat together on its edge. "It's all right," he continued to console. "It's okay to cry, Arlo. A terrible thing happened in front of you today, and tears are a perfectly healthy, natural reaction."

"I didn't even know the girl."

"Do you need to know a person to feel sympathy for them? You're kind, Arlo, and you feel things deeply. That's not something to be embarrassed about, you know? There's a great many people who go their whole lives without ever learning to feel that compassion, and in my opinion, it's better to feel too much of that than to look on at suffering and feel nothing at all."

Arlo thought of the girl—the one in black, whose magic had been so violent, so volatile, that Arlo had been able to feel it like a physical wound; the girl who'd been virtually unaffected by the death of such a young child and had watched it go down like some grade-school science project.

The girl in black, who was quite possibly the one behind everything happening to the ironborn community lately . . . the one the folk had labeled their unlucky Dark Star.

Arlo's tears stemmed into sniffles.

"Can I talk to you about something?"

"Of course you can," Celadon replied. He didn't need it spoken to know she wanted to talk in private. Glancing over at Elyas, he said in equal gentleness, "Elyas, why don't you go warm up those cinnamon rolls we brought? I'm sure Arlo could use a sugar high right about now."

Elyas wrinkled his nose at Arlo. "No one buys *me* cinnamon rolls when *I'm* upset," he teased, as he usually did whenever he wanted to defuse a situation and bring a smile to Arlo's face. "When did you become the High Queen?"

"Shut up," Arlo teased weakly in return as she wiped the tears from her eyes. "Go warm me a cinnamon roll like you were told. The last time you were sad, Celadon bought you a *horse.*"

Unable to deny this fact, Elyas shot his tongue at Arlo and took his leave.

"All right. It's just us now," said Celadon. "What did you want to talk about?"

"It's . . . about the café."

"Yes?" Celadon prompted patiently.

She launched into what had gone down at Good Vibes Only, her encounter with the girl in black, and what had really happened to Cassandra, who was maybe ironborn but whose death didn't quite match up to the pattern of what had claimed the others. "—and then she just started glowing."

Celadon cocked his head in confusion. "What do you mean she started glowing?"

"Like . . . her veins. There was something in her veins, and it started glowing this really bright red, and then she collapsed. It faded when she . . . But it wasn't a trick of the light," Arlo added hurriedly. "It wasn't my imagination, I swear, that little girl was *glowing*. And I don't have any proof apart from what I felt, but I *know* the girl in black had something to do with it. So, I . . . uh, followed her."

"Excuse me, you did *what*?"

"Let me finish!" Arlo held up a hand. "I followed her—she tried to leave, and I don't know, I guess I was just upset, I didn't really think about what I was doing—"

"You don't say."

"But I caught up with her on the street and . . . well, tried to get her to come back to the palace to talk to the king, and one thing led to another and just, it's . . . *very* possible the girl in black is the Dark Star, is what I'm trying to say."

If Celadon had been wearing pearls, Arlo had the distinct impression he would be clutching them right now in horror. "The Dark Star," he repeated faintly.

"Yes."

"She was in the café."

"I'm . . . fairly certain, yes."

"The café where a little girl *died*."

"Yes."

"The Dark Star, who is currently under suspicion for the involvement in *several murders*, was in a café where *someone lost their life* and you thought you'd just . . . try to arrest her all on your own? And what, march her up the palace steps and present her to my father?"

Arlo took a breath. "It . . . does sound stupid when you say it back at me like that, yes, but you're missing the bigger picture here, Cel."

"No, no, I think I have a fairly accurate idea of the picture, Arlo. Do you realize how dangerous that was? Do you realize you could have been *killed*?"

Arlo swallowed, fear catching up with her at last. "I realize that *now*. I'm sorry."

"I'm just . . . *Cosmin*, Arlo, I'm just glad you're all right." Ah, he was really worked up about this incident. Celadon didn't invoke the UnSeelie folk's patron god (however much out of show this worship was anymore) unless he was genuinely upset.

"You . . . you believe me, though, right?"

Celadon gave Arlo a pointed look. "Who do you think I am? Of course I do. I don't like what you put yourself in the middle of, but I believe it happened. And if you say that girl was the Dark Star, then that's who she was. It *is* strange, though, you feeling her magic that acutely."

Arlo nodded. "I've never *felt* another person's magic before. Not like that. And this was twice in one day, if you count whatever I felt outside the café before we went in. Two different auras . . ."

"Even we don't share that sort of bond," Celadon finished, his tone gentle in contemplation. "I'm closer with you than anyone else. We've spent almost all our time together since you were born. You often don't even need to focus to pick up on my aura now, and the same for me with you. But we don't feel each other's magic any more than usual. It's completely possible you one day could, given how strong that talent is in you, but to feel a complete stranger's magic so profoundly and nothing from your own family . . . well, it's not exactly normal."

Arlo flopped back on her bed. She felt exceptionally drained now that she'd offloaded this information she'd been carrying around and was actually looking forward to the Cinnabon cinnamon rolls Celadon used emotional crises as an excuse to buy.

"Maybe I *am* cracking up."

"Maybe you're coming into your magic. I mean, detecting auras that profoundly is more of an immortal talent, not something generally found in the folk, but it's still *magic*. It could even be a Gift."

"Wonderful. My only superpower is painful sensitivity to others. I'll have to swear off society altogether and live the rest of my days as a hermit. I'll never be able to buy my own Pumpkin Spice Lattes again—you'll have to do it for me."

"Only if you promise to never again chase down wanted criminals." Celadon rose from the bed. Softer, he added, "In all seriousness, are you all right, Arlo? When Thalo came to tell me what happened, she was very worked up—I thought at first something had happened to *you*."

Staring up at the center of her canopy strung with a mobile of glow-in-the-dark stars, Arlo nodded. "I'm all right. No harm done. I'm not the one who died."

"No, you aren't, and I'm going to be glued to your side for the next little while to remind myself of this fact. But witnessing death is corruption of its own. Whether you notice it yet or not, a part of you did not survive your encounter with what you saw today."

For some reason, his words made Arlo laugh. "Wow, easy on the wisdom, Gandalf. You've been reading too much human literature again. The death of innocence—that's William Blake's Songs thing, right?" Celadon frowned, probably at her butchering of one of his favorite author's titles, which only made her laugh again. "Thanks anyhow, yeah?" she added when she calmed. "I think. Even though you more or less just called me corrupt?"

"Arlo," a voice sighed from the doorway. Arlo lifted her head to find Elyas returned. "We have a long way to go before you unlock *that* achievement."

Arlo glanced up at Celadon. "This is why my mother says they should stop letting you babysit him."

"I know," Celadon chimed happily, his way of showing he wasn't concerned about something that might actually be concerning him. "Come on, let's go out to the kitchen and gorge ourselves on baked goods. And I'll talk to Father about what you said. It wouldn't hurt for you to tell Thalo, too. If the Dark Star *is* here, we'll find her, so try not to worry, all right? If we need your help, we'll let you know. For now, I think you've been through enough."

Nodding, Arlo peeled herself off the bed. She'd done what she could, passed her knowledge on to the ones who could actually use it. There wasn't anything else for it now but to wait and see what the High King did.

Hopefully it would be *something*.

The folk labeled the High King's behavior of late erratic, what with him spending more effort chasing down the Assistance than the ironblood killer and naming a veritable ghost the culprit, but Arlo believed he had his reasons. He wouldn't allow a lead like this to go ignored. He wasn't the unfeeling monster the folk were starting to call him. He cared about the ironborn community just as much as he cared about everyone else under his protection. He'd never once been unkind to Arlo, even if he'd been distant, and the Dark Star . . . Now that she was here, he'd be able to capture her, and the whispers would stop—the folk would remember how good their High King was, both to them and at his job.

In the very least, they'd make some progress. Arlo might even learn a few answers to the questions starting to burn in her mind.

For instance, if Cassandra was ironborn, what had all that glowing been about? Had that happened with the others? Would that girl in black have somehow stolen Cassandra away to *mangle* her, as every other victim suffered? *Why?* And underneath all this, if it was so unusual to actually *feel* auras of the folk—if that was a talent better attributed to gods—was it possible what she felt hadn't been one of the folk? *Arlo* was no immortal. Her mother was fae and her father was human, but they knew next to nothing about the Dark Star.

They didn't know who she was. They didn't know *what* she was. The Dark Star's background was a complete mystery to them, and no one had any idea of what they could possibly have done to earn her very apparent contempt.

What if in addition to Arlo's magic getting stronger, the Dark Star was someone who shouldn't be here—an immortal in breach of the treaty that kept them out of the Mortal Realm? What would it mean for Arlo's world if she was?

Arlo followed her cousins out of her room and to the kitchen, a whole new concern blooming inside her chest. She could only hope that her instincts were wrong and it wasn't the beginning of a crisis *worse* than the one they were currently in.

CHAPTER 8

Vehan

⌁

I<small>T DIDN'T SURPRISE VEHAN</small> that the Forum Shops at Caesars were busy. They were *always* busy, especially this time of year. This expansive luxury shopping mall attracted a lot of attention, and not only because of its location in the heart of the Las Vegas Strip or its impressive showcase of designer human fashion.

No, what made the Forum so enchanting was the presentation of it all.

Its entrance greeted visitors with grandeur reminiscent of an ancient Roman palace. It had high-flung ceilings and gleaming white columns, a sunken fountain, stunning classical architecture, and sculptures of human philosophers and heroes. A spiral escalator carried people up to other levels, and it was here the Forum truly became itself—here that cracked-stone flooring and glowing lampposts guided patrons from one thematic shop to the next, everything framed by gilded stuccowork and exquisite carvings and yet more marble columns.

What Vehan found more exciting than anything else was the barrel-vaulted ceiling overhead. There, painted clouds and clear blue sky were somehow made to simulate the various times of day—the finishing touch to this out-of-doors atmosphere. Glowing bright through morning and noon, dimming soft once twilight fell, this display of ingenuity was a perfect reminder that humans weren't as helpless as they seemed . . . and a challenge the folk couldn't let pass to prove they could do better—Seelie Summer had pulled out every stop in the market they'd built to compete with this.

"All right, if I were the Goblin Market, where would I be . . . ,"

Vehan mused. To Aurelian, he added, "You know, I'm surprised it took us this long to think of coming here—especially when you consider how much time we used to spend in this mall."

Overcome by a sudden surge of memories that simply being here invoked, he paused outside a shop window, where several mannequins in various wardrobes looked sightlessly down at him.

Once upon a time, he and Aurelian had been much closer than they were now. Once upon a time, they'd been best friends. They'd watched shows together on Aurelian's laptop so late into the night they often fell asleep in a huddle around it. They'd snuck into the kitchens after everyone else had gone to bed to feast on the cakes and tarts and sweets Aurelian's parents purposely left out for them; delectable things, those goods, and the very reason Vehan's mother had poached Aurelian's parents from Seelie Autumn with an offer of a Royal Warrant of Appointment—an award that proclaimed them the official pâtissiers of her Court—when she and Vehan had first tasted them on years-ago vacation abroad.

Vehan and Aurelian had played together, trained together, laughed and learned and explored *together*. One of their favorite pastimes had been coming here to the mall, because Aurelian was fairly obsessed with all things human and Vehan was fairly obsessed with *him*, this first-ever person who seemed to like Vehan for Vehan and not for the trimmings and trappings and privileges that made a "prince."

Why that changed, Vehan had a good guess.

When it changed, he knew clearly.

It was right after his mother proclaimed Aurelian as Vehan's steward, turning their friendship into a shackle—and never mind that the role was far from what Aurelian wanted for himself. From that moment on, Aurelian could barely look him in the eye. These days, Vehan tried to make the duty that bound them together as painless and impersonal as possible to give Aurelian the space he obviously wanted, but it was hard to forget he'd been half in love with Aurelian once upon a time.

Even harder to forget he was still very much so now.

"We were never looking for the Market back then," came Aurelian's placid reply, and Vehan startled, remembering only now that he'd asked a question.

"Correction: *you* weren't looking for it. *I* was—it's the *Goblin Market*. What sort of kid doesn't want to go someplace you can trade memories for wishes or locks of hair for ambrosia, or buy dwarven weapons, or drink salted ale with merfolk, or—"

"Found it."

Aurelian pointed across the way.

In between a store selling shoes and another selling lingerie was a door no more exciting than that—a door. It was solid and narrow, upholstered in pearl-white velvet, but despite its uniform color, it looked out of place next to everything else around it; magic bent the light around it to ever so slightly set it apart from the mundane.

"*Finally,*" Vehan said through a sigh. "This would have been so much easier if the entrance just stayed in one place. Well, let's go find our trouble, then."

Only those with magic in their blood would be able to locate this door and open it. Of course, the Goblin Market was firm about their age restriction. Any human or underage child of magic who looked at its entrance saw plain white-painted metal and STAFF ONLY stamped across its surface. If they tried to enter through it, all it led to was a flight of stairs that would take them back outside, but for folk who were Mature . . .

Vehan and Aurelian pushed through and found themselves in a compact reception.

The floor was carpeted in plush dark gold.

The walls were plastered with shimmery paper, depicting a bamboo forest bathed in dawn, which swayed and rustled and made all the same noises as though it were real.

There was seating provided, soft with the same pearly velvet as what had been on the door, but these Vehan ignored. He made straight for the counter stretched along the right side of the room. "Hello," he greeted her warmly. The faerie girl behind it looked up from the magazine she'd been reading. She had emerald-green hair and bright lavender skin, cat's ears twitching on her head, and the brilliant multicolored hue of her eyes meant she was most likely a shifter. She blinked at Vehan, and then at Aurelian, and a moment later her entire expression brightened.

"Hello, handsome," she purred. "Here for the Goblin Market, or is there something else I can help you with?"

There was very clearly something else she was prepared to offer, her unspoken proposition easy to read. Vehan was used to this sort of interaction, even when people didn't recognize who he was. He was handsome and he knew it—on the prettier side, as were many of the fae, and an awful lot of the world was weak to a pair of bright blue eyes, black hair, and the casual flirtation Vehan employed in his easy smiles.

"Another time, maybe." He winked, earning a laugh from the faerie girl and the barest hint of a groan from Aurelian, who stood a step behind him. "Just the Goblin Market today, I'm afraid."

"Well, all right. You know where to find me if you change your mind." She gave him another glance over—Vehan could see she was trying to determine why he looked so familiar—and then a second look at Aurelian that said she wouldn't mind at all if *he* took up her offer as well (which Vehan didn't like half as much, and made his smile shrink a molar). Then she pointed back at the door where they'd entered. "You're free to go on through."

A popular trick in the magical community, these doors that led to different places depending on the way you turned their knobs, or where you knocked, or how you described where you wanted to go. They were mostly reserved for things like this—for places that saw a lot of magical traffic that needed conducting but weren't a government practice that could afford police or Court involvement.

"Thank you," he said.

They made for the door.

There had been no knob on the outside; all they'd needed to do was push for the door to let them through. There was one on this side, though, and just above it was a sign in braille, a button that would read the sign aloud, and on top of that, the same sign again, written out: FORUM on the left and MARKET on the right.

At the moment, FORUM was lit up gold. When Vehan turned the knob right, it flicked over to light up MARKET.

"Are you ready?"

Aurelian rolled his eyes at the excitement in Vehan's voice. He couldn't help himself—he'd been wanting to come here for so long, and until now, hadn't been able to for everything going on. He opened the door, and as soon as he stepped out the other side, it was as though he'd been sucked into a completely separate dimension.

COME BUY, COME BUY—this tongue-in-cheek wooden sign stood before them, little wooden hands pointing off in every direction. Beyond it was the Forum, completely altered.

The ceiling was no mere painting any longer but actual sky, trapped in twilight, scraped from the heavens and plastered above them.

The bulbs in the numerous lampposts had been replaced with real fire.

The shops weren't merely fronts now, but entire buildings of all shapes and colors—red and blue and green and lilac, large and small and bulbous and narrow; some made of stone, some made of wood, others bits of vibrant canvas and swatches of luxurious silk; some were only visible if you caught them at certain angles, or, as Vehan had been told, the stroke of every hour.

Set against yet more of the shimmery forest that papered the walls of the Market's reception, it seemed to Vehan as though this space stretched on forever, filled with the scent of pine and crisp fresh air, woodsmoke streaming from scattered chimneys, and the savory, spicy, mouthwatering scents of various faerie foods.

"This way," said Aurelian, touching Vehan's elbow as he passed to draw his attention. "We might as well start our search with this floor."

They'd never been here before. They didn't really know what they were looking for, apart from some sign that someone might know anything at all about what was going on with the human kidnappings and dying ironborn.

However hard the Courts worked to regulate the magical community—to ensure the folk conformed to modern codes and practices—there was no stamping out "the old ways" altogether.

There was always some unsanctioned revel the Falchion Police Force had to disband. Turf wars broke out on a regular basis between the many faerie gangs over every oak and ash and thorn they could stake their claim on. Household sprites—those gentle faeries who took to hearths of happy, cozy human homes—were constantly getting into places they shouldn't and forever needing to be chased back to pre-approved, ironborn hosts.

Even the fae found city life difficult. The folk detested money, for a start—considered it offensive to trade things for *cash*. While interaction with humans any more than necessary was discouraged, it couldn't be avoided altogether. It was almost a daily occurrence, therefore, that one of the folk would try to make purchases in human stores with gems instead of proper currencies, or with things like spider's silk or even a "blessing," which was nothing more magical than a faerie they'd later bully into paying special attention to the human's land or helping them along with something.

The folk were a stubborn people.

They rebelled in many ways against their continuously evolving lifestyle. It allowed them to keep their existence a secret, yes, but every tradition they were forced to shed for the "good of the Courts" stirred more and more agitation among them.

Goblin Markets had become a refuge of sorts. They were more than just the obvious collection of vendors. The folk had more than enough stores at their disposal, glamoured to look like condemned buildings to human passersby. They had vendors on the streets whose wares were magicked to be wholly unappealing to human senses, but to the folk were all manner of faerie-made items. But *Goblin Markets* . . . Even the most uncompromising of Councillors was loath to disband a place where anything the heart desired could be obtained, and if what the heart desired was information . . . well, there was no place better to find it.

As Vehan trailed behind his retainer, his head turned this way and that.

COME BUY, COME BUY—these signs were everywhere, stamped on posts, scrawled over doorways, winking down at them on fluttering banners. Vendors shouted it out at the street. They passed a menagerie where caged birds with rainbow plumage and actual flaming tails had been trained to call it out. There were other shouts too: promises of dreams come true; of fruit that melted like honey in your mouth; of tailors who could spin a dress or suit out of *anything*, from petals and glittering insect wings to moonlight and morning fog. Vehan overheard a diminutive faerie (who looked no older than a child but had eyes as old as earth and skin the color of rubies) inform passersby that his business would give them cents more than the banks in their American currency exchange.

"Come buy, come buy, no questions asked! No trade denied! Is your neighborhood scheduled for Inspection? Don't want the Falchion to find those old alchemy textbooks you have tucked in your homes? A cursed amulet to dispose of? A bit of vampire blood to spare? We'll take it all—your goods for human cash, ten cents more on the exchange, come buy, come buy, we can't be beat!"

The Forum statues had taken on life, Vehan noticed as they walked on. They added to the chatter, conversing with one another, arguing, providing running commentary on the people below them and sparking fights between easily riled faeries who needed very little encouragement to turn nasty on one another. These statues were no longer the likeness of Roman figures but illustrious folk long dead. When Vehan and Aurelian reached the Forum's Fountain of the Gods, in place of the Roman deities that stood there on the human side were colossal sculptures of Urielle, with her robes of fire and water and wind, a crown of light atop her head; Tellis, with her gown of moss and leaves and fur, hers a crown of stone; and Cosmin, draped in starry night, beset with his crown of bone—the Great Three, western gods of old that the folk in this portion of the world had once worshipped above all others. There were other gods for other Courts, whose statues probably stood in their Markets just like this.

Vehan had never seen such grand and undefiled depictions of the Great Three, though. The gods had been driven from this realm by the Eight Founders of the Courts, those heroes he most looked up to who'd unified the folk against these immortal sovereigns and together devised a way to free mortals from their tyrannical rule. These statues glared down at Vehan as he passed, made him feel uneasy and small and hot around the ears, and he pressed a little closer to Aurelian, who must have been feeling the same as well, for he allowed it without comment.

The farther they walked, the harder it was to remember why they'd come.

They passed vendors selling apples red as wine and every bite just as intoxicating; stalls selling vials of unicorn tears, which would allow the user temporary clairvoyance; shadowy nooks where one could purchase roses grown on the graves of beautiful people who death had stolen in their prime, and anyone the buyer gave these out to would supposedly attract untimely demise.

One of the courtyards they came across had a massive aquarium at its center, and in it was an actual *mermaid*, with sea spray–white hair, sunset-orange skin, large yellow eyes, and a long iridescent tail the color of newly fallen snow. Vehan couldn't help but gawk— understandably, he felt, as merfolk didn't leave their waters often and were therefore a rare encounter. Not to mention their voices were a magic designed to produce such a reaction.

If Vehan listened long enough, she could convince him to do

anything she willed into her song. At the moment her song was a jingle—living advertisement for the Mermaid Tavern then, which Vehan suspected must be somewhere nearby—and suddenly, *desperately*, he wanted to visit. He only startled out of his "appreciation" when Aurelian cleared his throat.

"Do you think Mother would let me bring Zale as a date to the Solstice, if I promise to dance with whoever she wants me to?" Vehan asked, more to fill the awkward silence than anything.

Zale—the only mer Vehan had ever seen besides the one in the tank—was conveniently in his mother's employ. He hadn't been Vehan's bisexual awakening (even Aurelian didn't possess that "honor"), but he'd been the first of the folk to consistently knock Vehan on his ass any time they sparred together. This hadn't changed over the years. No matter how good Vehan was with swords and magic and hand-to-hand combat, Zale was always *better*, and apparently, Vehan's attraction to other people correlated directly with how much they frustrated him.

Aurelian frowned.

It was very unfair—another one of those frustrating-slash-attractive things, and something Aurelian did a lot these days. It certainly didn't help Vehan's whole "try and get over your hot best friend" thing any. "I think you don't have a choice about the dancing," Aurelian replied. "And Zale is almost thirty."

Vehan snorted. "So? My mother had way more years than that on my father." He waved a hand. "At a certain point, people stop caring about age so long as it's all consensual and both parties are Mature."

"To a degree, sure. You're not at that point yet, though."

Vehan rolled his eyes. Aurelian was always touchy on the subject of Vehan's attraction to Zale. "Okay, *Dad*. But . . . I suppose I don't want Zale to lose his job or die in the murderous rampage just *asking* that of mother would probably set off. Do you think she's given High Prince Celadon an invitation?"

"To the Solstice?"

"No, to the open season on my hand in marriage." He laughed, but that was more or less what this was turning into—his mother announcing his Maturity to all the fae elite like he was some blushing debutant and her only purpose in life was to see him make an "excellent match." However much she despised the High Prince—and the Viridian family as a whole for their patriarch, Azurean, beating her to challenging his father for the crown that made him High King—Celadon was young enough and well enough connected that it would be foolish of her not to consider him.

Riadne Lysterne was many things, but foolish she was *not*.

To this, though, Aurelian said nothing. A muscle leaped in his jaw, which meant his silence wasn't for lack of comment, but where once Vehan hadn't been able to get his friend to *stop* talking (about video games and human technology and oh goodness, did Aurelian ever find *space* and *Star Trek* fascinating) but now conversation was like pulling teeth. Vehan considered himself lucky they'd been talking as much as they currently were.

A splash broke their conversation, followed quickly by whoops of laughter and vicious delight. Vehan turned to look—a large and grisly canary-yellow redcap had apparently done something to irritate the on-duty mermaid, because she had lured him up and over the tank's ledge, lion's tail streaming behind him as he sank down to his grave. His scythe, sharp and well-maintained, glittered on the cobblestones where he'd dropped it. His crimson hood, stained dark by human blood, floated atop the tank's rippling surface. The laughter turned into cheers when the mermaid unsheathed both claws and teeth and lunged at her prey.

The tank was instantly filled with vibrant blue blood.

Vehan shook his head at the spectacle. Granted, that redcap probably deserved what he got, but the folk were getting nastier and nastier to one another the longer they went denied of their long-ago freedoms. Murder was just as illegal in the Courts as it was in human society, but here in the Goblin Market, so long as the Falchion were handsomely paid off, law was content to look the other way—and it was expected of Vehan to do the same.

A little less interested in the sights and a little more subdued, he fell into step beside Aurelian, and together they wandered the Market in deeper silence than before. Until . . . "Hang on, that looks promising."

VERY SLIGHT FORCES, read the shop's name. Beneath it: PSYCHIC READINGS.

An oracle.

The shop was small, slotted in between two other much larger businesses, but quaint. It had large frosted windows, and a lavender-painted front door, emerald shutters, and a matching slanted roof. "If anyone knows what's going on in the world, it would be an oracle . . ." Vehan looked to Aurelian.

His retainer looked back at him, molten gold eyes as fathomless as they were intense.

Aurelian was . . . gorgeous. A lot of folk—particularly of the fae variety—would look at his tattoos and piercings as obscene, too human for their tastes. There were many things the folk appreciated about adopting human ways, but this wasn't one of them, and the people at the palace were constantly getting after Aurelian for things like his ripped skinny jeans and the brown and black shirts he favored, colors of Autumn, not Seelie Summer's white and gold. They'd been quick to stamp out his German accent; quick to counteract the human public school education he'd preferred with enrollment in the Nevada Fae Academy; quick to deny the things he enjoyed—his hopes and ambitions, like attending human university and pursuing those sciences he loved so fiercely—all because it "wasn't suitable for someone in training to be the future king's steward," a role Aurelian had been forced into when the queen realized how *good* he was with her son.

Vehan had never been one of those people to look at Aurelian and see any of his passions as "wrong." Aurelian had always been beautiful, even more so when he was free to be himself. But of course, he *wasn't* free, not anymore—not thanks to Vehan, who could no longer meet his gaze without feeling gut-wrenching guilt. He hated what had become of their relationship, and hated even more his bitterness about being punished for something that wasn't his fault.

It was hard to pretend things were fine between them with all of this, yet pretend he did.

"Want to check it out?" he asked, swallowing down his rampant emotions.

"If you do, Your Highness."

Ignoring the way Aurelian's use of this title made his skin crawl, Vehan nodded and started forward. As soon as he entered Very Slight Forces, he was overwhelmed by incense. Despite the Market's dim lighting, this shop was even darker, and it took a moment for his sight to adjust to the gloom. Once it did, he found himself in an open-concept room. The front was lined with shelves against the walls, stuffed with jars of animal bits, insects, and plants; crystals of every size and hue; delicately painted tarot cards; candles; books. Hanging from the ceiling were various dried herbs, a pair of pixie wings (which would fetch quite a lot of money and just as much jail time for possession alone), as well as antlers and horns and teeth and pelts from all manner of creatures, magical and otherwise.

Off to his left, a wooden staircase wound up and disappeared into a second floor.

At the back of the shop sat a glass-case counter with more occult paraphernalia, but before Vehan could examine it too closely—

"I was beginning to think you wouldn't come," said the woman standing behind it.

Vehan stared.

She was old enough that lines had set permanently around her eyes and mouth and nose, but young enough that gray only streaked her dark brown hair in muted wisps. Fae could easily live for hundreds of years, some nearing close to a thousand. Many faeries could as well. The rest merely enjoyed a life extended by a handful of decades, with better health and less wear. This woman's eyes were bright, her features handsome, but something about the rosy glow of her emerald-tinted, snake-scaled skin told Vehan she was ironborn—and a practicing one, at that. The items for sale in her shop made sense now; these were all things that went into potions and spells, those books most likely tomes of arrays and enchantments. Behind the woman was a fireplace—a cauldron set in its unlit heart—with symbols stamped into the wood that Vehan recognized as alchemy from all the secret research he'd done of late.

An alchemist who was also an oracle . . . This was almost a little *too* lucky. If this woman knew what was happening to her *own people*, chances were she wouldn't charge as steep a price as others might to give Vehan the means to help.

"Hello," he greeted her warily. The folk were tricksters at heart, particularly the faeries, and the Market could be a dangerous place, existing outside the law as it did. It was possible this woman wasn't who he thought she was, and if she wasn't, how she knew he would be coming was concerning. "Expecting us, were you?"

"Yes and no," the oracle said with a smile. "Just because I saw you coming doesn't mean you'd choose this path. The future is no certain thing, you know, even for those to whom it speaks."

Oracles. Vehan resisted the urge to roll his eyes, but he had a feeling Aurelian wasn't taking such care behind him—quite the skeptic, his retainer, when it came to those who predicted futures.

These days, true oracles were rare, almost nonexistent. With the gods now banished from this realm, this skill could no longer be given out to their favored worshippers, as it had once been. It had to be inherited from ancestors of those the gods had blessed long ago, and Aurelian wasn't the only one whose first reaction to someone claiming their art genuine was unflinching doubt.

"It's not every day you meet a one-day king. Come closer, boy—let me get a good look at you."

Vehan stepped forward as bidden. Aurelian followed fast at his heel. Whatever hurt existed between them, he knew Aurelian wouldn't let him come to harm and was very suspicious of situations in which harm could easily reach him.

"Just as pretty as they say you are."

"Thanks." He grinned, though the action wasn't up to its usual brilliance. "I try not to disappoint."

"Yes . . . you do, don't you." Both tone and smile curled around some private amusement; she was no longer talking solely about Vehan's appearance. "So eager to please, to prove yourself worthy . . . Welcome to Very Slight Forces, Vehan Lysterne, Crown Prince of Seelie Summer. My name is Lydia. What brings you here today?"

"What," Vehan joked, unable to help himself. "You don't know?"

"Yes and no," Lydia replied serenely. If she was at all nervous about a pair of royal fae visiting her very illegal shop, she didn't show it. "I'd like for you to say it."

"Very well. I'll get right to it, then. I'm here because ironborn children have been dying. I'm here because humans have been disappearing from the streets, kidnapped and never seen again. I'm here because I know it's connected. I know it isn't another human doing this, like the High King has ruled, or the Dark Star, whom everyone is looking to blame. I know this is all serving some magical plot, I just don't have any *proof*, and I would like to know where that can be found. Will you tell me?"

"I will indeed, Little Light, but nothing comes without a price."

Vehan knew that well. The entire magical community was built on the concept. "I'm aware. Name your trade."

A moment of silence filled the shop while Lydia thought on her reply. There were a number of things she could easily request of him— as a prince, he had so much more to give than her regular clientele, not least of all a geas that was no small thing to hold over him. Vehan had had more than enough time to weigh what he would and wouldn't be prepared to give for answers today, but for some reason, on the cusp of learning just what this quest would cost him, he felt a little anxious.

"Why does it matter to you, a *fae*, that ironborn are dying and humans are going missing?"

Vehan almost laughed. Was this question her price? It was nothing.

He was asked this often, every time *he* asked another person about these events or voiced his opinions about them. "Why?" he scoffed. "I'm the prince of Seelie Summer. These are *my* people being made a target. They are all folk, and it's my duty to protect them."

Lydia laughed where Vehan refrained. "A noble sentiment." She came out from behind her counter at last, pulling her brown cable-knit shawl tighter around her wide-set frame. "Very noble, my Little Light. Our estimable Court Founders would be so proud to hear you spout this—but they're just words. Why does this matter to *you*?" she repeated.

"Is this your price?" he asked, wariness seeping back into his tone. He wanted to be clear on their trade, before she could decide on something else once terms were met.

"This is my price. A truth for a truth."

Vehan sighed. "It's not just words. It *is* my duty. Did you know I was the one who reported the first ironborn death?" He glanced at Aurelian, unsure as to whether he should continue. But it wasn't as though this information was a secret, and if this was all she wanted in exchange for what she knew . . . "It was a few years ago now, three maybe? Aurelian and I were walking home from school when we noticed an ironborn teenager slumped over on a park bench. Aurelian said he was *glowing*, something red in his veins that was quickly fading. I couldn't see it at all, but Aurelian is lesidhe, his magic is different and allows him to see things sidhe fae can't—things like active alchemy, for instance. I didn't question it. We went over to help the boy, but by the time we got there, he was already dead. Shirt ripped to shreds, chest scored with bloody lines, and gore under his nails . . . The next thing we knew, the human authorities were there and ushering us back, but before we were forced to leave, I was able to glimpse what had caused him so much pain and had driven him to try to claw his way through his breast—because, yes, he had done it to himself."

Death hadn't been all that real to Vehan until he held the lifeless body of that ironborn boy in the park. It had only existed as a concept. His father had died when Vehan had been too young to make much sense of it other than the fact that he was gone and no amount of waiting in his personal rooms, morning and night for a whole month, would see him returned. "It's my duty to see this resolved," he said with renewed conviction. "I was there in the beginning. I couldn't help that boy, but I can stop it from happening to others. Please, do you know who's behind this? Do you know where I can go to look for answers, if you don't?"

"I do," Lydia replied. "But why does this matter to you?"

Vehan gritted his teeth. There was nothing for it.

He would have to show her—in the very least, this secret should satiate her thirst for private information about him.

"You want a truth?" He stepped forward. Yanking his white cotton shirt at the hem and up to his shoulders, he bared his chest for the woman to see. Aurelian startled, made a noise of protest, but in his current irritation Vehan didn't care how highly inappropriate this scene would have looked to anyone walking in on it. "There. You see it, right? An array. The exact same array that the ironborn boy had. It's mostly faded now—hard to tell it's there, I know, or even what it is—but I've had it long enough to recognize it anywhere. I'm branded, just the way every other ironborn who's died was, I'm sure of it, and no one can tell me *why*." He righted his shirt, glaring now at the oracle, daring her to tell him this wasn't enough of a trade.

Still, she said nothing.

Vehan shook his head in frustration. "It hurts, you know? It doesn't glow, but it hurts at random. I never thought much of it before now. When I first asked my mother about it, she told me it was just a scar. She told me I had been injured as an infant, grievously so— an attempt on my life gone wrong—and that injury had left a mark they'd never been able to fully heal. I never had cause to investigate what sort of mark this could be. I'd been content with that answer. But some magicks, Madam Oracle, leave indelible impressions. That boy, like me, must have come into contact with something dark, and

I want to uncover what it was. Will you *tell* me," he repeated, firm and commanding as the future Head of Seelie Summer that he was.

Lydia stared at his chest, expression guarded. Vehan considered it a win that her smile had finally fallen, until . . . "Interesting. But it's still not the truth. Why does it—"

This insufferable woman! Was that not enough? What was she looking for him to say here, that this matters to him because . . . what, he has some secret fetish for dead bodies she could one day use against him?

"I'm sorry, people are *dying*. Why *shouldn't* that matter to me?"

"If you want to know the truth, you'll have to give a truth in exchange. A price must be paid, Prince Vehan. Why does this matter—"

"Because it *does*!"

"Why?"

"Because I care?"

"*Why?*"

"Because no one else does!" he shouted, taking even himself by surprise. But he was at the end of his patience. "Nobody cares! People are dying and nobody *cares*. An entire community of people made to feel that they don't matter—it makes me sick. It *eats* at me, because feeling that? The soul-crushing hopelessness that drowns *everything* else inside you and tells you you're totally and completely alone, that you're nothing but a tool, a means to an end, a *burden*, and no one will really miss you when you're gone? I know exactly what that's like."

His mother, who constantly moved her expectations of him higher and higher each time they were met, always convinced he could do better . . .

His best friend, who resented him and no longer wanted anything to do with him . . .

All the people around him—his schoolmates, his advisors, his tutors, his family—*everyone* looked at him like a thing to be used, molded, endured, *eliminated*, even, to get what they wanted. . . .

Vehan wasn't *happy*. He had a good life, a life people envied, full of wealth and security and anything he could ever want except a single gods-damned person to genuinely care he existed at all, and he *was not happy*. The amount he was not happy was growing quite difficult to manage, in fact. Normally he could hide it away behind his smiles and easy charm, but at the moment, forced into this hideous game he should have known better than to undertake so lightly . . .

"Feeling that?" His voice cracked. "It's awful. I'm selfish, is that what you want to hear? I'm projecting. This is all about me and my pathetic emotions—I just want to protect someone the way no one wants to protect *me*."

Tears threatened to fall at any second. Vehan wanted nothing more now than to leave. He'd never meant to say any of that, would never say it in front of his mother, who would only reaffirm he was being ridiculous, and he'd never absolutely *ever* wanted to admit such things in front of *Aurelian*. He didn't want Aurelian to feel like it was his fault Vehan was unhappy, that he shouldn't want a life that was his own, that he owed Vehan anything more than he'd already given.

There was silence.

His confession rang louder in his ears for it.

"There it is," said Lydia at last. Her gaze had turned on Aurelian, though, and Vehan couldn't say why, only that he appreciated the chance to collect himself. "For a people who it pains to tell lies, you're very bad at admitting truths." She turned her attention back to Vehan, a softness in her expression now that almost looked like pity. It made him feel worse. "The price is met. Word in the Market is that folk are being offered large sums of gold in exchange for people no one would miss. The facility you'll find right here in the Nevada desert—iron teeth will show you the way. But know this: only once the stars align will you receive the answers you seek."

Vehan clenched his fists. "Wonderful. Very helpful."

He had many questions. Why oracles insisted on imparting their wisdom in riddles . . . He would have appreciated if she'd been straightforward with him, but it didn't matter right now. He'd worry about that later. Right now, he was done. He abruptly turned to leave, decidedly not meeting Aurelian's gaze, when—

"Excuse yourself, watch where you're going. This suit is very expensive."

—he ran right into the chest of a middle-aged man standing in the doorway, wearing black leather gloves and a very nice midnight-black suit indeed, his equally black hair glossy and carefully groomed. "I'm sorry," Vehan choked out, hardly able to hear his own words.

"Don't be sorry, boy, be *careful*," was the man's withering reply. The way he looked down at Vehan hinted he knew exactly who he was—he simply didn't care. It was unsurprising. In the Market, where the common folk ruled supreme, royal sidhe status was more of a hindrance than anything else.

"Ah, Mister Aurum—right on time. Here to restock already? My, but you've been busy lately," Lydia said, looking quite pointedly at Vehan as she spoke, clearly wanting him to leave before he caused a scene.

"Good day, Madam Oracle," Aurelian interjected, striding forward now too. He took Vehan by the shoulders and guided him carefully from the shop, and Vehan did his best to avoid looking up at his face their entire journey home.

He didn't think he'd be able to handle what he might find in his former friend's expression, the pity, the dismay . . . or worse: confirmation that Aurelian didn't care about him at all.

CHAPTER 9

Arlo

T HE VERDANT PALACE OF Spring—named the Reverdie by
its Viridian Founder—was a beautifully sleek construction
of curved glass and steel. It wasn't all that different from
everything else where it was stationed on Bloor Street's crowded stretch
of high-end outlets and commercial buildings, but the multiple glamours concealing its appearance rendered it invisible to anyone who
didn't know it was there.

Arlo loved the Reverdie.

Its wavelike shape had been designed to resemble a curl of breeze—a
tribute to the element of air that UnSeelie Spring fae commanded—and
it was every bit as opulent on the inside as what humans always described
of faerie palaces: walls and floors and high-reaching columns of green-
tinted soapstone, marble, and jade; enormous chandeliers dripping crystal like the ice their season melted; gold-leafed carvings and tapestries of
living butterflies that fluttered from place to place; fan-vaulted ceilings
painted to resemble forest canopies, which actually rustled and swayed
in breezes and shook in passing storms.

The palace was decadent—a spectacle at every turn—but the carpets of moss and the lush profusion of plants and flowers that grew
over every surface lent it the appearance of having been plucked out
of a long-forgotten time.

This impressive, sprawling overgrowth was the High King's influence.

As one of the two Heads of Spring, wherever he went, so followed
verdant life. It was the same for all the Heads of the Great Courts
(though for the High King, as sovereign over all, this effect was to

a much greater degree). Winter trailed frost, Summer radiance, and Autumn a colorful decay. The Reverdie was Arlo's only encounter with any of these formidable Gifts; it was, after all, only in a Head's close vicinity that this magic was ever this noticeable.

What she could do without was the feeling of the High King's magic stripping away her glamour, as it did for any and all who entered the palace. The sensation, quite like stepping through a gust of wind, always left her tingling and raw. Beyond the slight sharpening of her features, pointed definition to her ears, and a little more vibrancy to her eyes, she never looked much different on the other side of this trick either, so it was more than a touch disappointing—especially considering what it did to everyone else.

"Afternoon, Arlo," said Dag, waving her through the Tower's second set of glass front doors. "Here to visit High Prince Celadon?"

Arlo nodded.

"Good," he grunted.

Dag was a dwarf. He was just over four feet tall and built like a boulder, with most of his warm brown face consumed by his copper hair and matching, bushy beard. Random braids were twisted throughout, no doubt left by his partner. It was a faerie superstition to which even fae subscribed, most believing the braids offered their loved ones protection from ill intent.

Dag was perhaps Arlo's favorite guard—the only one who didn't press beyond what his job demanded whenever she came to visit—but today she felt even more grateful to see him than usual.

What had followed the ordeal at the café had been comparatively uneventful. Spending that awful night with her cousins, binge-watching feel-good movies on Netflix with cups of warm cocoa and Celadon's cinnamon rolls, left Arlo feeling much more like her usual self.

Now, a few days later and in better spirits, her thoughts were able to wander back to curiosity. The High King had yet to act on the knowledge passed along to him, this further proof that the already suspicious Dark Star might know more about what was going on than she'd been letting on.

At least, he hadn't done anything publicly.

This wasn't too concerning to Arlo—not yet. The High King, who commanded all; the Heads that served him and ruled their Courts according to his wishes and whatever freedom he otherwise allowed; the Fae High Council that served as the only voice the rest of the Courts had in the decisions the High King made—they all had been tight-lipped from the start of this matter. There was much going on behind the scenes that Arlo wasn't privy to, she knew that, but still . . . she'd rest easier if someone could tell her something was being done. The longer this silence stretched on—when one day turned into two, and neither Celadon nor her mother had any update to share with her other than the fact that Cassandra had indeed been ironborn, as Arlo had suspected—the more impatient she became.

What if that girl in black decided to go into hiding now that she knew Arlo was onto her? What if this was their only chance to fig-ure out who was killing ironborn children and *why*, and it slipped between their fingers because Celadon had forgotten to tell his father a key piece of information that might have incentivized the High King to act quicker? That Cassandra had been *glowing*, for instance, or that Arlo had been able to *feel* the girl in black's magic much more than a slight tingling or pressure . . .

No one could bring her the answers she needed; Arlo would have to get them herself. If she pretended she was only here to visit Celadon and kept her ulterior "prying into private Court matters" motivations to herself, even the guards that harassed her the most couldn't send her away—she was still a member of the royal family, after all, official Viridian or not.

"You should visit more often," Dag added, giving her a pointed look. A vine of ivy had begun to creep over his bulky shoulder, extending from the pillar just behind him, but he swatted it back with practiced ease and stepped forward. "Maybe then the High Prince would actually stay put when he's supposed to, and we wouldn't have to chase him around the city just to drag him back to work."

"Yeah . . . sorry." Arlo laughed. "Poor Celadon, he hates paperwork almost as much as he hates being indoors."

"Yes, poor Celadon. Definitely not poor *me*, who wasn't told a thing about your little café episode the other day and therefore foolishly tried to stop your cousin from barreling out the door—as the High King himself instructed we do with his 'easily distracted' son—under the assumption he was trying to escape from another meeting."

Planting himself in front of Arlo, Dag stared hard up into her face, his dark brown eyes brighter than usual. Arlo winced—she knew how Celadon got when he was worried. "Sorry," she apologized again. "He's been acting really weird lately. Worse than normal. I hope he wasn't rude to you—if he was, I promise to yell at him for you."

"Ha—like that would do him any good. Fae and their moods . . . I'm far too used to it to care anymore. Still. I hear the High Council might grant you that fancy VIP status, eh? You should consider moving into the palace if they do. Then some of us might be able to retire." He paused to double down on his meaningful look, and Arlo gave him an awkward chuckle in return—she'd almost forgotten about the Weighing with everything else that had happened since, but she still didn't think it was very likely she was going to develop enough fae qualities for the Council's liking. "All right," he said, a touch more firmly. Drawing himself up to full height, he kept her gaze and said, "You know the drill."

Arlo nodded.

"State your name."

"Arlo Cyan Jarsdel."

"Your purpose here today, Arlo Cyan Jarsdel?"

Arlo willed her pulse to keep a calm and even pace, fighting the magic that compelled her to answer honestly. "I'm here to visit High Prince Celadon."

Dag twitched a nod and stepped out of her path, pressing no further than this.

It was one of the oldest tricks in the book, the Thrall. Anyone with even a drop of magic in their blood was subject to its rule. Fae and faeries alike found it difficult to lie by nature—it made them uncomfortable, and the greater the lie they tried to weave, the worse the resulting tension festered. Better instead to tilt the truth to flattering light, the magical community had discovered, and soon, their clever games of convolution and careful omission became the common practice. Soon, the magical community stopped telling outright lies altogether, but the fewer they told, the greater the power of truth became.

Names—one of truth's greatest weapons—had become a means of control.

The folk had taken to choosing second ones once they reached Maturity—true names, given out only to those they trusted with their lives—so as not to leave themselves vulnerable to harm. Arlo didn't have a second name, not yet, not until the Fae High Council granted her official status in the community as either fae or common citizen. But she was still subject to this magic even with only her birth name.

Fortunately, she had her protections.

There was iron in her blood.

If Dag decided to press a little harder with his questions and unearth the other half of her true purpose here today, she could count on her very human advantage. For all that lies indeed made her uncomfortable, it was nowhere near enough to force her to avoid them altogether. She could still tell them—she *did* still tell them—but Dag, it seemed, was happy to take her words at face value.

"Keep out of trouble, you hear?"

Arlo nodded again. Shooting him a thumbs-up, she scurried past him into reception, an enormous room carpeted by moss and pockets of springtime flowers, with towering oaks that grew in place of random pillars, the wise spread of their branches adding to the magicked canopy. In addition to this, an honest-to-gods thunderous waterfall had been built into the far opposite wall, and several pure gold statues of all the previous High Sovereigns stood along the perimeter like overly resplendent guards.

The Reverdie was busy today, but no more so than usual, given the hour. As the first few floors of the palace were given to public services, anyone was welcome to seek an audience with the High King or apply for approval for portal travel, trade, or various other licenses. Customs and Immigration always saw the most traffic, with folk seeking visas to travel to other Courts for prolonged periods of time or citizenships to move between them. There was even a Tim Hortons off to Arlo's left, the Falchion Police Headquarters right beside it. Beside *that* was the home branch of the Court of Spring Bank, which everyone simply called "COS Bank" and which operated much like a pawn shop. Here the folk could trade possessions for human currency, or exchange the money they earned from human jobs for trinkets and gems and bits of gold to spend at folk-run shops.

Twittering birds of various breeds and colors darted from one perch to the next overhead, and among them hummingbird-like faeries flitted about—their lustrous plumage iridescent, their limbs slight as toothpicks—tending to the plant and wildlife with strength enough to lift things ten times their size.

A rainsquall was moving across the ceiling. The rain that would soon fall from it was magicked to evaporate before it touched anything, but the show always made people stop and gawk, causing even more congestion.

A crowd had formed around the information center in the middle of the room, patrolled by burly ogres in Falchion Police Force garb. Numerous folk of a wide variety waited in the lavishly decorated sitting area for their turn to meet with the High King. The folk formed a veritable rainbow: pale peach and golden brown and jewel black, but turquoise, violet, and shocking pink, too; muted butter yellow, diamond blue, and forest green. Some had features like tails and claws, some were tall enough to brush the canopy, and some folk were so small Arlo had to watch where she stepped to avoid trampling them.

She followed a sizable family of ink-blue, spindly-limbed imps barely tall enough to reach her knees to the elevators that flanked the waterfall. Once upon a time, this had all run on magic. These days, much of the palace ran on electricity—part of the High King's attempt to show the magical community the benefits of relying less on magic that might give them away. The elevators on the right led to private and more specific government offices, but the elevator on the left led to the high floors of the Reverdie, devoted to the private home of the royal family and the library they kept for their personal use.

It was here Arlo needed to go.

"Afternoon, Arlo," greeted Cali, the fae on today's elevator duty. Her long, violet hair was twisted into a tight bun behind her head, and her emerald and sage uniform was perfectly pressed and pristine.

Arlo rarely saw any of the palace staff outside the building, where they could hide behind their glamours. She wondered if this was why she found their true appearance less disconcerting than what she sometimes saw elsewhere. Cali's unglamoured beauty was sharp—avian, in a way—and ethereal to an almost unsettling degree. Her alabaster skin possessed a milky, sapphire-blue tint, and her white-less eyes were a deep plum verging on black.

"Hello, Cali," Arlo greeted politely in return. She stepped into the elevator, and Cali closed the grate behind her. "Floor ninety-six, please. Off to bother Cel for a bit."

Cali beamed—it was no secret she was part of the fan club that had built itself around Cel—but before she could comment or push the button for Arlo's floor, the elevator's grate was forced back open.

"Oh! Lord Malachite," Cali spluttered, startled. She bent into a deep bow of apology. "I'm so sorry, I didn't mean to close the grate on you—I didn't see you coming."

Malachite Viridian-Verdell—Arlo's uncle, and her mother's only brother—glared down his prominent nose at Cali, but whatever comment he might have made in return was forgotten when he noticed Arlo. *"Arlo,"* he gasped, his enthusiasm as false as the smile that plastered itself on his ageless face.

Much like the rest of Arlo's family, Malachite was tall and extraordinarily handsome. When he was without his glamours, as he was currently, the twilight glow of his royal status lent a greenish, pearly sheen to the blue flush that bled through tanned skin. A distinct vulture-hunger warped the aquiline edge of his features, with his grin showing off the tips of his much-too-sharp teeth. "Are they training you for palace service too?" he asked her, then flickered his gaze at Cali. "As happy as I am that they've found a use for you at last, maybe I should talk to someone about pairing you with better instruction."

Cali practically wilted under Malachite's tone. He didn't seem to notice in the slightest. Wafting into the elevator, he jerked his head at the grate, indicating for Cali to close it behind him. Once settled into place at Arlo's side, he threw an arm around her shoulders. "Come on, don't look so down. There's nothing wrong with honest work! Briar tells me you made a bit of a fuss at your Weighing—I think, considering that, you should be grateful you're allowed a position in the palace at all." His grin grew a little sharper, the green in his eye so bright it was almost a fire. "I mean, we can't all be foreign diplomats like High Prince Serulian or world-renowned Trackers like me."

The flare of Arlo's anger was a familiar thing by now.

She wanted to say something. She *always* wanted to say something whenever people like Malachite said such terribly rude things to her and the others around her, but the words would never leave her tongue. Every time she felt them bubbling up inside her, those good intentions turned to cowardice and were swallowed once more by nerves.

Because Celadon and Elyas were anomalies. Most of Arlo's family pretended she didn't exist. The High King was kind enough on the rare occasions Arlo met him, and the Crown High Princess Cerelia had always been cordial to her, but Arlo's maternal grandparents had been so displeased with Thalo's choice in husband that Arlo only really knew them from pictures. High Prince Serulian acted like she was invisible when they crossed paths here at the palace. She had several other cousins and relations (however removed) who came and went, passing winds who thought nothing of asking rude and prying questions into her life and made very little effort to keep their whispers about her to themselves. But all of that was preferable to the way Malachite treated her right to her face—as though she was less than nothing, and her humanity made her inadequate. His every comment was designed to fluster her too much to fight back.

And that Malachite took so much pride in his profession was just about the best indication of his character as Arlo could find. Trackers were the magical community's police force for the creatures that didn't quite qualify as the Courts' standards of "people," and Malachite took perverse pleasure in being the one they often sent to "neutralize" what they deemed a threat to their peace.

"Better an attendant than a murderer," she said under her breath.

"What's that now, darling niece?"

Malachite had heard her. There was no way he hadn't, given his fae-enhanced senses. But what Malachite perhaps hated more than Arlo's ironborn heritage was the fact that, with her mother's high position and Celadon's affection, *she* was the one with more power.

If only that actually helped her where it mattered.

"I said what floor do you want?" Sliding out from under her uncle's arm, she made for the panel of buttons on the wall. The look on Malachite's face said he was disappointed Arlo hadn't risen to his bait—that he knew full well Arlo wasn't in training with Cali and had meant his "assumption" as an insult. Malachite had insulted Arlo to tears so many times before that this pathetic jab was almost laughable—but the look on Cali's face made Arlo's stomach clench around her anger.

"You'll have to work on that bedside manner," he replied stiffly. "Floor twenty-three. I'll pass the news of your new *ambitions* on to Councillor Sylvain—he'll be glad to hear you're taking so well to your common station."

"I'm sure he will." She pressed his number, then her own.

Shooting Cali an apologetic look, Arlo settled between them once more. Determined to make up in *some* way for her appalling family members, she pulled out her phone and held it awkwardly between them. "We went to Niagara Falls for Celadon's birthday. He got really drunk and tried to liberate the sea life at Marineland. We're banned for life—want to see pictures?"

Cali nodded vigorously.

CHAPTER 10

Aurelian

I *JUST WANT TO PROTECT someone the way no one wants to protect me.*

There were times Aurelian almost hated Vehan for not being able to see through an act that kept him up at night out of fear the prince would do just that. There were times he wanted to take him by the shoulders, shake him, yell at him, ask him how he could think so little of their friendship that it had been that *easy* to convince him it was over.

I just want to protect someone the way no one wants to protect me.

Until recently, Aurelian's moments of weakness could always be quelled by way of the simple reminder that Vehan would want to know *why* all this pretense had been necessary—and Aurelian could never tell him the truth.

He couldn't shatter that last bit of innocence the prince so desperately clung to—the hope that despite whatever else Riadne was, she was still a mother who loved her son. Aurelian never knew what was worse when he played this scenario through in his head: that the prince might send him away for slandering the queen, leaving Vehan even more vulnerable to her manipulations than he already was, or that he'd *believe* him. That he'd confront the queen and risk her shedding the minimal kindness she pretended toward her own flesh and blood.

I just want to protect someone the way no one wants to protect me.

Until recently, fear had been what maintained his resolve. He could push Vehan away if that distance kept him safe. He could let Vehan think that he blamed him for the duty Aurelian had been forced into, for the loss of a future he would have instead pursued, if it meant

Vehan wouldn't pry into what was really going on around him.

But now he had a new fear, and this one *weakened* his resolve. There had been a note of something dangerous in Vehan's voice back in the Goblin Market when he'd spoken about feeling alone—a note of something Aurelian might have picked up on sooner if he hadn't been so preoccupied with keeping tabs on every other threat to notice *this* . . . an isolated boy standing on a precipice, starved for affection, silent as ever because Vehan *never* asked others for the help he so freely gave. What if Vehan soon came to think—or worse, worse, worse, *already* thought—that the only way off this lonely ledge was to fall?

Do you know why I brought you here, Aurelian?

He shuddered.

"Is it some sort of lesidhe custom to mash one's food into a pulp before it's eaten?"

Aurelian looked up from the bowl of spinach salad he'd been absently grinding under his fork. Seated in the Nevada Fae Academy's too-bright cafeteria (with its arched floor-to-high-pitched-ceiling windows and beechwood tables and gray bamboo flooring), he'd been so absorbed in his spiraling thoughts that he'd managed to tune out the sycophants that followed Vehan wherever he went to the point he only just remembered they were there.

He didn't dignify the question with a response. Kine, a porcelain-white and blond-haired fae who liked to tell anyone who'd listen how *close* he was with the prince of their Court, had also never made it secret that he greatly disliked Aurelian.

The feeling was mutual.

"Racist," hissed the golden-haired, equally fair girl beside him—Fina, Kine's twin sister, whom Aurelian might have liked a bit more if she wasn't all-around awful and would accept the fact he was very gay and very much *not* into her attempts at "conversion to bisexuality."

"I am not—it was a genuine question! I'm trying to understand his culture. It's called having an open mind, *Fina*."

"An empty mind, you mean. Do you even pay attention in our

sociology classes? Honestly, sometimes I wonder if you're half-troll, the stupid things that come out of your mouth. Ignore him, Aurelian, my brother is being an ass—we all know the lesidhe can be perfectly civilized. But don't worry." She winked at him. "I like my fae with a bit of the *wild* left in them."

"Great," said Aurelian. He stabbed a spinach leaf and shoved it in his mouth.

Normally, he took lunch elsewhere—the roof of the school was his favorite place, but also in the theater or the music rooms, and sometimes the garden, if it was quiet enough. Adapting to this all-fae school had been difficult at first—before this, his parents had allowed him to attend a human elementary—but eventually he'd formed his own group of . . . well, not quite "friends," but people he could actually stomach to be around. He wasn't the only lesidhe fae enrolled in the Nevada Fae Academy, despite the fact that, for the most part, the lesidhe had chosen to keep to the forests and their own society outside Court territory. He wasn't even the only student who'd come here from a different Court. The folk bounced around just as readily as humans did these days, especially those like Aurelian with magic strong enough to translate both human and folk foreign languages for them (though Aurelian had gone the extra mile to actually learn the human English and Northwestern Seelie dialect that were the official languages of this Court). The folk married and moved abroad, settled down in different places, studied through exchange, traveled around on work visas. . . . It was no longer curious to come across a djinn outside their native UnSeelie Summer territory, and the trolls of Seelie Winter were everywhere you looked these days.

Aurelian was far from a spectacle. But to the spoiled, elitist children of sidhe fae parents (whose entire upbringing had been under the belief that, because the Founding Eight had been sidhe as well, it was they who were by default *best*), anything that wasn't "them" was novelty they oh-so-graciously permitted in *their* community.

"Guess what, bitch," Kine snapped. "That makes you half-troll too." He threw a leaf of his own spinach at her, causing her to shriek as though he'd thrown a slug and dive behind Theo, the boy beside her.

Theo looked far from amused. Fina's theatrics had dropped a spoonful of butternut soup in his lap. "If we have to spend any more of this break listening to the two of you argue over who inherited the *one* brain in your family," Theo drawled, "I'm going to have my parents banish your entire line to the Arctic."

Theo was . . . all right.

Of all Vehan's "friends," Aurelian genuinely liked this one, however begrudgingly. He was exceedingly beautiful, even for fae, even next to Vehan, with short, tight curls of black hair, full bow lips, and high-swept cheekbones flaring to sharply pointed ears. The copper warmth of his dark brown skin glowed ever so faintly, because Theodore Reynolds was also (technically) a prince, the eldest son of one of the three Seelie Summer royal families. Theo was someone Vehan could actually relate to in a way he couldn't with anyone else, and that was *good*. Vehan needed someone who understood the things even Aurelian never could. But it was no secret that Riadne had encouraged their friendship because of the potential benefits the joining of their two houses would afford her. And Aurelian wasn't a saint; he was allowed to be jealous, to envy how *right* Theo and Vehan looked together.

"Try it, Your *Nothingness*." Kine sneered. "Your family can't do shit without the Lysternes' permission, right, Vehan? It's a joke we even still call you a prince, Theo."

But Vehan wasn't paying attention. He'd been staring at his phone throughout the entire conversation, which explained his silence where normally he'd be quicker to Aurelian's defense when his friends got away with themselves. But it was odd behavior. Vehan was *terrible* at remembering to bring his phone when he went places, and he didn't spend much time on it when he did.

"Isn't that the UnSeelie Spring capital?" said Danika, a black-haired, amber-skinned girl leaning into Vehan's space to see what he was looking at. "Toronto! It is—that's the aquarium. I've been there on vacation. Wow, what happened to it?"

"Didn't you hear? Court News Network did a whole segment on it. They say there was a *Reaper* attack."

Court News Network—a website owned and run by the magical community, and just about the only thing Vehan used his phone for. It was accessible only by way of invitation and the Identification Number all folk of the Courts were given at birth or registry.

"Seriously? A Reaper in the Courts?"

"In the *capital*." Kine sucked air between his teeth and scoffed. "The High King's becoming a joke. Your mother should Challenge him and put him out of his senile misery, Vehan. This would never happen with *her* in control."

Vehan looked up from his phone with a glare.

A Challenge—Aurelian knew it was coming, they all did; it was only a matter of time.

The High King's role as Head of the Great Courts wasn't one that could be passed along through succession. It had to be won by a very specific set of rules, and only by certain few.

Only fae of royal blood could contend for the Bone Crown's possession—that gift the gods had given the Founding Eight fae when the immortals left this realm. Aurelian wasn't quite convinced the Crown was a gift at all, from what he'd heard of it. He wasn't alone in this suspicion.

Only fae of royal blood could pose a Challenge, and the Challenger was allowed to pick the time—within a year.

They were allowed to pick the place—anywhere at all.

They could choose to undertake the Challenge themselves or appoint a Champion in their stead, but there was no backing out once the terms were set, and it was a battle to the death that decided the victor. If you lost, your life was forfeited. If you won, the crown was yours. Azurean Viridian had been a formidable fae in his prime—had maintained his crown long enough that it had been Aurelian's entire lifetime since anyone dared try to take it from him. But his prime had clearly passed. Azurean was showing sign of more than weakness these days.

His god-given crown exacted a hefty toll, the rumor went, on any who even once dared to wear it. It had never been meant for mortal heads and was said to whisper madness in their ears. And that speculation was boosted by the fact that each High Sovereign that *didn't* meet a quick demise grew erratically unstable in exactly the same way. The folk were convinced that these whispers were the voices of the Crown's previous possessors. Instead of being ferried away to the stars after their death, the soul of every High Sovereign was thought to be consumed by the Crown in the gods' last play of cruelty against them, forever trapping them in an object they couldn't help wanting because this hefty toll was always eclipsed by their desire for power.

High King Azurean had been a legend even before he claimed the Crown that amplified his magic. As young as Riadne had been at the time of the Crown's changing of heads, she'd still been more than a match for Azurean's age-worn father, but she'd needed to bide her time where Azurean was concerned. That time was coming. Everyone sensed it. Riadne's resentment toward the Viridians had only grown stronger over the years, and the folk were waiting, watching, morbidly fascinated by the long-term game they were fully aware she played in secret. Aurelian knew once she made her move, the spectacle of this battle was going to make Challenge history . . . but this had always been a touchy subject for Vehan.

If Riadne won, he'd become High Prince.

If she lost, he would lose his mother.

"Maybe don't say things like that in front of Tulia." Vehan's reply was cool enough that Kine ducked his chin to hide a flinch. Vehan set his phone down on the table, glancing briefly over to where Tulia Viridian—one of the High King's many nieces, however far removed— sat holding court of her own group of sycophants. "Also, in case you've forgotten, High King Azurean has done a lot of good for us."

"Yes, yes," Fina sighed, waving a hand, speaking over her brother. "We're extremely grateful for his human protection acts and those faerie public schools he had built throughout the Courts. Hooray to accessible education for the masses."

"And health care," Theo added. "Free public health care in every Court has been a pretty big thing among the faeries."

"Yeah, it's free because there's double the tax on *us*. The fae are the ones who pay for it, who are expected to give more of our goods to the palace stores during Tithe Season to compensate for this. And for what?" Fina sniffed. "Faeries are forever going on about how unfair things are for them. They're ungrateful. We let them live in a society *we* built, so of course they're going to be expected to adapt to *our* ways—and I don't know, maybe stop buying things you can't afford if you're too poor to pay medical bills? Like, get another job or something."

A few of the others gathered nodded agreement with this sentiment. Some looked distinctly uncomfortable but kept quiet.

Aurelian often wondered what exactly he'd done wrong in his previous lives to wind up with this one. The fae were a privileged lot, the sidhe fae especially, and many of them took that for granted. That privilege didn't make them bad, but hells, the ones who thought it made them *better* . . .

Vehan, outrage painting him blue in the face despite his glamour, opened his mouth and was about to launch into what Aurelian knew was sure to be an impressive tirade on his opinion of Fina's spectacular ignorance—he'd never been known to hold back any other time she showed it—but Theo held up his hand. "Please, Your Highness, allow me." He turned to Fina. "Fina, your mother should have swallowed you."

This comment opened the floor to several minutes of waspish remarks, threats, and further heated argument. Aurelian used it as cover to choke back a laugh.

"Okay, okay," Vehan said a few moments later to wrangle in the conversation before their break was over. "Fina said something inappropriate. It's been addressed. Let's let it go. There was actually something I wanted to ask you all before we break off for class."

A Reaper could have plowed through the cafeteria wall and no one would stir for how immediate and fixed the entire table's attention had turned on Vehan. No doubt they thought he was about to ask them something pertaining to the Solstice, but here it was at last—the reason Aurelian had subjected himself to this lunchtime torture to begin with. Vehan usually had others to watch over his safety during the lunch hour, the stern-faced palace guard by the cafeteria door being only one of them. Aurelian's presence wasn't normally necessary, but . . .

Iron teeth will show you the way. But . . . only once the stars align will you receive the answers you seek.

No amount of digging had clarified what Lydia the Oracle had meant by this riddle. "Once the stars align" might have been an instruction as simple as only being able to find this mysterious facility she'd mentioned at night when stars were visible in the sky. Iron teeth, though? They were completely stumped on that.

It had been Vehan's idea to ask his peers their opinion. Aurelian had to admit it wasn't the worst plan he'd ever come up with, and he was just as interested in solving this riddle, even if he pretended not to care. As painful as it was to listen to this particular collection of faé gossip and argue and complain about petty things, they were still teenagers—they knew a lot of things adults wrote off as unworthy of their time.

"So, Aurelian and I went to the Goblin Market the other day—"

"Oh my gods, did you really?"

"How was it?"

"I'm so jealous."

"Did you buy anything?"

"Oh, please, you *have* to come with me when *I* Mature."

Vehan waited out the comments far more graciously than Aurelian felt they deserved. "It was . . . interesting. We didn't have much time to look around, though. I was there for a different reason."

"Was it for the Solstice?"

"My family sent in our RSVP as soon as we got our invitation—Vehan, you'll save a dance for me, won't you?"

"Tell me you at *least* stopped at the Honeytree. They have these cakes there—gods, they're *sin*. My mother brings them back for us every time she goes. No offense, Aurelian, I know your parents are—"

"Would you let him speak?" Aurelian snapped. It didn't matter to him where any of them shopped or that most of them pretended to adore the queen's selection—his parents—for her royal pâtissiers, but whispered among themselves how scandalous it was that she hadn't bestowed that honor upon talent from her own Court.

Their break was almost over.

Vehan was far too nice to people who were too happy to walk all over him; he needed to hurry this along.

The prince ducked his head, just enough to hide a grin so brief and fleeting, it could easily have been Aurelian's imagination that it had been there at all. Then, to the table, he said, "It wasn't anything exciting, but I was looking for something, and someone told me I'd be able to find it if I followed 'iron teeth.' I have no idea what that means, though, and was hoping one of *you* might?"

Ah, to prove oneself useful to the crown prince in a time when everyone's thoughts were on marriage. If only Vehan applied a little more of the manipulation he'd learned from his mother to *other* areas of his life, Aurelian wouldn't have to worry so much about him.

"This might work better, Your Highness, if instead of dancing around the truth, you told us exactly what you want to know."

Aurelian studied Theo. Theo studied Vehan.

Theo hadn't spoken once since Vehan had called for their attention. He had sat and listened, no doubt reading many things between scant lines, clever as always—the perfect balance, really, to Vehan's naivete.

No one said a word while they waited for Vehan's response.

"All right." Vehan folded his hands on the table and sat a little straighter. "Rumor has it there's someone out in the desert trading gold for humans. Does anyone know anything about that?"

Again, no word. The gathered fae looked to one another and shook their heads.

"Come on . . . nothing at all? I'd be indebted to you, of course, if you could point me in the right direction. I'd *really* like to find where this is."

The look of longing on Kine's face and several others made Aurelian itch to tell Vehan to retract such an offer.

"Iron teeth, huh?" said Carsten Odelle, a burly boy who was more muscle than brains, with sandy-blond hair, lightly tanned skin, and a resting expression that had earned him the nickname "Grim." If Aurelian recalled correctly, his highly decorated father served under the Seelie Summer faction of the Falchion.

Grim didn't speak all that often, only slightly more than Aurelian did. It was curious, but so was the look he shared with the reedier, gaunt boy beside him—Jasen.

"Yes?" Vehan perked a little more to attention. The rest of the table did too.

It was Jasen who responded, nervous and extremely hesitant to do so. "You're not going to tell my parents where you heard this, are you?"

"I swear to you, I will not."

Jasen shook his head. "Tell my parents—you have to say all of it. A proper promise or I'm not saying a word."

"I, Vehan Soliel Lysterne, will in no way betray to your parents how I've come by the information you have to trade."

"And you'll owe me a favor."

Vehan nodded. "Whatever is in my power to grant, of equal weight to what you tell me, if it's what I'm after."

Biting his lip, Jasen reached into his pocket. Looking around to make sure the only eyes on him were the ones at this table, he leaned a bit closer and slapped something down on its surface.

A packet, filled with ashen powder.

Aurelian recognized it instantly.

"Is that . . . Faerie Dust?" Fina asked, leaning in for a closer look.

It was. Aurelian had tried it once in a fit of rebellion. He'd tried a number of things, but Faerie Dust had been the worst by far—a psychedelic that started out a lot like the mixture of DMT and ecstasy he'd also tried until it warped into a nightmarish horror and triggered all manner of negative effects like nausea, panic attacks, extreme paranoia, aggression, profound terror, and suicidal ideation.

It was also extremely addictive and cheap, and its high was so indescribably *wonderful* once the body adjusted to the poison and those side effects lessened to almost nothing.

The Falchion had its hands full with the stuff, more of late than usual. That Jasen had this on him, at the Academy no less, was an incredibly risky move.

But there, a symbol on the packet—the seller's signature: an open set of teeth, drawn in black, the incisors of which gleamed iron silver.

"Jasen," said Vehan, no louder than a whisper. He slid the packet closer on the tip of his finger, and Aurelian had to restrain himself from physically recoiling. "I think we have a deal."

CHAPTER 11

Arlo

〜

"WHAT ARE YOU DOING?"

"Arc-welding," Arlo replied, glancing up from the book she was very obviously reading.

Celadon's rooms had always felt most like home to her at the palace. The elevator opened up into a large, airy parlor where multiple windows had been stamped into pale green walls to reveal a stunning wraparound view of Toronto. Directly across from the elevator and situated between two of these windows was a golden-jade granite fireplace where she and Celadon had spent much of their youth, curled up in front of it with cups of cocoa and human fantasy books they read aloud to each other.

There were all the usual fixtures of a palace drawing room in here: a grand piano that Celadon couldn't play to save his life but pretended he thought himself a genius at when people he didn't like imposed themselves on him; settees and divans and armchairs and couches upholstered in sumptuous emerald fabric; handsome vases and gorgeous sculptures and golden-framed oil paintings of things both sublime and romantic.

The doors to the right would take one into yet more rooms devoted to various forms of entertainment, but the doors to the right were for Celadon alone—his personal chambers. Here there was a black marble bathroom, larger than many of Toronto's whole apartments, with a sunken hot tub, a glass-encased waterfall shower, and windows enchanted to look out over a tranquil forest dipped in twilight; a dressing room with racks upon racks of clothing and shoes and jewels and accessories; a private library; a meditation room; a gaming den; and another, smaller parlor.

It was the bedroom Arlo had chosen to haunt while waiting for Celadon's return—his four-poster bed, specifically, big enough to comfortably fit three full-grown people and outfitted with cotton sheets like melted butter against Arlo's skin.

Rolling his eyes at her response, Celadon threw himself down beside her, making her bounce. She glared at him, though the action lacked heat.

Celadon frowned at the book in Arlo's hands (some particularly dense and rambling tome about the magical bonds), then pulled toward him another book she'd grabbed to pass the time—this one selected on a whim, lying on the rosewood desk (infused with the scent of actual rose) off by the open balcony doors. Celadon had clearly been in the middle of reading it, and that was initially what drew her attention, but the black-and-gilded serpent winding up the leather spine, weaving through a string of several golden orbs, was what had made her want to examine it further. That symbol seemed . . . strangely familiar.

"You know, most people don't spend perfectly lovely spring days holed up indoors reading Nicholas Flamel's *Exposition of the Hieroglyphical Figures.*"

"Is that what that one is?" Arlo asked distractedly, turning her nose back to her book and flipping the page. "Haven't gotten to it yet. Is it good?"

"If you like discursive, prolix fanaticism, yes. A wonderful read. Arlo . . ."

Arlo glanced up once again. His choice of words raised her brow—the schooling that fae received made them all sound like the ancient scholars who taught them—but the meaningful expression on Celadon's face distracted her from comment.

"Not that I don't love you terribly, but why are you here?"

Sighing, Arlo closed her book and sat up to tuck her legs beneath her. There was no beating around the bush. Celadon already knew why she was here, judging by the wariness in his expression. "Has there been *any* word on what the High King is going to do about what happened in the café?"

"Arlo—"

"*Cel.*" She stared him down.

Celadon slipped off the bed in a huff. "You know I can't tell you. You're not an official member of the Courts yet, and it's classified information, besides. He's put a summons out for her—"

"Yeah, ages ago. That isn't anything *new*."

"What do you want him to do, put a Mark on her?"

Arlo winced. "Well, no . . ."

A Mark . . .

Once, the gods had taken a much more active role in mortal affairs and were able to come and go as they pleased. But even by fae standards, their rule had been too cruel—too capricious and austere. Eventually, the folk had decided enough was enough.

Eight fae had come forward—eight champions, eight soon-to-be founders of the Courts of Folk—their magic undiluted by years of iron exposure, their unique Gifts the most impressive talent folk back then had ever known. They'd united the magical races, led the assault on the temples and shrines the folk had long maintained, because gods . . . they were power unrivaled. They blew and shook and flooded and scoured the earth in their anger over this rebellion, but that power? It depended entirely on mortal worship.

Without worship, the gods were nothing—they diminished, faded, shrank to pitiful, powerless creatures. To preserve themselves, the gods agreed to a treaty that they would pass their days in the Immortal Realm of the Titans. They agreed to keep out of mortal affairs any more than permitted, in exchange for the folk's promise of continued worship, though less than what it once had been—only enough that would sustain them.

Arlo only really knew about a handful of the gods. The war had happened so long ago that most of the others had fallen into obscurity.

The Great Three of Western worship were Urielle, Goddess of

Chaos and the Elements, said to have formed the mortal world and infused it with light and magic; Tellis, the Goddess of Nature, said to have given the world life; and, of course, Cosmin, Lord of the Cosmos, who'd divided day with starry night, and balanced his sister's life with death. His cadre of immortal hunters was vast and had been depicted throughout faerie legend as harvesters of souls. They roamed the skies, chasing divine quarry, and only showed themselves to the recently deceased when they came to collect their souls and ferry them back to Cosmin's realm.

Of the many in his employ, four stood out above all others—the Wild Hunt, they called themselves.

The crown that Arlo's great-uncle currently wore did more than make him High King and put UnSeelie Spring in power over all the others. Given to the Founding Eight by Cosmin himself as a token of peace between the two realms, the Bone Crown also placed him in command of this legendary troupe. Even though Arlo had never seen a Hunter for herself, she knew as well as anyone else they weren't to be taken lightly. There was no escaping them once they'd been set after you.

And if the High Sovereign Marked you, the Hunt was permitted to chase you down however they wished . . . to tease you and torment you and make the last moments of your life a living hell. . . .

This was not the fate Arlo wished on someone she couldn't say for certain was the murderous culprit they were after.

"Arlo." Celadon said her name much softer now, stepping forward to place his hands on her shoulders. "I know you're anxious to see this resolved. Trust me, I am too. I don't like how close you've come to danger here—and how much danger you're still in every day this is allowed to continue. But this isn't for you to worry about." He lifted a hand to tug on a strand of her hair. Arlo swatted it away, however half-heartedly. "Please allow me to take care of this. You're my family, my best friend, and I love you like a sister . . . maybe better than a sister, because I have one, and let me tell you, she gets on my nerves a *lot*. So let me protect you as I've always protected you . . . as I'll always continue to do."

Damn Celadon, he was far too good at getting his way. Arlo knew he meant every word he said—there wasn't anyone in the world she felt safer with than him, no one in the world she loved better, no one in the world who loved *her* better in return—but that didn't mean he didn't also know by now exactly what to say to soften her obstinate moods.

"Fine," she sighed. She could *feel* her fight draining out of her. "You win."

"This isn't about winning." Celadon dropped back onto the bed. "This is about you living long enough to give Councillor Sylvain an aneurysm when you're named an official Viridian."

Arlo snorted.

She knocked her shoulder into his. Celadon swung like a pendulum out and back against her side with just enough force to topple her over. He grinned impishly at her glower. "Seriously, though," he added as soon as Arlo righted herself. "We'll get to the bottom of what happened in the café. Leave Nausicaä to us."

Nausicaä?

"Pardon?"

The shock on Celadon's face was enough to know that he'd let something slip he hadn't meant to. Arlo felt her fight stir instantly back to life. "Nausicaä—is that her name? Do you know who she is? Is she actually the Dark Star?"

Celadon looked an odd combination of furious and horrified at himself. He sat on the edge of his bed, blinking at her. Arlo had *never* seen him caught off guard like this before. Normally, he was wit she couldn't keep up with, and three steps ahead of every conversation.

"Is that her name?" she pressed a little harder, surging forward to crowd her cousin's space.

"I . . . *yes*. Okay? It's her name. Now let it go! Arlo, *what are you—*"

"How do you know it?" she demanded, draping herself across his shoulders. There was no way she'd be able to physically wrestle information out of him he didn't want to tell, but she could certainly annoy him into relenting. This was important—this was *progress*. If Celadon knew the Dark Star's name, he undoubtedly knew other things about her too, because the High Prince's Gift—the extra ability his strength of magic afforded him—was the ability to hear things that had been said long after their saying. Words left impressions on the air, hung around like ghosts to haunt the space in which they'd been spoken. No secret was safe from someone with this talent if they knew where to apply it and did so before those ghosts could fade.

"Arlo, you're wrinkling my suit! Get off."

"Tell me what you know about Nausicaä!"

"No."

"Do you know where she is?"

"*No.*"

"Don't make me use *your* name . . ."

"You wouldn't dare!"

"You are *unbelievable*."

Arlo nodded. It was fair. There were times (like now, for instance) she couldn't believe her persistence either. "Uh-huh. I know. Now, are you really sure you can't come in with me?"

Celadon drew a breath as though to calm whatever reply he'd like to make instead of, "I'm sure. The Faerie Ring has a strict 'no sidhe fae' policy. I physically cannot enter. Also, can I remind you again that this place is *incredibly illegal and very dangerous*, and if anyone finds out about this . . ."

The Faerie Ring was more than just a nightclub. That was just its official face. Its true nature was right there in the title, though that, too, was rather fluid.

Originally, faerie rings had been altars to Fate. As a Titan—an immortal even older and more powerful than a god—many had paid her worship, though that worship wasn't necessary to sustain her or any of the other self-reliant Titans the way it was for the gods.

An endless loop with no discernable ending or beginning, rings had become something of her symbol, and it was here that faeries brought their prayers and sacrifices to earn her favor.

After the gods were expelled from the world, certain faeries had taken to warping these rings into traps, imbuing them with a magic that would lure unsuspecting humans from their paths and straight into the ring's clutches. Once captured, that human would be enslaved to faerie whim until released, but often this total servitude was a lifelong sentence.

The Courts didn't allow faerie rings within their territories, along with many other tricks invented for human torture, if only because it drew too much attention to what they were now attempting to hide. For the most part, most rings had all been destroyed. Only the ones in the Wild were left untouched—and *this* one, the nightclub Arlo was about to enter. Rumor said it was the very first altar Fate had erected, and even the High King was wary of offending the being said to control destiny.

Arlo waved her hand, dismissing Celadon's very valid concern. In truth, now that she was here, the nerves that normally prevented her from doing foolish things like this were finally starting to agitate.

This was well outside her normal behavior, the very sort of thing *other* people did—people who were brave and not at all timid balls of worry and apprehension like she was. Hells, she didn't even like to jaywalk, let alone infiltrate expressly out-of-bounds dens of human torment.

But Celadon knew who the Dark Star really was.

He knew where she could be *found*.

A summons wouldn't be enough to bring in "Nausicaä Kraken," not with what Arlo knew of her personality from their brief interaction, and overwhelming was Arlo's even greater anxiety that Nausicaä would get away in the time it took the High King to realize he needed to take better action.

It would have to be Arlo who found the undeniable evidence the High King seemed to be waiting for.

She'd survived the encounter once—the Dark Star hadn't been half as frightening as her legend made her out to be, possibly because Arlo had never imagined her to be so young and . . . well, relatively gorgeous. She could survive the encounter again. If everything went according to plan, they wouldn't run in to each other at all—what were the odds that Nausicaä would be present this time of not-quite night? What were the odds she was still here in the city at all? Arlo needed evidence and nothing more. If she could find a faerie in the club who could confirm Arlo's theories and stand as witness before the High King . . . "We're young." She shrugged. "Impulsive . . . The Courts never take pre and newly Mature fae seriously—not until we're at least half a century old. If this turns south and we get caught, the High King will give us a very stern talking-to and we'll promise never to do something so stupid again in our lives. It'll be *fine*."

The knots twisting up her stomach screamed a different story.

"Yes, except you're probably going to *die* before you get to make any promises of intent on better behavior."

"Don't be so dramatic, Cel. Nobody's going to kill me. You said so yourself, there's a 'no killing other folk' policy within the club. And you'll be right here waiting for me when I'm finished, right?"

Celadon grumbled his affirmation.

"I'm not going to be on my own any place where there might be actual danger."

That was the plan, at least. Now that it was being put into action, Arlo had much less faith in its perfect execution—of course, she wasn't going to let Celadon catch whiff of this and double down on his efforts to change her mind.

"You're going to infiltrate what's probably the most notoriously dangerous club in the *world* to prod a bunch of notoriously danger-ous criminals for information on someone who is quite possibly an assassin, and gifted with strange, magical death powers." Celadon's jaw clenched. "Yes. That sounds fine. This is one hundred percent an activity safe for all ages; nothing could go wrong."

Unhelpfully, Arlo's mind decided now to remember that they would also have to do this all before her mother came home. It was still quite early in the evening—the sun had barely hit the horizon—and Thalo had a few more hours yet before her usual return from leading the Royal Guard through training simulations, doling out and checking on assignments for the Falchion factions, and generally storming around wherever the High King went as an extra bit of muscle. Still, there was always the chance she'd cut her workday short.

Arlo sighed, trying to ignore the swell of nausea.

"If she's there, I'll leave," she reminded him. "If there's any trouble at all, I'll *leave*. I know this is dangerous, Cel. I know this is . . . yeah, okay, sure—I'm one of the folk, no matter what the Courts say. No one can try to kill me inside the Ring. But that doesn't mean they can't hurt me or follow me out if they feel like reminding me they're a bunch of murderers, thieves, and criminals."

"This talk is having the opposite effect of what you wanted."

Arlo looked her cousin in the eye. She didn't *want* to get this involved, to run around after possible killers and throw herself from one fire to another. She would give anything to be at home right now, safe and unconcerned about what was going on in their community, to leave this problem to other people, but *other people* were doing just the same. Those other people weren't doing anything, and Arlo just couldn't shake the sound of Cassandra's mother crying. She couldn't shake the sight of Cassandra's face, frozen in pain . . . her body, lifeless . . . the Dark Star, so infuriatingly flippant about it all. Every time Arlo closed her eyes, she relived what had happened in the café and wondered if she could have done something more to prevent it from happening at all. She wondered if maybe *she* really could be next to die, as Celadon already seemed convinced—and hells, it could have easily been *her* on that café floor. She was iron-born, just like Cassandra. She'd been seated right beside her, in the midst of a killer who could apparently strike whenever and wherever they wished.

How many people would be relieved if she were gone?

Who would bring *her* justice, where Celadon and the too few others she mattered to couldn't because of the rules that bound them?

Family, classmates, the Fae High Council . . . Arlo could have died, could still die—others were *going* to die—and nothing would be done about any of it because nobody really cared about the ironborn.

Arlo was all Cassandra had, it seemed. Arlo wasn't going to let the not-too-insignificant fears inside her keep her from doing this one little thing that might actually help, and once again there was that hopeful little feeling inside her: *What if . . .*

What if this could all be over now?

What if *she* could *do* something?

"I have to do this, Cel."

Celadon was quiet as he studied her expression. As always, Arlo appreciated that she rarely had to speak her thoughts for him to understand her. "I'll give you one hour," he relented. "Anything that tries to hurt or follow you out of that club will find themselves at war with the entirety of the Eight Courts. If you feel unsafe at *any* point inside the Faerie Ring, the mission is off. If Nausicaä Kraken is there, you are not. Do you understand me? You are *not* to draw any more of her attention than you already have."

Arlo nodded mutely.

"Fine. I'm still not happy about this."

"I know."

"One hour."

"Got it."

"Do not dance, drink, or eat *anything* while inside the club. You're human, too, and that's still a ring—they might not let you go if you do."

"Yeah, I'm really not feeling those options at the moment, anyhow."

"Arlo?"

Facing her cousin once more, Arlo's mouth pressed flat together. Celadon's expression was so uncharacteristically heavy that seeing it made her hesitate all over again. There was a fine and fragile line between the things that made a person brave and the things that made them fools—so far, she had a sinking suspicion their plan belonged to the latter category.

"Yeah?" she inquired softly.

His protracted silence wore on for what felt like another full minute before he allowed his concern to dial down. Only when he relaxed his hold on the steering wheel did she realize he'd been gripping it tight enough to turn his knuckles white. "Be careful, please. Don't do anything stupid."

Arlo rolled her eyes. She had to do this before she lost her nerve completely. "We're there, Cel. We've reached 'stupid.' You know, you're not even twenty-one yet. You're going to look like you're younger than that for a solid twenty-one to come. I'm further along in my timeline than you are—one of these days, people are going to start saying *I'm* the bad influence on *you*."

"Excuse you," Celadon huffed, more of his usual spirit restored. "I'm the very and incredibly dated definition of 'adult.' I have a house and a job and at least three potential life partners who haven't yet met me in person and therefore haven't learned that all the rumors about me are more or less true."

"Uh-huh. What *is* your job, even? Making sure budget report meetings don't end in casualties?"

Making a show of thinking this over, Celadon frowned. "You know, I can't really say. Is keeping myself and the Viridian name out of scandal a job title? Because I'm fairly certain that's the reason they're forcing me into the High King's advisory to being with."

Snorting, Arlo threw open her door. She stepped out onto the sidewalk, but before she closed the door behind her, she bent to catch Celadon's gaze. "If it is, you suck at it, and they're probably paying you way too much."

Celadon ignored her statement by way of reaching for the lever that adjusted his seat and reclined, clutching his Venti S'mores Frappuccino as though it were something stronger.

Shaking her head, Arlo closed the door.

She felt much older than she actually was in the black jeans, hot pink heels, and dark gold sequined top she'd purchased expressly for this little adventure just after their conversation at the Reverdie. It had taken almost a full hour and several YouTube videos for her hair to match this image, half tied back in an elaborate knot meant to resemble a rose, the rest left to drape in flaming, loose curls down her back. She was almost proud of the end result, though.

It wasn't often she felt so beautiful. It wasn't often she felt like she could hold her own—even somewhat—beside her stunningly gorgeous fae family. Catching a glimpse of herself in the reflection of a dark window she passed, she felt like an entirely different person.

Her outfit was like armor. Wearing it, she could almost wield her strange new confidence like a weapon.

Of course, when thick cement replaced the various shop fronts she passed, that weaponized confidence began to waver. Her destination was coming up quickly—a derelict overpass covered in bits of overgrown weeds and graffiti—and casually leaning against the barren stone was someone who looked like a little determination was all they needed to bend Celadon's car in half.

Gut instinct told her to tuck her chin closer to her chest and scurry past this veritable mountain. Their olive toned arms were so thick they strained the cotton of their plain black shirt, and a woven pattern of tattoos stood in place of the hair on top of their bald head. They were the sort of person with whom very few—including Arlo—would be comfortable making eye contact, but the flick of a glance when she drew nearer was all it took for her awareness to catch on a peculiarity that made her stop in her tracks.

Faeries were excellent at spinning illusions, casting their glamours to warp their appearance into something so human no one would notice without close inspection. But there were always tells. Even in the fae, whose magic was the strongest of the faerie races, there was *always* a trace of a signature.

Something in the back of Arlo's mind suspected, though, that the fathomless black in this particular person's inhuman eyes wouldn't have been noticeable if they hadn't wanted her to see it. They were their only tell. The harder Arlo looked at them—really looked at them—the harder their illusion cemented around them, and no one's glamour was *that* good, let alone the faerie those eyes and that bulk suggested they were.

A *troll.*

Under a bridge . . . of sorts.

Arlo wasn't about to point out the irony in this just in case the troll thought she found it funny—this sort of faerie had a tendency to kill the things that sparked their live-wire irritation.

Rallying every ounce of courage she possessed, Arlo forced herself to face them fully, inflating as tall as her five-foot-four height could manage. "Hello," she said, pitchy and overly cheerful. Not that she'd doubted Celadon and his wealth of knowledge that he probably shouldn't have, but if a troll of this caliber was standing around out here in the middle of nowhere, she had to be in the right place.

This was most likely the Faerie Ring's "bouncer."

"No." The troll shook their head.

Arlo blinked. "But I didn't even ask you anything yet!"

"You didn't have to. The answer is no."

The troll had a way of speaking that made them hard to understand. Their words grated together, not exactly accented, but dull and deep, and the way they echoed in the pit of their baritone voice, Arlo felt as though she were conversing with a cave.

Scrambling to keep hold of her wilting courage, she tried again. "Okay, but I'd really like to get inside the club, please. It's important."

"I have no idea what you're talking about, little girl. Go home."

Damn it, this wasn't working at all.

"Listen, Mister," she said as firmly as possible. She really hoped she wasn't making a scene for nothing—that the troll was just being difficult—because if it turned out this one just liked standing under bridges, she was about to badger something twice her size and far less concerned with the consequences of public disembowelment. "I know what's here. I know you're guarding the Faerie Ring, and I want in. I'm one of the folk; you have to let me in. Um . . ." Her hesitation resurged. "Don't you?"

The troll waved dismissively, neither intimidated by Arlo's tone nor overly worried that she'd caught them twisting the truth. In fact, if anything, Arlo would swear amusement lit a glimmer in their unnaturally dark eyes. "First of all, I'm no 'Mister.' My genders may be fluid and many, but my identifiers are neutral."

"Oh! Sorry," Arlo apologized. "Won't happen again."

The troll nodded. "Second of all, you're fae. Sidhe fae. They might not let you wear their name, but it's in your blood all the same . . . blood that smells like iron." The troll's face was heavy-lidded, squashed, and square. When their wide mouth curled into a sneer, Arlo could almost see beneath their human mask to the blunted lower canines jutting into their upper lip. "Fae *and* human, and neither of those are very welcome where you think you want to go."

Arlo deflated, but wasn't entirely ready yet to give this up to defeat. It wasn't anything she hadn't been expecting—a club that was smart enough to flout Court law was smart enough to hire someone who wouldn't let in just anyone claiming to know it was there. "I'm not officially recognized as anything. I'm one of the folk, that's it. There are plenty of us who have no Court affiliation at all."

"And . . . what? You've decided that since you're nothing more than the 'lowly masses,' you might as well aim for banishment?" The troll raised a brow, eyeing Arlo critically. "Do you even know what the Faerie Ring is, little girl? It's not just some nightclub for your entertainment. Just because you're not good enough for the VIP section of the Courts doesn't mean they won't come down on you like the crumbling heavens if you get caught here. This isn't a place for someone like you."

"No, you're right, it's not," Arlo agreed, folding her arms defensively across her chest. "I know exactly what this place is, and it's *definitely* not for me. But it's where I need to be right now, and you can't deny me entrance."

The troll considered Arlo with flickering interest. "Why is this where you need to be?"

"It's secret."

"You don't say." They twitched a grin. "Who is it that you're after?"

"I . . . never said I was after anyone."

Silence stretched between them, though it wasn't really silent.

The traffic on the street behind was loud and bustling with end-of-day commuters, and the first stirrings of Toronto's Friday night-life. Somewhere in the distance, a heartbeat of music pounded out of someone's car stereo, and a group of human teenagers, too wrapped up in their boisterous conversation to notice anything else around them, filtered past between Arlo and the railing dividing sidewalk from road.

When the last of the group trickled by, the troll pushed off from the wall and took a step toward Arlo. This seemed to make them grow several inches taller, and Arlo wasn't ashamed to admit the effect was highly intimidating.

Their black eyes locked onto hers.

She wanted to look away, but a small voice inside her said that if she did, she might as well *walk* away too.

"All right, Arlo Jarsdel. I will let you through."

The use of her name surprised her. Stunned, she tried to think back to when she could have possibly given it. The troll mistook her stark silence as need for clarification. "You can go inside, if you're sure that's what you want."

She wasn't sure. Not at all. Her certainty in *that* was about as close to sure as she was of anything at the moment. "A-all right," she replied. "Yes. Thank you."

Snorting at whatever in her statement they found amusing, the troll nodded acceptance of this verbal contract. They dropped back to the wall, but before they could reach it, stepped aside, and the patch they'd been previously guarding revealed itself as . . . merely that.

A patch of wall, no different from the rest of the cement around it.

"Um . . . how do I get through?"

"Well, it's not Platform Bloody Nine-and-Three-Quarters, so I don't suggest you barrel off at it."

Arlo rolled her eyes at the blatant sass in this statement. The magical community—however much they grumbled about their growing reliance on technology and assimilation with human culture, their love for human art was evident in the amount of times they referenced it in casual conversation.

"Put your hand on the cement. The door will open. A *proper* faerie would have known that."

Doubtful, but Arlo wasn't going to start that argument.

She could do this. She'd made it this far. All she had to do now was walk through this magical door and she'd be able to uncover more information about the mysterious young woman from the café—it was that easy. The time for hesitation was past. With a minute nod to herself for encouragement, Arlo stepped forward and did as the troll instructed.

At first, nothing happened.

Then, just as she was about to prod for a little further guidance, a portion of the cement beneath her fingers caved inward with a heavy *thunk*. A moment later, the doorlike impression shifted back, then slid aside, and in the space behind was revealed a narrow passage climbing down into darkness so thick, Arlo couldn't see anything beyond the first few steps.

"Are you sure this is the Faerie Ring?" she heard herself ask faintly.

"I never said it was to begin with."

Arlo glared at them.

The troll was toying with her, if the glint in their eyes and fern curl of their grin was anything to go by. This *was* the Faerie Ring, and she didn't have time for her overactive imagination to invent another reason why she shouldn't do this.

Eyeing the passageway mistrustfully, Arlo sighed and squared her jaw at the dark unknown. "It's a nice, quiet life for you after this," she promised herself. Lifting a foot, she crossed the threshold onto the first stone step.

The second joined the first.

She didn't realize she'd been holding her breath until she felt it rush out of her aching lungs. She'd been expecting something to happen— something a lot like what had happened to the thief at the beginning of *Aladdin* who was devoured by the Cave of Wonders for daring to enter when he wasn't the "diamond in the rough."

Arlo wasn't faerie.

She wasn't "properly" fae.

She wasn't "properly" human.

Arlo wasn't properly anything, and she sure as heck wasn't hero material like Aladdin had been and maybe like what this investigation really needed. She'd have to save the teenage angst for later, though, because whether or not she was right for this job, she'd already taken it on. Turning back now would be more than an embarrassment.

The troll appeared behind her, clutching the doorframe in a squat-fingered hand. "I hope you find what you're looking for, Arlo."

She whirled around. "Okay, *how* do you know my name?"

The troll merely grinned. Their impossible glamour wavered, allowing slate-gray skin and bone-crushing teeth to bleed through the flickering moment. Somehow, equally impossibly, Arlo was struck with the impression that this trollish image beneath was a glamour as well.

The black of their eyes flared cold and infinite, marbled now with blue and red and violet and white—an iridescent cosmos, drawing Arlo deeper the longer she looked, and only when those eyes blinked did the veil of a troll fall back into place, and she was released from their thrall.

"Good luck," the troll rumbled, fingers peeled away, the door already beginning to close.

Arlo watched them disappear into a sliver and then . . . they were gone. In a matter of moments, the cement wall had resealed itself completely. All around her was darkness. She could barely see a hand in front of her face. The unease she'd been feeling before started to swell again like a balloon in her chest. "A nice, quiet life, with lots and lots of lighting."

Clinging to this promise, she spared one last pause to appreciate how totally and truly she'd screwed herself over. Then, stretching out her hands to either side, she used the walls to guide her slow descent.

CHAPTER 12

Nausicaä

~⌒~

A WIDE FLIGHT OF WOODEN stairs was all that separated the Faerie Ring's VIP landing from the rest of the club—that and a pair of vampires.

There weren't many vampires that Nausicaä was on good terms with. This brand of folk was the result of long-ago fae experimentation with blood magic. The stories said that a handful of them had gotten together to try to make themselves like the gods they'd kicked out of their world, and it had worked . . . in a way. Their inventive ritual had slowed their aging down to what was almost a complete stop and enhanced their already remarkable speed, endurance, agility, and senses. Of course, it was some next-level dark magic that had given them these powers, and dark magic was much like a parasite. It latched on to its host and fed.

In some, it fed until that host became a mindless husk, and that husk became an instrument of harm, and Nausicaä (as Alecto) became the intervention that brought it to an end.

Nobody liked interventions, no matter the good they served.

The two vampires that flanked the stairs before her were obviously newly made. Blood magic was a finicky thing and required a fresh and constant supply of folk blood to maintain it. The longer it was maintained, the more it altered the host's appearance. Taller ears . . . longer fangs . . . sharper bones and thinner, sallow skin . . . These two still looked fae—the only race of folk who could be turned into a vampire—their eyes bright blue and not navy as midnight, like their color would mellow into over time. Newly made meant fierce dependence on their Maker to supply their dinner and keep them from falling into mindless bloodlust, as was easily done at this age. And it was just Nausicaä's luck that the "they" these two were guarding was a "they" who probably liked her least of the bunch, which meant neither of *them* would like her either.

But it was this "they" who Nausicaä had been stalking at this all-hours faerie revel, and she was far too used to being disliked these days to let that turn her off.

"Hellooo," she drawled, her voice pitched low and sultry. With her hands on her hips and as charming a smile as her unreliable memory of such things could help her craft, she looked between the two young vampires. "I need to have a chat with your Maker."

The vampire on the left—wiry, chestnut-haired, grayish-white skin the color of pale stone—shared a look with his partner. It was the partner—stronger, hair a deeper brown, earthen skin a deeper shade of gray—who replied. "Do you have an appointment?"

"Appointment? Ha, what is this, the dentist? No, I don't have a fucking appointment. I'm also just being polite. *Move*—I need to talk to someone with more than two brain cells to rub together."

She pushed her way between them. For all that it was like cleaving a mountain in two with her bare hands, they parted, and the shock on their faces was mildly satisfying.

"Stop!" said the right-side vampire, darting for her arm.

Nausicaä stopped. She turned to face him. "I'll give you ten seconds to think about how attached you are to that hand," she threatened, not at all a fan of being grabbed by strangers.

Her "captor" snarled, baring pointed teeth that could tear out a throat as easily as blades could shred a sheet of paper.

It was adorable, like a cub playing at fearsome with a lioness.

Nausicaä snarled back at him, shedding a piece of her glamour. It was enough for her true appearance to show through: for her mouth to split too-wide across the severe angles of a hollowed face and fill with sharpened teeth; for her height to flicker taller, and threads of black-like-smoke to trickle out behind her, slowly weaving the image of wings. The vampire released her with an alarmed cry, recognizing if not *her*, then at least the distinctive features of a Fury. He scurried back, knocking into his equally frightened companion.

Nausicaä reeled her anger back under the surface of her glamour, knit both her composure and softer appearance back together, and laughed. "You should see the looks on your faces."

"Your theatrics are quite unbecoming, Nausicaä Kraken."

Her laughter melted away. "Of what, Pallas?" Nausicaä whipped her head back around to face the top of the stairs, and the vampire looking down at her. "A *lady*?"

The vampire, Pallas, sighed. "Honestly, the way you fight me, one would think me the horrible misfortune of being your father."

"Ha! You wish."

She stomped up the stairs.

"And I meant it unbecoming of your mastery. You are a god. You should be above our mortal passions."

"Fuck you." She glared as she pushed past him. It was that mindset that reinforced the deities' stubborn belief in the same. It was that mindset that had led to Tisiphone's depression going ignored and untreated for so long. It was that mindset that tore at Nausicaä's sanity, because as much as she knew it was wrong, she couldn't drown that toxic voice inside her head insisting it was also right. "Looks like I was interrupting a good time."

The landing was an arrangement of fine tables, crushed-velvet divans, and wide-cushioned sofas in each of its four pockets. At the center was an island bar, staffed by a human man with dyed-green hair and wearing a plain white shirt that was rumpled and torn in several places. This glazed-eyed, slack-faced captive of faerie whim wasn't what made Nausicaä raise a brow, though.

Only one pocket of the landing was occupied. Pallas had full reign of this space when he was present in the Faerie Ring, given he was its current "king." A collection of faeries of various genders in various states of undress were reclined on the provided sofas, and scattered around a space that had clearly been Pallas's command until Nausicaä's arrival drew his attention. Ivory and onyx, red and navy, pale lime and morning-yellow limbs twined together, both muscular and slight. A lizard tail flicked lazily on the floor. A curtain of willow vines draped over an arm of the couch. None of their owners seemed much aware of what was going on, their heady bliss a side effect of the magic in vampire fangs, which to anyone other than fae was nothing more than a highly addictive drug.

Pallas waved a hand, drifting back to his vacated seat. "You're always interrupting something, I find. What is it you want, Nausicaä? I'm told you've been persistently present in my club these last few days. I prefer you weren't."

"Then tell me what I want to know, and I'll get out of your ridiculously perfect hair."

No amount of time could drain Pallas fully of the former beauty he'd clearly possessed in his time as a fae. His skin was thin as a pixie's wings, showing off all the bones and spidering veins that held him together beneath, and it was so bleached of sapphire life that he was white as marble stone. A walking mausoleum, he looked to her, ancient even by vampire standards, but prettiness lingered in the russet hair that curled around his nape and ears, the heavily lashed purple eyes that hinted at once being jade, and the airy elegance in his movement. "What is it you wish to know?"

"I take it you've heard about the recent rash of ironborn deaths?"

Pallas inclined his head. "Of course. My concern lies with the common folk now. I take any harm that comes to them to heart."

Nausicaä snorted. "No, you don't. You just don't like to share your food. Can't drink human blood—all that iron is bad for your diet. And the Courts would come down on you like flaming shit if you turned your fangs on their fae, so good luck when they discover Thing One and Thing Two down there, by the way. It's faeries or nothing for you lot—you forget I'm not an idiot."

"*You* forget you wish for my help."

"Urgh, *fine*. I'll say it nicely. Please, oh great and terrible Pallas Viridian, most beloved brother of he who founded the UnSeelie Court of Spring. Reveal to me, a most lowly creature, the knowledge that your many years and handsomest beauty and hair like burning bronze and—"

"Are you done?"

"Hang on—and fangs to rival that of the great and terrible Jörmungandr, bringer of the end of days—"

"There is a Reaper in the city. I do not know who its guardian is, nor do I know their aim apart from the fact it's playing cleanup for its master, and whoever that is, they possess power enough to operate directly under my many-greats nephew's nose—power that stems from an art the Courts have rightly forbidden."

Nausicaä drew a breath and released it loudly through her nose. "I *know* all of that already. Someone's making a bunch of philosopher's stones. They're using kids to do it. Kind of fucked, but hey, I've come to accept mortals are weird like that. Is that seriously all you have for me? Vampires can lie—you gained that ability back when the Alecto before me broke your bond to proper magic." Because the sort of magic that changed a being into something else entirely, like a fae into a vampire? It was a form of altering destiny, and the previous Furies— the ones Nausicaä and her sisters had challenged for their roles, as was the custom of their kind, and what they'd spent their entire life training to do—had been forced to punish accordingly. "Remember: not an idiot."

"And do *you* remember Noel?"

The entire room fell still. The sofa-bound faeries were still unfocused and uninterested in their conversation, but even they would be able to sense the shift in Pallas's mood. Nausicaä knew from memory the way it would have bled into the room a stench like sour milk and layered his tone with the undercurrent of the storm he'd once been able to conjure.

Noel. Pallas's fae lover. The first he'd ever turned vampire, flouting

Court law. It was Pallas's status that had saved him from the execution his actions demanded, and however much the vampire virus was still dark magic, now that it had been called into the world, it was no longer a form of altering destiny. Fate could spin it into whatever possibility she pleased from then on, but none of this could do anything to protect Noel when Pallas's bite broke his mind and sent him down a murderous path that ended with his death.

"Noel abducted a bunch of humans and sacrificed them to resurrect his own personal undead army," Nausicaä replied dryly. "He was trying to, and I quote, 'erase the sun and drown the world in a feast of enemy blood.' I'm sorry, Noel was insane. Necromancy is against the Law. I was a Fury. I was doing my *job* in bringing him in, nothing more."

"You did your job with *relish*, spiteful thing," Pallas hissed.

Nausicaä folded her arms over her chest and glared. "Hard disagree with you there. Can't relish something you don't give a shit about—yeah, I *liked* being a Fury. I was good at it. It's what I was created for. It's what I spent my entire life in preparation to become. But I didn't know you *or* Noel. It wasn't personal. It. Was. My. *Job.*"

"Leave my sight!" Pallas snarled, leaping to his feet. The faeries around him gasped, stirring at last. One dove for cover in the arms of the faerie beside them; another fell off the end of her divan. The enthralled human at the bar fumbled the glass he'd been washing, shattering it on the ground.

He didn't so much as flinch when he walked across the shards to find a broom—when he came out from behind the bar, Nausicaä noticed that he was barefoot and trailing bloody footprints behind him.

The things the Ring got away with, all because the humans its patrons lured in for "entertainment" were given the freedom to reject whatever temptation was used to get them here. All because—after these humans served their purpose and their faerie captors grew bored—they were released back into the world (if they didn't die first) without a single memory of what had happened. "Alien abduction," many of them reasoned this gap in their recollection as. Nothing the Courts could do if they wanted. Nothing the Furies could do about it either.

"Leave! You had every ounce of sympathy for your own plight but *none* for mine. You do not care about these ironborn! You do not care about this realm! You have no care for *anyone* other than your miserable self, and whatever else I know about this situation, I would rather suffer the terrible end that's on its way than divulge anything to you. *Leave.*"

"You know what, curse you!" Nausicaä spat on the ground, sealing what she spoke. "I hope you lose even more than Noel."

The faerie with the lizard tail gasped.

Even Pallas looked taken aback.

To curse someone was no light thing, however little it needed of oneself to make it happen: saliva, a trace of magic, conviction—belief was a strong thing. It could be bent to just about anything to serve a terrible purpose. Nausicaä knew all too well how curses could cycle back to harm the one who cast them just as deeply as they harmed the intended victim. She didn't care. Pallas made her furious enough as it was without him ripping open old wounds.

"The gods should have Destroyed you when they had their chance," he said, barely above a whisper.

"On that we totally agree!"

Nausicaä stormed back down the stairs, knocking roughly into the two who'd earlier barred her way just because she could. She was tired of this. Pallas, the insufferable asshole that he was, was right—this was none of Nausicaä's business. What did it even matter to her that a bunch of effing ironborn were dying? What did it matter that someone might just be using this particular dark magic to pull something into existence that this realm would never survive? She should *welcome* this, if anything. She had no one she cared about to lose in this war, and no one to care about her if she bought into the "wrong side."

To hells with this!

That Reaper and its master could kill a hundred thousand mortals right in front of her, and she could spit on them, too, for all that would matter to her—this wasn't her job anymore. She was *done*.

She had no idea what drew her attention to the row of booths that lined the far wall. Luck, she supposed. It was nothing but luck that made her cast a glance in that direction as she plowed through dancing faeries, disgruntled cries and swears and threats buzzing in her wake like wasps. But what she saw there made her freeze.

Nausicaä could hardly believe her eyes.

There, stalking between tables, was a creature tall as she in her true form. It was enormous. The sharp bones of its emaciated, long-limbed body protruded under stretched-taut skin, and though something had caved in its skull and taken the creature's sight, it seemed to have no problem getting around.

A Reaper.

Her Reaper.

She could smell it now, from all the way across the room. No one else even twitched with notice, and that was odd, because even the most ghastly of folk would panic in the company of *this*. Which meant . . . "Do they just not see you?"

Was a Reaper honestly glamoured so well that nothing in a den of the world's most wicked creatures could pick out its presence at all?

Nausicaä stood a moment, simply staring the Reaper down, finding this all quite hard to believe. She followed its slow winding trek toward the back of the room, baffled by the fact that it was here at all—Reapers were one of the few things even the Ring rejected—let alone completely at ease here.

"Excuse me . . ."

"*What?*"

Nausicaä wheeled around. She'd stomped a decent way through the dance floor before the Reaper had stalled her, making for the exit and scattering faeries as she went—all except one, apparently. A very gruesome one, a globular mess of matted hair and scarred flesh, and a mouth the size of a tire in the center of its body.

An anthropophagus.

A *polite* one at that.

Nausicaä felt a little dismayed that the reveling faeries had most likely scattered less because of her fury and more because of this cannibalistic creature. "Well?" she prompted when the anthropophagus merely stared, like *she* was the one who went around gobbling up her fellow folk.

"Er . . . you're the one who's been askin' around about these, right?"

He held something out between them in his massive, gnarled paw. It was smooth and gray and shot through with black veins and twisted up in similar colored tubes, a stone at first appearance, in the shape of a mortal . . . "Is that a heart?"

"It used to be."

Nausicaä felt her own begin to hammer in her chest. Anthropophagi weren't as wildly unhinged as their Reaper cousins, but they were definitely dangerous and just as driven by their hunger for flesh. This was . . . odd. Everything happening right now was odd. Of all the faeries she'd figured to be useful to her, this one wouldn't have made her list even if she knew they were here.

She glanced back across the room. The Reaper was nowhere in sight now—almost as though it had never been there at all. Even the stench of its rot had vanished; had she been seeing things? Nausicaä didn't normally doubt her own eyesight like this, but seeing things that weren't really there was much more believable right now than a whole freaking Reaper partying it up in a club of people who would normally be screaming if it were.

"Where did you even get this?" she asked, turning back to the anthropophagus.

"Won it." The anthropophagus laughed, a garbled sound that reeked of stale gore. "The rest of him went down easy, but I've got no taste for *this*. You do, though, as I hear. I also hear you like your cards."

"I'm sensing a proposition here, my good . . ."

"Cyberniskos."

Nausicaä bared her teeth in a grin. "Cyberniskos. You hear correctly. I'd very much like that used-to-be heart in your hand . . . as well as whatever you know that made you so sure I wanted it to begin with. Your terms?"

It was Cyberniskos's turn to grin, and it wasn't a pretty sight. "Word has it you're a Fury."

"Mm-hmm, and I'm guessing you've never dined on *that* before." She could already see where this was going, and damn it all if she wasn't the tiniest bit excited. It was also the perfect excuse to hang around a bit longer in case her Reaper really *was* about. She'd never had an actual conversation with an anthropophagus before—never played one in a game of poker for their worldly possessions either. Here at last was a sliver-thin promise of answers, which was more than she'd come by since arriving in this deities-forsaken Court, and further, she couldn't deny a certain thrill derived from threats and danger. "I'm supposing this will cost me an arm and a leg quite literally, won't it."

Cyberniskos chuckled. "They never said the Dark Star was funny."

"Yeah, they never do."

CHAPTER 13

Arlo

❧

THIS WASN'T THE FAERIE Ring. The passage that Arlo climbed down was the stairway to hell, and nobody could ever convince her otherwise. She had no idea what she was going to do when she finally made her way out of her nightmares incarnate, but she was absolutely certain she was never setting foot in this darkness again.

Because it wasn't mere darkness.

The air here was impossibly dense and far too damp and cool for the shadows to be lack of light alone. Darkness didn't fill a space like liquid tar poured into a mold. It certainly didn't throb like a fizzling energy against Arlo's skin, static-shocking shivers down her spine. Darkness wasn't a living thing that whispered in her ear, planting panicked thoughts not quite her own in Arlo's mind, hurrying her down slick steps with nothing but the vaguely slimy walls to guide her, because the darkness (she suspected) had also killed her phone and the flashlight it came equipped with.

Every step was paired with an increasing urgency to *turn back around*, as though the passageway itself tried to dissuade her from her course of action. Why, she could only guess. Maybe it was a test. Maybe it was magic meant to keep humans from following whatever lure faeries used to draw them into this spider's web. Maybe it was just a product of her damned imagination, but when the disembodied, not-quite-Arlo voice in her head started hinting that, if she didn't leave at once, she would suffocate and die—forever entombed in this gods-awful place—she didn't care; she desperately wanted to do what it said, turn right back around and leave.

"I can't," she chanted under her breath. "I can't, I can't."

Turning around would be smart. It would be an excellent idea. Arlo suspected people braver than she wouldn't continue on at this point. The passageway was a level of horror she'd never before encountered, but if she turned back around, she'd have to face that troll again. She'd have to face their smug superiority and give them the satisfaction of confirming that she didn't have what it took to enter the Faerie Ring.

She might as well be fully human, after all, if the presence of magic alone—however inordinately powerful—was enough to scare her off.

Arlo pushed herself to continue on. She doubled her pace, flying as quickly as she could safely manage down the rest of the stairs, and the moment she cleared the bottom step, the entire world lurched around her. Only when color and sound burst to life in her senses did she realize the passage had stripped these away to begin with. Arlo was left feeling as though she'd just been strained through a particularly elaborate sieve. The faintest ringing in the depths of her ears made her wonder if she'd ever forget the experience.

"I'm going to kill Celadon," she muttered shakily. "Stupid magic passageway piece of garbage . . . A *little* warning might have been nice."

She hated her cousin with every fiber of her being at the moment—maybe if he'd told her about this passageway of doom, he'd have convinced her to sit this plan out—but it was over. She was here.

The Faerie Ring sprawled out before her.

It was a club like any other in construction—not that Arlo had been to any, considering she was underage by human standards, and didn't have friends apart from Celadon to go with, besides. There was a circular bar in the center of the room and a dance floor off to her left, packed full of bodies, writhing and lurching around one another. To Arlo, they looked like a sea of worms, rising and falling on waves of beats that poured from the live band at the back of the room, just beyond a set of stairs that led to some private landing.

Overhead lighting threw a rainbow of colors around the open

space, glancing off the dancers and the mist that curled between them. When she tried to focus her senses, the jumble of auras was as impossible to untangle as the bodies to which they belonged.

It was the cages overhead that set this particular club apart from others run by the folk. The cages, gleaming gold, suspended from the ceiling by thick chains—there was a human in each, blissed out on the food and drink they'd been tricked into consuming. Feathers had been stuck to them, a parody of birds as colorful as the flashing lights, and when one of them stopped singing (their throats either too dry or bodies too fatigued, some even beginning to surface from their stupor), the crowd below would hiss and boo, throw more bits of food or the contents of their drinks to prod them on.

It was the platform back by the band, where scantily clad humans danced like marionettes, wide-eyed and blank, splashed with glowing paint and grime and undoubtedly worse. Arlo noticed they were bruised and scraped and worn for the carelessness they had no idea they suffered.

It was the yet more humans trapped on the floor, so giddy on faerie food that they'd dance themselves to collapsing, if they were lucky. The wholly preserved heads mounted on the walls, hung the way hunters collected trophies from their favorite kills—catches these vicious faeries liked too much to release back to their lives.

Arlo tried to look away, but one terrible sight replaced another in every direction. Here, in this gathering of the worst of their kind, where the Courts held no rule, folk were allowed to vent their frustrations with the life they'd been forced to give up, all for a peace they didn't want. These humans were made to pay a terrible price for whatever pitiful thing they'd been promised—money that would shrivel up into leaves, gems that would rot into mushroom caps, a beautiful face that wasn't so beautiful underneath its glamour, every promise disguising a sting, and many wouldn't survive the days they gave in trade to receive it.

"Just keep moving," she muttered, suppressing a shudder. "Just . . .

don't think about it, and keep moving." She knew what she was going to find here—both Celadon and rumor warned her. The Courts couldn't intervene in anything that happened here, this crack that fell outside their control, as technically it belonged to the Wild. There was nothing *she* could do, and she would lose her nerve if she didn't keep moving.

Head down . . . Don't attract too much attention.

There was seating to her right. Dozens of tables stood littered about, all the way to the far wall and the row of booths that lined it. These were also packed with folk, and it was here that was probably the best place for Arlo to gather her information, but it occurred to her now she'd actually have to go up and *talk* to some of these faeries, and she had no idea how to start the conversation she needed to have.

Have you seen a blond young woman with gray eyes? Wears a lot of black? And, perchance, do you know if she's been going around killing people lately?

Yeah. No, she'd sound too much like a member of the Falchion— the magical community's standard police force. In a place like this, that was only going to land her in the trouble she was trying to avoid.

"Gotta start small . . . ," she said to herself.

The staff (at least the ones who weren't humans made to shuffle around like animated dolls with trays) would probably be the best place to start—with a table, she could flag one down under the pretense of placing an order. "But of course I picked the busiest night to do this . . ." She sighed.

The Faerie Ring was a popular place for the criminal lot, and it wasn't hard to understand why. As a faerie-exclusive club, where glamours could be shed completely without risk of being caught, it was a place of respite. Here, no one had to exhaust themselves on the human standard of appearance, which strict, unforgiving Court law dictated they use their glamours to weave, and many struggled to maintain for lengthy periods of time.

On her way through the tables in search of a vacancy to claim for her own, Arlo passed a group of gnomes: squat, knobbly men with great graying beards, orange-peel leathery skin, and stubby limbs. They were as rampant as rats in the cities these days. These were all nursing tankards bigger than they were, and none of them were tall enough to actually see over their table.

Arlo's focus moved to the next table, occupied by something that looked a lot like a rose-pink elephant in a crisp white suit, and sporting so much gold they glinted blindingly every time the rainbow lights bounced their way. Their partner was a rather splendid-looking woman, with four pairs of beetle-black eyes, long navy hair, and gem-blue skin that shimmered like the scales of a fish. Arlo had no idea what either of them was, but it was possible they'd followed the Ring from one of its previous haunts, and therefore weren't something normally found in Spring territory.

Another table she passed hosted a giggling group of faeries Arlo *did* recognize—dryads. All of them were gorgeous, with teak and oak and willow brown bark for skin and petals sewn together for clothes. They were tall and supple and attracting a great deal of attention from a group of citrine-yellow, lavender, and pastel-toned pixies seated a few tables off, whose iridescent wings were perked to full mast in the attempt to attract some of that attention back.

At last, after a few more minutes of winding through the crowd, she spotted a vacancy in a far row of booths. It was a little out of the way, but that might actually be a blessing, as it would be much harder for anyone she didn't want the attention of to notice she was there. She pushed ahead and would have made it without trouble had a hand not darted out to catch her wrist and halt her in her tracks.

"Hey!" Arlo whipped around. Her indignation wilted the moment her gaze met cold black. "Uh, weren't you just . . ."

The troll from outside the club was now seated at a table, watching Arlo carefully. Gone was their glamour—at least, the one that made them human—and their bulk was revealed to be distinctly rocky under olive skin that was tinged pine green. The runelike tattoos etched across their head were still visible running down their neck and under the collar of their shirt, but now two blunt horns no more than five inches tall protruded from their temples. These horns were the same volcanic-glass black as their eyes and nails, which one free hand drummed on the table.

It was clear they intended Arlo to take the chair opposite them, the only other one at their table. She hesitated. They'd gotten here too quickly—without Arlo even noticing. Faeries were pretty good at moving unseen, but trolls (especially the size of the one before her) shouldn't be capable of practically popping up wherever they pleased.

She wasn't sure what to make of this abnormal behavior.

"Sit," said the troll.

"I'd really rather not . . ."

The troll dropped Arlo's hand and jerked their chin at the vacant chair. *"Sit,"* they repeated, and Arlo found herself complying despite her reservations. Appeased, the troll relaxed. "I like you."

Arlo wrinkled her nose. "You have a funny way of showing that. What do you want with me?"

"What *I* want is irrelevant right now, Arlo Jarsdel. The real question is, what do *you* want?"

What did she want? Well, an answer to the things she asked would be a wonderful place to start. "How do you know my name?"

The troll lifted their shoulders in a casual shrug. "I know much more than that, but that's irrelevant at the moment too, if you haven't already figured that out." Looking off over Arlo's shoulder, they jerked their chin again at something behind her. "There's an exit at the back of the club. Do you see it?"

Arlo turned in her chair. Between flashing lights and countless other heads and limbs and antlers and horns, she could just make out a door concealed in the shadowy distance, marked by a glowing red sign. "Yeah? I see it."

The troll grunted again. When Arlo turned back around, they jerked their chin at something else, this time off to her right and close to the bar. "That dryad there, do you see her?"

She scanned the crowd.

There, four tables away, sat a dryad all on her own. She was hunched over her drink, slim, rosewood shoulders pinched up at her ears, pansy-black hair hanging around her like a mourning veil. Her tension seemed to coil tighter with every venomous glare she shot off across the room. She was beautiful, just like the other dryads Arlo had passed on the way here, but something about the way she held herself made her look tired and brittle.

"Yeah, I see her, too. So what?"

"If you go through that door behind you, you'll find yourself on a path that may very well unravel the mystery behind what claimed that ironborn child's life back at that café."

Arlo sat a little straighter at attention.

"Choose instead to speak with that dryad, and you'll find yourself on the path of justice. The dryad knows the answers to the questions that brought you here tonight—how *fortunate* you are, that you chose the same night she did for your visit. What she can tell you will undoubtedly lead to the capture of your quarry. What she can tell you will right a wrong that's been left to fester for just over a century and put to rest an ancient grudge that even gods cannot appease."

Cocking her head, Arlo considered the troll in a new light.

Their behavior was growing odder and odder. In addition to their unusually strong, strange glamours and lack of detectable aura, they were quite a bit more eloquent than she'd ever imagined a troll to be. According to pretty much everyone, they weren't the most verbose of creatures. "Why are you telling me any of this? What's in it for you to help me out?"

"The door or the dryad—these are the options Fate has allowed you in coming here," they went on to explain. "But they aren't the only paths available to take." They leaned forward. At some point in this conversation, their fingers had ceased drumming. They seemed at last to be arriving at their point, and despite the insistence in the back of her mind that this faerie was the sort of danger she'd been warned to avoid, Arlo was eager to find out what that was.

"In the simplest of terms, you are at a crossroads, Arlo. Fate has already decided on your future, but there are certain moments in your life—such as now—where she gives you the chance to choose the path you'd like to take to get there.

"Lucky you, this moment is occurring in a faerie ring. *The* Faerie Ring. I am certain you weren't aware that faerie rings are one of the few spaces deities can visit in the Mortal Realm these days without invitation. It's *lucky* that you came, because these moments of choice are something else as well. These moments are the only time one's destiny can be exchanged for something made by someone other than my Titan sister, and it's been some time since I've had a proper player on this board—not to mention one that Fate would have otherwise made into a hero."

Arlo stared.

". . . You're not a troll."

The troll grinned, revealing more of the blunt boulders that served as their teeth. As it drew across their face, their image flickered, just as their human mask had done before.

There was Arlo's answer.

That flicker didn't last nearly enough time to make sense of what she saw, but the impression of a much sharper face, green-fire hair, and tiny twin galaxies petrified in obsidian stuck in Arlo's mind long after the image had gone. It was all she needed to know that she wasn't speaking to your average, everyday faerie—and certainly not something as simple as a troll.

But what did that make them? she wondered. Their *Titan sister* . . . Was this troll some sort of *god*?

"So . . . let me get this straight." She shoved aside the millions of other questions clamoring in her brain and focused on her companion. "Fate has decided I'm going to be some sort of . . . hero? And right now I'm at a 'special moment' in my life that's going to determine how heroic a hero I'm going to be, depending on what I choose to do. *And* one of those things I can choose is going to tell me what caused Cassandra's blood to glow."

That "what if" feeling of hope, both back at the hearing and before her arrival in the club—had it been leading her to this moment? Had everything that had happened recently been nudging her in this direction—not to a life of a fae, but to the life of a hero?

The not-troll nodded.

"Yes. Fate is rather determined you play a bigger part in the story unfolding around you. Choose the door or choose the dryad—both are her will, both are meant to shape you into the grandest role your future holds, in different ways, of course. It all depends on the work you put in to become what Fate intended."

Arlo could almost feel the blood drain out of her face. "You mentioned something about exchanging fates, though. What if I don't want to be a hero?"

She cared about what happened in the Courts. She cared about what had happened to Cassandra. She wanted to help, wanted to bring this terrible chapter in the lives of the ironborn community to a close. She loved reading stories about people taking off on adventures, discovering they were natural leaders born to make a difference in the world, but a hero?

Heroes went through so much hardship.

Heroes were the stuff of *tragedies*.

They took charge of situations and challenged authority and made decisions not only for themselves but on behalf of other people too. Arlo . . . Arlo could barely make up her mind about going to *school*. She was a disappointment in pretty much every area of her life, and she'd only disappoint at this, too, because this . . . this was more than poking around for clues to pass off to other, more competent people. This was choosing to be responsible for other people's *lives*, to keep them safe, to be their *hope*. Arlo was firmly an extra, a background character, the healer of an adventuring party if anything at all. She simply didn't have what it took to be anything else, no matter what Fate seemed to think.

But given the way the troll across from her smirked, she'd apparently said the right thing. Too-black eyes flickered even darker, revealing another glimpse of fathomless infinity. Their grin curled a little sharper. "Well then, that would bring us to your other options."

"Which are . . . ?"

"You could leave. You could choose not to be a hero of any kind and simply force Fate to reset her plan. Force her to find you a new role."

Arlo's gaze darted over the troll's shoulder to the Faerie Ring's entrance and the darkness waiting to receive her exit.

"Fate has already given you her warning for this, her temple, as she warns all. Once is all you get. You won't have the same experience should you choose to leave the way you came," they explained, picking up on her hesitation.

"And that's it? I can just . . . get up and walk away, and I don't have to be anyone's anything?"

Was it really that simple? Could she leave through the front door, and in so doing, leave the heavy burden of her supposed destiny behind?

Would she do it was the real question.

Was she really selfish enough to walk away from something she'd not only been so determined to help resolve in coming here but that also needed her so badly it was willing to make her into a hero for her help? Did it actually matter what she chose, or would this situation find someone else to play the role instead? Just because Arlo apparently fit the requirements for this part didn't mean she was the only one who did, and surely there was someone out there better suited for playing savior than she was.

"It's as simple as that," the not-troll confirmed. "However, in the spirit of fairness, I'd like to draw your attention to something else."

They lifted a black-nailed hand. This time, they physically pointed across the sea of faces and tables to the booth Arlo had been previously heading toward. The one she'd wanted was still unoccupied, but from this angle, the one in front of it was no longer obscured. Her mouth parted in a silent gasp when she recognized one of its two occupants.

The girl in black.

Nausicaä Kraken.

Her aura was once again wholly undetectable.

Like everyone else, she looked different in the Faerie Ring. She was a little too far off for Arlo to make out anything definite about her face, but she still wore that air of nonchalance like a cloak around her, and sprawled as though that booth of hers was her throne. She was still clad entirely in black; her legs were stretched out under the table and seemed even longer, thanks to the tight bind of her leather pants and the lethal points of her red-soled stilettos.

Much more of her was on display than when she'd been in the café, her leather jacket traded for a scanty top of lace and mesh, baring her strong shoulders. In this lighting, her unbound sand-blond hair was an ever-changing rainbow of colors. On anyone else, this might have been a whimsical effect, but on this girl—on Nausicaä—it did nothing to mute the serpentine deadliness at rest beneath her casual facade; in fact, it made her appear even more wraithlike than before.

She was playing cards and looked to be far too comfortable both with the things that should be weighing on her conscience—like Cassandra's murder—and her partner. This said loads about her character, in Arlo's opinion. If it had been *her* seated across from that globule, gargantuan mass of blood-crusted skin and broken teeth, she wouldn't be half as calm as Nausicaä, who'd just now pitched back her head to bark out laughter in response to something that creature had just said.

Arlo turned back to the not-troll with a familiar, anxious nausea churning in her gut. "She was kind of the someone I was hoping to avoid tonight, you know."

"The Dark Star. Yes, I do know."

"But you want me to go talk to her," she concluded.

"Yes," replied the not-troll. "I do. What Nausicaä is—what she's capable of—I would very much like to collect for what's coming, and before the others realize they ought to try to do the same. She is the future I'm willing to offer in exchange for the one you currently shoulder. This is the option *I* would like you to take."

Ah, so it wasn't Arlo whoever-this-was was actually after. Once again, she was only the means to get to someone else. "You know she's probably a murderer, don't you?"

"Oh yes, she is that, and her darkness has made her legend in certain circles. But she's not the one behind the crimes you wish to lay at her feet."

"Oh?"

That wasn't exactly comforting, however otherwise informative.

So, Nausicaä hadn't been the one behind Cassandra's death? Wonderful. She was still a murderer by this mysterious faerie's own confession. Arlo was no hero, but she was no villain, either; she didn't want to keep that sort of company. "Well," she announced. While she still had the confidence to walk away from this, she pushed back in her chair and rose from her seat. "Maybe you should talk to her, then. I don't want anything to do with Nausicaä Kraken, or really, anything to do with whatever you're working up to asking me. I've learned what I came here to learn—that the Dark Star isn't behind the ironborn deaths."

It would have to do.

She wouldn't abandon this cause completely; she'd still help any way she could, but she couldn't go through that door in the back of the club or talk to that distressed dryad. She couldn't condemn the folk to *her* as their "savior." It would have to be someone else—someone like the High King, born to wear the mantle of the hero . . . someone who wasn't a teenage girl.

"You're leaving, then?"

Arlo nodded. She slid out of her seat. "I'm leaving. Thank you for making me aware of my options. I realize you didn't have to do that, and I'm grateful. I just don't want to be anyone's hero—not even yours. I don't want to be a pawn in some game, or one of your *Avengers*, or whatever you're trying to do here. I'm not . . . cut out to be the person someone *needs*."

Fate had made a mistake; there was no other explanation.

She wasn't special.

She was Arlo—*just* Arlo—and the life she had was pretty good. Why would she want to shake that up for all the stress that came with getting involved in life-or-death matters?

"You misunderstand who I am."

"That's probably because you never told me."

The mysterious troll-god shook their head. "I don't want you to be a hero, Arlo Jarsdel. What I want you to be is something a bit less tangled up in rules. What I want you to be is my Hollow Star, as my husband has taken to calling the children I adopt—someone whose future is *severed* from Fate and tied to Luck instead. Someone who can alter the outcome of any decision, to form as many destinies for themselves as they can dream."

"That sounds like it's actually harder than being a hero." She pulled a face. "Endless possibilities? Luck? Yeah, I'm not so sure I have much of that. So, um, thanks but no thanks." Nodding farewell, Arlo stepped around the table.

Once again, her wrist was caught in the not-troll's lightning-quick grip.

"Take this," they said, gentler than they'd spoken all evening.

There was a sudden weight in the fold of her fist, and when the not-troll released her, Arlo lifted her hand to unfurl her fingers and examine what they'd magicked into her hold.

"A die?" She looked back at the not-troll, raising a brow.

Was this some sort of joke? The die was beautiful, carved from jade the exact same color as Arlo's eyes, and each of its twenty sides was marked by pure gold numbers. But it was still just a die . . . wasn't it?

"A die," the not-troll confirmed. "And it's all yours. I made it specially for you."

"O . . . kay. Well, thanks, but I already told you I wasn't going to help you."

"And if you never use it, that's entirely up to you. But it's yours, and it will work for no other. If you ever decide you'd like to take me up on my offer, all you have to do is say so, and give it a roll."

Arlo nodded. She pocketed her gift—had a feeling that insisting they take it back would only end in a headache, and she could always pitch it later when they weren't around to catch her. "All right, well, noted. Don't hold your breath or anything, though."

The not-troll merely shrugged in response. Arlo decided to take this as permission to leave. She spun back around, ignoring the urge inside her to glance back at that door, to wonder a little more after that dryad and what she had to say, because no . . . she couldn't. She couldn't let herself get pulled in by curiosity.

In her haste to escape before the not-troll came up with another way to detain her, it was only in her periphery—a glimpse too quick to process—that she noticed the way the not-troll's black eyes flashed; the pulse that rippled through the air and tugged ever so slightly at proceedings; a faerie leaving their table in a huff the *exact* moment Arlo *happened* to step forward. With no more warning than this, the two of them collided, and the remainder of the faerie's drink sloshed over the rim of his cup, soaking the front of his shirt.

"Watch it," he snapped. Arlo, who'd very nearly toppled over, could only stare.

She'd never met a lesidhe fae before this moment, at least not to her knowledge. They didn't tend to like the Courts and crowded city spaces and had little desire to play at politics and mingle with society outside their own—just about the only reason it wasn't the lesidhe sitting in control of things instead of the sidhe, as was the general consensus, as their magic was considerably more powerful.

The surprise of their collision knocked his human glamour of a middle-aged man away to reveal his blazing amber eyes and frost-blue skin. His aura—discernable from the too-many others only because of their close proximity—sat like a barely-there wintery pine in her nose and practically shimmered in the fringe of her Sight, which a sidhe fae's had never done.

"I-I'm sorry," Arlo stammered.

The lesidhe and the sidhe . . . They didn't get along all that well—so little, in fact, that the lesidhe almost preferred to go by the distinction of faerie and were generally welcomed as such in rings and other like spaces. The lesidhe thought the sidhe every bit as arrogant and cruel as the gods had been and hated being forced into strict regulation just to be able to live in the Courts. Conversely, the sidhe couldn't stand knowing that the hierarchy they enjoyed could be easily toppled if the lesidhe decided they were tired of their forests and the rules that bound their strength.

Arlo could see by the way this one narrowed his eyes that he'd finally realized what Arlo was. "Piss off," he grunted, his mood curdling further. He shoved her farther away from him.

Arlo stumbled again. The lesidhe's actions had been too quick for her to defend against. The force of his push sent her into the table where she and her mysterious companion had just been sitting. The not-troll was gone now, but the hard wood was still present, and it hurt like hell to hit so harshly against it.

The screech of scattering chairs scraping the floor was enough to draw the attention of several others around them, but no one moved to help. The only reaction was a few cheers and whoops of laughter as spectators toasted the altercation.

Groaning, Arlo gingerly pried herself off the wooden surface, her palms smarting. She was a little more durable than an ordinary human, but that didn't stop anger from sparking through her enough that heat crept up her neck and bled into her cheeks.

"That wasn't very nice," drawled a throaty voice.

Arlo recognized it instantly.

"Yeah? Maybe next time she'll watch where she's going," the lesidhe growled out.

It was a little difficult to be offended when Arlo's brain was busy trying to work out how her murderer-turned-savior had gotten to her so quickly. But it *was* Nausicaä who'd come to her aid. And with her standing as close as she currently was, Arlo could see that her face was still the deadly weapon of sharp angles and proud features it had been in the café. The steel eyes considering the lesidhe before them were still dagger-lethal.

Her aura was still noticeably absent.

Something had changed, though. She'd definitely been wearing a glamour back in the café because here, now, in one of the only places that discouraged doing so, the dark and skeletal horror Arlo had only glimpsed before was far more pronounced.

Clearer.

Like a high-definition image set beside standard resolution.

Nausicaä was still gorgeous without her glamour, but the nine rings of hell couldn't come up with anything more terrible than the way her grin split across her face like razor wire catching skin and tearing it apart.

The transformation was oddly arresting—*Nausicaä* was oddly arresting—though why noticing this should make Arlo's breath catch in her chest, when heavens knew there were many people in her life outright stunning in *their* unglamoured glory, eluded her completely.

"Maybe," Nausicaä replied, the steel in her eyes glinting. "I don't know if you'll be able to say the same."

The fae cocked his head. He was clearly trying to work out how much of a threat Nausicaä could really be to him. When he squared his jaw and opened his mouth to growl out a retort, he'd clearly come to a conclusion—but the flare of his temper died on his lips.

Finally surfacing from her momentary stupor, Arlo leaped back in alarm.

The fae stiffened.

The several who'd been following this exchange from their tables started in their seats, upsetting their drinks and knocking their limbs painfully against the furniture. Others took much keener interest in what was now the good possibility of a fight.

Nausicaä had drawn a weapon she hadn't been holding a second ago with such speed that Arlo could swear she'd pulled it straight from the air itself. Unsheathed, the point of her katana's long black blade hovered perilously close to the lesidhe's left eye. If she so much as flicked her wrist, he'd be instantly blinded.

Her darkness has made her legend in certain circles.

The mysterious troll's words surged to the fore of Arlo's mind. She swallowed against the swell of her fear.

Nausicaä might not be the one behind the death at the café, but she wasn't innocent. No one who stood with such presence behind an actual, gods-damned sword could be innocent, and Nausicaä looked happier now than she had all evening.

"Hey," Arlo heard herself say. Quite without permission, she lifted a (slightly) trembling hand to the arm that held Nausicaä's blade. "Stop it! Don't hurt him. I really wasn't watching where I was going, and I think he's just drunk."

There was the barest spark in their initial contact, but more alarming was when Nausicaä's gaze shifted to lock with hers. Arlo's stomach clenched against the painfully uncomfortable sensation of stabbing magic. "Why does it *do* that?" Arlo wondered aloud, more to herself than Nausicaä, whose dark blond brows furrowed over the question.

If she had a reply, it was cut off by the resurgence of the lesidhe's mood. "I don't need your help, sidhe bitch," he snapped.

Nausicaä flicked her wrist.

Fortunately for the fae, she'd altered her target from his eye to his mouth, and the resulting damage was nothing more sinister than a nick to his lower lip, though the wound was deep enough to draw a hiss of pain along with a trickle of sapphire blood. "FYI—you really did," Nausicaä scathed. "This ring? It doesn't bind my violence the same way it does yours, and I don't unsheathe Cate without intent on taking a life." Whistling precision brought the point of her katana to the stone floor. In the next moment, everything from blade to hilt burst apart into ink-black smoke, and "Cate" dissolved into the air. "Piss off," she added in a sneer, hurling the fae's earlier words back at him.

With a hand pressed to his lower lip, the lesidhe glared over blue-stained fingers, first at Nausicaä, then at Arlo. "If you think you can attack and threaten me without consequence—"

"*Attack* you? *I* didn't attack you," Arlo spluttered.

"Oh, for fuck's sake." Nausicaä took hold of Arlo's shoulder and spun her around as easily as though she were a rag doll. "Go find somewhere else to throw your tantrum, asshole. And get your lip looked at!" she added over her shoulder, already leading Arlo away. "I can't remember which one of my weapons I edged with poison."

Barking out more laughter at the look on the lesidhe man's face, she committed herself fully now to directing Arlo back to the booth she'd come from. The grotesque creature Nausicaä had been sitting with tracked their return with a curious gaze. "Geez, Red," Nausicaä said, back to her throaty drawling. "Granted, the lesidhe aren't the cuddliest of woodland creatures, but most are pretty chill. How do you even get one to go all rage-monster on you? You must be next-level irritating—I'm impressed."

"Um, wh-where are we going?"

"Back to the card game you so rudely interrupted. Cyberniskos was trying very hard to win his dinner."

"Kiber . . . Kiber *what*?" That thing at her table had a *name*?

"Cyberniskos. Interesting fellow, really—once you get past the smell. Between him and you, tonight's been full of fun little surprises."

And suddenly Arlo was at her limit with blithe behavior and not-quite answers. She was tired of being pushed around like a pinball in a machine, bouncing off one interaction after another, and further-more, her position hadn't changed. She wanted nothing to do with whatever Nausicaä was involved in—with what Arlo suspected was that not-troll's attempt to get her to do what they wanted by sending Nausicaä to her rescue. She wasn't about to let this whirlwind of a girl sweep her up into this mess. *"Stop,"* Arlo ordered.

Nausicaä stopped.

At the very same moment, the door at the back of the club flew open—the very same one that mysterious not-troll had pointed out just minutes ago.

It struck so loudly against the wall that the crack of wood meeting stone echoed across the tables. Everyone within earshot winced. The band at the opposite end of the room killed their music. It was only the entranced humans who continued on as if nothing had happened, though with the wave of someone's hand, the ones in the cages fell silent. In moments, the steady hum of conversation was silenced as well, and everyone slowed to a standstill, gaping at the stringy-haired and lumpy mauve goblin standing in the rear exit's threshold.

"AN IRONBORN HAS JUST BEEN MURDERED!" the creature cried. His shrill voice, magically amplified to fill the room, bounced off the walls with the ever-roaming rainbow of lights. "GO NOW IF YOU DON'T WANT TO BE CAUGHT—THE WILD HUNT IS ON ITS WAY!"

Tension rang in the punctuating silence.

A glass, too absently set on some distant ledge, wobbled to the floor and shattered. With it, the spell over the club had broken.

Chaos took its place.

"Does it ever bother you that the people you've been using for your experiments are exactly what *you* used to be?"

Hero looked up from the body laid out on his operating table. He didn't *need* to look. He knew the voice that had spoken almost as well as his own now, and no other made his pulse flutter in such a way. But look he did, and was unsurprised to find his Hunter standing opposite him, grinning as though he'd been there all along and hadn't just materialized out of nowhere after weeks of absence and no word on where he'd gone or what it was he'd been doing.

"People just like you," the Hunter continued to muse. "Once upon a time. The lonely . . . the forgotten . . . the *pitiful*—"

"They're human," Hero interrupted bluntly. He had to clamp down on the rush of elation he felt at seeing the Hunter to hold on to his irritation with him. "We aren't the same at all, and never were."

Which was true, in a way, but also a lie.

True because Hero had never been solely human. He was iron-born, an alchemist, human and magic *both*.

A lie because while the fodder his employees collected for his use were exactly that to him—fodder—they were also more. They were *him*. They were the helplessness and hopelessness and pointlessness he'd felt back in a life he'd lacked the power and means to escape on his own. They were control. It didn't bother Hero to take these people apart and fit them back together as something better, to play their savior the way his Hunter had done for him. It *relieved* him. It quieted an anger nothing else had been able to purge, a grief he tried to ignore, a hunger that had grown insatiable of late . . . but such was the price of grandeur.

"True." The Hunter flicked the body between them, the minute action still enough to slice through skin and bone with the claw on the tip of his finger. Hero sighed. He'd have to get one of his employees to patch that up. "What does *this* matter? You certainly didn't seem to care when it was a little ironborn girl you were carving into—"

"Where were you?" Hero blurted. His face had grown warm. His hands itched under their gloves.

His Hunter had followed through on every promise he'd made him—had given Hero the means to become greater than he'd ever dreamed possible. Creating a philosopher's stone had been no easy task. The process had already been started by someone else (and it needled at Hero more than he cared to admit that the Hunter wouldn't tell him *who*). His lamb had already been primed for slaughter, branded by an array; Hero had spent the better part of sixteen years waiting for it to mature and learning how to activate it when the time to do so finally came. So intricate was the formula that shaped it; so powerful were the symbols that gave it fuel. Each of those symbols had needed taming like a living wild creature before he could even begin the grueling process of mastering them.

And then, his Hunter had brought him an ironborn girl.

The array carved into her chest directly over her heart had been put there at birth by someone else's experimentation—the reason (it had been explained) being that the heart required time to adjust to its magic and accept what it would become. An adult's heart was already too hardened and rejected this particular magic outright, but children . . . they were wondrous; *impressionable*; full of belief and acceptance and trust. They had to be ironborn, of course, because this magic relied on the host to sustain it, on alchemy to help it grow, and yes, it had been a difficult hurdle for Hero to overcome—sacrificing someone so young, so very much like him, to his own personal gain—but Hero had been so eager to please.

She'd been the first life he'd ever taken.

The deed had grown considerably easier after that, but he didn't like talking about *her*—didn't like remembering what he'd lost to get this far, no matter the payoff; no matter the reward his ambitions had earned him, and the way his Hunter looked at him now whenever he remembered to visit.

"Where were you?" he repeated. "You've been gone for nearly a month. I thought you were going to help me improve my cava's plating?"

"Oh, I've been here and there," the Hunter replied, peeling away from the table to poke around at the various other instruments in Hero's workshop.

"You've been disappearing more and more, longer and longer—have I done something?" The very idea made his heart constrict and flooded him with anxiety that left him slightly breathless. "Are you . . . unsatisfied with me?"

The Hunter laughed. "Unsatisfied?" He picked up a flask, filled with an acidic solution Hero had been toying with in his spare time, for closer examination. "No. No, you're doing just fine. You're everything I hoped you would be, my Hero." He set down the flask and turned his attention back on Hero, where it *belonged*. "But I have other projects on the go. Other people that need me—"

"*I* need you." He sounded every bit as possessive as he felt, but for all he winced to hear that so bald in his voice, he couldn't bring himself to regret his comment. He didn't like sharing. He didn't like being compared to a "project." He didn't like that the Hunter's interest in him was clearly waning, regardless of what he said. "We're supposed to be a team. You're supposed to be here—let me guess, it's Arlo again, isn't it."

The Hunter never lost his amusement, even if it did frost over. "Be careful how you speak to me, Hieronymus. I would hate to think you *ungrateful* for all I've done for you."

"I'm not!" Hero hurried to console. "I'm not ungrateful, I'm just . . . confused! You've been obsessed with this girl for as long as I've known you. I just want to know *why*. Why are you giving her so much of your time? She's barely fifteen, hasn't even been Weighed yet, and people gossip—I *know* she isn't worth the interest. She's nothing—no one! An embarrassment, and it's not like you've ever talked to her, have you? All you do is *watch*. So what are you looking for?"

"*Looking* for?" The Hunter scoffed. "Nothing. *Waiting* for, on the other hand . . ." He crossed the lab and placed his claw-free hand on Hero's face. It was cool, as always, in the rare instances the Hunter touched him, yet despite this, the contact heated Hero's skin like fire, and Hero never noticed until these fleeting moments how starved for warmth he was. Instinct nearly made him forget himself—he almost leaned in but caught himself just in time. "I've told you before, there's great potential in Arlo Jarsdel—something impressive that might become quite useful to me later on."

"*I* can be useful to you," Hero breathed, words trembling. "You don't need her."

Hero raised a hand. The Hunter never let Hero touch him in return, but perhaps this time?

The Hunter stepped back. Stung by this rejection, Hero let his hand fall back to his side. "Jealousy bores me." He started off toward the door. "Let me know when you're ready to prove that usefulness."

"Wait!" Hero cried, then bit his lip to clamp down on what else he wanted to add. He'd made the Hunter angry. That wouldn't do. He had to fix things and put himself back in the Hunter's good graces. Maybe if Hero did exactly that—maybe if he proved just how much the Hunter needed him, how useful Hero really was, the Hunter would stop looking elsewhere for the things he could find *right here*. "Wait—I want to show you something."

The Hunter paused, then turned around and raised a brow in silent inquiry.

"A gift," Hero added. "For you. To help you with your . . . other projects."

"I'm listening," the Hunter purred.

And Hero showed him.

He led him out of the workshop and down the hall, down to another floor where he kept his more sensitive "endeavors"—to the room where he kept his Reaper, a creature that hadn't been easy to come by, harder to capture, and even more difficult to break to his complete control. "The children . . . those others you've branded for your experiment, many of their arrays have started to mature. The ones who won't survive the strain of this transformation . . . they're going to draw an awful lot of attention, I think. In fact, whispers have it the Seelie Summer prince and his young retainer have recently found one such ironborn boy dead in the park. By their recount of the incident, he'd been glowing quite the unusual color."

Hero placed his gloved hands on the bars of the Reaper's alchemically reinforced cage. It rumbled at him, stirred, but made no move to attack him—an impressive show in itself, as Hero kept him starved for better meanness. "You're going to need help if you don't want anyone finding out what's really going on."

He snapped his fingers.

A pair of goblins entered, dragging between them a teenage ironborn boy whose parents were still tearfully begging for his return on the human news—"Wherever he is, whoever has him, *please*, give us our son back." His pale face was streaked with tears, his body bruised and right arm broken. He cried out for help, cursed and spat and struggled against the hands keeping him captive—a missing child the callous, fickle world would soon forget the moment something else came along to seize their attention.

Hero stepped aside, dissolving along the way the array that kept the cage secure. Its door swung open.

The Reaper tore out at a lunge.

The room filled with screaming, but only the boy's—Hero had conditioned his monster to touch no one other than ironborn prey.

"You're going to want to teach it to only go after the ironborn we've marked with arrays, of course," was all the Hunter said, watching the gruesome scene before him with something that looked a bit to Hero like longing. But then he lifted his gaze. "It can only go after the failed stones. It needs more training."

"Of course, Master Hunter." Hero smiled. "Whatever you require."

The screaming stopped.

The Reaper crowed.

With a sickening crack of bone, it broke through the boy's chest and began to devour his innards, heart and all.

A moment passed, and then finally the Hunter smiled back. Full and wide and glinting, it was a terrible thing, an arresting thing, a thing Hero craved—both poison and elixir, there was often no telling which, but he drank in the attention all the same.

"I think it's time you call me Lethe, don't you?"

Hero smiled, and he smiled, and he didn't stop smiling until long after *Lethe* left.

CHAPTER 14

Arlo

A RLO SPUN ON HER heels to face Nausicaä. "They think it's *you*," she panicked.

"They *what*?"

It only struck her now just how much taller than Arlo this mysterious faerie was. The shoes certainly added a few inches, but even without them, Nausicaä had to be at least six feet. At this proximity, it forced Arlo to tilt her head quite far back to meet that quizzical stare. "The Wild Hunt—they're on the way, and everyone thinks it's the Dark Star killing ironborn. And . . . well, I *might* have told some people that I saw you at the café where that little girl died. I might have also told them it was possible you were responsible for that death? So, uh, it's going to look *really* hecking suspicious if they find you . . . here . . . where another person has just died . . ."

If the not-troll was right, Nausicaä was innocent of that particular crime. If they were right, then Arlo had been wrong—had once again *disappointed*, had tried to help and only made things worse. Now, thanks to her meddling, very scary people with very real power to very thoroughly ruin Nausicaä Kraken's life thought with much more conviction than before that Nausicaä was the culprit they were after.

"Who the hell did you tell that that would even matter, the High King?" Nausicaä laughed as though even the possibility of Arlo doing that was absurd.

Arlo winced.

". . . You told the High King."

"I told the High King."

"What the fuck, Red! Why do you even think this was me, to start with?"

"I don't *now*."

All around them, faeries flew in all directions, some of them quite literally. Many made for the Faerie Ring's entrance, filtering out through the passage in droves, but many more made for the wall on the opposite side of the dance floor. As soon as the goblin had made his warning, panels in that wall had sprung open to reveal themselves as portals. The emergency had triggered their activation, and the majority of the club now slipped away through these magicked door-ways, which led out into deserts, forests, other cities, and one—Arlo noticed—straight into the depths of an ocean.

A handful remained in the club along with the human captives; while most merely stopped whatever it was they'd been doing to stare blankly ahead, the ones on the floor were still caught up in dancing to music only they could hear. Arlo could see now a ring of mushrooms and tiny flowers mapping out that floor's perimeter, trapping them in until the faerie who'd lured them there, or another who was stronger, let them back out.

Much of the staff had no choice but to stay behind, though they hunkered down behind the bar and other large fixtures. Most had undoubtedly come from elsewhere, many of them probably banished from the Courts; getting caught in the street would land them in even more trouble. The gnomes Arlo had passed earlier were bliss-fully unaware of proceedings, unconscious under their table. Nausicaä seemed more concerned about the fact that Arlo was going around telling people she murdered children than she was about the impend-ing arrival of the Wild Hunt, but then again, she was the *Dark Star*— she had her own infamy to make her bold where others weren't.

"But you have to admit," Arlo added, defensiveness creeping into her tone, "you were being sort of sketchy. You just sat there, staring at that girl, not even a *little* upset that she was dying right in front of you. And then there was your magic, of course."

"I *beg* your pardon?"

It was the politest Arlo had heard her speak yet, and hands down the most aghast. "Your . . . your magic," Arlo repeated, a lot less sure of herself this time around. "I couldn't sense it at first because you were doing such a good job of concealing it—but then I felt it! I've never *felt* magic so . . . so violently before. Yours was . . ." She pressed on her stomach, summoning the memory, at a momentary loss for words.

For a few seconds, all Nausicaä did was stare.

"*Tch,*" she snorted, recovering quickly from whatever had caught her off guard about what Arlo had said. "Figures. Kids these days—"

"I'm eighteen!" Arlo corrected.

"—no respect for their elders—"

"No offense, but you don't look much older than I am."

"—runnin' around accusing perfectly innocent assholes of assholery they've been actively trying to avoid."

"What? You mean you *normally* feel like picking off children?"

"Uh, I'm currently really considering it." Nausicaä equipped her statement with a pointed glare. "But I meant the murdering business in general."

Arlo sighed. "Right, well . . . this is a problem. The Hunt is on its way, and I'm really not supposed to be here." Gods, the night wasn't going at all how Arlo had planned. In fact, it was derailing in a direction she hadn't even imagined in all the possibilities her panic had invented to try to dissuade her from following through with this stupid idea.

Nausicaä's steel eyes searched Arlo's in a deep inspection.

Whatever Nausicaä was looking for, she apparently found it; the glint in her gaze was now one of minor, personal victory—a suspicion proved true—half-baked disapproval quick on its heels. Quicker than Arlo could escape, Nausicaä darted out a hand to catch her by the chin. "Those eyes are a pretty shade of green, Red," she said in what would have been a singsong tone from anyone else. "I think I've seen it somewhere before. Guess I know why you went straight to the *High King* just to tattle on me."

"Yeah, well . . . ," Arlo grumbled, shaking herself free. "We should *both* probably get going."

She made to push past Nausicaä but only got a couple steps away before she realized Nausicaä hadn't followed. Arlo turned around.

"Oh yeah, *you* should definitely get going, Your Highness. Wouldn't want to get caught in a place like *this*, you naughty thing."

Nausicaä dropped a wink; Arlo rolled her eyes in response. "I'm not *that* royal. Are you coming or what?"

"Coming . . . what, with you?"

"Yes?" She didn't know why it came out a question, but the longer Nausicaä stood there, staring back at her as though Arlo had suggested they run down the street in their underwear, the more she began to doubt herself. Was she not supposed to invite another faerie to leave the Ring with her? Was this some sort of rule Celadon had forgotten to warn her of? Was she moments away from tying herself irrevocably to a murderous faerie villain or something?

Nausicaä bit her lip, her gaze flicking toward the exit where the goblin had been but was now no longer there. She looked to be weighing her options, wrestling with something difficult, but just before Arlo could rescind her offer, Nausicaä finally replied, "Group activities . . . not really my thing. Thanks for the invite, but I'm pretty sure there's a Reaper out back, and I've been tracking it for a while, so I'm going to go do . . . that. Good luck with your stuff, though. The not getting caught and . . ." Arlo almost laughed at how awkward Nausicaä suddenly sounded, pairing her stunted farewell with a double shot of finger guns, just like Arlo did when she was nervous. But then comprehension of what Nausicaä had said finally dawned on her.

"I'm sorry, did you say a *Reaper*?"

Was there really one here?

Her mother had told her all about what had happened at the aquarium, that witnesses reported that disaster as the work of a Reaper, but since it had fled before the Falchion could arrive to capture and confirm this, rumor was all that story was.

Besides, a Reaper in the *Courts*? Impossible.

Arlo received no response. Nausicaä had already fled, her blond hair bouncing behind her as she made for the back exit and disappeared through the door the not-troll had pointed out as one of the paths that would make Arlo a hero.

It was exactly what Arlo should be doing—heading for an exit—the one at the front, obviously—and never looking back. Reapers were dangerous. Nausicaä was dangerous. This whole hecking club and everything that was currently happening was *dangerous*.

She turned to leave.

The Wild Hunt—they're on the way, and everyone thinks it's the Dark Star killing ironborn.

She froze.

The Wild Hunt . . . If they found Nausicaä back there at the scene of the crime, it would do nothing to help clear her name, and this was Arlo's fault—she had to do *something*.

"Dang it, dang it, dang it," she chanted under her breath as she flew off in the opposite direction toward the exit at the back of the club. "Please don't be a Reaper, please don't be a Reaper, please don't be a Reaper," she begged as she threw open the exit door. "This is not me choosing to be a hero," she added in case Fate was getting any funny ideas. "Nausicaä went through first, pick her!"

She stumbled out into the back alley.

Twilight had fallen during the time she'd spent inside the Ring. The night was cool on her heated face, a light and crisp contrast to the heavy humidity that weighed on the air in the club. The alley was narrow, sunken in the shadows of surrounding buildings. Shards of light darted into its depths like a serpent's tongue, from traffic that passed by its open, opposite end. Not far from her stood Nausicaä, staring at the ground—at something that pooled out around a large metal garbage bin.

Blood.

Arlo grimaced. She tried very hard not to think about what all that darkening red meant. "Please don't be a dead body . . ." She started forward. "Nausicaä," she said a little louder, "I don't think we should be here—the Wild Hunt, remember? They think you're behind this? If they find you here—"

Nausicaä whipped around so quickly it shocked Arlo into silence. Once again she found herself frozen in place, wondering if maybe the Dark Star would attack her after all, because really, what did Arlo know about this veritable stranger? Maybe this whole thing had been a ruse to lure Arlo out into a dark, secluded place and pick her off as well for getting too close to her.

"They were already here."

Suspicious, Arlo narrowed her eyes. "How do you know?"

"The body's gone. So is the Reaper. Damn it, I knew I wasn't seeing things! I should have gone after it earlier. I should have . . . never mind." She shook her head, her frustration narrowing into a glare of her own aimed directly at Arlo. "What are you doing out here? Do you normally plod off after things that could kill you? Do you just not know what a Reaper is? What it can do? *You* shouldn't be here. I don't need your help. Go *home*, random faerie girl."

Embarrassment conspired with indignity to make Arlo's face grow warm. She balled her fists, taking a step forward. Her whole life, people talked down to her, sent her away, excluded her from things because she was too young, too human, too *different* to "fit in" or to "understand what was going on." A disappointment. Not good enough. For some reason, it hurt just a little bit more to be on the receiving end of this from Nausicaä. "Fine! I'll do that, then."

"Good!"

She didn't budge an inch. "What do I care if you get dismembered and eaten by a Reaper?"

"I really couldn't tell you." Nausicaä took a step forward, expression darkening, her temper unfurling to pit itself against Arlo's.

Things were just bubbling up to the surface now. Arlo heard herself say, "Just because you didn't kill the girl in the café doesn't mean you're a good person," and instantly felt a touch of remorse with the way it very clearly struck something fragile in Nausicaä. But when Nausicaä shot back with, "Yeah? Well, I'd rather be an amoral murderer than a stuck-up, pampered, irritating princess like *you*," she lost herself once more.

"What is *wrong* with you?" Arlo fairly shouted. Through her frustration, she thought she noticed a crack in Nausicaä's composure. The steel in her eyes didn't seem all that hard in this fleeting moment. In fact, they seemed a little glassy, as though all that metal had melted and threatened now to spill over. "I'm sorry," she said in a softer tone. As quickly as her irritation flared, it deflated.

"Don't be," Nausicaä huffed, crossing her arms over her chest. "I often wonder what's wrong with me, too." Restored to her wholly untouchable, unaffected self, she'd resumed glaring Arlo down, but Arlo sensed something balanced precariously on the precipice of all that swagger. Whatever had happened between them just now had nudged it closer to tipping the wrong way.

"Do—" The sound of something suctioned peeling off the wall behind her made Arlo pause her awkward patch job of the rift between them. A chill spilled down her back and shivered across her skin. The hairs on the backs of her arms stood at frightened attention. Nausicaä, whose eyes had grown a fraction wider, stared off over Arlo's shoulder.

"You should . . . come here, Your Highness. Very quickly. And probably don't turn around."

Arlo turned around.

Whatever was there, she couldn't see it clearly. The alley's gloom and its exceptional glamour distorted it too well, but a pungent scent of rotting corpse and fishy, foul decay flooded her senses, making her gag; she didn't need to know what defined the hulking shadow creeping forward to also know she didn't want it to catch her.

"Pretty petal . . . little alchemist . . . Are you the one? Come here and let me taste you," it rasped.

Arlo screamed. Instinct made her grab for something she could defend herself with, but there was nothing around her except—her die! The not-troll had given it to her. Maybe it was a weapon?

Backing away from the Reaper, she reached into her back pocket and lobbed the die at the space she hoped was the creature's face.

The die made contact.

It bounced off the Reaper and rolled onto the cement.

Nobody moved, stunned by how underwhelming this play had been.

"Quick question," said Nausicaä, breaking the baffled silence. "What the fuck was that supposed to do?"

"Well . . . not that," Arlo admitted. "I was kind of hoping for something more—"

The Reaper hissed, cutting her off, and Arlo screamed again, scrambling backward.

"Okay, time to go!" Nausicaä said firmly.

"Wait!"

Nausicaä looked at her as though she'd grown two heads. They didn't have time for the resurgence of Arlo's hesitations. Between what was undoubtedly the Reaper making its grand reappearance and someone who was some sort of (possibly) reformed murderer, she'd have to take danger over immediate death. Shaking her head, she took Nausicaä's outstretched hand and followed her flight toward the opposite end of the alley. "I'm sorry," she apologized along the way. "It's just . . . you better not be luring me away to kill me somewhere private, because I swear to *Cosmin* I will use my entire afterlife to haunt you, if you are."

"Not the time for this, and I don't mean to ruin your dreams or anything here, but that's a competitive market, and you might want to have another ambition to fall back on." Nausicaä stopped them on the alley's cusp, tugged Arlo closer, and proceeded to wrap an arm around the small of her waist, hauling them flush together. "Better ask yourself if I'm worth that kind of eternal commitment, besides," she added in a slightly huskier tone.

Arlo glared, ignoring the heat that fluttered through her at both the insinuation and their current proximity. Nausicaä's coyness took on a razor edge, yet this expression was infinitely more amusing than the last. "You're not as funny as you think you are," Arlo said. "Also, what the hells are we doing?"

Were they actually taking time out of their desperate flight to . . . what, hug and make up?

"You cannot run from me, pretty petal . . . I'll find you no matter where you go. I know you now. I know your scent . . ."

Arlo peeked around Nausicaä. The Reaper's obscured form had taken clearer shape now to extend a hand so close to reaching them that it brushed the strands of Nausicaä's hair. "We really need to go now!" She tried to pull away, but Nausicaä kept her firmly in place.

"Hang on a little tighter than that, Spider Monkey."

Before Arlo could make any comment on the reference, smoke like what Nausicaä's blade had shattered into burst out from her back. It shot into the air behind them like fingers, reaching back at the Reaper, then arched and curled toward them.

Arlo couldn't help her reaction. She screamed again, stiffening in Nausicaä's hold, burying her face instinctually against her. But the blow she expected never came, and with her eyes so tightly shut (as though that too might protect her from the spears of smoke hurtling at them), Arlo couldn't see those shadows-like-fingers take hold of them—but she could feel them. They wrapped around her body and *squeezed*, feathery, leather soft, and cool.

Her ears popped.

Dizziness grew overwhelming.

Arlo gasped for breath as though it had been knocked from her chest. The pressure that built around them began to ring. She felt sick, and shaky, and moments away from passing out, and it reminded her a great deal of what she'd felt in the café those handful of days ago, to an even more forceful degree. Then, the world bottomed out beneath her feet, striking Arlo with the dual sensation of falling and floating away.

It wore on forever, this rushing-floating-falling, but when it stopped, Arlo found she preferred it immensely to what took its place—a feeling like being hooked on the end of a line and steadily reeled in to shore.

Whatever was going on, she would give anything for it to stop.

Finally—blessedly—it did.

The smoke dissolved, scorching and crumbling apart like ash in the wind, and the pressure relented. The ground returned just in time for Arlo to collapse to her knees and vomit off to the side.

On the . . . grass?

She glanced around, waiting for her nausea to settle before she got back up to her feet. No longer were they in the alley. She was still outside, but in a small park, by the look of things, nestled right into the corner of a busy intersection. It was nothing more than a square of space sectioned off for a swing set and slide, but she recognized it by the replicated statue of Peter Pan erected at its center—the same as the one in London's Kensington Gardens, but paired with a double check of the cityscape around her, Arlo knew where she really was.

Toronto.

They hadn't gone far.

Breathing a small sigh of relief, her nerves still trembling from what she'd just escaped and how she'd come to be here, she returned her focus to Nausicaä and narrowed her eyes.

"Why do they always vomit?" Nausicaä wondered aloud, frowning down at Arlo.

"What the hells was *that*?" Arlo half rasped, half shouted as she shakily climbed back to her feet. "Did we just . . . did we just *teleport*?"

The thing was, teleporting wasn't exactly impossible, but it wasn't something your average folk could do. It wasn't even something most *fae* could do—in fact, Arlo had yet to hear of anyone that could.

Many of the folk used ragweed brooms and steeds glamoured as cars these days to get around, but portals had become the preferred means of transportation across long distances for the wealthy. Magically transporting oneself from one place to another required such precise understanding and skill that it might as well be impossible. To scramble yourself in one place, then piece your body back together in a different spot entirely was so difficult an art that, so far, the only people Arlo knew of being able to do anything at all like whatever Nausicaä had done were the Wild Hunt.

And Nausicaä had gone a step further: she'd brought someone else along for the ride.

"What *are* you?"

Sucking air through her teeth, Nausicaä replied in her driest tone yet, "Hasn't anyone ever told you it's rude to ask a faerie what they are?"

"Like hell you're a faerie! Are you fae?"

"Are you going to answer that, or what?"

Confusion etched a crease across Arlo's brow. "Answer what?"

But then she felt it—the phone vibrating in her back pocket. Apparently, it was working just fine now that it was no longer in the Faerie Ring. She'd forgotten she'd set it to vibrate only, and with the rest of her body still vibrating from the foreign experience of honest-to-gods *teleporting*, hadn't noticed the insistent, incoming call.

"Oh no," she groaned.

Tonight was going from bad to worse.

Celadon hadn't been far off from the club. No doubt he'd seen the mass exodus streaming from the Faerie Ring's front entrance. There was no way something like that wouldn't cause him to freak out.

Fumbling her phone out of her pocket, Arlo looked down at the screen. Sure enough, it was Celadon.

He was going to be furious.

"Hey . . ."

"Arlo!" Celadon gasped, though it sounded more like a strangled, breathy sob. The absolute relief in his tone ratcheted Arlo's guilt up to maximum level. "Arlo . . . Arlo, where are you? Oh Cosmin, but you're okay, right? You're safe? You're not dead in bloody pieces in an alley behind the club?"

"What? No, Cel, I'm sorry, hey—"

"Where are you? Are you still inside the Ring? Listen, Arlo, I need you to come back outside. I'm coming to get you. I'm sorry. The Hunt . . . They know you were in the club. Your mother called; she told me another girl was killed. The Hunters have been tasked with keeping tabs on ironborn deaths, and Thalo passed the news on to me because she knew I was helping them look into it, and just . . . gods, Arlo, she said it was right outside the Faerie Ring. A red-haired ironborn girl—I panicked! I thought she was talking about *you*, so I told her everything! I'm so sorry. I'm trying to get into the club, but it's fully locked down, and . . . Arlo, are you still inside?"

Celadon rambled when he was well and truly terrified. It was something of a family trait.

"Um . . . no." She glanced over at Nausicaä, currently studying her nails in a show of spectacular boredom. The state Celadon had already worked himself into said loud and clear that if she told him she'd nearly been eaten by a Reaper on top of everything else, he'd probably pass out. *She* felt like passing out whenever she thought about how close a call that had been. "No, I got out. I'm . . . I think I'm at Glenn Gould Park. The one with the Peter Pan statue? Will you . . . come pick me up?"

There was silence over the phone. Arlo could hear Celadon's labored breathing and the sounds of traffic in the background. When he found his voice at last, it was faint with incredulity. "How in the *world* did you get all the way over there?"

"It's . . . a long story. But I—"

The phone was plucked out of Arlo's hand.

"Hello? Who's this?" Nausicaä held it up to her ear, her other hand extended to hold Arlo off from snatching it back. "Celadon? Like *High Prince* Celadon? Man, and she said she wasn't that royal. Arlo? Who's Arlo?"

Arlo paused her attempt to win back her phone to glower when Nausicaä's gaze cut once again to her.

"There wasn't much time for introductions. So, hey, are you coming to pick her up? 'Cause you can take me with you, if you are. I change my mind about ignoring your little summons; I want to have a talk with your old man. Me? Nausicaä. Wha—I'm not going to *hurt her*, what the fuck? Hey!" She held the phone out in front of her, blinking at the screen. "He hung up on me! Rude."

Snorting her distaste, she tossed the phone back at Arlo. *"Not that royal,"* she added in a sneer. "You never said the freaking High Prince of Spring was your father—who wants you to wait here, by the way, unless I turn into that murderer everyone's accusing me of being today and try to kill you. Then I imagine he'd want you to run."

"First of all," Arlo corrected, "Celadon isn't old enough to be my dad. You're probably thinking about his older brother, Serulian—also not my father. Second of all, Celadon's my cousin. My dad is *human*, so no, I'm not *that* royal, and I have no idea why I'm explaining myself to you. Third of all, why do you want to talk to High King Azurean?"

Nausicaä's expression arranged itself seriously. "Don't worry, you'll find out soon enough."

Arlo's frown deepened. "Does it have to do with why there was a freaking *Reaper* behind the Faerie Ring tonight?" There were only a handful of faeries banned from the Courts and forced to live their lives in the cracks and shadows and neutral spaces between them—Reapers were perhaps the most notorious of that lot. It was deeply concerning, to say the least, that one had slipped between the many defenses in place around UnSeelie Spring's capital that had been designed specifically to keep them out.

Nausicaä said nothing.

The Dark Star opting to bring herself to the High King was the best thing to come out of this disaster of a mission. She'd be able to fill him in on exactly what was going on—whatever she knew, at least, if the High King didn't already know what she had to tell him—and this was much better than the meager findings that Arlo had to report back with herself. But for just once this night, she would love if someone bothered to answer at least *one* of her questions.

"Don't give me that wounded look. I'm not the biggest fan of repeating myself, is all. I'd rather wait until I have a full audience."

"*Urgh*, you know what? Fine. This has all been too much anyhow. My mother's going to kill me."

"I take it she doesn't know about your moonlit career as the world's worst detective?"

"No," Arlo snapped before her temper dissolved into more groaning. She replaced her phone in her pocket. "I'm so dead. I survived a Reaper, and I'm still going to die. They're *all* going to kill me, and then ground me for the eternity of my afterlife."

Rolling her eyes, Nausicaä ended their conversation by sauntering off toward the statue behind her, where presumably she was going to wait for Celadon's arrival. It was a thoroughly graceless exit—the thin spikes of her heels sank right through the soft earth. Eventually, she stopped to rip the shoes off her feet, growling out another choice expletive.

Arlo turned to face the road, shaking her head. She'd actually like to remove her own footwear, her heels sinking uncomfortably into the dirt as well, but because Nausicaä had done so first, she stubbornly refrained.

Her attention wandered skyward.

It was shaping up to be a beautiful night, but the last vestiges of day still clung to the horizon in a faint twilight-blue glow. The many buildings set against this otherworldly hint of light were cast in darkness so austere they seemed more like silent, formidable giants crowded all around. The way they looked down on Arlo was as though this park were a stage and something momentous was a breath away from taking place.

Unnerved, she dropped her gaze back to the street, where the wash of twilight muted the dance of the busy intersection to varying shades of navy and steel. Through it, dozens of pale yellow headlights beckoned like will-o'-the-wisps between the trees in their woods.

In no time at all, an emerald Audi peeled off the road and up onto the sidewalk. Despite her familiarity with this car, Arlo was genuinely surprised to see Celadon stumbling out.

The vehicles he cut off in his haste to get here honked as they passed by. Several shouted out their windows their opinions on his reckless driving. He ignored them all, tearing toward Arlo with a cry of her name, looking paler and more harassed by his own terror the closer he drew. His residual fear transformed him from the Celadon she knew—all confidence and composure and every hair in place—into someone she barely recognized, and his rain-and-cedar aura hit her with the force of a tsunami before he physically could himself. "Arlo, thank Cosmin you're all right."

He tugged her into a fierce embrace the moment he reached her. Once again she found herself winded by the strength of someone's hold, but Arlo hugged him just as tightly back as she could manage, images of that Reaper's creeping shadow impossible to shake from her mind. "Sorry, Cel. I didn't mean to make you worry."

But Celadon made no reply.

When the silence grew a little too lengthy, and the air fell suspiciously still, Arlo pulled back as much as their embrace allowed. What she found was her cousin glaring at the statue—at Nausicaä, folded casually against it. "Hi," Nausicaä greeted in that obnoxious, almost singsong taunt of earlier, paired now with a dismissive wave that was little better than a flick of her fingers. "I like your car."

Celadon growled.

There were many ways that fae were a lot like humans.

There were many ways they weren't as well.

Celadon growled again, and it was not the imitation of annoyance. It was a genuine rumbling thing, deep in his throat, and reminded

Arlo strongly of an agitated demon. Fae could only make the sound when they themselves were deeply unsettled. Arlo had never seen Celadon so ruffled as to actually do it himself, because most of the sidhe fae considered the behavior to be highly uncivilized.

It was a mark of how dangerous fae in such a state could be that even Nausicaä yielded, and whatever the poor humans passing by on their nighttime stroll made of the sound, Arlo knew that no one would try to disturb them now.

"The High King has summoned you for questioning." Celadon's tone was dark and silken, almost a complete contrast to the growl still echoing in Arlo's ears. "I suggest you find a bit of deference before this meeting."

Nausicaä shrugged, but it wasn't the easy thing her actions so far had been. "Deference, huh? It's in here somewhere. So, after you, I guess?"

"*Not* with *us*." That inhuman rumbling finally began to chip away at the smooth threat in Celadon's voice. Meanwhile, unnatural darkness spilled across the night. Like ink bleeding from a well, it blotted out the twilight, and the formidable sentry of surrounding buildings shrank back from it in fear. Stunning outrage spread like poison across Nausicaä's face, disfiguring her beauty into something so monstrous the sight of it forced Arlo's eyes away.

Then the night began to swell, and that's when Arlo knew—the Wild Hunt was here.

Shuddering, she winced an apology at Nausicaä. "We should go," she said to Celadon.

"Yes, we should," was Celadon's clipped reply. He spared a few more seconds to glare across the way at Nausicaä, then fell back from Arlo just enough for her to take his hand.

Nausicaä would be all right for now. The Wild Hunt wasn't collecting her from the scene of a murder. But if Arlo wanted to make things right, it wouldn't be done by lingering to argue with a troop of heartless immortals. She had to hurry before it was too late. Before

Nausicaä could be taken to the High King and tried without defense. Behind her, the swelling reached its limit and burst apart, and four shadows emerged from the obscured heavens to descend upon the park, invisible to all but those with Sight.

"Can we go back to the palace too?" Arlo asked the moment they were closed inside Celadon's Audi. "I have to talk to the king. I have to tell him . . ." She had to tell him this wasn't Nausicaä. She had to fix this. Her heart thudded so hard in her chest that her vision swam for reasons other than tears now. Already her nerves clamored over what she was about to do—another stupid thing, as was the theme this evening—and none of it was helped by what had transpired outside.

Celadon released a weighted sigh. "Yes, we can." He reached for his seat belt. "Funnily enough, he wants to talk to us, too, Arlo."

. . . Damn.

They were in so much trouble.

But so was Nausicaä if Arlo didn't repay her debts, and soon.

CHAPTER 15

Arlo

W HERE CELADON WOULD HAVE stopped any other time to chat, tonight he only spared a nod of greeting to those who bowed as he passed through reception. Arlo trailed behind, miserable and apprehensive.

She wished he would say something. The last time she'd been on the receiving end of his silence, they'd been six and nine respectively, and Arlo had cut a sizable chunk of his hair while he'd been sleeping to use in an art project. But she didn't blame his reticence now. She didn't feel much like talking to herself at the moment either.

Arlo was in *so much* trouble for what she'd done, but the worst her great-uncle could do to her was chuck her out of their lives for good, as had been the threat her entire life, really, so this anxiety wasn't all that new to her. For the son of the High King, though—who couldn't be blotted off the family tree, stripped of his knowledge and power, and disowned quite as easily—"worst" would have to get much more *creative*.

And once again, this predicament was all Arlo's fault.

First with Nausicaä, now with her cousin . . . Every time Arlo stuck her nose into something she should have left alone, innocent people paid the price.

How could Fate have ever thought *she* could be a *hero*?

Finally, they reached their destination. Two stern-faced fae, resplendent in gold-embellished uniforms of emerald and sage— the official colors of UnSeelie Spring—bowed them through handsome oak doors to the throne beyond. With its green marble floor and sparse trimmings, this room was a lot like the one in which Arlo had faced the Fae High Council, save the overgrowth of vegetation clinging to its pillars and beams and gilded fixtures and the strip of moss that rolled like a carpet from door to throne. In place of stands sprawled a gold-edged dais supporting three high-backed chairs—the thrones, formed out of twisted branches and tangles of ivy and vines.

All three chairs were occupied.

The High King was present, his distinct, grassy aura almost as familiar to Arlo as her mother's for its prominence in nearly every room in the palace. There was his queen, Reseda, to his right. On his left sat their eldest daughter, Cerelia, heir to the UnSeelie Spring throne. If Arlo gave her gift a nudge, she'd be able to pick out their respective auras of citrus blossom and earthy forest.

Thalo stood just beside the queen, looking whole worlds of furious, despite the puffy blue that rimmed her eyes. Behind her and their sovereigns, concealed in shadows and standing still as death, were four figures Arlo actively attempted to avoid gaping at—she had a feeling she knew who they were, despite the fact she couldn't sense any of their magical auras at all. Their presence was far from comforting.

The Wild Hunt.

Celadon veered, moving to stand beside the only other person in the center of the room: Nausicaä, completely unchanged by the magic that had reduced everyone else to their unglamoured state. Arlo had no idea whether she preferred this to mean there was nothing underneath her surface beauty, as opposed to what certain moments hinted, or that Nausicaä's powers were strong enough to withstand the king's. Regardless, her hands had been bound behind her back by rope specifically designed to detain the folk. She was barefoot still—where her shoes were now was anyone's guess—and staring just as furiously up at the head of the room as she'd been at *them*, when Arlo and Celadon had left her to her Wild escort.

The moment Arlo fell into place at Celadon's side, the king lifted his chin. "Explain," he commanded.

"It's entirely my fault, Father."

Azurean sighed, his mouth twitching amusement. "Celadon Viridian, I am not surprised at your involvement, but I would hand my crown to the Seelie Queen of Summer myself if your statement was *entirely* true."

Celadon and his father were mirror images of each other, reflecting different stages of the same life.

Azurean was old, even by fae standards. His neatly trimmed beard had wholly conceded to the gray that streaked through his curling hair, and the lines in his face were those that only decades of stress could etch. He was a handsome man, tall and willow lean, much like his youngest son, but he carried with him the presence of a mountain, and in his prime, no amount of the wind that UnSeelie Spring fae commanded would ever have been able to bend his knee.

Whispers wondered whether the same could still be said of him now.

"It's true enough," Celadon went on to explain. "This *was* my fault. I was the one to tell Arlo where the Dark Star could be found. As much as I didn't want Arlo any more involved in this than what she already is, I *allowed* her to go to the Faerie Ring. I allowed this to take place. I didn't want to risk our quarry's escape, not when the lives of our ironborn people were on the line, not when Arlo herself could become a target." He paused to swallow. Arlo eyed him sideways, concerned by the way color drained down to silvery distress in his face. "This is upsetting to me. You know it is. You yourself allowed me to keep closer watch over my cousin these last few weeks to ease some of this worry, but my desire to see this matter resolved as quickly as possible made me reckless, and I apologize."

Arlo's heart gave a lurch. She'd been so flippant with Celadon when he tried to tell her his reason for following her around lately. She hadn't taken this situation seriously, and now here they were.

"You let your emotions rule too much of your judgment, Celadon," said Azurean, not unkindly, but with a certain amount of disapproval. "To what end, might I dare ask, did you send your younger cousin off to the thick of our criminal underworld? I refuse to believe you intended her to confront the Dark Star all on her own?"

"For information," Celadon quickly supplied. "No, I didn't want Arlo to apprehend our suspect. The plan was to investigate whether or not we were wasting our time pursuing someone of the Dark Star's . . . caliber."

Nausicaä snorted.

Azurean shifted his focus to her, and his expression hardened to stone. "And here we are, the Dark Star. You certainly took your time in responding to my summons, Nausicaä Kraken."

"I never intended to at all, Your Majestic High Prime Lordship, Sir. I don't 'respond to summons.' I don't really think you wanted me to either."

The High King frowned. "You think very highly of yourself, don't you, young woman."

"Or very lowly," Nausicaä replied, grinning. "Either way, neither space is yours to command." She dropped a wink, and Arlo might have rolled her eyes if she wasn't just a little bit horrified by this level of disrespect for someone the magical community held in importance above all others. "Listen, I have places to be. Things to do. Children to *not* murder, thank you very much. I'd like to get on with the show now that all the company's arrived."

"Sire," a new voice interrupted, drifting from the shadows along with one of the figures.

It had never occurred to Arlo that members of the Wild Hunt could speak.

She'd simply never thought about it, could honestly say her imagination would have conjured something cold and airy if she had, not the silken bass that poured from this particular Hunter, filled with such distaste that Arlo cringed. She wasn't the only one to do so. The Hunter strode to the front of the dais and knelt before the king, and Queen Reseda flinched for his nearness. It was still impossible to make out anything of his appearance from Arlo's side of things—his cloak was like woven, glittering midnight draped around his long and powerful body, and it concealed him from head to toe—but his presence was distressing enough that she didn't envy what Reseda could probably see if she dared to look.

"You should know who this is."

Azurean nodded permission to go on.

"Your affairs are not our concern unless you task them so, Sire. The Mortal Realm is not our place to interfere, but the person here before you is a plague that knows no bounds, and—"

Nausicaä gasped, so suddenly it startled the entire room. "*Eris.*"

The hooded figure stiffened, and Arlo realized "Eris" was the Hunter's *name*. "That's, like, the nicest thing you've ever said about me. If I didn't know any better, I'd say you miss me."

Miss her?

Was Nausicaä some sort of disgraced member of the Wild Hunt? Arlo eyed her with fresh curiosity.

The Hunter—Eris—ignored the disruption, though his tone did freeze a little for the taunt. "Just as the Mortal Realm is not our concern, the affairs of the other realm are not yours. It was determined unnecessary, upon the initial banishment of this particular immortal, to make you aware of her true nature. Circumstances force our tongue. This is the former Erinys Alecto—a Fury, though she holds no longer the rank or title."

So, Arlo had been right to be concerned—Nausicaä *was* someone who shouldn't be here.

A Fury. She'd read a bit about these immortals, but oddly enough, most of her knowledge on them had come from human sources—school, for instance, when their drama class took a brief detour through ancient Greek plays. "Erinys" . . . It was a title meaning Fury, though fear and belief that speaking this name could summon them meant they were also known as the Eumenides—the Kindly Ones. They'd been painted in Arlo's mind as angry goddesses of death and revenge, a bit like harpies, with batlike wings and bloody claws and matted heaps for hair, grotesque and terrifying monsters born in hell.

The fae didn't talk about them, mostly because—much like with the Hunt—the general fear was that mention of their name was all it would take to draw their attention. The way Nausicaä stood before them, too perfectly human to be something so ancient and nebulous and godly, made it difficult for Arlo to believe this claim.

"A Fury?" Azurean eyed Nausicaä. "Yes, I know a little of their kind. I've never actually seen one before now, though . . . You do tend to keep to yourselves, when here."

Eris nodded. "As they should. The Infernal Sisterhood—the Kindly Ones—one of the few like us that magic demands be allowed wherever it exists, regardless of the treaty. They are daughters of the Goddess Urielle, born from the elements she commands—from magic itself, given life to ensure its laws are properly kept."

Eris rose to his feet. He kept his back to Arlo and the others at the center of the room, but his words were easy to hear, regardless. "They are, by your terms, police of the realms. Three sisters—Megaera, Tisiphone, and Alecto, these titles handed down to each successor. When one is challenged and defeated, Destroyed or cast out for whatever reason, another is chosen to take their name and place."

Azurean lifted a brow, green eyes glittering. He looked impressed by the prospect that here before them was an immortal about whom their people knew so little, but warning glinted beneath; the gods were no more welcome here than they'd been when they were driven out, long ago. "And what have you to say for yourself on this matter, former Erinys Alecto?"

As though her secrets weren't being aired one by one in front of ten other people, Nausicaä shrugged. "That you can call me Nausicaä?"

"He can call you murderer and suspect," Eris interjected, whirling around. With his hood drawn low over his face, it was still impossible to see what he looked like beneath. Arlo couldn't find it in herself to be too upset by that. His tone was a barely controlled icy fire, and she had no desire to see that reflected in his face.

He was frightening enough already.

"There is more you must know about the shame that stands so proudly before this court," Eris continued, turning back to Azurean. "*Nausicaä* was banished for taking the lives of eleven mortals before their designated time of death. Nausicaä is the reason Your Majesty exhausts himself on keeping an ever-burning ship secret from human discovery. She is the reason that ship is haunted by pain, and violence, and rage."

In the face of these accusations, Nausicaä merely grinned. There was nothing "mere" about the action, though. When a quiet, singular note of smug laughter escaped through Nausicaä's nose, Arlo had to look away from that razor-torn smile.

"You're welcome," Nausicaä fairly purred.

More than terrified by the revelation of Nausicaä's crimes, Arlo felt . . . disappointed. She couldn't say why. She'd *known* Nausicaä was a criminal—that not-troll in the club had said as much—but it was one thing to know a matter in abstract and another to know it in detail.

In the end, Nausicaä was a murderer, and it was disappointing to realize that Arlo had actually become a little fond of the wildly unstable immortal being beside her.

Azurean knocked his golden staff against his dais like a judge banged their gavel for silence. "Enough. I have no patience for personal quarrels. Thank you for bringing this to my attention, Eris, but I'm afraid even I cannot punish a person twice for the same crime." Quieter, but no less clipped, Azurean continued. "I respect that you were once a greater being, Nausicaä, but here in my realm you will respect *me*. You have come to tell me something. I suggest you plead your case before I find myself inclined to believe my Hunt's suspicion of your guilt."

Nausicaä looked to be weighing her next words carefully. "Do you mind releasing my hands, then?"

Azurean's brow quirked his skepticism on the matter—skepticism that she even needed his help with that to begin with—but he waved the hand not clutching his staff. The ropes binding her hands behind her back slithered untied and dropped to the ground.

"Thank you." She worked the stiffness from her wrists before flicking a hand through the air. Where there was nothing before, a rock appeared in the palm of her hand, held out for the king's examination.

All ten of the room's other occupants leaned in for a closer look.

The stone didn't seem all that special to Arlo, who peered around Celadon to view it. It was little more than a misshapen oval chunk of gray stone shot through with the occasional black vein.

"You're, what . . . a hundred, Your Majesty?"

Azurean ruffled. "Three hundred and twelve."

"Right. My mistake," Nausicaä amended graciously. "My point is, you're young. Older than I am, sure, but I'm pretty young myself compared to certain legends."

The king examined the stone a little harder. Eris, despite himself, seemed mildly interested too—at least, Arlo assumed that was what his silent hovering meant. He might have fallen asleep for all that she could really tell.

And then, too suddenly, the king reeled back in his throne. Recognition flickered in his eyes, along with a nameless fear, but then was quickly shuttered away. His regard for Nausicaä turned inexplicably cool—which only seemed to delight her. "See, I knew you'd recognize it too."

"I do not."

"Wow," Nausicaä snorted. "How much did it hurt to tell *that* lie? This isn't just some rock—this is a philosopher's stone, and you know it."

This was not the dramatic revelation Nausicaä had probably intended it to be.

Queen Reseda groaned, deflating in her seat. She rolled her eyes as though people walked in every other day with legendary magical rocks, and Cerelia twitched a grin over the sheer absurdity.

But Celadon had drawn noticeably stiff beside Arlo, and King Azurean sat suspiciously still. He seemed to Arlo as though trying for nonchalance, but his grip on the arms of his seat was far too tight, and tension made his posture rigid. *Was* he lying? He certainly could be, judging by his unease, and really, as High King, he had the fortitude to pull it off. But to outright lie in so many faces, over something as important as murder . . . he wouldn't. Nausicaä had to be mistaken. "However enchanting certain tales may be," Azurean clipped, speaking at long last, "they are still, in fact, *tales*. A magical stone that turns lead into gold and grants the possessor life eternal? Fiction. Even faeries have their fantasies—the philosopher's stone is not real."

The wince he almost succeeded at hiding—the telltale pain that laced a lie—filled Arlo with as much dread as it did confusion.

Nausicaä seemed completely unperturbed by this aggressive dismissal; her smile smoothed out into perfect serenity. "Bullshit." She turned to Arlo. "Hey, Red, do me a favor and hold this for a second, will you?"

Arlo perked to attention at being so suddenly addressed. "Um . . . no?"

"I promise it's not going to *kill* you. Please? This will only take a second."

"Mmm . . ." Arlo peered at the stone, doubtful. "If I do this, we're even for all the stuff back at the Faerie Ring, okay?"

"Yeah, yeah, even for the Faerie Ring. Here."

Arlo stepped forward and took the stone . . . and nothing happened.

"Okay," she said after a moment of silence and too much of the room's focus, which made her face begin to heat with embarrassment. "Now what?"

"Now look at me."

Drawing a deep breath, Arlo did as instructed. The moment her gaze locked with the hardened gray of Nausicaä's, she nearly dropped the stone to the floor.

Nausicaä had released whatever had been concealing her magic. The force of it overwhelmed Arlo, stabbed her through with jagged relish. As pressure built in Arlo's head, eating away at her vision, its woodsmoke-and-iron scent filled her nose.

Somewhere in the distance, she heard shouting.

After a moment, or an eternity—it was difficult to determine which—the air behind her surged under Celadon's command, rushing past her so firmly that if she had been the target, it would have knocked her clear to the opposite wall.

Nausicaä, however, merely stumbled. The disturbance was enough to sever the connection, and it was only then that Arlo surfaced from Nausicaä's violent aura, tingling and a little dazed.

In her hand, the stone that had once been dull now glowed a vibrant red.

"Arlo?" Celadon took hold of her shoulders, turning her to face him. He didn't once glance at the stone. "Arlo, are you okay? You cried out—you looked like you were in *pain*. What happened?" He glared over his shoulder at Nausicaä. "What did you do?"

Arlo blinked up at Celadon and then slowly surveyed the rest of the people in the room, statue-still in whatever action they'd been about to perform before the High Prince's elemental power burst out of his control.

Finally, she looked to Nausicaä. "You said that wouldn't hurt!"

A bit of the tension bled from the room, and its occupants reluctantly settled. Thalo, however, never lost the look on her face that said she was ready to do more than hurl a breeze at Nausicaä—which wouldn't be difficult, and quite a lot more damaging, considering her Gift allowed her to gather air in the palm of her hand and wield it like a steel-tipped whip.

"False—I said you wouldn't die."

"Take it back! Why is it glowing?" She held the stone out to Nausicaä, slightly panicked that something would happen if that glowing went on any longer—that seemed to be her luck with things lately.

"Hype down, it's fine. It's just a response. It's only glowing because you're an ironborn with strong magic, and it still has a bit of juice left."

Arlo actually laughed at how far from correct that statement was, despite the situation—her magic, *strong*? Hardly.

But Nausicaä ignored the outburst and turned back to the dais, blond hair wildly disheveled by the gust Celadon had summoned. She waved her hand at the glowing stone in Arlo's hand—a glow no one but the Hunt and their king seemed able to see. "The lesidhe; the ironborn; immortals—those are the only three who can see the glow of alchemy, can see when one of these stones is fueled up enough to activate . . . or spoil. But that crown of yours makes you special, doesn't it, Your High Majesty? You can see it too." Her grin returned, no less sharp for however muted it was compared to before. "Technically, you're right—this *isn't* a philosopher's stone, not a proper one at least. It's a dud. The ironborn heart required to make it just couldn't withstand the stress of the transformation."

The stone in her hand was a *heart*?

In disgust, Arlo dropped it on the floor. Nausicaä sighed. She stooped to snatch it up before anyone else could, and not long after, the glowing began to recede back to gray.

Glancing up at the throne, Arlo noticed Azurean poised on the edge of his seat, his face gone a sour, milk-pale blue. "That is *enough*," he bit out, something under his tone making the hairs on the backs of Arlo's arms stand on end.

Nausicaä jutted her chin in defiance of Azurean's oddly brittle mood, almost as though she were purposefully goading him into losing his composure. "No, I don't think it is. I didn't come to tell you something, Azurean Viridian. I came to ask why the hells you're pretending this isn't what you *know* it is?"

"I will not tell you again to drop this. Philosopher's stones *are not real*."

"Don't get me wrong," Nausicaä continued blithely. "I don't care, but some dude made *one* of these things *centuries* ago, and you all got so freaked out about it that you outlawed an entire branch of magic. So don't tell me you aren't concerned. Don't tell me you haven't at least *suspected* these ironborn deaths could be the result of alchemy. There are signs, you can't have missed them, you're not stupid, so why are you passing this all off as *me* and then just . . . ignoring it? You could have dragged me in here long ago for confirmation, but all you issue is a fucking *summons*? You don't even *want* to look into this, do you? You're ignoring it. *Why?*"

A minute ticked by.

A second one followed.

No one spoke. Everyone watched. The room's attention had turned to the High King, and everyone waited for his response, but none was forthcoming. His face took on sapphire outrage, growing darker by the second. Arlo had never known her great-uncle for being a man so quick to temper. He was passionate enough, sure, and didn't suffer nonsense lightly, but Arlo had never seen him this *angry*—not once. Even when Celadon did his best to provoke him, Azurean Viridian was a man who preferred gravity over hysterics, sharp words over shouting.

"No comment, huh?" Nausicaä tapped her chin. "Interesting. You know, with a Reaper running around your heavily guarded city, gobbling up the ironborn, destroying the proof that what I'm saying is true so no one else asks these difficult questions you're oh-so-desperate to deflect . . . it's all a little *convenient*, don't you think? What with your insistence that everything's fine, that this is all the work of some human serial killer, the Dark Star, or heck, maybe that the ironborn are just dropping dead of their own accord—what excuse *haven't* you tried to distract the magical community from what's really going on? This Reaper . . . It couldn't be *yours*, could it?"

"ARREST HER!" The High King tore from his chair, spittle flying from his lips.

Arlo jumped, nearly colliding with Celadon, who'd startled as well. They weren't the only ones caught off guard by Azurean's reaction. Queen Reseda and Cerelia both flinched, and Thalo had actually drawn the jewel-hilted dagger she carried at her side, immediately poised to take down a threat that wasn't there.

Nausicaä laughed. "A *coward*—the great Azurean Viridian is nothing but a shivering little *wood sprite* hiding away in his tree."

"ARREST HER! I WILL NOT BE SPOKEN TO LIKE THIS IN MY OWN HOME! ARREST HER—SHE SPEAKS TREASON AGAINST YOUR KING!"

Eris was all too happy to oblige.

As soon as the order was given, he made for the step leading down from the dais. The other three Hunters glided forward, spurred into action by their king's command. They poured out around the throne like dark mist.

Celadon retreated instantly from Nausicaä, clearing their way. Arlo wanted to do the same—rather desperately, she might add—but her feet wouldn't move. The Hunters descended, and their aim was the person who, so far, had done nothing more tonight than keep Arlo safe.

"ARREST HER!" Azurean stamped his foot, and around it burst a carpet of deeply purple iris flowers. Royalty . . . wisdom . . . it was part of her teachings, as a child of Spring, to learn the language of flowers—so was it Arlo's imagination, or did they look a little . . . shriveled? "ARREST HER!"

The Wild Hunt descended the dais, fanning into formation. Eris stalked forward.

"W-wait!" Arlo cried, quite without her own permission, but that was apparently the way of her bravery. "Wait, please don't! Nausicaä . . . she isn't—"

"SILENCE!"

Arlo's mouth snapped closed, the command so forceful no one would be able to ignore it.

The High King panted like a winded beast, his cheeks flushed so dark a blue it couldn't be healthy, and Arlo's bravery fled in the face of such feverish ire.

She couldn't make sense of this.

Azurean was a fair king. He was a good man, a kind man, someone who'd entertained and investigated claims on shakier grounds than this before, and this behavior . . . this *madness* . . . it wasn't him at all!

Arlo watched as her great-uncle threw himself back in his seat and brushed the tips of his fingers against his crown, that simple twist of ivory-white antler bone that made him lord above them all. "It's fine," he muttered. "It's fine. We're fine." Then, with all the swiftness of a flick of a switch, he was back to his normal, calm temper. "Arrest her. She is to be placed under temporary custody on the grounds of suspicion of collaboration and withholding pertinent information to ongoing crimes of abduction, murder, and magical misconduct. Conviction pending formal hearing—a hearing," he added pointedly, "that will only commence when the accused has shown a better willingness for cooperation and *respect* for the situation in which she finds herself."

Finally, Celadon snagged Arlo and pulled her back from Nausicaä, who'd been oddly calm about this entire thing. In fact, all she seemed to Arlo was vaguely pissed that the king had the nerve to place her under arrest.

"*Tch.*" She flicked her hand once more, dismissing her stone heart back to the void where, presumably, she kept her swords and gods only knew what else. "I guess it's true what they say about power." She tapped her head in the very place a crown would sit. "Fine. Live in your fantasy world. I have better things to do than decorate your prison. Later, assholes."

Tossing her hair over her shoulder, she turned on her bare heels. Before Azurean could draw on his magic to detain her or order a little more haste in his Hunt, the same shadowy darkness that had transported them away from the Faerie Ring shot from her back. It folded itself in a bubble around her and compressed down to a *pop* of nothing, and in a matter of seconds, Nausicaä was gone.

Azurean, as stricken as Arlo had been by the realization Nausicaä could teleport so easily, sat once again tense and poised to spring, as soon as he remembered how to move.

Eris paused as well, though he and his companions seemed wholly unsurprised by Nausicaä's abilities. In fact, one of the Hunt cared so little about the turn of events that they weren't looking after her disappearance at all—they looked instead at *Arlo*, as though she was just as curious a thing as they were to her.

At least, Arlo assumed they were looking at her. The opening of their black hood had turned in her direction, that much she could say for certain. Another shudder—with little warning, the air took on a cool, crawling damp quality, and a sickly sweet scent just faint enough to stir a memory she couldn't place. She'd sensed this before, but where? Whose aura was this? Not one of her family's . . . not Nausicaä's . . . Did it belong to one of the Hunters? The one watching her? But if it was theirs, why couldn't Arlo sense any of the others?

"Sire?" Eris turned to face his king, his hesitation merely lack of direction and not the amazement that gripped the rest of the room. "I regret to inform you I cannot Mark another immortal. Do you still want us after her?"

Arlo breathed a sigh of relief.

"The Dark Star is your new priority. I want her brought in—alive, please."

The Hunt's compliance was immediate. They swept past Arlo and Celadon, and Arlo could feel the Hunter watching her until the very last second, though she tried her best to avoid gazing back. Finally, in a stream of fluttering cloaks, they took their leave of the room.

When Azurean turned his hard stare on Thalo, Arlo's mother stepped quickly toward him. Arlo looked on in rising dread as Thalo bowed low in deference to her king, employer, and esteemed uncle. "Your daughter has demonstrated a foolishness that will not be again abided," Azurean said. "As she was not found in the Faerie Ring and was herself responsible for none of the harm that's been done tonight, I will leave it to you to dole out the punishment her actions demand. Take her and go, Thalo. You are both dismissed."

Nodding gratefully, Thalo straightened and took immediate leave of the dais. She swept down the steps, every bit as intimidating as the Hunt had been, and made directly for Arlo.

Arlo, meanwhile, was too caught up in a curious concoction of weightless relief, paralytic foreboding, and residual horror to move. "Your High Majesty," she ventured, her words sticking to her throat. "Please, I *am* responsible. This was all my idea. I made Celadon tell me where the Faerie Ring was, I made him come with me, I—"

She didn't want to leave without making sure Azurean, in his current and unusual temper, wouldn't punish Celadon too harshly. Celadon hadn't actually done anything, and she wouldn't let Celadon take more of the fall for this than she—but Azurean held up his hand and leveled her a look of distaste she was wholly unaccustomed to seeing from *him*, a look more appropriate of Malachite. "My son is my concern, not yours, Arlo Jarsdel. Remove yourself while I still permit it. That was alchemy you performed in this room just now—I have half a mind to arrest you, too."

Arlo's heart stuttered and nearly gave out.

All she'd done was hold a stone . . . She hadn't meant for it to glow, hadn't used any magic. Nausicaä had said it was just a response. Surely the High King couldn't *throw her in jail* for something like that?

"Arlo," Celadon urged, voice pitched low. "It's all right." His pallor suggested he didn't quite believe that. "Thank you, but you should go with Thalo. I'll come see you later, okay? I'm just relieved you're okay—for a moment tonight I thought I'd lost you, and . . ." His mouth formed a false, weak smile. He shook his head. "You're okay. No punishment could be worse than the opposite."

Thalo reached them at last, glaring so coolly at Celadon that Arlo worried this was something the relationship between her mother and her cousin wouldn't be able to withstand. That maybe Celadon had "lost" Arlo after all in whatever fallout would come of this. "We're leaving, Arlo," she frosted.

Mouthing another apology, Arlo turned from her cousin. Celadon nodded back an apology of his own before kneeling on the ground to await the High King's verdict.

Azurean wouldn't banish him, would he? His own son? For something as trivial as playing getaway driver for a shoddy investigation? But the person sitting on the throne wasn't the High King that Arlo knew. She couldn't say with certainty what he would or wouldn't do.

As impossible as it was, she stumbled after her mother and out of the throne room, more anxious and afraid and terribly, wretchedly *guilty* than she had felt upon entry.

CHAPTER 16

Vehan

⌁

THE SEELIE FOLK WEREN'T known to pay much worship to night's beauty. Their power came from day—from the sun and light and warmth it offered—and it was therefore day on which they spent their pretty exultations. For the prince of the Seelie Court of Summer, this way of life was more like law, but even Vehan had to admit their current view was stunning.

"Look at all those stars," he marveled, folded over the steering wheel of his SUV to peer through its windshield. "There must be *millions* up there. . . ."

The sight reminded Vehan of some cosmic, ethereal garden the way hyacinth blue and verbena purple swept through endless orchid black, those stars like glittering dew on their petals.

"There's more than 'millions'—over two hundred billion in our galaxy alone, is the current estimation," Aurelian corrected, looking up from his phone at them too.

"Did you learn that from Google?"

A snort—"Don't look so pleased with yourself. You barely understand what Google is."

His tone made Vehan laugh, its hint of petulance reminiscent of the days when this sort of banter had been the usual between them. "I can't be perfect, you know," he teased. "I have to have at least one character flaw."

"It would certainly make things easier, yes."

"Pardon?"

Vehan examined his friend. The statement confused him. Aurelian hadn't spoken it loudly, had punctuated this quiet admission with a wince that told him, more than likely, he hadn't meant to say it at all. And he looked spectacularly uncomfortable now. There was no better description for it. Night blended with dashboard lighting to pitch the lavender tint of his hair even darker, to smooth his already-perfect skin, to cast shadows across features Vehan would know with his eyes closed for how often he stared when his friend wasn't looking, and sometimes when he was. Aurelian was beautiful, always, but a little more so in this moment, because that discomfort was so clearly visible—a genuine, open expression—and it had been so *long* since Vehan had been allowed to see anything other than emotions that shaped a frown.

He recalled, suddenly, their very first meeting.

Before Aurelian and his family had come to the palace. Before every tension and every sigh and every hurt that now stood between them, there had just been *them*. Vehan—the little boy clinging to his mother's skirts, sullen, silent, and all-around miserable, trying his best to make sense of his father's recent passing; Aurelian—the little boy in the tiny shop that doubled as his home, offering Vehan a sugar cookie he'd frosted himself, nothing but gentle words and warmth and the biggest, purest smile on his face.

"For you, Your Highness."

Vehan peered up at the slightly taller boy. His smile was so bright, Vehan thought for a moment it was magic like what his mother could do. "Thank you," he replied in the smallest voice, more like a mouse than a boy. It had been weeks since he'd been able to say anything to anyone—at first because he thought maybe a tantrum would bring his father back, and then . . . because he'd been too sad.

"You're welcome. Do you want to go play?"

Vehan peered up at his mother. She was looking at the smiling boy too. Thinking. His mother was always thinking. "Well?" she nudged, and Vehan shuffled forward. He took the other boy's outstretched hand very cautiously, and when they returned several hours later, Vehan was also smiling—flush in the face, happy, laughing.

"Mister and Missus Bessel," he overheard his mother saying. *"I have a proposition for you."*

"Vehan."

Vehan shook himself out of his memories, of that fateful vacation he'd taken with his mother to Germany after his father's funeral. Of coming across a bakery said to be the best in the Seelie Autumn Court. Of his first encounter with the Bessels. But now Aurelian had spoken, had sobered into a seriousness that was unusual even for him. Aurelian dropped his gaze from the heavens to meet Vehan's staring, and the look in his eyes was so intense it would have been impossible to look away even if Vehan should want to. "Since we have a moment, there's . . . something I would like to talk to you about."

Oh hells . . . This was going to be about what he'd said in the Goblin Market. This was going to be about his minor breakdown about feelings and loneliness. Vehan had been all kinds of embarrassed about that particular incident—had lain awake the last few nights recalling in painful, vivid detail how *pathetic* he must have looked, crying about the unfairness of a life where he was a flipping *prince*, for Urielle's sake.

He'd been careful to keep himself busy, to avoid any possibility of this confrontation. Normally, Aurelian didn't try to talk to him about things anymore, and for once in the two years their relationship had taken a noticeable turn toward irreparable, Vehan had been *relieved* by that. But Aurelian was a good person. He'd feel duty-bound to inform Vehan he wasn't alone, that he had people around him, that his mother was strict but she loved him, but if he ever needed someone to talk to, Aurelian would listen. For some reason, the thought of hearing Aurelian play pretend in exactly the same way his other friends did made Vehan cringe.

"Uh . . . okay, but listen, if this is about the Goblin Market, I—"

"I don't hate you, you know that, right?"

Despite himself—despite the fact that "I don't hate you" was by no means a passionate confession of deeper feeling, or hardly any feeling at all, really—Vehan's heart leaped into his throat. His eyes stung a little, and he blinked them furiously, turning his gaze immediately back to the windshield to hide this ridiculous reaction. "I know you don't." He gave the scenery a smile. "But you don't like me very much anymore, do you."

It was the first time they'd ever said any of this out loud—of course it was happening *now*, in the middle of a desert, where they were meant to be waiting to meet with a drug-dealing goblin. "Pincer" didn't know who they were, only that they'd been referred by Jasen, were interested in making a "considerable purchase," and preferred to do so as out of the way as possible. The desert had been Pincer's idea, and Vehan wasn't foolish enough to think it likely they were anywhere near the facility he needed to find, but if they could just *meet* this goblin . . .

Iron teeth will show you the way.

If they couldn't bargain for the information he needed, hells, the goblin might just *sell* it to him. That seemed to be his thing, if he was indeed one of the faeries getting paid to kidnap humans.

"I . . ." Aurelian seemed at a loss for what to say, unable to lie but apparently unwilling to speak the truth when he thought Vehan so vulnerable—which was definitely worse, in Vehan's opinion. "Vehan, I don't—"

"I hope our goblin shows soon."

He couldn't deal with this right now. He didn't have it in him to listen to Aurelian explain why their friendship had failed, especially since he'd soon have to plaster charm over his heartbreak so he could wheedle information from a dangerous criminal.

Aurelian hummed, a noncommittal response that said he'd heard (and accepted) Vehan's unspoken plea for mercy.

"This meeting was more appealing when it was theory. Trekking through the desert to the middle of nowhere on a school night was . . . poor planning, really. I can't believe you agreed. And we're coming up on half an hour past when Pincer was supposed to meet us. Are we sure we're in the right place?"

"I'm sure," Aurelian sighed, looking back down at his phone. His expression had closed into unreadable stoniness once again. "Unless this Pincer has changed his mind or gotten his own directions wrong, this is where we're supposed to be."

Goblins weren't the brightest of faeries. It was possible Pincer had gone to the wrong place.

Sighing deeply himself, Vehan dropped to rest his chin on his hands on the steering wheel, intending to ride this out a bit longer.

He was so tired of false leads—of hunting a truth that proved more and more convoluted the more of it they unraveled. He was tired of no one believing that something was going on to begin with too. If Pincer turned out to be another dead end, he didn't know how much more of the world working against them he could take.

"Vehan."

A hand shot to his shoulder. Vehan looked up to find Aurelian tense and deeply alert, like a cat that had spotted some distant prey. "It's him."

The matte-black Hummer approaching on their right had apparently doused its headlights long back, but the cloud of dust its speed kicked up behind it negated this bit of stealth—the dust, and the death metal music. Vehan could hear it now that he was paying attention; a *human* would have been able to hear it, so cranked was that stereo's volume.

"Hey, look—someone else who thinks screaming is music. Maybe you guys could be friends."

Aurelian pointedly ignored Vehan's comment and threw open the passenger door. Laughing under his breath, Vehan followed suit. He exited the SUV and crossed around to lean against its hood, where Aurelian already waited. With Aurelian's stark-white shirt sleeves rolled up to reveal his tattoos and his silver piercings gleaming in the moonlight, he looked more like Vehan's hired muscle than his one-day steward, whose job would be not only to manage both Vehan's schedule and household but to also act as Seelie Summer King in his stead—regent, should Vehan travel abroad for any prolonged period or become in some way temporarily incapacitated.

The entire Court had been shocked when the queen bestowed this honor upon someone who was not only lesidhe, not only common, but also *not a fae of Seelie Summer*. Aurelian faced no end of scrutiny for Queen Riadne's decision—no end of jealousy, hostility, and unkind gossip—and the palace council had done their best to dissuade her from it, but Vehan's mother was stubborn. When she wanted something, she got it by any means necessary, and for some reason, she'd *fiercely* wanted Aurelian in Vehan's life even more than what he'd already been.

The Hummer tore past them, circling behind the SUV to loop back around. Its windows had been rolled down so two of the vehicle's passengers could hang out the back and leer, and the driver could hold his sleek black AK-47 against the outside of his door.

"Guns," Vehan muttered distastefully. The fae, on a whole, detested this sort of weapon—found guns to be crude and extremely "impersonal," as killing had never been a sport for them the way it seemed to be for humans and other folk; they viewed the taking of life far more seriously, and if it had to be done, it was usually because of some hideous wrong against them.

And for a hideous wrong, most fae preferred to be more "hands-on" than what a gun allowed.

Aurelian straightened. He wasn't Vehan's muscle, but the lesidhe were strong—stronger even than their sidhe counterparts—and nobody wanted to mess with one that could glower as well as Aurelian could. It was just about the only reason the queen allowed Vehan to run around without a bodyguard, never mind however well it was known that any lesidhe who lived in Court territory had to swear an oath of restraint to their respective sovereigns—an oath that forbade them from utilizing any more strength than the sidhe.

"Behind me," Aurelian ordered, stepping forward.

Vehan remained where he was, lounging against his vehicle. The goblins' Hummer skidded to a stop, fishtailing to face them. The music cut off. The dust settled. Four black doors burst open and multiple pairs of boots hit desert ground, and when those doors slammed closed once more, Vehan counted five fully grown goblins staring back at them, all various shades of purple.

Each carried a gun—the one who'd been holding his out his window actually held two, with another strapped to his back. This had to be Pincer. When he grinned, Vehan could see the bits of iron implanted in place of incisors.

"You're Pincer, then?" Aurelian called.

Pincer lifted his gun and aimed it at Aurelian's chest, and Vehan pushed off from the SUV so aggressively the air crackled around him. He extended a hand, aimed right back at Pincer, was poised to fry him with a snap of his fingers, but Aurelian placed a hand on his arm to stall him.

"You must be Jasen's *friends*," Pincer sneered.

He whistled. Two of the three goblins behind him prowled forward, yipping and slapping at each other, snapping their crooked teeth at Vehan and Aurelian as they passed to inspect their vehicle.

Goblins—one of Vehan's least favorite of the faerie races.

They weren't much to look at between their leathery skin, bulbous features, and ears like bat wings, but Vehan's dislike stemmed more from the fact that they were a nuisance. Their gangs operated much the way the factions had before the Courts had been established, forever at war with one another over territory they lost and gained and lost again. They didn't care about anything other than money— human cash or gold or jewels; if it was currency, they coveted and fought over it, killed one another and backstabbed and *lied* for it.

They had very little magic (which they'd never cared much for, anyhow). Because of this, they had taken to city life like a kelpie to water since iron barely fazed them, and violence was rampant, and they could lord like underworld rat kings in their sewers and alleys and holes with guns and explosives and chemical gases that gave the Courts no end of grief trying to manage.

Pincer—a lilac-toned, particularly mean-looking goblin—wore combat boots, a leather jacket, and a dark green top tucked into camouflage-printed army pants. He was taller than Vehan by a couple of inches, the average height for goblins, but he would've been more of a threat if goblins weren't incredibly lacking in intelligence. Still, Vehan knew Pincer would have no problem shooting at them if Vehan or Aurelian gave him reason to.

"Don't mind *my* friends. Just gotta check to make sure you ain't got any other little faelings hidden away."

Aurelian jerked a nod. "It's fine."

"What's your names?"

"Aurelian," he said. "Vay," he added, tugging Vehan slightly forward and closer to his side.

Vay—what Aurelian had once called him, what he *hadn't* called him in so long. Vehan didn't realize just how much he'd missed hearing it until now.

"Vay the fae!" Pincer laughed uproariously. "Vay the fae—what a stupid name!"

The goblin behind Pincer joined in this humor, working himself into a wheeze that morphed into a coughing fit. The pair behind Vehan snorted, and Vehan felt this was extremely rich of someone who went around calling himself "Pincer," but held his tongue.

The goblin who stood on the side of the Hummer opposite Pincer frowned. "I don't get it."

"It rhymes, you moron!"

"Oh!"

"All clear." The two conducting the investigation of Vehan's SUV declared it safe, and stomped back to their Hummer. Pincer lowered his gun. "So, you're lookin' to buy some Faerie Dust, are you? Jasen said you was looking to buy a *lot*."

"That's right," Aurelian confirmed.

"Ha—spoiled little richies like you are my favorite, you know? What, Mommy and Daddy don't love you enough? Need a bit of

248

attention? Don't worry, you got the cash, I got the goods, but you ever use this stuff before, *Aurelian*?"

Vehan realized with a sinking sort of dejection that he honestly couldn't answer this question about his friend. There was so much he didn't know about Aurelian anymore. The friends *Aurelian* kept weren't the ones who'd burrowed in close and planted their roots and refused to budge an inch unless it was to somehow creep closer, wrapped around Vehan to the point of suffocation. . . . Their quieter, milder classmates—the ones Aurelian spent his time with—didn't stand a chance against people like Kine and Fina.

A muscle leaped in Aurelian's jaw.

"Ah." Pincer snickered. "You have. You got the look. It gets ya. It gets everyone. Try it once and ya never forget it. Terrible, isn't it? But you want it again—you always want it, you never stop wantin' it, and by the second taste you're hooked. There's no getting over Dust—she's a bitch, for sure, but hells if she doesn't make you feel like king of the fucking *world* before she ruins you."

The goblins all cheered. Two of them rose their guns in the air and fired off a shot, and Vehan startled, which only seemed to amuse them further. "Princess here don't look like she knows what she's in for," Pincer added, his slightly protuberant eyes now sizing Vehan up. "She *does* look familiar, though. Loogie—doesn't Vay the fae look familiar to you? Hey, Vay, where have I seen you before?"

"Ha! Hey Vay—that rhymes too!"

Perhaps they should hurry this along. Vehan had been hoping to win their information without revealing who he really was (it was surprisingly easy to roam around unrecognized, for how little people expected their prince to be out and about in public), but he had a feeling if he allowed this to continue much longer, someone was either going to get shot or electrocuted.

"Yes, well," he said, stepping away from Aurelian to draw himself up taller. "Actually, my name is—"

"I don't *ducking* believe it."

"For the last time, Bludge, 'ducking' isn't a swear word."

"Duck you, my phone says it is, and I like it!"

"Are those *Flamethrowers*?"

Heads turned. Every pair of eyes fixed on the glowing orange light off in the distance behind the SUV. Vehan cocked his head, wondering what on earth this could be, growing bigger and brighter until suddenly he realized it was another vehicle making its approach, and that glowing orange was revealed to be streams of actual fire. The engine revved like a rumbling beast—another Hummer, bigger and glossy black, with spikes mounted on its front grill as though it were built for war instead of city driving.

"It is!" Pincer shouted. "It's the Flamethrowers—we've been set up! Vay the fae set us up, they're working with the Flames! It's a turf war, boys, open fire!"

Oh . . . good. A goblin turf war. The Flamethrowers must have been a rival gang. This was exactly the opposite of what they needed, and now a bunch of riled-up faeries with guns thought Vehan had orchestrated some coup against them.

One moment he stood gaping at this turn of events, the next . . . he lay sprawled on the ground, Aurelian flat against him, shielding him from bullets that whizzed far too close over their heads for comfort. This was not the moment to be keenly aware of how *firm* Aurelian's muscles were under his hands, instinct having forced him to grab Aurelian's biceps on their way down. But he was saved from embarrassment by Aurelian hauling him far too easily to his feet, and ushering him back toward the driver's side door.

"Wait!" Vehan cried. "*Wait.*"

This was going to end with answers or a hole in his head—those were the only options, damn it.

He tore out of Aurelian's clutches and made directly for Pincer.

Pincer shot at him—the others were more preoccupied with shooting at the second Hummer, now upon them, goblins armed with actual blazing flamethrowers hanging out the windows.

"This ain't your turf!" shouted Bludge.

"This ain't your turf either!" shouted one of the Flamethrowers.

"This wasn't me!" Vehan snarled over the din. He kept his hands raised. Drawing on the electricity in Pincer's Hummer to fuel a force field between them, he deflected Pincer's bullets, and they whizzed off in various directions.

Electricity.

The element of Seelie Summer.

The well in which this power gathered had grown considerably deeper inside Vehan, since his coming of age. He was still in training, still learning how to control his abilities, which were so much stronger than ever before but nowhere near all he'd be able to wield as he got older.

"This wasn't me—stop shooting! My name is Vehan—Vehan Lysterne. I'm your *prince*, so stop shooting at me and listen!"

Pincer stopped shooting, but it was only to chuck his gun at Vehan's force field. When that, too, failed to break through it, he turned and scrambled back into his Hummer.

"Stop!"

Vehan lunged. The door slammed closed before he could reach it, but Pincer wouldn't get away. Vehan had leached a little too much life from the Hummer's battery—could feel it buzzing inside him, sparking and eager for use. He had to be careful, because that eagerness could rebound if he didn't find an outlet for it soon, but spending it in his current state—a novice wound up on stress and adrenaline—could be just as dangerous.

"Duck."

"Language," Vehan sang, teasing Aurelian for his wording. But he didn't need telling twice. Vehan dropped, and his retainer slammed the side of his fist against the Hummer's reinforced window. He reached through shattered glass to unlock the door, but Pincer had finally given up on starting his vehicle. Diving for the opposite side, the goblin kicked the door open and fled.

He was fast.

Vehan was faster.

Pincer didn't make it far into the desert before Vehan tackled his legs, but Pincer had an advantage. Sure, Vehan was used to fighting. He was used to Zale wiping the floor with him, and hand-to-hand combat training with Aurelian had once left him with a bruise around his eye and he'd laughed for how dark it had been (and Aurelian had felt so guilty for it, he'd removed himself permanently from their sparring sessions).

So yeah, Vehan could spar—but he'd never had to fight anyone in earnest, and Pincer was well versed in this art where rules were for people whose lives weren't on the line.

He swung—clipped Vehan square in the jaw with enough force that snapped his head back. Disoriented, Vehan released him, and Pincer clawed his way to freedom and tried once more to flee.

Aurelian had found himself with a problem of his own, detained by one of the Flamethrowers who had decided anyone who wasn't them was an enemy. They aimed their flamethrower right at his face, and Aurelian didn't need his assistance—had magic of his own to knock this pest away—but Vehan couldn't help the way his heart clenched to see his friend in danger.

"Look out!" he hollered, and tossed out a hand.

Electrical current shot for the goblin like a bolt of lightning. It shocked him, lifting him off the ground and flinging him back. He moaned—alive, thank goodness, Vehan had managed *some* restraint then—and writhed on the ground, but he didn't get back up.

Aurelian rushed to him. Vehan pulled himself to his feet. His jaw ached, but he barely noticed it. "Pincer!" he called over his shoulder. "He's getting away, come on!"

They ran.

The dark was nothing to fae senses. Vehan could see the direction Pincer had fled just fine. The only distinct landmark that identified this meeting spot had been the wide sweep of solar panels up ahead.

Contained within four bright stadium light posts and secured by nothing but a bit of wire, this undoubtedly belonged to the human government, not Seelie Summer, but that didn't matter. What mattered was that Pincer was already in the process of heaving himself over that fence, clearing it just as Vehan and Aurelian reached this hurdle too.

What was the point?

Where was he going to go?

Goblins—how brainless were they that this one had accidentally trapped himself so easily?

"Come on," Vehan urged again, and hauled himself over the fence with ease. Aurelian did the same, but as soon as their boots met the earth, the ground trembled. It was far too subtle for human notice, but Vehan felt it—the quick draw of something sliding open.

"What the hell?"

Pincer had stopped. He stood not far from the solar panels, stomping impatiently at the ground, shouting at something to "hurry up," and that's when Vehan realized—

"A door . . ."

A door indeed.

Flashing a grin at Vehan, Pincer dove through the door leading underground to, what? A secret facility hidden away in the desert?

Iron teeth will show you the way.

Vehan shot forward. "Aurelian, this is the facility, the one the oracle mentioned—*we've found it!*"

He skidded to a halt.

The moment Vehan breached the pools of light around the solar panel field, their stark-white glow snapped to bloody red, and a high-pitched shriek split the night. The door Pincer had disappeared through snapped closed, and from this distance, Vehan could only just make out a pattern carved into its surface of odd symbols and looping writing contained within a circle.

Alchemy—that pattern was an array, an alchemic seal, he was

sure of it. After all the research he'd done of late pursuing his many theories, there could be no mistaking it, and it was one more piece of evidence in a long string of worrisome clues that pointed to a much more sinister something waiting to close its jaws around them.

He filed this information away for later, though. He didn't have time to ponder this right now. They'd tripped an alarm, and the noise was bound to draw attention, if not damage his hearing. "What's happening?"

"We have to leave," Aurelian yelled over the alarm. "Right now. Something's coming. We need to get back to the car!"

Lesidhe fae senses were stronger than sidhe and could detect movement farther off than sidhe fae were able. Vehan would have to take his word for it. He turned with every intention of taking Aurelian's outstretched hand and making their retreat, but once again, surprise trapped him in place.

"Tsk, tsk, tsk."

Aurelian whipped around.

Even he hadn't noticed the appearance of the faerie behind them, and that was deeply concerning. Too tall, too thin, too oddly built—like driftwood shaped by unkind waters—the faerie was . . . well, Vehan wouldn't call him beautiful, but he couldn't look away. Not from the skeletal sharpness of his face, or his wide poison-green eyes, or the lethal silver trimmings of his darker-than-black tunic, which glinted dangerously in the light. "Whatever is His Highness doing all the way out here?"

Vehan frowned. He took a step forward, but Aurelian was faster—he threw himself like a shield between them. "Let us leave. We don't want any trouble."

The disconcerting faerie tipped his head in the opposite direction of his one-sided grin. "You want no trouble, and yet you're here, stirring up exactly that."

Whatever Aurelian had detected coming toward them, Vehan heard it now. He turned, pressing his back to his retainer's, and watched in mounting horror as the door in the ground snapped back open and something began to spill from its depths.

It wasn't Pincer.

At first, Vehan thought it was some massive, many-legged spider unpacking itself from its den, the way its limbs flailed about and stretched to heave its body through, but it wasn't. Those limbs belonged to multiple bodies—bodies with weapons that glinted just as deadly as their mysterious, green-eyed faerie. "Let us leave," Vehan growled, tossing out a hand to draw on more current. Sparks of electricity crackled at his fingers. "Move, or we'll have no choice but to make you."

The mysterious faerie laughed, a sound like creaking floorboards. "I'd *love* to let you give that a go. Unfortunately, tonight is not the night we test your mettle, Prince Vehan."

The swarm of hulking humanoid shapes jerked and twitched ever closer to where Vehan and Aurelian stood. They didn't have time for this banter, but just as Vehan felt his weapon beginning to take shape in his hand, the night fell from the sky.

This was the best he could describe it.

The glittering cosmos melted, dripping tarlike black around them, oozing from the sky to wrap them both up in its sticky, cold embrace. Vehan cried out in alarm—Aurelian gasped—but as quickly as the night swallowed them whole, it spat them out, unharmed.

The solar panel field was gone.

The lights . . . the creatures creeping toward them . . . the shrieking alarm . . . all of it was gone. They were back by their car. Pincer's gang and the rival Flamethrowers were gone as well, the only evidence they'd been here singed earth and six motionless bodies.

"What in the name of *Day* just happened?" Vehan wondered aloud.

He blinked up at Aurelian. They stood rather close, Aurelian's arm slung tight around Vehan's lower back, his other around his shoulders—protective. Vehan's hand, pinned between them, was clenched fast to Aurelian's shirt, and it took a moment for his brain to catch up with how intimate this might look, but through his daze found he didn't care as much as perhaps he should.

"Are you all right?" Aurelian inquired a little breathlessly.

"I'm okay. You?"

"Confused, but otherwise, yeah—I'm fine."

"*Well,*" said a third, obnoxious voice, reminding Vehan they weren't alone. "Here we are, safe and sound." He looked at the corpses around him and sighed. "The ones who matter, at least. I hope you'll excuse me, Your Highness—duty calls. I'm sure you'll be able to see yourselves home. . . ."

Vehan untangled himself from Aurelian and stepped toward this stranger. "Who are you? Did you know we would be here? Do you work for my mother—did she put you up to this?"

The faerie looked down his nose at him. For a long and deathly silent moment, they stood matching glares—acidic green clashing against electric blue—and said nothing. Then the faerie lifted a silver-clawed finger to trace ever so lightly down the length of Vehan's nose. He grinned, revealing two dozen teeth that could tear Vehan's flesh to ribbons. "Good night, little princeling. I'm sure we'll meet again."

Aurelian growled low in his throat, and Vehan shook his head. The featherlight, threatening scrape of that claw tickled his skin. The faerie retreated—one step, two. Aurelian called after him to wait, but in the span of a blink he seemed to dissolve back into the darkness, taking the fallen goblins with him, and they were alone once more.

Gone . . . just like that.

No faerie or fae Vehan knew could vanish into thin air. Nothing tonight made any sense.

For a moment longer the heavy silence left in the faerie's wake persisted. Then Vehan heard the crunch of gritty earth beneath Aurelian's boots as he made his approach. "We need to return to the palace, Your Highness. Whoever that was . . . how they could come and go so easily . . . what happened here tonight—all of it. It's . . . it's been enough. Let's go home."

"'Tonight is not the night we test your mettle,'" said Vehan, murmuring the words he couldn't seem to get out of his head.

Something about their faerie savior . . . something about the things he said, the way he said them, what lurked beneath their surface, unspoken . . . a memory, there and gone in a glint, flashed through Vehan's mind, but trying to hold on to it had been like trying to cup sliver-thin minnows in water.

"Pardon?" Aurelian said.

Vehan shook his head. "We knew this was big." He turned around at last. "We knew there was something going on." He clasped Aurelian on a shoulder that was far narrower than his own, yet so much stronger. "There was an alchemic array on that door, did you see it? Every step we take in this investigation, we encounter something that screams alchemist activity. Mother can't ignore this. She *can't*."

Aurelian nodded, a single dip of his head and nothing more, his gaze never breaking from Vehan's own. But Vehan knew him well enough still to tell when he was holding his tongue.

"You think she will."

"I won't speak poorly of your mother," was all he stiffly replied.

"You still don't think she'll listen."

Aurelian stared at him.

Heaving a sigh, Vehan dropped his hand. "Her heart's in the right place. She's busy is all, and we can't expect her to leap at every suspicion two teenage fae bring her, besides. But this . . . she has to listen to *this*."

Perhaps it was the note of plea in Vehan's voice he couldn't seem to shake . . . Perhaps it was simply Aurelian's neutrality reserving his judgment. Whatever the case, Aurelian yielded. "As you say. We should get back."

He turned for the car. Vehan watched him go. *Tonight is not the night we test your mettle.* "You're not as much of a stranger as you should be," he mused under his breath, barely registering the words he spoke. "I know you . . . but how?"

"Does it hurt?"

Vehan's gaze shot up to find Aurelian staring. He stood by the driver's door, expression tight, the only indication that he did actually care a bit if something happened to his prince.

Ah.

Vehan had been absently rubbing his chest—rubbing the brand that wasn't a simple scar, no matter what everyone else told him. "No. It's fine. Come on, I want a bath—and burgers. Let's stop for food along the way."

"Fine. You're driving."

Vehan laughed—of course he was. Aurelian loved most human inventions, but driving seemed to unnerve him. "*Anything* for you, *Your Highness.*"

Later that night, when he was in bed replaying this interaction ad nauseam, he'd curse himself for letting a bit more sincerity show through this joke than he'd intended.

How far Hero had come from the boy who'd once had nothing, from the life he'd spent entirely on other people and working past exhaustion just to barely scrape by.

His memories were filled with things like skipping school (which he'd always enjoyed) because one of his siblings was sick and needed care; the months he'd been shy on rent and had to pretend he wasn't home until he could pay it (no lights, no water, and very little heat, sneaking in and out like a squatter in his own apartment); clothes and shoes and coats that didn't fit right, were either too small or too big, ugly and cheap, rough against his skin and yet threadbare, because as much as he hated them, he couldn't afford to buy better things.

Now, in a dimly lit passage of metal floors and glass walls, Hero looked out at his empire. The goblins and orcs and imps down below went about their business, inspecting Hero's prized creations and putting them through their paces, but for all Hero stared, it wasn't this he watched—his own reflection had caught his attention.

A man in his forties—flushed with life and health, no longer ungainly and skinny but strong, fed with prime cuts of meat and expensive wines and fresh, organic produce.

Clean-shaven . . . no more bags beneath his eyes . . . skin no longer parched and sallow . . . his rags replaced with riches, wearing a suit the High King himself would envy, cut from night and tailored to his every curve and angle; it was just as much a robe to Hero as what fae royalty paraded around in—but far more valuable.

"Whatever are you going to *do* with them all?"

Turning his face to examine the line of his jaw, Hero chuckled.

"Sell them, of course. To the world's highest bidder. Was there something you needed, Lethe?" Not that his Hunter wasn't welcome here whenever he chose to visit, but in this current, final stage of operations there was no real need for surprise appraisals, and Lethe rarely did anything without a purpose.

A hand planted itself on the glass beside his reflection. The muted glow of floodlight caught on long and pointed filigree claws. They pricked through the glass as though it was made of sponge, and made Hero turn at last from his self-admiration to find himself half-caged by a closeness that was highly unusual. Lethe's arm stretched firm and unrelenting as an iron bar, but the length of his body had curved against him into something that could almost be intimate, something that made warmth ignite in Hero's veins and bemusement unfurl a smile. "Yes?"

Green eyes bore into his.

Hero drew a breath.

It sat in his chest—wary and waiting—as one moment turned into two, turned into more, and green held him captive. Hero's thoughts narrowed to one. . . . He lifted a hand. It pressed flat against Lethe's chest. This was more than he'd ever dared before, more than he'd ever been allowed, and when Lethe raised his free hand, Hero flinched—was convinced that Lethe would slap his away, or push him back, or *something*, anything other than cup it over Hero's and hold it closer.

"Hero," Lethe fairly purred.

"*Yes?*" Hero breathed. His heart raced for the intensity this gorgeous being angled down at him, for their proximity, for this entire heady situation Hero had no idea what to do with or how he wanted it to proceed, if he even wanted it to proceed at all.

"I wish to tell you a story."

"Okay . . ."

"About a boy, who was so good at taking lives that when death came for his, he made him a deal."

"Is this boy you?"

"Shhh," Lethe hushed, gentle as a mother soothing her fussing babe. "Just listen. This boy, whom death loved dearly for his years of worship, for the souls he'd sent like offerings to death's altar, made him a deal—an offering of his own: immortality, for service. The boy would be made like a god, given the rest of his days to take lives in the name of the stars. The very first Hunter. But deities . . . they like their games. Death? His gift was no gift but a *leash* for this boy. The years became years became years became more. Death plucked many others for his glorious service, made many more Hunters. The boy was held above them all, a shining example, along with three others too foolish to see this platform for what it was—to realize this was only meant to shackle them further."

Hero looked into those green eyes that seemed to him suddenly, impossibly old. Impossibly tired. Hero sympathized. He *empathized.* He knew what that felt like, that weariness, that sank down to bone and rooted itself even deeper, inextricable. Lethe . . . Had he ever had anyone to care about him as Hero did? This story, this boy, it had to be Lethe—had he ever had anyone other than Hero to tell this to?

Lethe . . . He had to be so lonely to have lived so many years with no one. It was good he was finally opening up to Hero. His Hunter—changeable and sometimes cruel, but good, so good, beneath it all.

"You deserve to be free," Hero told him.

"I do." Lethe squeezed his hand, a little too hard, and Hero winced, but his Hunter was so much stronger than he was and sometimes forgot that. It was fine. He ignored it. "I'm glad you think so too. Perhaps you can tell me, then, why you let your Reaper get so close to my only means of achieving that?"

Hero blinked. "What?"

Lethe drew himself a little taller, bending over Hero with too much threat for him to mistake it as anything else. "Your Reaper. It seems to be getting a little . . . carried away with itself."

Oh.

"This is about Arlo."

"This has *always* been about Arlo," Lethe hissed, the green in his eyes flaring toxic bright.

Tearing himself out of Lethe's hold, Hero stepped back and rubbed his smarting hand. Would he find bruising, he wondered, when he later looked beneath the gloves that protected the world from his touch? Incensed to be abused over *this* of all things, he snapped, "What does it even matter? You can't tell me she's still important to you—not after her Weighing! She barely made it out of that. I don't even know how she got through at all, to be honest. She's worse than I was at that age. She's no one! What does it matter if my Reaper—"

Lethe lunged forward quicker than Hero could comprehend. His hand clutched Hero's jaw in a vise that threatened to crack bone. "It matters," he rasped, breath spilling against Hero's face cool as a shiver. "The world was once *full* of us immortals. I am not the only one who craves freedom. It. *Matters*. I am not the only one invested in Arlo Jarsdel's future, so do not touch her—do *not*, or you won't survive it."

Hero glared. He couldn't speak, so he let his eyes spit the vitriol he knew he could never say to this person he was so indebted to—a person who, much like what death had given that boy in that story, had perhaps never been the gift he pretended to be in Hero's life.

"Your Reaper was at the Faerie Ring tonight. It almost killed Arlo. This will not happen again. Fate has given immortals *one* advantage, Hieronymus—one little mortal, perfectly malleable champion of their return. If you mess this up for them, I can promise you, it won't be me carving out your punishment, but oh, you'll wish it was."

He released Hero then, tearing away. With a sweep of his cloak he vanished, leaving Hero on the floor. Trembling . . . *furious* . . . after all he'd done for Lethe, after all that had happened between them . . .

No.

He drew in a breath.

He released it through his nose.

This was more than Lethe had ever told him about himself, personal information Hero had never had until now; a window into the

Immortal Realm through which few—if any—were privileged enough to peer. What Lethe meant about this talk of Fate, Hero only had the vaguest sense. The Immortal Realm, they were planning a comeback? Fate had made Arlo into something they could use for this?

She was weak. She was nothing—useless. She'd only disappoint the too many people who thought otherwise. And Lethe, it was no wonder his moods were so fickle, why he snapped at Hero every time Hero reminded him that he deserved someone better than Arlo for his savior. Because Lethe saw it—he *had* to. He had to spend so much of his time and concern on shielding her from harm—on worrying over her—but he had to know, deep inside, that he deserved better.

"I could give him better."

Hero stared down at his hands—lost in thought—at the gloves he wore, the only things that wouldn't turn gold when he touched them; this alchemically reinforced leather was all that acted as barrier between the unique magic his philosopher's stone granted him and the rest of the world.

Hero could give Lethe better, could give them *all* better. He could be the Immortal Realm's champion—he already was, they just couldn't see it because they were too focused on this *child* to realize what they had!

He wouldn't call off his Reaper. Lethe didn't have to know he'd given it additional purpose in sending it out into the world. It was no mistake it had gone after Arlo, and now that Hero knew just what was at stake, he was more determined than ever to take care of this problem for his Hunter. But first . . . maybe a peek. Maybe he should pay Arlo Jarsdel a visit in person, just to see if there was something his reports weren't telling him.

Arlo would die, no matter what.

Lethe would be free.

A little peek wouldn't hurt anything, would confirm what he already knew, and everyone would realize it was Hero that they should look to, Hero that they should give both their protections and their—*"Gah!"*

He clapped his hands around his ears, wincing at the shrill sound of the alarm that had suddenly gone off.

The lights turned red.

He scrambled for the elevator at the end of the hall.

Someone had just come across his laboratory who didn't have his permission to be here. His night had started out so well—how had it devolved to this?

"Doc!" a goblin shouted the moment Hero exited the elevator back onto the main floor. This one he knew by name—Pincer, easy enough to remember, thanks to the iron incisors he'd had Hero implant to "make me look more intimidating to our rivals." Had he caught fire? The tail of his cloak was singed. "Vay the fae just tried to fucking kill me! He killed my brothers—I want more guns, I want *revenge!*"

Hero could only stare. "I'm sorry, who?"

CHAPTER 17

Nausicaä

⌒

D AMN IT!" NAUSICAÄ SWORE. "Damn it, damn it, *damn it!*"
She fisted her hands in her hair. She'd teleported out of the
High King's throne room with no real thought as to where
she would go, only that she wanted to get away—away from the High
King, crumbling apart beneath the weight of his heavy crown; away
from the Hunt, too stuck in past grievances to cut her any slack; away
from Arlo, who was definitely the mysterious "someone" Haru had
intended her to help in bringing her here.

Nausicaä groaned.

Her fingers gripped her hair a little tighter.

She'd rematerialized atop the hub of Toronto's CN Tower, the city's
tallest structure, sprouting from its core like a massive concrete thorn.
It was about as far "away" as magic would let her fly, because Haru was
a jerk, and her debt to him had yet to be fulfilled.

Arlo . . .

With her Viridian green eyes and fire-bright hair, and all that
rose-pink glow under lace-white skin, Arlo looked nothing like
Tisiphone to her now, to a point it was laughable Nausicaä had ever
seen a resemblance between them to begin with.

And she *liked* her.

That was probably the worst of it.

Nausicaä actually *liked* this Arlo Jarsdel. She didn't know her all
that well, but in their brief acquaintance so far, Arlo had shown a stub-
bornness, a determination, a ferociousness that reminded Nausicaä
strongly of herself. But there was gentleness to her as well, and loyalty, and love—things Nausicaä had once possessed but lost when

Tisiphone had died; things Arlo had no idea she probably shouldn't wear so boldly on her sleeve for how cruel the world was to any shred of goodness.

That was Red, she was learning—*good*. Sheltered, sure, and extremely timid in certain moments, but no less strong for that hesitation.

Then there was the fact that she'd come after Nausicaä in that alley behind the club, never mind the Reaper, and the Hunt, and the dead body, and the fact that Nausicaä was a stranger Arlo had not long ago suspected of murdering children. There was the fact that she'd tried to stand up to the High King and vouch for Nausicaä's innocence, which no one—*no one*—had done since everything had gone to absolute shit in Nausicaä's life.

Remember our deal.

You'll know when you meet them.

You'll help. I'll take you.

"*Damn it*, Haru!" Nausicaä slammed her hands on the stone ledge that fenced the top of the tower's bulbous hub. The changeling boy's words floated back to her—the deal she'd struck with him in exchange for bringing her here—impossible to forget, impossible to escape without consequence, the sort even Nausicaä wouldn't want to pay. "I'm never making another deal with a changeling—ever," she growled under her breath. "Nothing has gone right since coming here!"

She was no closer to catching her Reaper or discovering the identity of its master. For all that talking with Cyberniskos had been interesting, she hadn't learned anything new from their game except that there were so many more people walking around with half-baked philosopher's stones in their chest than she would have guessed, and none seemed to know they were there. She had no answers, no direction to go from here, and on top of it all, she'd pissed off the High King enough to sic his Hunt after her.

Was this even worth it anymore?

She'd started after this Reaper as a way of drawing the immortals' attention and making them regret sending her here. At the moment, though, the only person regretting anything was *her*. After all the distance she'd tried to put between herself and her past, the investigation this curiosity had turned into was too much like her previous life for her comfort—and now, if she wanted to continue with it, she'd have to play it cautious.

Caution was something Nausicaä had never been much good at observing.

"I'm starting to take this personally," she muttered at the stars. With a sigh, she deflated and slumped over the tower's ledge. "What did I ever do to you?"

A crow landed beside her, not far from Nausicaä's arm.

She rolled her head to gaze at it sullenly. "There's sure been a lot of *you* around here. Precious little spring flower Arlo . . . Hard to believe she's UnSeelie born like the rest of you big bad nightmares."

The crow cocked its head.

It wasn't really a crow. It was far too big and far too black, and its eyes were such a deep shade of claret they too might pass for black at a glance, but Nausicaä knew better. The sluagh croaked and clicked its beak, and its tiny shards of wicked-sharp teeth glinted in the moonlight overhead.

"Eat anyone exciting lately?"

The sluagh croaked once more. Then, with a ruffle of feathers, it leaped into the sky and took off as silently as it had arrived. Nausicaä watched it swoop back down into the city, oddly elegant for a vicious demon that preyed on the souls of dead folk, but that was the UnSeelie faction—elegant, vicious demons the lot . . . except maybe Arlo. And not that the Seelie were much better, for all they took pains to pretend otherwise.

Nausicaä sighed.

Toronto was vicious elegance too. From way up high, the city looked like an open maw. Night draped ebony velvet over the fang points of its numerous buildings, disguising their promise of death, and the many glowing lights woven into this deceptive veil reminded Nausicaä of the souls the stars kept watch over.

It was beautiful.

It was deadly.

But it was nothing she hadn't seen before—cities were all the same.

Far down below, a streetlamp popped. Nausicaä watched it fall to darkness, her sight much stronger than anything a mortal possessed but still not as good as it used to be. "I'm just so *tired* of all of this," she grumbled.

She missed her old life.

It wasn't often she allowed herself to admit this, but she missed being a Fury. She missed having sisters, a mother, and friends, and people who cared whether or not she lived or died. Of course, outside of Tisiphone, she'd apparently never had any of that to start with—Megaera, Eris, her mother, the immortals and deities and various Others she'd counted as her "people" hadn't cared a lick about her in the end. When all she'd wanted was someone to understand why she was upset, when all she'd needed was their sympathy—a freaking *hug*, damn it, would have gone a long way—the people she'd once thought loved her had only turned their backs and branded her a monster.

Arlo was nice.

It didn't matter.

She was probably going to die because the Courts were an absolute mess and their government was horrible, and all that impossible, immortal strength inside this mortal girl—which Nausicaä still didn't understand why Fate had given her, but *whatever*—was going to rebound eventually. Arlo wouldn't be allowed to give that power a proper outlet. The Courts would never let her practice alchemy. Her own magic would destroy her the moment she Matured into it, and if she somehow survived, the immortals and their insatiable hunger would ruin her in its place.

Another streetlamp popped.

Nausicaä raised a brow.

Another popped . . . and then another.

Lifting her head, Nausicaä watched the admittedly weird phenomenon with budding interest. The streetlights continued to blow, and the traffic beneath them came to a halt. Honking horns and disgruntled shouts perforated the city's baseline din, the sudden loss of light enough to startle drivers into a steadily growing pileup. Darkness swept through the street like an illness, dousing more than lamps but also the lights in the buildings now too. Confusion and murmurs and fear wafted up to Nausicaä's haunt, but most curious of all was when that darkness veered, pouring straight into the depths of a random alley, filling it like a well, and went no farther.

". . . Huh."

Was this magic or a simple power outage running wild with Nausicaä's imagination? The question answered itself almost as soon as she thought it. That darkness continued to expand in the alley, and every crow in the city that wasn't a crow took to the air. The sluagh rose up around Nausicaä, heavy as a cloud of swarming locusts, and the glee in their deafening caws jumpstarted her adrenaline.

It was magic, then.

The sluagh converged over the alley, circling above as though a storm.

She couldn't *not* go see what caused such a stir in the local wildlife, and so she leaped from the tower.

Like crumbling rock, she plummeted toward the street, air streaming past her with the force of rushing water. As she fell, she unspooled. Her own brand of darkness burst from her back—her wings, or at least, as much of them as she could bring herself to use anymore. What they'd been reduced to . . . It hurt her too much to see, reminded her too acutely of what she'd lost. But these shadows still served their purpose. Flaring wide, they mediated her descent, and as soon as her feet hit the ground, she took off at a run.

Whatever this was, it was big. The Falchion Police Force would arrive before long. All she wanted was a peek—maybe the faerie responsible for causing this stir would be willing to have a chat if she could whisk it off to safety.

She skidded to a halt outside the alley. She couldn't sense magical auras by scent anymore as she'd been able to do as a Fury, but whatever seethed in this darkness, its magic prickled the back of her neck, cool as death. It was almost familiar. She tried to focus her senses and search for a threat of clarity, but whatever masked this magic's identity was strong.

It was almost like someone *else's* glamour had been thrown on top of this aura.

"Are you kidding me?"

Excitement thrummed even headier in Nausicaä's veins. Throwing one's glamour over someone else's magic was a talent not many could perform. Throwing one's glamour over someone else's magic with enough strength to shield that magic from immortal detection . . . It was the very thing that would help, oh, perhaps a Reaper roam unchecked through the greatest Court of Folk?

She didn't think it likely the High King could actually have anything to do with this—the Reaper, or the dying ironborn. His sanity was slipping, yes, but he'd always seemed proud of his position, fond of his people, determined to do right by them. Still, pretty much everything going on now was absurd, and really . . . it wasn't her wildest theory.

The High King couldn't perform alchemy, but how difficult would it be to hire someone who could? And it didn't take iron blood to *use* a stone. In the twilight of his life . . . any time now, someone would make a play for his crown . . . It wasn't totally preposterous that he could want to try to keep it long as possible, and what better way to do so than with a philosopher's stone to serve as additional amplification of his power?

"Guess we'll find out." She stepped into the alley. "Please be the Reaper, please be the Reaper, please be the Reap—"

The darkness exploded.

Nausicaä blew backward, hardly able to make sense of events. All she knew was that one minute the pricking on the back of her neck spread cold as icy water over her body—and the next, she was blinking up at the sky, ears ringing. She lay on the sidewalk clear across the street, the clean-shaven face of a young man peering down at her.

"Easy now," the man cautioned when Nausicaä shot upright. "Hey, are you okay?"

Nausicaä shook her head, hoping to silence the ringing in her ears. "What happened?"

"What *didn't* happen." The man shook his head as well. "Gas leak . . . power outage . . . pileup . . . reports of a minor explosion too, in that alley over there, but . . ." He gestured behind him, at the perfectly undisturbed alley, no sign of the darkness that had lashed out at Nausicaä. "Could you look over here for a moment, please?"

Nausicaä looked where instructed. The man was dressed in uniform, reflective bands around his dark navy pant legs and sleeves, and a badge up by his shoulder that marked him a paramedic. She swatted him away. "I'm fine."

"Well, I don't think that's likely. You were unconscious. Can you follow my finger, please?"

"Can you follow mine?" She shot him the one in the middle.

Despite himself, the paramedic laughed. "Okay, your teenage moodiness isn't broken. What about the rest of you? How are you feeling?"

"Annoyed." She got to her feet. The paramedic protested loudly, but Nausicaä didn't have time to assuage his concerns. Yes, she looked like a teenager. Urielle had made her this way. Yes, she was technically still teenage by immortal standards too. Yes, she was going to spend the rest of her eternity here being coddled by adult strangers centuries younger than her. Sometimes it worked in her favor. Sometimes it got in her way—like now, when all she wanted was to get a good look at the alley now swarming with police. "Gas leak," she snorted. "Humans."

"Wait, Miss, you shouldn't—"

Nausicaä crossed the street, pulling her hair into a bun behind her head and tying it off. If the human police force were here, then so was the Falchion. Many of its members acted as double agents, working both teams to ensure the magical community would be first on any scene that might need covering up. She'd have to steer clear of them; if the High King had an arrest warrant out for her, drawing their attention would mean never confirming what had been in that alley, among other problems.

If she still possessed her former powers, she'd be able to warp herself completely invisible and poke around at her leisure. Fortunately, she could still rely on other tricks.

"What a mess," Nausicaä grunted, coming up beside a human officer making notes on a pad of paper.

The officer looked up. He was a Black man, fresh-faced and umber-eyed, with buzzed short black hair, a strong, clean-shaven jawline, and thick arms—tall, too, but so was Nausicaä, and the strength in her own build played nicely into her facade. When the officer looked at her, he didn't see a teenage girl in dust-coated leather pants, no shoes, and a black mesh top that was now torn in various places. Nausicaä looked to all the world like another human officer, her powerful glamour weaving the mask of a pristine uniform and unscathed skin.

"Tell me about it," the officer replied. "Have you seen inside yet?"

"No time like the present, eh?"

The officer jerked his chin at the alley. "Hope you didn't eat a heavy dinner." He went back to making notes on his paper. Nausicaä hadn't really expected it to be *this* easy to get past the security keeping the rest of Toronto at bay, but if Officer Brown-Eyes didn't care enough to question a uniform he'd never seen around before, Nausicaä wasn't going to argue.

"Evening," she bid to the two other officers positioned outside the alley. Both were human. The Falchion members were gathered around a squad car; she could pick them out by the hum of magic in the air around them. Sharing coffee from a thermos, not at all interested in the alley or what the humans were doing in it—odd behavior, considering it was definitely magic that had caused so much chaos tonight.

"Badge?"

Finally. It was no fun playing at someone she wasn't if nobody would let her spin the lies that immortals could weave just fine. Reaching into her back pocket, she fished out the badge she'd nicked from the previous officer. The person protecting their Reaper wasn't the only one who could throw a little glamour on something else. When she handed over her badge, the officer checking it saw Nausicaä's made-up info and nothing of the Greg Jordan it actually belonged to.

The officer nodded and waved her through. Nausicaä pocketed her badge and passed between them.

Gone was the darkness that had filled the alley before. Most of the sluagh had disbanded too, but dozens remained on the lips of surrounding buildings, watching the scene in their crow disguises. Sluagh excitement was a sure sign of magic; they only went after its children, the folk—or, more precisely, their souls. As they were scavengers, their meals depended on them being quicker to reach the dead than Cosmin's Hunters, so if sluaghs were still hanging about, then so was that prize they were after. Did the Falchion truly find nothing worth their attention here?

She pressed past the CSIs and other officers hard at work destroying the scene. The focal point was a mangled body—young, female, red-haired, and pale even for a corpse—undeniably victim to her Reaper's wicked purpose, just like all the others. For a split second, Nausicaä could swear it was Arlo. She had to shake her head to clear the image.

"Hmm."

One of the officers—a woman with golden-tanned skin and short auburn hair pulled back behind her head—looked up at Nausicaä. "Hmm, what?"

"They're kind of . . . old to fit the pattern, don't you think?"

273

"Pattern?"

Nausicaä rolled her eyes. "The bodies in the news, of course. Mostly teens and children. Mangled . . . torn apart . . . just like this one, except whoever this is must be close to thirty. Have you checked inside their chest?"

The officer pulled a look of disgust. "Uh . . . no? Hang on, wait! You can't just—"

Nausicaä had crouched down and, amidst several cries of alarm, thrust her hand inside one of the body's gaping holes. "What are you *doing*?" Nausicaä rummaged around. Her fingers closed over the organ she sought, but unlike the others, this one was warm, slippery, and fleshy soft in her grip.

"It's just a regular heart!"

"What the hell were you expecting?"

She withdrew her hand.

A quick scan for residual magic told Nausicaä that the victim had a modest amount of it while alive. White, female, red hair stained even darker for the bloody pool around it . . . *red* blood. This was definitely an ironborn member of the folk, but she was perfectly ordinary. The Falchion's disinterest meant she'd most likely been designated fully human on her Weighing by the Fae High Council, yet this was without a doubt the work of Nausicaä's Reaper.

"But you didn't have a stone," Nausicaä mused. "Why did it go after you?"

"Listen, I don't know what you're going on about right now, but you can't just go around sticking your hand inside dead bodies. I think you need to leave."

"Yeah," said Nausicaä, astonishment soft in her tone. "Yeah, I think I do."

None of this made any sense. This change of pattern . . . Had her Reaper just been hungry? Had this even been a Reaper attack at all? Nothing about this latest victim's lingering aura suggested she'd ever practiced dark magic, but that didn't mean these creatures wouldn't go after anything else if their preferred meal couldn't be found.

And the way this young woman had been splayed in death, it was too similar to the way *her* Reaper killed for this to be anything else, unless there were a whole-ass *two* of these monsters roaming around Toronto, chasing separate goals. But Reapers were intelligent enough to keep their out-of-bounds creeping to lower-profile cities. And no one would be stupid enough to try to wrangle more than one Reaper to whatever their evil scheme was and then parade them *both* through the High King's very congested capital. The Hunt would notice . . . the Furies would notice . . . *people* would notice—they should all be noticing now a hell of a lot more than they were, and—"*Urgh*, I'm so confused! What is even happening here?"

She stalked out of the alley, frustration sprouting an ache in her temples.

This didn't add up. . . . She was missing some very important clue. It was staring her right in the face, and she couldn't see it—she was too close.

Which meant it was time.

Nikos wasn't going to be happy—they hadn't parted on very good terms. But it was time to talk to someone who actually cared about things, someone who made it their business to keep an eye on *all* the communities, not just the fae.

At some point, Nausicaä was going to have to make "friends" with someone who *wasn't* steeped in illegal activity, if only to give her life some variety.

CHAPTER 18

Arlo

~~~⟡~~~

"Y OU WILL *NOT* BE seeing Celadon for a while," Thalo
announced the next morning, storming into their condo's
kitchen of black-granite countertops, heated hardwood
flooring, and pristine stainless-steel appliances.

"*Mom—*"

"Don't you 'mom' me, young lady." Blustering around the island
at the center of this room—where Arlo sat gloomily prodding her
bowl of Cheerios—Thalo planted herself directly opposite her daughter and glared. "I am *appalled* by your behavior last night—the *both* of
you. I know Celadon isn't much older than you are. He's still a teenager for all it counts. But he's also a prince, and he should damn well
start acting with the responsibility of this station. He had no business
pulling you into this! That it even *occurred* to him . . ." She trailed off
in a frustrated growl, resuming the task of angrily gathering her russet
hair into a tie behind her head.

"And this isn't the first time he's done something like this! The
two of you when you get together—I've made my allowances,
considering . . . but I've had it! The Fae High Council . . . the other
royal families . . . hell, most of the Courts find Celadon Viridian an
obnoxious, spoiled child. He's so puffed up on his own perceived
intelligence and importance that he doesn't stop for a second to
think of the way his 'jokes' and 'tricks' and clever little 'plans' affect
other people. Innocent people! His own *family.*" Her tirade ended in
another snarl that took a moment to calm.

Arlo's feelings about what her mother had said must have been
too clear on her face, though, because Thalo revved back up again

with, "Don't you look at me like that. You think he doesn't see how you idolize him? You think *I* don't see it? How every passing year you become more and more like him and that poor nephew of his. That Serulian and Elexa leave their young, impressionable boy to the worst caretaker they could possibly choose out of anyone in the palace when they go away . . . if it were up to me—"

"Well, it's *not!*" Arlo asserted hotly, throwing her spoon into her bowl. "It's not up to you who looks after Elyas—a perfectly kind and wonderful boy, *by the way*, just like Cel—"

"This hero worship is exactly what I'm talking about—Celadon can do no wrong, can he?"

Groaning, Arlo slid off her stool and onto her feet. "This isn't Celadon's fault. I'm the one who—"

"Not entirely, no, but he should have done more—anything—to stop you. Do you realize what you did? Do you realize that after all the stress of your Weighing and all that's been done to keep you in this family, you could have ruined everything completely with this stunt? And Celadon did nothing but encourage you. He's forced my hand here. You will *not* be seeing him until the both of you get your act together, *and* you're going to live with your father in the fall."

Arlo's face fell. "What?"

"This irresponsibility, Arlo, makes me seriously question whether you're ready to live on your own. If you decide to go to school in the fall, you're going to spend the first year with your father, where he can keep a better eye on you than I apparently can. Once you've demonstrated sufficient maturity, you'll be able to move into residence. You're also going to make some more friends. *Different* friends. I mean it, it's not healthy having only Celadon to hang around with, especially since his influence is the reason behind your spectacular immaturity last night."

"What, so you're kicking me out now?"

"No, that's not what this is, but—"

"I'm eighteen, so where I live if I go to school is my business! And while we're at it, if I want to see Celadon, that's *also* my business."

"Yeah? Well, you're my daughter. You're always going to be *my* business, and so long as you're living under this roof, you're going to have to abide by *my* rules. If you think your father and I aren't both going to keep a closer watch on you now, you've got another think coming." Thalo's disapproval etched deep into her face. "School aside, you and Celadon are banned from spending time together right now—that's final. And the next time you want to play detective with a bunch of criminals, Arlo, maybe you'll remember that your actions have consequences. Somebody *died* last night, do you understand that? That somebody could have been you."

"Well, it might as well have been!" Arlo shouted, throwing her hands into the air and marching out of the kitchen. She knew she was being childish, but she didn't care. Her mother's words were a painful reminder of what she found the hardest to shake: that people were dying; that she'd *witnessed* that death; and that very easily, Arlo could have been a target, could still yet be, because really, how did she know *she* didn't have a stone inside her waiting to go off?

For the first time in her life, Arlo was genuinely afraid of the magic she'd wanted so badly.

For the first time, she wished she were human and nothing else.

"Don't say that!" Thalo hollered after her, following close behind. "And don't you walk away from me—"

Ignoring her mother hot on her heels, Arlo stormed down the hall and back to her bedroom. She understood that Thalo was angry, but that didn't mean she had to like it. It wasn't okay that her life was being decided for her, and that suddenly there was an embargo placed on her friendship with one of the incredibly few people who took active interest in that life to begin with.

How many private lessons had Celadon relayed to try to help keep her up to speed with what the Courts demanded she learn? How many of his days and nights had he spent keeping her company in this lonely apartment when work kept her parents too busy to be at their respective homes? How much of his time had he sacrificed over the years, trying to coax just a bit more magic from Arlo so that she could impress the Council enough to let her stay? Even when Arlo had given up on herself, Celadon hadn't.

Celadon meant just as much to Arlo as her own mother and father. He was family. He loved her and supported her and never once made her feel like she was weird or didn't belong, or that she owed him anything for his attention.

She knew her parents loved her. She knew her mother worked tirelessly at her job, not just for her own sake but for Arlo's, too, and that good standing with the High King was the reason their lives were so comfortable. She knew it had to be hard being a single parent, and that it wasn't anyone's fault she was an only child who had to do so much on her own. Thalo was reacting this way out of fear for Arlo, but that didn't make any of this easier to swallow. In her current temper, Arlo didn't feel like giving her mother an inch.

"Just go to work," she snapped. Finally, she reached her bedroom door. "Leave me alone."

Thalo halted a few steps behind, stuffing a hand onto her hip. "There will be no more interaction between you and your cousin until I say so, understood?"

"Fine."

"And you're grounded."

"I figured."

"That means no going out anywhere unless it's to school, work, or your father's place. I'll know if you do."

Of course she would. Part of Thalo's job as General of the Falchion meant that if Arlo pushed her luck any further, her mother could have each and every step Arlo took shadowed, despite the fact that this technically wasn't allowed; law forbade tracking the under-age. "Got it." Drawing a breath through her nose, blinking furiously to hold back her tears, Arlo kept her face angled to the door. "Are we done?"

Her mother's reply was simply to spin on the heels of her boots and stalk back down the hall. Clenching her teeth, Arlo kicked her bedroom door open and slammed it closed behind her. Crossing her room to fling herself on her unmade bed, she snatched her phone off the table beside it, knocking the die she'd received from the not-troll to the floor.

She watched it roll to a stop, landing on the number four.

I don't want you to be a hero, Arlo Jarsdel . . . , the not-troll had said before giving her this mysterious gift. *What I want you to be is my Hollow Star.*

A hero . . . a Hollow Star (whatever that was, really) . . . a responsible adult, but also, *keep out of trouble, Arlo, you're just a child and we know best.*

She'd be a little more offended that nobody seemed to want her to just be herself if she even knew who "herself" was. Tired . . . lonely . . . *afraid . . .*

A disappointment.

"Wait a minute . . ." She shot back upright.

That die shouldn't be here. She clearly remembered throwing it at the Reaper and obviously hadn't paused her flight to pick it back up. Was this some sort of magic? Was this stupid thing spelled to follow her around for the rest of her life?

Grumbling—wondering why she'd even accepted the useless thing to begin with, because it certainly hadn't done much for her so far— she leaned over the edge of her bed to scoop it off the floor and dump it into her bedside table drawer, then went back to her phone.

11:53 p.m. Dad: Just got off the phone with your mother. You and Celadon snuck into a nightclub? Thalo is livid. I'm not that impressed myself. We need to have a chat tomorrow, young lady.

12:28 a.m. Elyas: Grandpa's been yelling at uncle cel for like 10 years. They took his phone away. MUST BE SERIOUS!!! What did u guys do now?

12:40 a.m. Elyas: Srsly are u oaky?

12:40 a.m. Elyas: *okay?

News Top Stories:
Gas leak in downtown Toronto to blame for serious accident leaving one dead, numerous injured.

Arlo read the messages on her lock screen and sighed. She hadn't looked at it all night, and in her miserable self-pity had trudged out for breakfast without a glance at the screen. Apparently, the world carried on regardless of personal distress.

It would be interesting to hear how her mother had spun this particular act of "teenage rebellion" into something Rory would understand. But even if her father most likely thought this nothing worse than an attempt at underage drinking, she still didn't want to listen to his disappointment with her either.

Then there was Elyas, who, by now, must have been fully apprised of the situation. Arlo felt guilty all over again for her part in causing this argument between not only her family, but the young prince's, too. Tapping his message, she unlocked her phone.

Arlo: Thanks El, I'm okay. Sorry to worry you . . . I feel bad. Messed up and things got intense and now I'm under house arrest until I die or decide to go to uni. Something like that. Is Cel okay? He isn't in too much trouble, is he?

Her heart raced, watching the blinking ellipsis spring into the bottom corner of the screen. Arlo feared the worst for her cousin but was hopeful that, since Elyas wasn't all that panicked about his uncle, his punishment hadn't been quite as severe as the High King's mood could have made it.

Elyas: There was SO MUCH YELLING. Oh my gods, I've never heard grandpa that angry before. Pretty sure that WAS the punishment too, because ive never seen uncle cel cry either and his face was really wet when he came all winded bull troll out of the throne. I think they were both just scared about you being in danger. Grandpa likes you, you know he does. You're family. He likes Uncle Cel too and he's ALWAYS an idiot. So, he's been grounded, and forbidden from talking to u and going over to your place for a while, but nothing like super terrible. Actual quote forbidden tho. When grandpa stopped yelling to let him go ur mom called to yell at him and now everybodys mad at everybody else and we'll probably grow up estranged and see each otter in twenty to fifty years.

Elyas: *each other

With another sigh, Arlo dropped her phone to the bed and flopped onto her back, staring up at her ceiling.

Wonderful.

A family feud.

If Arlo had just minded her own business, hadn't tried to play that hero Fate had wanted her to be, had just let Celadon and the others take care of things like they promised they would, then they wouldn't be in this mess.

If she'd just been a little more decisive back with the not-troll, or maybe watched where she was going after to not run into that lesidhe man, or hadn't followed Nausicaä into that back alley where a Reaper lay in wait, she could have left the club like she'd intended instead of throwing her entire night into chaos. If she hadn't been at that café . . . if she hadn't been an ironborn . . .

This wasn't the first time Celadon and Arlo's mother had gotten into a spat over something—it wasn't even the first time they'd gotten into a spat over Celadon's "reckless endangerment" of Thalo's only child—but it was certainly the angriest she'd ever been, much like the

High King, who'd actually threatened to *arrest her* if Arlo didn't watch her step from now on.

There was nothing else for it; "watch her step" was exactly what she was going to do.

Fae were incredibly patient—unsurprising, in a people whose lives spanned hundreds of years—and Thalo was particularly good at holding on to a grudge when given cause to be difficult. But if Arlo played by her mother's rules and kept her nose out of trouble for a while, this would blow over.

It had to.

Her phone vibrated again, alerting her to another message. She fished it out from her duvet to check.

Elyas: I can feel you panicking about this from here. Don't worry Arlo. Everything will be ok. It's Saturday, you work today right? Double shift right? Yuck have fun! Cel said to tell you sorry btw.

Arlo: Thanks El. Love you both. And IM the one who's sorry. Cel didn't do anything wrong

She slid her phone back onto her bedside table and hauled herself upright. She did have to get ready for her usual Saturday shift at Starbucks, which would start in a couple of hours. After the night she'd spent furious and scared and crying into her pillow, she definitely needed a shower first.

"No more trouble," she said to the innocuous stars dangling from the center of her canopy netting.

Arlo wanted no more part in the things that were happening around her.

Whatever the reason for the High King's refusal to investigate Nausicaä's claims, whatever the story behind these so-called philosopher's stones and the Reaper and the reason why people were being used to grow dark magic in their very hearts, Arlo was done.

She wasn't going to involve herself in this danger any longer.

She was no hero. She was done with all the mystery and death that had started taking over her life, with making things worse every time she tried to make them better, with drawing attention to herself in all the wrong ways. The adults could decide what to do about the dying ironborn, and potential alchemy, and terrible threats against them. Arlo would focus on school and life as it had been before the café. She'd force herself to channel her energy toward something other than her fears, and in time, both her mother and the High King would forgive her.

In time, she could put this entire chapter of her life behind her, and Cassandra's face would no longer burn in the fore of her mind; Cassandra's mother's crying would no longer ring in her ears; the hulking shadow and gory stench of a Reaper would never again haunt her nightmares, as it had done last night.

In time, Arlo would no longer worry whether the flutter that had just passed through her chest at the reminders of all the things she wanted to forget was anything more sinister than anxiety.

CHAPTER 19

Vehan

THE ENDLESS ATRIUM WAS Vehan's favorite room in the Luminous Palace of Summer. It was cavernous, a vast expanse of polished white soapstone, marble, and granite under a dome of diamond glass. Beautiful sunbursts and clouds so airy light that they could hardly be mere depictions had been carved into the walls, all of them leafed in the same brilliant gold as what filled the fissures-like-bolts-of-lightning that streaked through the floor.

It was here where every corridor led. It was here where some began, accessible by no other means than this room, as though the Endless Atrium were the heart keeping the palace alive, and these corridors were arteries. Vehan had spent much of his childhood exploring the halls of his home and still he suspected this heart contained secrets he'd yet to discover—much like his own, and perhaps that was why he liked this place so much.

"Do I want to know what you promised the guards to get them to let you do this?"

Vehan craned his head and grinned. "Probably not. It isn't my firstborn son, if that's what you're thinking."

"Funny," Aurelian said, looking wholly unamused. "Fine. I'm not going to stop you if they won't."

This was something of Aurelian's motto. While he'd never allowed Vehan to come to harm, he never held him back from trouble either— not recently, at least. He'd been a little more concerned about things in the height of their friendship. Perhaps Aurelian hoped that by proving himself an ill fit for Vehan, incapable of controlling his charge and keeping him safe, the queen would retract her honor and strip him of his role. Perhaps he just didn't care.

Vehan had yet to summon the courage required to determine which "perhaps" it truly was.

He turned his attention back to the mirror, the only object in the room. No other decoration existed apart from this—no other embellishment or fixture, not even a rug on the floor or potted plant against the wall. The Endless Atrium was home to the mirror it was named for and that alone, and though every sovereign of every Court possessed an Endless Egress, there were only the eight of them in total.

A portal.

A *true* portal—not like the glass they sold on mass production that could only take a person from their home to limited, predetermined locations and under strict conditions of operation. An Endless Egress was a mirror made of stardust from the stores the gods had left here in the Mortal Realm, pillaged when the Great Rebellion drove them out. An Endless Egress could take one anywhere they wished to go— even, many theorized, to realms outside their own. It was also a direct connection between the eight Courts and *their* mirrors, and for this it was kept under careful guard.

Fortunately, Vehan was on excellent terms with much of the palace staff, including Zale—with his beach-glass green hair, wide gray eyes, shell-brown and shimmery-toned skin—the current guard on mirror duty. Resplendent in his pearl-and-citrine ceremonial armor, Zale stood by the mirror pretending rather pointedly that neither Vehan nor Aurelian was here without permission. He stared at his perfectly manicured nails, examining their gloss in various slants of light. Never once did he look up, most likely for the cover of "No, I haven't *seen* your son, Your Majesty," should Vehan's mother come asking after him.

"Why doesn't she listen, Aurelian? Why doesn't she believe me? It's not like I can lie to her . . . Why would I even want to? If she'd just send a few people out into the desert, she'd be as sure of this as I am."

Aurelian took his time in replying, his very apparent desire to maintain distance between them at war with what Vehan knew to be a kind heart. "The disappearances . . . the glowing we saw in that boy . . . the bodies in the news . . . the alchemic symbols and that *thing* on your *chest* . . ." He paused to fix a pointed stare at Vehan's heart. "Your mother undoubtedly knows there's something more going on here, but getting any further involved means seeking permission from the High King, and you've heard the Summer council. His High Majesty has been acting 'strangely.' He hasn't been accepting audience with any Court official."

Vehan sighed.

If the High King had written this whole thing off as trivial simply because he didn't want it to be true, it would only lead to further problems. And if it fell to an eighteen-year-old, newly Matured fae barely old enough to carry the title "Crown Heir of Seelie Summer" to make their Head Sovereign see reason? So be it. Vehan wasn't going to let some aging king's paranoia lead them to destruction. But still, there were times he felt the weight of this task a little . . . unfair. "This would be so much easier if the adults would just act like adults right now," he muttered.

"Agreed."

Vehan sighed, rubbing his chest in thought. "Seelie Summer and UnSeelie Spring . . . Our two Courts have never been on the best of terms."

"Also agreed."

"It's a very bad idea to portal to the Spring Palace unannounced and demand an audience with the head of the entire magical community when he's clearly expressed his desire to be left alone."

"It is."

Biting his lip, Vehan cast a look up at his retainer. "This is dangerous. We could get into a lot of trouble—you might get more than fired as my future steward if you come with. I should order you to stay."

"I wouldn't listen."

He held his ground, despite the fact that what he was about to say might further the rift between them. "You would if I used your name."

"We have a deal." Aurelian looked down at him, expression tight and posture stiff.

They did. The lesidhe considered their true names even more precious than the sidhe did. They only gave them to those they cherished deeply, and in swearing allegiance to Vehan as soon as Aurelian had Matured, Aurelian had been forced to betray this belief and offer up his name—another strike against Vehan, another thing that drove a wedge between them. Vehan had sworn his own oath, had given his own name in exchange to lessen the blow, and promised that if he ever used Aurelian's name against him—for anything—that it would release Aurelian from his duty afterward.

There were times Vehan was close to giving him what he wanted, to spending his name on something inconsequential and setting him free, but it would never be that simple. Aurelian's family would suffer for this slight against the queen's "generosity"—would face even worse judgment and gossip for being let go in such a manner—and both of them knew it.

Zale coughed.

It was then that Vehan realized he and Aurelian had been standing and staring at each other, wasting valuable time. "Right," he said. "Well, we should do this now, if we're doing it at all."

Giving himself a little shake, Vehan focused once more on the mirror. He placed a hand on its glass. It was warm under the touch, smooth, and somehow fluid, as though he'd placed his hand on the surface of calm water. He closed his eyes and called to mind exactly where he wanted to go. An Endless Egress could summon any place the traveler could picture, but there was no need for such direction when it came to traveling *between* them. As soon as his thoughts turned to the Reverdie and the mirror there contained, it rippled into view under his fingers.

"Ready?"

Aurelian nodded.

Vehan stepped through the glass, the surface giving way as easily as liquid. It was cool and slithery against his skin, but otherwise not unpleasant. Stepping out the other side, however, came with a colder, prickling sensation of the High King's magic stripping them of their glamours, causing him to shiver.

Vehan's true appearance was hair deepened to a black so dark it devoured the light around him; eyes brightened to blue so electric they almost sparked; porcelain-blue skin glowing soft as the dawn his faction worshipped; ears narrowed to noticeable points. His bone structure changed as well, taking on an ethereal, avian sharpness, and in his dark gold pants, cream-white shirt, and soft beige knee-length robe emblazoned with the sigil of Seelie Summer on its back (a sun, the beams of which were streaks of lightning that shimmered and crackled with every movement), there was nothing left to disguise who he was.

Beside him, Aurelian had also changed.

The fae didn't shed their glamours often, even in the privacy of their own homes. It was something of an unspoken challenge among them to see how long they could go without dropping their illusion, how far they could push their limits until resting was no longer optional.

Vehan didn't know whether lesidhe were similarly competitive or if Aurelian had adopted this behavior to fit in, but it was rare he got to see him like this, his tanned complexion now tinged with blue, his golden eyes molten hot, his leanness harder and angles sharper. None of his appeal was diminished by the formality of his current outfit—his palace uniform of straight-legged brown slacks and a white shirt, crisp in both cuff and collar, and an enamel sun pinned over his heart (the only designation of a station that Vehan's mother's steward had allegedly poisoned someone to obtain).

In fact, as ever, Aurelian was nothing less than beautiful.

There were times Vehan honestly thought his retainer was the most beautiful person he'd ever—

"Prince Vehan Lysterne, right on time."

Vehan tore his awe from Aurelian, startled. The UnSeelie Palace of Spring kept their Endless Egress a little differently. The room they now stood in was a much smaller chamber, carved from green instead of white and carpeted by a deeply emerald velvet that sank like mossy earth beneath their feet. Like the Endless Atrium, its ceiling was made of glass, but here those windows spilled down the walls, revealing the whole of Toronto beyond, and the limestone between them had been overtaken by twists of ivy, hanging vines, and vibrant bursts of flowers.

This room was more like a hothouse, located at the very top of the Tower. Only those of the highest clearance were permitted to use the mirror it housed in its center. As a prince of Summer and heir to his faction, Vehan was allowed such clearance, but he hadn't sought to secure it today. He shouldn't be expected . . . shouldn't be "right on time" according to anyone's schedule.

Drawing himself tall, Vehan eyed the fae before him. He was dressed in a finely tailored sage-and-charcoal suit that paired quite nicely with his lily-black skin, a darker tone of sapphire flush to him that marked him UnSeelie. The stark silver of his hair made his dagger-point features even more cutting, and poured full and thick and slightly waving just past the sharp flare of his shoulders, yet for all of this, the smile that played in the corner of his mouth was soft and genuine. "I wasn't aware there'd be a reception," said Vehan.

The unfamiliar fae folded his hands behind his back. "Your mother, Queen Riadne, sent word along that we might expect you," he explained simply, as though everything were fine and they hadn't been turning away delegates and concerned royalty alike for the last few weeks. "My name is Lekan, Head of House Otedola. If you'll follow me, I would be happy to escort you to more comfortable chambers. The High King has graciously accepted your mother's request for an audience when she explained how upset you've been made by certain events."

His mother?

His mother had arranged this? Vehan looked to Aurelian, who shrugged but said nothing.

Appreciation flared in Vehan's chest, alongside embarrassment. His mother was strict and didn't suffer his foolishness lightly, but she was a good person. She was helping him in her own way, and Vehan felt a bit of his faith in her renewed. "Excellent. Well then, yes, I've come to speak with His Majesty the High King. I . . . apologize for the short notice? I'm honored that as House Head, you'd go out of your way to receive me."

"Nonsense. And no apologies necessary. His High Majesty wishes only to assuage you of your worries—the children of his Courts should never suffer such concern. Come."

Vehan followed, Aurelian close at his back. The doors that led from the mirror's chamber opened into an elevator of even more limestone, glass, and verdant greenery. In silence they descended the Tower's many levels. It surprised him when they stopped much sooner than anticipated, among the floors considered private residence. This space was reserved for the Viridian royal family, his favored Houses (like the one Lord Lekan belonged to), the UnSeelie Spring representative on the Fae High Council and *their* family, and whoever else the Viridians deemed important enough for extended stay.

It was not a space for Vehan.

So far removed from the rest of them was the High King that when they stepped out of the elevator, it felt a bit to Vehan like stepping into the home of a long-ago god.

The hall that Lekan led them down was wide-flung and long, out-fitted in various tapestries and rugs, expensive artwork, and the occasional chandelier that looked more like upside-down hanging trees alight with countless fireflies.

They came at last to a room. Lekan pushed open the heavy doors and swept them through, giving Vehan very little time to run his fingers over the foliage and vines and blooming roses carved into its wooden frame.

"High Prince Celadon, what *are* you doing?"

Vehan choked on his breath, stopping so suddenly Aurelian nearly collided with his back.

The room was beautiful, every bit as much as the rest of what he'd seen of the palace. It was large and carpeted in the same plush moss that had been in the portal chamber, and the massive window at the opposite end allowed for a great deal of sunlight to filter in. Directly opposite him was a fireplace that could easily swallow ten of Vehan abreast, the mantel barely visible under ivy so dark a green the leaves dripped from it more like tar. Between this and where they stood was High Prince Celadon Cornelius Fleur-Viridian, poured over an emerald sofa, legs thrown over the back of the seat and russet head pointed at the ground.

"What does it look like I'm doing, Lekan? I'm waiting for my father."

Lekan sighed. "Your Highness, really, what more are you hoping for right now? You know His High Majesty has declared this matter concluded—"

"Concluded?" The High Prince forced a laugh that made Vehan wince, and spilled completely into the sofa to right himself around. The carelessly elegant movement tugged open the emerald silk housecoat he wore, revealing more of his pajamas: a plain white tank and sage silk sleep pants—not at all what Vehan expected of a fae well-known for his meticulously groomed appearance. "Concluded! There's a Reaper roaming the city, and Thalo won't let me anywhere near Arlo, possibly ever again, and my father refuses to . . . who is this?"

Vehan felt his eyes grow a fraction wider, realizing the brush of the High Prince's hand indicated *him*. Aurelian snorted. He alone knew Vehan perhaps sort of only a little bit completely worshipped the youngest son of the High King—he had been Vehan's first crush.

Celadon Viridian was handsome, charming, and wickedly clever. He made people laugh so easily, and despite all the mischief he got up to, was still somehow the darling of the magical community.

Of *course* Vehan was going to look up to that!

So what if he'd joined the fan club that had built itself around the High Prince? How else was he supposed to learn how to be like a fae he'd never met? And . . . okay, yes, he did have a poster . . . or two . . . but it was the High Prince! People had posters of all kinds of things, so why Aurelian found any amusement in this was beyond him. Aurelian's posters were all of things like human rocket ships and planets and something called the "periodic table," and in Vehan's opinion, that was the odder behavior.

He stepped forward. "Vehan Lysterne, Your Highness. Seelie Prince of Summer. This is Aurelian Bessel, my friend. We're here to meet with your father."

"Vehan?" The High Prince peered at him a little harder. The closer scrutiny made Vehan feel like melting through the floor. "Sorry, I didn't recognize you."

"That . . . that's all right! I was pretty young when you last visited the Luminous Palace. I didn't expect you to remember."

"Mmm, I'm sure. No one ever expects anything of me at all until it's everything at once."

Vehan floundered. He wasn't sure what he was supposed to say to that.

"Celadon," Lekan reprimanded firmly. To Vehan, he said, "The High Prince apologizes. Ignore him. He's wholly unpleasant when he's pouting."

"Oh, piss off, Lekan, I can apologize for myself."

"I don't hear you doing so . . ."

The High Prince groaned heavily. "I'm so sorry for directing emotions at you, Prince Vehan."

"That was not an apology."

"Uh . . . we can come back another time, if that would be better?" Vehan hedged.

"No, we can't," Aurelian asserted, and when Vehan whipped his head to stare, found him glaring down the High Prince. "We came to speak with the High King, not his petulant son. High Prince Celadon can come back another time, if that would suit *him* better."

Vehan's eyes grew even wider. Aurelian's comment caught him between amazement and horror. One the one hand, it was oddly pleasant to have Aurelian defending him; on the other hand, Aurelian had just mouthed off to the *High Prince*. "What my friend means to say—"

"Your friend said what he meant to say," the High Prince cut in, his tone indecipherable. His expression looked just as set to declare the Seelie Court of Summer excommunicated as to ask after the weather there.

"All right, yes, he said what he meant to say." Vehan squared his jaw, firm despite his nerves, and added, "Should we leave?"

The High Prince glanced between them, then sank back against the sofa. He appeared . . . exceptionally drained. "I'm sorry. Don't leave. My comments were uncalled for. You came to speak with my father—what about?"

Vehan hadn't intended to share the particulars with anyone other than the High King. Who knew who they could trust? How far this deadly plot had reached? He didn't want to risk the wrong ears overhearing how much they'd already discovered, but the High Prince— the High royals, in general—possessed a command none of the folk could ignore. They didn't need to speak a name to inspire compliance. Vehan would have to be a little more truthful here than he liked. "It concerns the deaths in the human news. I have information he may be interested in learning."

The High Prince stared at him.

The look wore on long enough that Vehan felt the need to add, "I know it's not my place, I'm not the head of my family yet, or my faction, but there's so much more going on here than I think you realize, and all these deaths in the news . . . We both know this isn't the cause of some human serial killer?"

The High Prince said nothing. He only continued to stare. Vehan felt his heart begin to race, his mouth about to spill more secrets his brain wanted to keep to silence.

"It's not," said the High Prince at last. "It's my firm belief that our ironborn are being targeted by someone within our own community."

"There *is* something going on with the humans, though. They're disappearing. Abducted off the streets . . . bought and paid for by someone hiding deep within the criminal underworld, someone dabbling in this."

The High Prince cocked his head.

Reaching into the back pocket of his pants, Vehan extracted a piece of paper and held it out in front of him—a drawing of the symbol that had been etched on the door in the desert ground. He hadn't slept at all last night, had busied his hands with sketching out what his mind refused to let go of for rest.

The High Prince nodded to Lekan to bring it to him, and when he saw what was sketched on its surface, his back snapped immediately rigid.

Vehan blinked. "You know what that is?" Whatever higher clearance the High Prince enjoyed, alchemy had been stamped out of practice hundreds of years ago—well before his time. He shouldn't know what this was, not without having gone out of his way to familiarize himself with it.

"I do," replied the High Prince, his tone faint. "I think. It's . . . an array. All these symbols and this writing . . . it's alchemy."

The room fell entirely still. Even the air sat heavier.

Despite this, relief washed over Vehan like bathwater, warm and soothing. "That's what we thought too. The High King will help us, won't he? In the very least, we're hoping he'll give us permission to look through the alchemical tomes and notes he guards, from the alchemists who used to serve the Courts. Maybe if—"

"Oh no, he absolutely won't."

Vehan's mouth fell open. Before he could ask why he wouldn't, the High Prince rose from his seat. Gone was his fatigue. Even his mood seemed to recover. The wind he commanded stormed fierce and bright in his jade-green eyes, and the twilight glow to his sapphire flush darkened into navy night. The High Prince moved with frightening grace to hand Lekan the paper, and they shared a look between them. Lekan nodded, and the High Prince spun to face them. "My father won't help. He's . . . well, when you've finished your talk with him, I suggest you take a stroll with Lekan. We were going to meet with someone today—someone who knows much more about what's going on than we do, but maybe she'd respond a little better to you. The Dark Star and I . . . our first meeting didn't get off to a very good start, and ended even worse."

"The *Dark Star*?" Vehan blurted, looking at the High Prince in astonishment. "The Dark Star is *here*?" Had they finally managed to catch her and learn something substantial?

The High Prince nodded. "She is."

"She isn't seriously the one behind this, is she? I . . . didn't think my mother would actually be right about that." This really didn't seem to fit what he'd known of her, but then, what did Vehan know about anything anymore?

"I don't believe so, no. But that's true . . . Your mother did accuse her of being a murderer. I suppose she must dislike us equally, then." He sighed, then pursed his lips, looking Vehan over so intensely that Vehan had to fight the urge to smooth out invisible creases in his clothes, and held himself at stiff attention.

The High Prince could gather secrets from the very air, if he knew where to look and what to ask for—that was the rumor, at least. It had never been confirmed. But Vehan couldn't help wondering at the moment whether he could also read minds, and really hoped that if he could, he wouldn't press far enough to discover he'd starred *very* inappropriately in many of Vehan's dreams when he'd been younger. And hells—now he was panicking harder. Thinking about it made it even clearer in his mind, even easier to overhear!

"I still like our chances better with you than me."

Vehan almost blew out a breath and sagged in visible relief when the High Prince had spoken and carried on with no mention of Vehan's embarrassing thoughts.

"Besides, it might be better if I don't risk getting caught in the place you needed to go. Go with Lekan. Talk with Nausicaä. If this *is* the work of alchemy, it's gone ignored long enough. The Dark Star might be our only hope to salvage this situation. I'm sorry"—he bowed to Vehan, which had taken him so off guard that Vehan almost forgot to return the gesture—"I must take my leave. There's something I have to do now. Lekan will give you my cell so we can talk about this further, later. Excuse me, Prince Vehan. Lord Bessel."

He left the room, emerald robe billowing in his wake.

So sudden was his exit that for a moment, all Vehan could once again do was stare. Then, he stuttered, "Did . . . Did I just get the High Prince's phone number?"

"A hurricane, that one," said Lekan in a tone of exasperated fondness. "His cousin is the only one to ever find their way into its center. Come, sit! You're best to at least try your story out on the High King. I'll send for some tea—and Timbits. His High Majesty is quite fond of Timbits. When your meeting is through, we can see about getting the answers you seek."

Timbits, Vehan mouthed. He had no idea what this word even meant.

In something of a daze, he wandered to the sofa the High Prince had just vacated and took a seat, Aurelian doing the same beside him. Even if the High King didn't believe Vehan, High Prince Celadon was now on their side. Whatever that meant, it was something. It was a start, at long last. For the first time in a long while, when Vehan drew a breath, it actually felt like breathing.

CHAPTER 20

Arlo

———◦⌒◦———

"HELLO," SAID ARLO TO the middle-aged man who approached her counter. "What can I get for you today?"

"A latte."

Arlo suppressed a sigh.

One of the drawbacks to customer service was having to deal with people in a bad mood, as this man clearly was. In his midnight-black suit, black leather gloves, and a sharp gold tie paired with perfectly groomed, glossy black hair, he gave off the air of someone important— and with the sour turn of his pinched mouth and glittering, hard stare, he was clearly an *unhappy* someone important.

Best to move this along quickly.

"One latte." She punched it in. "What name can I write on the cup?"

"Hero." His frown etched further into a scowl. "Your customer service is atrocious."

"I'm . . . sorry?" She had no idea what she'd done to offend him. The man was clearly looking for someone to take out his mood on.

"You know, you should smile more. Girls are much prettier when they smile, and you could certainly use that help. To think I came all this way for *this*—I don't even know what he sees in you. You aren't a threat to me at all."

"Uh . . ." Was this still about her? "So you can pick your drink up over there . . ."

"That's all you have to say? Goodness, girl, I'm *insulting* you. Don't just—"

"My dude," drawled a voice from behind the man. "Methinks the lady doth say fuck off."

Arlo's heart tripped over its own beat. Her eyes grew wide. Her breath tangled up in her throat and caused her to choke on a cough, because she knew that voice—would probably never forget it for its haunting new role in narrating her previous night's nightmares—and when the man at her counter turned around, it was indeed Nausicaä standing next in line.

"Excuse me?"

Nausicaä beamed—Arlo hoped to never witness her do so again; it was more than a little terrifying to see such threat behind false cheer. "You heard me. Pay for your drink and move along, asshole. It's my turn to terrorize the barista."

"You *will* regret talking to me like that."

"Um . . . should I—"

"Promises, promises. Take your mood and go." The man continued to stare her down long enough that Arlo considered flagging over one of the other staff. Nausicaä maintained her smile. It was no human thing. A hint of what lay behind her glamour bled through her image—a grin that split from ear to ear, crowded with vicious teeth, as though she could swallow the man down in shreds. "You know," she added, that ghostly overlap of truth moving in sync with her lips, "you should smile more. You'd be prettier if you did, and my ego's incredibly fragile. I rely on vulnerable people to validate my shitty existence."

Arlo wasn't surprised when the man threw a couple toonies on the counter and stormed to wait by the bar. If Nausicaä had ever looked at her the way she was at him, Arlo would most likely pass out. One problem solved—but only to make way for another.

"Thanks." She blew out a breath in relief, then added, "What are you doing here?" She lowered her voice to whisper and bent across the till. "Isn't the . . . you know, *Hunt* after you?"

Nausicaä shrugged. "*Tch*—probably? I don't know, who cares. Listen, what time are you getting off work?"

"Uh . . . why?" While she appreciated the rescue, both now and back at the Faerie Ring, the trouble Arlo was in was still fresh in her mind. So, too, was her promise to stay out of any more, and trouble seemed to follow Nausicaä like a curse.

"I'd like you to come somewhere with me."

Arlo was grounded.

A not-insignificant part of her was terrified of this exceedingly bold and vulgar girl.

She'd spent a solid hour the previous night looking for any trace of something out of the ordinary on her chest and all over her body. She'd found no array—whatever that was supposed to look like—but that didn't mean Arlo wasn't now acutely aware that whatever had been piling corpses up in pieces on the news was apparently lurking right here in the city, using a Reaper to hunt down people just like her. Arlo was so incredibly *not* brave, and on top of all of this, her only Gift appeared to be the ability to make bad situations worse—she didn't want to tempt her death *or* promised fate any more than she'd already done these past couple weeks.

And yet, despite all the reasons to tell Nausicaä *no*, she still heard herself say, "I'm done in an hour. Go with you where?"

"I'm so glad you asked! There's a certain someone and his friend who'd like to meet you, and as it's incredibly beneficial to my interests to introduce you to them, I told them I'd see what I could do. So, what do you say to making me one of those obnoxiously sweet Unicorn Frappuccinos, and I'll hang out until you're done and give you a few more details then?"

No, Arlo's mind scolded. *You have to tell her no. Whatever she's caught up in, it probably has more to do with that philosopher's stone business, and the last time you went along with something she was after, you nearly got eaten by a Reaper. Do you* want *to attract the attention of a serial-killing lunatic?*

"What size?" her traitorous voice asked aloud.

"Fucking kill me."

"I . . . don't think that's one of the options on my screen."

"Oh, it is. You call it 'Venti.'"

Arlo punched the order through. Nausicaä paid for it, dropped her change into the tip jar, and stalked off to wait for her drink at the bar.

The final hour of work passed uneventfully.

Arlo glanced Nausicaä's way often, where she sprawled in a chair by the window, because for some reason, she could never sit normally in any seat. She nursed her brightly colored drink and passed the time on her massive teal smartphone, and only looked up when Arlo dropped into the opposite seat at her table, tired and sweaty and finally finished with her shift.

"So, who's this somebody and his friend you want me to go meet with you, and why?"

"Vehan Lysterne. Did you know he's here in Toronto today?"

Arlo stared.

Vehan Lysterne was prince of the Seelie faction of Summer. One of two royal families that reigned over the Season, the Seelie faction held its court in America—Nevada, if Arlo remembered correctly. The UnSeelie faction was currently somewhere in India. That was all Arlo knew of him apart from the rumors that boasted him as handsome as he was gifted with the electric element that Seelie Summer fae commanded.

"Uh . . . no, I didn't. How did *you* find out? How did you even talk to him in order to set up this meeting? Shouldn't you be in hiding or something? More importantly, why does he want to talk to *me*?"

"Honestly, I don't really know. He wouldn't say. We made a deal: I bring him you, and he'll tell me how he knows about philosopher's stones."

She knew it.

Arlo's heart clenched around resurgent fear. She wasn't a target, she reminded herself. She didn't have an array, and by Nausicaä's own admission, that was how the hearts she'd found turned into stones. But it occurred to Arlo then, as bad thoughts did when panic took the helm, that this might not be the only way. "I definitely don't have a stone inside me . . . right? I'm not going to die, am I? That's not why he wants to talk to me, is it?"

Nausicaä waved her hand between them. "No, no, you're all right. At least, I think you are. I don't sense anything off about your magic. Don't have an array on you somewhere, do you?"

Arlo shook her head. "That's the only way to make a stone out of a heart?"

"The only way."

She breathed a sigh of relief. "Okay. But still, shouldn't I not get involved in this? I mean, for starters, I don't really want to. I don't know if you've noticed, but I'm not really the go-get-'em adventurer type, and things tend to go terribly, horribly, very badly wrong whenever I get involved. Also, you said so yourself, just because I'm not a target now doesn't mean I can't become one if I continue to stick my nose in this."

"These are all perfectly valid concerns, Arlo," said Nausicaä, setting down her phone to fold her hands on the table. "I'm kind of hoping you'll ignore all that. You might not be the adventurer sort, but I don't actually know of anyone better suited to help in this situation."

"I'm also grounded, you know."

"I'll have you there and back in no time—I can teleport, remember? Just tell your mother you got held up at work or something. This won't take long, it's just a meeting. I'm not suggesting we run away to Vegas together."

"You also realize my mother is head of the magical community's top police force and can check like *that* to see if I'm taking advantage of loopholes to lie." Arlo snapped her fingers to impress upon Nausicaä how easy it would be for Thalo to confirm her fib.

Leaning back in her seat, Nausicaä grinned. "Yes, your ability to lie. So much potential . . . so little proper guidance. There's a lot I could teach you, Arlo. We'd make quite a team, you and I . . ."

Arlo staunchly ignored the part of her that took that statement as a compliment. "A wanted ex-Fury and a magically stunted ironborn girl—yeah, quite a team." She rolled her eyes. "If it's really just a meeting—if Prince Vehan just wants to talk—then . . . I don't know, I guess. Sure. It'll have to be quick, though. Like, an hour, tops. But seriously, why *me*?"

Arlo was nobody. She'd never met Prince Vehan before in her life, and knew no possible reason for him to want to change that, now of all times. She didn't know anything about philosopher's stones, or alchemy, or whatever else was going on. What would be the point in meeting her at all?

"Again, no clue. If they're wasting our time, I promise to exact revenge and lure them out to Cyberniskos's lair."

Cyberniskos, the card-playing faerie cannibal that had been at the Faerie Ring?

"What? No! Nausicaä, you can't kill the Seelie Prince of Summer just for 'wasting your time,' you . . . do know that, right?"

"Mmm, better come along, then. It's hard to keep track of all these made-up rules on my own."

She waggled her brows.

Arlo sighed heavily through her nose.

Part of what had attracted the UnSeelie faction of Spring to set up court in Toronto was the city's human diversity. As it was one of the most multicultural cities in the world, people from all over could make home within its many pockets and retain some semblance of their roots.

Plus, with so many different people packed in close together, it was much easier to maintain their secrecy. Arlo had once stood in a line at Tim Hortons behind an entire human group of Final Fantasy cosplayers, and no one had batted an eye. Their presence meant the ogre behind her whose malfunctioning glamour revealed a glimpse of impressive tusks went completely unnoticed.

But the largest part for choosing here was pride.

The Seelie faction of Spring held court in the English countryside, where carpets of emerald grass rolled like a sea over waves of hills, and everything turned profoundly green as soon as winter melted.

Here in Toronto, a city whose winters could freeze quite harsh and summers could heat quite hot, claiming a place for spring was no small achievement. War had to be waged on an annual basis against the ice and snow that loved this country dearly, and any time their season won had to be used efficiently before high and humid temperatures could steal it for their own.

The result was a majesty only UnSeelie Spring could unfurl—vibrant jeweled fields of tulip flowers, frozen lakes warmed sapphire bright; snow-capped mountains rose high into clear blue sky off along the western coast, and to the east, swaths of forest draped jagged, winding cliffs in verdant luxury. Spring was a wick already half-burned by the time this region claimed it, but Azurean Lazuli-Viridian hadn't come to wear his crown because he feared a challenge.

"It always surprises me that Canada can be so *warm*," Nausicaä complained.

Arlo eyed her companion.

It was the middle of May, but the first spells of summer's heat weren't uncommon for this time of year. Arlo was already sweating in her work clothes—black skinny jeans and a matching black polo—but Nausicaä had to be dying in the exact same outfit she'd been wearing upon their first meeting.

"You could maybe lose the leather jacket."

"Excuse you, I can't just take something off. This is my *outfit*." She pulled a look of extreme affront. "Also, temperature doesn't really bother me. It was just an observation. I thought this place was mostly snow and plaid and maple syrup factories."

Arlo shook her head. "So where are we going?" They'd teleported out of an alley close to her work and right into another on the Danforth, an arterial street that cut through what had come to be called Greektown. It was a thriving avenue, restaurants, businesses, and numerous pubs stacked one after the other. It was loud and always busy, no matter the time of day and well into the night, and not exactly the first place she'd assume a visiting prince would go.

Nausicaä led them to a crosswalk, weaving through the crowds of pedestrians like a plume of smoke. "That, over there." She pointed to a shop across the street.

"What, Chorley's Curiosities?" Arlo frowned. "It looks like a pawn shop."

"Ah, but you already know that looks can be deceiving in the magical community."

Chorley's Curiosities was a narrow slip of a building slotted in between an old used bookstore and a small souvlaki restaurant. Its sunflower-yellow paint had faded, peeling in many places, and the grimy front windows were plastered with various signs and old newspapers, and were crowded with bits of the wares its innards had to trade. On its equally shabby pine-green door hung its hours of operation . . . which apparently did not extend to the weekend.

"It says it's closed," Arlo observed when they reached their destination.

Nausicaä ignored the comment. She knocked on the door. It opened the opposite way Arlo expected, swinging inward at its hinges instead of the handle, and what lay on the opposite side left her stunned. She followed Nausicaä, stepping over the threshold and out the other side into . . .

". . . a forest?"

She gaped at the scene.

Gone was the Danforth. Gone was Toronto entirely. What stretched in all directions as far as the eye could see were trees— paper-white birches, fragrant cedars, and towering redwood *trees*. Each wore handsome mossy cloaks, and their dense, leafy crowns made a palette of the brightest, purest greens Arlo had ever seen.

Wind rustled through the canopy with waterfall tranquility.

Birds called a gentle, joyous song from their branches.

All around her seemed to be a faint and far-off tinkling, like glass chimes, and this taste on her tongue that sparked, and a crisp scent that sat in the back of her nose like winter.

Arlo had gone on many hikes with both her parents through some of the most beautiful forests this part of the world had to offer, but never had she been *here*. The stillness that stretched through this wood was a magic so ancient she felt it deep in her bones. But it was so peaceful—so restorative, so *good*—that more than anything else, Arlo wanted to sink into the sea of bluebells carpeting the floor and never leave.

"The Hiraeth," said Nausicaä. Her tone held something suspiciously like reverence. It was softer than Arlo had ever heard it.

"What's that?" Arlo asked drowsily. The longer she stood in this forest, the better she felt. It soothed every ache like a balm on a burn she didn't even know she had, but the effect was a little intoxicating. "What's a Hiraeth?"

Nausicaä turned to face her. Where Arlo was certain she looked as lethargic as she felt, there was a wild glint to Nausicaä's widely dilated eyes and a noticeably unnatural alertness about her. Each of her words and movements were executed with a care suggesting great restraint . . . but from what? Arlo couldn't summon up the energy to chase that thought. "It's what this place is called. Think of it like a vein that runs through all the worlds, connecting them together."

"All the worlds? As in . . . universes? Plural? There are others?"

Nausicaä hummed, nodding her head in slow affirmation.

Arlo turned back to surveying the forest. A lazy ribbon of mist curled through the trees, winding its way deeper into the forest's depths. In certain pockets, the ground seemed to move, trees and bluebells tilting side to side as the earth beneath them heaved—swelling and deflating, working like a set of lungs. "It's *breathing*!"

"Well, it's alive, isn't it? The Hiraeth is the birthplace of magic—the good old-fashioned pure stuff, which is why you're probably feeling a bit loopy right now standing around like this, breathing it in."

"This is where magic was born?" Wonder claimed her fascination, and suddenly, the forest seemed too vast to comprehend—like gazing into an endless pit, large enough to swallow a mountain, or standing at the foot of a building so tall it disappeared into the clouds.

Nausicaä snapped her fingers in front of Arlo's face, and Arlo blinked through her daze. "Come on, time to go. This place is specifically designed to strip immortals of their inhibitions. And it's Wild domain. Hunters come here to party. I'd hate to lose my cool and accidentally kill you."

She turned back around, and Arlo, surfacing quickly from her daze, did too—somewhat warily after such a statement. The door through which they'd entered the forest stood there still, along with the rest of Chorley's Curiosities, exactly as it had been on the Danforth except in far better condition. The paint was new, the windows clean, and gone were the trinkets obscuring their view. Through the glass, Arlo spied a collection of people that hadn't been there before.

Nausicaä knocked again on the door, and inward again it swung, this time the way it should. Together, they stepped into the shop, and when the door snapped closed, Arlo felt suddenly sucked into life and sound and movement.

The inside of Chorley's Curiosities was a charming construction of polished, dark-stained wood and quaint, rustic furniture. Off to the right was a homey space filled with beige sofas and antique tables, all arranged in front of a currently unlit pale stone fireplace. The left of the shop was devoted to shelving units stuffed with odds and ends, the price tags on each a clear indication that everything there was for sale.

At the center of the room sat a solid mahogany desk with numerous people gathered around it, deep in conversation.

Arlo stared.

The people weren't human—not fully, at least. There was a small and supple lesidhe woman, her hair a glossy black and eyes so light a gold they were almost white. Beside her was an older sidhe man, though she didn't need his sapphire flush, pointed ears, and avian-sharp features to discern this. The fae was someone Arlo *recognized*—Lekan,

Head of House Otedola, one of the High King's favored families.

"Lord Lekan!" She shot quickly into a bow.

Lekan turned, his expression closely guarded until he, too, realized who stood across from him. "Arlo Jarsdel?"

The room seemed to freeze.

"Jarsdel?"

The man that the two had been talking to—sturdy, middle-aged, with boar-black hair and a sandy complexion, his face showing every sign of its age—whipped around to stare at her too.

The fire-red pixie standing behind the desk perked their iridescent wings; the three fox spirits lounging on the sofas, with obsidian-glass hair pouring straight down their backs and snowy white tails fanned around their bodies, regarded her with curious, bloodred eyes; the pair of fae who'd been just about to disappear up the staircase behind the man who'd spoken whirled around on the steps.

Everyone had paused in the midst of what they'd been doing to turn their interest on her, and Arlo had no idea why.

"Uh . . . yeah? Hello." She gave an awkward smile to the room, clutching the strap of the tote bag she carried even tighter.

"Nausicaä," said the black-haired man, his tone turning severe. "What game is this? We're already playing host to Summer's royalty. The High King's blood is a step too far. Must I remind you this is a *secret* organization—and one we'd all earn the Wild Hunt's Mark for getting caught in its operation?"

Oh.

They recognized her by her ties to royalty.

Though for some reason, Arlo could almost swear the black-haired man seemed to know her by some other means. The way his eyes couldn't help but dart to her—human eyes, but the point to his ears said he was most likely ironborn—and the glimpse of awe she caught in them every time they did was different from how most people looked at her when they realized who she was.

Nausicaä snorted. "Hey, that was your soft heart that opened your door to the princeling and his babysitter. I'm just helping them get what they came for so that *I* can get what *I* came for, and *you* can go back to running your Rebel Alliance in peace."

The black-haired man huffed. "Stop calling it that. This isn't *Star Wars.*"

"Uh, Rebel Alliance?" Arlo raised a brow. "Where are we exactly?"

"The supersecret headquarters of the Assistance," Nausicaä was all too happy to supply. "Which is a stupid name, if you ask me. Rebel Alliance sounds much better. As the person who made your access to the Hiraeth possible, you'd think I'd have a say in titles." She rolled her eyes, then flourished a hand at the black-haired man and stepped aside to give proper introduction. "Anyhow, Arlo Jarsdel, meet Nikos Chorley, founder and facilitator of the largest magical organization devoted to inter–human and folk cooperation."

CHAPTER 21

Arlo

❧⟡❧

ARLO STARED AT NIKOS.

She obviously knew about the Assistance—who didn't, these days, what with the pressure they'd put on the High King to publicly acknowledge the ironborn deaths. But their roots dug back much further.

With World War II, the atrocities the folk had been forced to stand back and let happen "for the good of the Courts"—along with the unfair punishment any who tried to help had received—had sparked a growing number of the magical community to want to help humankind in times of need, to lend their power in any way they could, even go as far as to dispense with their secrecy altogether for a new age of unity.

It wasn't until the Assistance had formed twenty or so years ago that anything they'd ever done had survived the Heads' and the Fae High Council's efforts to keep the community in check.

But lately they were bolder by far than they'd ever been.

It seemed that now the Assistance was everywhere, on everybody's minds and tongues, where once not many paid them much attention because originally their organization had been quite small. A vigilante group committed to quieter things, they didn't have the means to do much more than support human protests for things like rights for women, BIPOC, and the LGBTQPlus communities; aid and form relief missions, which helped bring necessities to war-torn and weather-ravaged places around the world; build schools; track down and disband trafficking rings; protect the folk who chose not to or couldn't, for whatever reason, sign themselves over to the Courts.

They did their best to keep to the shadows, Arlo understood, to keep their names and their faces secret. Over the years, only a handful had ever been arrested by the Courts, and Arlo knew they cracked down hard on these "transgressors." Nikos could get in a lot of trouble for this, not to mention Lekan, a highly esteemed member of the Courts and husband to the High King's steward. If the High King ever found out he was here . . .

"I won't tell anyone!"

For a moment, Nikos stood unmoved. He shared a glance with Lekan, who shrugged at him in return. With a sigh, his countenance softened, and once again his eyes gleamed this odd sort of fondness. "Of course you wouldn't. You're a Jarsdel."

A Jarsdel? Well, yes, she was, but that had never mattered to anyone. None of her father's family lived in Canada. He was an amiable person, had his friends and the regular group of people he played trivia with at the pub on Thursday nights, but Arlo had never before encountered anyone who'd held her to the *Jarsdel* standard over the *Viridian*.

Nikos placed a hand on Arlo's shoulder, giving it a squeeze, and all she could do was stare up at him. "You must be Rory Jarsdel's daughter."

"I . . ." Arlo nodded, words swallowed whole by the rising tide of confusion.

"You look like him." He smiled down at her, the sort that made his eyes crinkle and laugh lines etched a little deeper. "Your father was a good man. If Arlo Jarsdel swears she won't betray us, that will be good enough for me."

It struck her as odd that Nikos spoke about her father in past tense, as though he wasn't alive and perfectly well and Nikos couldn't see him any time he wanted. But then . . . maybe Nikos had met Rory back before he'd given up his memories. Unless . . . No, it couldn't be, but she still had to ask, "My dad wasn't an Assistant . . . was he?"

Nikos held her stare a moment. That moment turned into two. In the next, it turned into laughter, so loud and rough around the edges, Arlo startled and jolted back. "No, no, nothing like that. He was just a good man with a good head on his shoulders and a good heart in his breast."

Arlo relaxed, confusion deflating, until Nausicaä clapped her hands together, reminding her she was there. "Wonderful. Everybody's friends. Now, if you don't mind, I need to make a delivery. Vehan's still upstairs, yeah?"

"He is," Lekan confirmed. "I'm afraid I really must be getting back now—this is all running a bit longer than expected, and I've other things to be getting on with today. But I trust you'll be true to your word and return our guest to the palace once you're through with him?"

Nausicaä nodded, waving off Lord Lekan's pointed look.

"Wonderful." He clasped hands with Nikos, then dropped a wink at Arlo on their parting. "Take care, Lady Jarsdel."

"You too, Lord Lekan," she bid with a bow of her head.

"Come on, come on, let's mosey." Nausicaä was already halfway to the staircase, forcing Arlo to scramble to catch up. Her gaze snagged on Nikos's penetrating stare. For a moment, he looked like he might say something else, but merely settled on, "Be careful, Arlo Jarsdel."

"I'll . . . try, thanks." She waved an awkward farewell, then took off up the stairs. "Is Nikos ironborn?" she asked as they climbed.

"Yeah. Never ever tell him I told you this, but he's okay. For an old dude. Spent most of his life advocating for unity between humans and the magical community, despite how much it's pissed off the Courts. I'm surprised they haven't pinned him with anything yet—gods know the Courts hold *zero* mercy for anyone they catch using magic to help a human."

They reached the top of the staircase and broke onto the top landing. A narrow, dimly lit hall stretched far off both left and right of Arlo, but it was the door directly in front of them that Nausicaä headed for.

"I return!" she shouted grandly, bursting into the room.

Arlo trailed after her, fighting the desire to roll her eyes at this girl for the millionth time.

The room was modest. Two sets of bunk beds pressed against opposing walls, a worn oval rug on the floor between them, and directly opposite the door was a window, under which stood a plain brown dresser.

Stretched on one of the bottom bunks was a boy roughly Arlo's age, dressed in a white shirt and gold pants, with a paler gold robe neatly folded at the end of the bed. When she focused her ability, she could sense his magic—a gingery, floral scent that fizzled in her nose—and with his floppy, charcoal-black hair, electric bright blue eyes, and the dawn-soft glow about his tanned skin, there was no mistaking who this was.

"You were gone for over an hour."

The reply had come from a desk back by the door, and Arlo turned to find the second occupant of the room, again not much older than she. Seated sideways on his chair, his long legs stretched toward the prince on the bed. He, too, was handsome, in a prettier sort of way, though also plainly dressed except for the abundance of silver pierced along the curve of his ears. His glamour concealed his aura surprisingly well—only a trace of autumn leaves and sun-warmed stone—but it couldn't hide the unnatural gold of his eyes.

A lesidhe.

The way those eyes fixed on Nausicaä was nothing short of a glare.

"Oh, I'm sorry. I didn't know this grand favor I'm doing you was on a time limit." She flipped the boy her middle finger. "You wanted an alchemist, here she is. Arlo, meet Vehan Lysterne, Seelie Prince of the Summer Court, and his incredibly pleasant bodyguard person, Aurelian. Guys, meet Arlo Jarsdel."

"Wait a minute—*alchemist*?" The High King's glare, his ferocious behavior, his threat to arrest her if she ever again performed the magic he'd forbidden, it all came back to Arlo at a word, and her panic ratcheted up to nausea quicker than it ever had before. "I'm *not* an alchemist. I don't practice alchemy. Have you been telling people I do? Is this payback for the whole 'I thought you were a murderer' thing?"

Vehan stood from the bed at last and crossed the room quickly. He stopped in front of Arlo, measuring her with a glance. At this proximity, Arlo was suddenly acutely aware of just how rumors did such little justice to his appeal. He had very pretty eyes.

Too bad she felt too much like passing out to appreciate them.

"Arlo? Not . . . not Arlo, as in the High Prince Celadon's *cousin* Arlo?" He turned pale upon connecting these dots and looked just as nauseated as Arlo felt.

"Yeah," she replied, however faintly. "That's me. I don't know what Nausicaä has been telling you, but I'm *not* an alchemist."

The prince turned a glare on Nausicaä. "I thought you said you could help? It's bad enough I'm involved in all of this—why are you dragging her into it too? Do you *want* the High Prince to hate me?" He actually shuddered.

"Listen here, Prince Charmless," Nausicaä snapped. "You wanted an alchemist—I presume you actually mean to *use* them, if you're going through all this trouble to find one? No, okay, that isn't exactly Arlo's regular day job, but wouldn't you know, not only is she a rare hand at this particular talent, but she's also not yet a legal citizen of the Courts."

Whatever reservations Vehan had about Arlo were quickly forgotten. "Which means the Courts can't track your magic yet!" His horror morphed into delight. "They won't know you're helping me. Oh, this is perfect! All right, then. Arlo—may I call you Arlo? What did Nausicaä tell you about why you're here?"

Arlo's gaze flicked briefly to Nausicaä. "Uh . . . okay, if we're just glossing over the whole 'not an alchemist' part, not much. Just that you needed to talk to me. She said you'd tell me the particulars."

"I will, but first, what do you know about philosopher's stones?"

Again, Arlo looked to her companion. When she met nothing in Nausicaä's expression that told her to guard her knowledge, she shrugged and replied, "I know what Nausicaä's told me. They're powerful. Someone tried to make one once. Someone might be trying to make one now out of ironborn people and alchemy and arrays . . ."

Vehan nodded. "Anything else?"

She shrugged. "The Courts don't believe that's what this is. I don't know why. Maybe they're too scared of what it means that this is happening at all."

"Oh, they might believe it," Vehan interrupted, a passionate crackle darkening his tone. "They might even want to act on it, if the High King would let them. He's forbidden the Heads from any further involvement—do you know how much fuss they collectively had to put up to get that meeting with the Fae High Council, the one where Nausicaä here was made their rabbit to chase?" He laughed, but the sound was far from humor. "You've heard his official statement. For the good of the Courts, Arlo."

This tragedy, while deeply concerning, has shone no evidence of magical origins. It is indeed the ironborn folk of our community made target, and the Falchion members of the human police forces will continue their tireless efforts to bring justice to the family and friends of those we've lost. But at this time, given the nature of this matter and the level of human involvement, and the lack of evidence to suggest the culprit is anything other than human themselves, I have decided to yield this to human authorities. I ask that we allow them the chance to conclude this without the considerable energy, resources, and risk our superseding would demand. This I have declared, for the good of the Courts.

Yes, Arlo had heard the statement, issued on every folk-exclusive website and streaming platform across the world. "For the good of the Courts"—the motto that much of the community was coming to detest. Many folk had been incensed by this statement. The fae, for the most part, had been appeased, but the majority of the faeries (and in particular, the ironborn community) had been quick to point out that no one would be weighing the "considerable energy, resources, and risk" if it had been the precious fae under attack.

Vehan shook his head, disgusted. "We can't engage with this at all, no one, not without his permission now, and it's unlikely anyone will get that anytime soon because that meeting with the FHC was the last he would hear about this issue. He's even started refusing to meet with anyone who wishes to discuss it. I have no idea why he agreed to meet with me today, what my mother had to threaten to buy my audience, but all he did was tell me to 'enjoy my youth' and to 'let the adults handle this situation while the burden is still theirs.' He wouldn't listen to a word I had to say." He scoffed under his breath.

Arlo's heart twisted around a concoction of resentment and grief. It really wasn't possible to ignore any longer just how unwell the High King really was, just how much he'd failed them—*her*—despite the good he'd done.

How much longer did he have left before someone decided to try for the crown? She hated thinking about it, about what that would mean, but it was coming whether she liked it or not.

"The evidence has been piling up for a while," Vehan continued. "People disappearing off the streets . . . ironborn glowing strange colors before they die—"

"Like Cassandra!" she blurted.

Vehan nodded.

"Yes, Nausicaä told us about that. It makes sense now, why I couldn't see it myself in our own, similar encounter when Aurelian could—lesidhe fae can see just about any magical aura. And I've suspected for a while that what's killing them is alchemy. But Nausicaä, you didn't mention Arlo was at the café with you."

"Sorry," she snorted, sounding anything but. "I didn't think it was important, seeing as it wasn't. Would you like to know what underwear I was wearing too?"

Sighing, the prince turned back to Arlo. "All ironborn folk possess a natural inclination toward alchemy, but even then, not all are able to make anything of it. Nikos, for instance, can barely even see its activation, let alone use it. Nausicaä seems to think you can do better, and if you already know as much as you do about what's going on, you may be just what we're looking for."

"Hooray." She didn't feel as fortunate as the collected enthusiasm suggested she should. "Maybe if you guys could actually tell me what's going on here, I can let you know if I even want to *be* that help you're after."

"Her royal sassiness has a point," said Nausicaä. "And you owe me a bit more info too. I delivered my end of the bargain, now tell me: What made you two suspect an alchemist was the person behind the ironborn murders? I mean, I'm older and wiser than all three of you combined, and *I* didn't even know this was going on until very recently. How the hell did *you* connect the dots?"

Vehan glanced to Aurelian and sighed.

"Well . . ." And then he told them, launched into his story of discovering an ironborn boy in some park a few years back, the glowing in his veins, his skin stamped with a brand that was too much like an array to be anything other than magic.

"Ah—and only alchemy uses arrays." Nausicaä nodded. "Well, you're not completely empty-headed, then. I'll give you that."

Ignoring this bait, Vehan closed off his expression completely. He stood in what appeared to be contemplation of his next move, weighing his options. Then, with a grim air of determination, he lifted a hand to tug at the collar of his shirt. It dipped down his chest. Revealed was a faded, pearly knot of scarring directly over his heart.

"It looks like a butterfly," Arlo observed, leaning closer alongside Nausicaä to examine it. She caught herself before her fingers could trace the barely-there lines of one of its wings. "What's all that stuff inside it? Those symbols and writing and . . . it looks like a weird math equation. Is that . . . It can't be *alchemy*, can it?"

"Holy shit, Vehan." Nausicaä's amazement turned her voice strangely breathless. "That's an array. That's a fucking *philosopher's stone* array—why the fuck do you have that? You're not ironborn!"

Jerking a falsely casual shrug, Vehan released his shirt, and the first alchemic array Arlo had ever seen slipped back out of view. "No idea," he replied. "Honestly, you're the first person who's ever told me it was anything other than a scar."

"Oh," said Nausicaä, looking a bit uncomfortable. "Well, maybe I'm wrong."

"You're not," said Vehan, his tone gone firm. "I've known for a while this is an array. It's relieving, actually, to have someone confirm that."

"All right, then, you're welcome. Congratulations on your magical death stamp. I hope you two are very happy together."

"That's not funny," growled the prince's bodyguard—Aurelian.

He'd been quiet up until now, hovering on the outskirts of the conversation, watching each person as they spoke. On Arlo his gaze was passive interest, on Nausicaä it cooled into disdain, but on Vehan, Arlo was reminded of the dark and hungry place inside her—inside everyone—where you hid the things you didn't want anyone else to know.

Vehan waved a hand. "It's fine. I'd rather people make jokes than ignore it."

"Not in front of me."

They frowned at one another. Aurelian had risen from his desk at last, a flintiness in his eyes that betrayed his otherwise unreadable expression as angry. Arlo noticed the twitch of his hand—as though it was far more in his nature to want to be more tactile, more involved in what was going on, closer, at least with Vehan. She wondered briefly what prevented him from doing so now.

"Why would someone do this?" was what she said out loud, to break the tension. "What exactly does a philosopher's stone do?"

Every legend Google provided on the matter told her the same thing—that a philosopher's stone could produce gold and make people immortal. Surely there were better ways of doing that than with something so dangerous and, by the sound of things, more myth than reality?

All eyes turned to Nausicaä. "Well," she replied. "The things pretty much everyone knows, from the last time someone attempted this. Even the humans noticed, when that went down—hence its prevalence in their culture. They turn things to gold, yeah, and grant immortality . . . but those are just perks, among many others. *Rewards* for successfully summoning one of these things into creation, meant to blind you to what you've actually done, and what you've lost in the process. Naturally, money and immortality is like, the only thing mortals all seem to get hot and bothered over, so I'm not surprised the finer points of this lore got lost over the years."

"Would you care to share how you know all this?" Aurelian prompted.

"And deprive your little detective agency of its game? Nah."

"We've told you what we know," said Vehan. "We're all on the same team, so why not just—"

"No, no, no—we're not on the same team," Nausicaä interrupted. "I'm no hero! Just because I'm not running around turning kids to stone doesn't mean I'm a fine upstanding citizen like Red and Prince Charmless here, and . . . I don't know, what fairy-tale character do *you* want to be, Aurelian?"

Aurelian cut her a deadly glare.

"And fucking Grumpy." She held up her palms in the air—the universal sign for surrender—and stalked back to the beds. "You lot are sticking your nose into this because you want to put a stop to it; I started chasing this because I wanted *in.*"

Arlo considered Nausicaä's statement. "Did you really?"

"More or less," she sniffed. "Originally, I wanted the Reaper whoever this is has been working with. Then this seemed like the sort of chaos at least worth checking out, and I don't know, maybe our murderous alchemist is okay underneath the whole . . . murdering children stuff. Everybody has a past with shit they wish they hadn't done. Stop looking at me like that."

Arlo pursed her lips, doubling down on the look Nausicaä now glared back at.

"You know, you haven't actually told us who you are, apart from your name," Aurelian reminded her.

"It gets less dramatic every time I have to reveal this."

Silence wore on between them long enough for him and the prince to conclude Nausicaä wasn't interested in divulging that information.

"Fine, whatever," Vehan snapped. "But if you still wanted in, you wouldn't be here having this chat with us."

"Maybe I'm just biding my time and seeing what you know before I pick you off myself?"

"Then why do you keep coming to my rescue?" Arlo pointed out. If Nausicaä really truly wanted to join forces with whoever was behind this, why didn't she just let the Reaper finish her off at the Faerie Ring? Arlo knew very little about the Fury before her, but she was starting to realize Nausicaä's words were just as much a mask as her glamour.

Nausicaä remained silent. She wouldn't answer any question she didn't want to answer, and Arlo suspected her moodiness was a silent tantrum, thrown over the fact that she couldn't comprehend why none of them wanted to believe her intentions nefarious.

"Okay," Arlo said before things could get any more heated. "Just . . . how about this: Can you tell me what you actually want from me, Vehan? Why you're even looking for an alchemist to begin with?"

"Oh! Yes, of course. Well, we tracked down this oracle who told us we needed to find this goblin who would take us to this facility that's been buying people off the streets for large sums of gold." He waved a hand. "Nausicaä can bring you up to speed on that later. Unfortunately, that facility's entrance is guarded by more than just a lock. There was a *seal*—an alchemic array, straight out of the books the Courts all want us to believe were destroyed. A seal that only an alchemist can deactivate. It's connected to all of this, somehow—I know it is—but I need to get in there to prove that. I have every intention of investigating that facility, Arlo, of getting to the bottom of what ties me to this mystery. I have no idea what's waiting for us inside, and there's no doubt it will be dangerous, but we'll never find out if we can't actually get into that facility. To do that, I need *you*."

Nausicaä didn't even pause to consider the application. "Well, *I'm* not helping."

"Oh, come on," Vehan broke down, pleading. He looked wildly between Arlo's paling horror and Nausicaä's flat disinterest. "Yes, you are. You want to know what's going on just as much as we do. So maybe you want to know if it's worth your good name to lend us a hand, but you still want to know. You want to check this out, and wouldn't it be nice to have some backup? Isn't a team of four better than a team of one?"

Nausicaä snorted, presumably at the implication that she had a good name or, even more probably, at the suggestion that any of them would be much help to her in a pinch.

Arlo had other concerns. "No. Absolutely not."

Vehan shot her a furrowed look. "What? Why?"

"Are you kidding?" she replied, as hotly as she could around her growing nausea. "First of all, what makes you think I can even get you in there? Again, I'm *not. An. Alchemist.* I've never used alchemy before! Second of all, are you forgetting what I am? Are you forgetting who's been made a target here? If I stick my nose into this any further than I already have—if I walk right into . . . into some . . . some *murder factory*—I could *die*! There's something out there picking people off, and I'm not some heroic prince with all kinds of magic to keep me safe from that."

If there was one good thing about Vehan's array, it was that it had relieved her of the lingering tendril of fear she felt wondering whether she might somewhere be carrying a deadly brand of her own. She wasn't. She had nothing like what Vehan wore anywhere on her, but that didn't mean she couldn't still get one if she did anything more to attract the wrong attention.

"I'm not helping if Arlo isn't," Nausicaä hurried to tack on, latching on to any excuse possible. "But also, Arlo, listen. Just . . . take my word on this right now, you can do this. Your magic? It might need a little nudge into action in its current state, but your magic . . . it's enough. What you've got inside you is more than enough. And it's honestly better if you use it. Plus, you're not in any danger. First of all, I wouldn't let that happen. Second—"

"A little hard to do, you know, if you're only in this to help the other side!"

Nausicaä looked taken aback by the ferocity in Arlo's retort, and the sight of this slip in her composure only served to make Arlo feel worse instead of better. But all the poisonous things that had been festering inside her had found their outlet—all her disappointments and fears and frustrations and *helplessness* in what seemed like every aspect of her life. Now that she'd begun, she couldn't get ahold of herself to stop.

She rounded back on Vehan, her vision growing watery, and it was only *slightly* satisfying that the prince's summer-morning glow began to dim in the face of her anger. "It might interest you to know that I'm also *grounded*—possibly for life, if my mother ever finds out about this little conspiracy meeting—and the only way I'm going to get *un*grounded is if I keep my nose out of trouble. This isn't my problem. There are other ironborn folk you can find to do your alchemy-whatever for you. I can't help you."

Arlo was fairly breathless by the time her words ran out, and her eyes were hot and stinging. She was close to tears, but she couldn't say why, because everything she'd said was true.

She couldn't help them.

She wasn't special, wasn't brave.

Arlo was just a girl with fancy connections and no real magic of her own, regardless of what Nausicaä thought she knew about her. She was no hero, no chosen savior, nobody but Arlo Jarsdel, ironborn *human*, and the sort of plots that involved princes and rogue Furies weren't the ones that could ever involve her.

Vehan maintained his stunned silence a moment longer. But then, very delicately, he ventured, "Why are you grounded?"

Arlo narrowed her eyes, daring the prince to make light of her anger.

Sensing the ice he stood on was very thin, the Summer Prince added, "Just making conversation! I was only trying to . . . smooth over the moment. I, uh, remember the one Solstice years ago when High Prince Celadon gifted my mother a deck of cards with bizarre animals on the front. He told her they were enchanted, and that all she had to do was throw them while shouting their names and the creature she wished to summon would come to her aid. She spent an entire *week* trying to summon something called 'Pikachu' before someone kindly explained to her what Pokémon cards were, and that they weren't magic. I'm pretty sure the High Prince has cemented his place on the top of her death list for that, but all the High King did was ground him." He chuckled, but the sound was much too nervous for the levity he'd clearly been aiming for. "What could you have possibly done that's equal to insulting my mother in her own house?"

Yes, Arlo recalled that specific event.

She'd been quite young at the time and so hadn't been in attendance, but it was perhaps the one prank that Celadon *hadn't* been punished for beyond a superficial reprimand. The Heads of the Courts all existed on a plane of mutual dislike for one another, but there was even less love to lose between Azurean Lazuli-Viridian and Riadne Lysterne, Queen of the Seelie Summer Court; Azurean had been beside himself with amusement over the whole ordeal.

"It's nothing," she sighed. "Just—"

"She snuck into the Faerie Ring to try and track me down under the suspicion that I was your friendly neighborhood psychopath."

Arlo shot Nausicaä a venomous look.

Vehan's mouth fell open. His eyes flew wide, a comical picture of shocked and impressed. "The Faerie Ring," he breathed, his excitement ratcheting up once more, his glow revived by this spike in his mood. "But that's illegal. Only criminals already in trouble with the Courts go to the Faerie Ring!"

"Stop it," Arlo cried. "Stop being impressed! It was stupid."

"Stupid, yes, but it *is* impressive—and now I'm even more confused by your reluctance to help. You've been to the *Faerie Ring*, Arlo. Surely you can muster up the courage to help us get into some random facility. You don't even have to come inside! *Please*, Arlo. We need your help. *I* need your help."

"Just find someone else," she yelled, her frustration blowing out of control once more. She blinked harder, because like hell she was going to cry in the middle of a room full of people who chased after danger like it was a ride in an amusement park. She still didn't even know why she wanted to cry in the first place, but the higher her frustration rose, the closer it brought her to doing so.

Vehan seemed to be feeling a touch of frustration himself. It creeped into his tone, honing the edges of his words into knives. "These are ironborn, Arlo, just like you. Humans. *People*. I don't understand why you won't come—why you won't try to help *them*, at least, even if you have no reason to care about what might happen to me. And you talk as though the ability to activate alchemic seals is commonplace, but it's not. We need you. If the gods-damned Dark Star says we need you, *we need you*. And all you have to do is come with us. All you have to do is open the door, *that's it!*"

All she had to do . . .

All she had to do was go to university.

All she had to do was be a normal human girl.

All she had to do was be a little more fae and a little less of an embarrassment to the family name.

Be magical . . . be special . . . be a hero, Arlo, but also keep yourself out of trouble.

Shed fate altogether and become some not-troll's Hollow Star.

All she had to do was use the power that—at best—could get her banned from the Courts entirely, never mind the fact that she didn't know how to use that power in the first place, and all at once, all the things she was supposed to be and do for other people came crashing in on her, and it grew more and more difficult to breathe.

"Arlo?" Nausicaä hedged, softer than she'd ever spoken to Arlo before.

"I need some air," Arlo clipped. She turned, and with nothing further said, strode out the open door and down the stairs to the landing below.

CHAPTER 22

Vehan

W ELL, THAT WENT HORRIBLY," said Vehan, anxiety ballooning in his chest. He watched the empty doorway, unsure as to whether or not he should go after the High Prince's cousin and attempt to smooth over their rocky introduction.

He was two for two now in the Viridian department.

He'd never met Arlo Jarsdel before today, though like any other self-respecting member of the Celadon fandom (more commonly known as "the Celadom"), he knew who she was. Pictures of her and the High Prince appeared quite frequently in fan websites and gossip magazines, and for this Vehan had been quick to recognize her when she'd arrived, but the entire encounter had caught him off guard.

Pictures didn't do Arlo justice.

Not that she was exceptionally beautiful in person. She was pretty, of course—how could she not be with her bright red hair and Viridian green eyes—but more, what wasn't done justice in pictures was how much she shared in common with the High Prince, beyond their appearance. Her mannerisms, her changeable mood, the way she held herself when she forgot what was clearly a great deal of insecurity in favor of imperious command . . . There was a point in their brief exchange where Vehan could have sworn the two were twins; the resemblance between them was so strong. How much of Arlo was learned from the High Prince? How much of the High Prince was learned from Arlo? How much was the fan club going to despise him when they inevitably found out Vehan had managed to piss off *both* of them?

"She won't go to that forest, will she?" Aurelian asked, turning to Nausicaä. "That place didn't feel like the safest space for 'air.'"

"I'm going to level with you here: probably. Arlo? Sweet girl, I'm learning—bad at keeping out of trouble. *Urgh.*" Nausicaä peeled herself away from the beds, groaning. "Okay, wait here. I'm going to go make sure my Zelda doesn't get herself killed or something."

"Right," said Vehan. Arlo's connections aside, he felt bad for trying to pressure her into something that made her uncomfortable. It was fair that she didn't want to risk her life for them—hells, Vehan probably wouldn't be doing this either if he wasn't so directly involved and gods-damned irritated with the High King. Always, *always* in the back of his head was the reminder that they were just kids, that none of this should fall to them; he couldn't fault Arlo for listening to that reason. He shouldn't have let his bullheadedness get away with him. "I'm coming with you."

"Nope, that's not what 'wait here' means, Charmless."

Vehan scowled.

"I don't know who you think you are," Aurelian drawled, his tone unusually sharp, "but you shouldn't speak that way to anyone, let alone the prince of Seelie Summer. Apologize."

"*Deities*—you lot are so annoying with your rules. Vehan isn't all that special. There are two other whole-ass royal families of the Seelie Summer faction, and either one of them could take the throne from the Lysternes. No one would even care, because that's how that game goes. So, thank you for your suggestion, but you can shove it up your—"

"Are you always this hostile?" asked Aurelian.

"Excuse you, don't interrupt my threats. But pretty much, yeah."

"All right, okay," Vehan placated. "I'm starting to see why you've had so much trouble finding someone to help your portion of this investigation, but this isn't getting us anywhere. We need to go and check on Arlo and make sure she's okay, preferably *before* something in that forest decides to eat her."

Nausicaä wrinkled her nose, looking down at Vehan in evident disgust. Why, he could only guess. She didn't like them—hadn't right from their introduction, and that was fair, because again, his mother had named her a murderer, and this was *the* Dark Star, she didn't have to like anyone she didn't want to. But judging by the way she acted with pretty much everyone other than Arlo, this wasn't a personal thing. Besides, he couldn't say he liked her all that much either. "Fine. Whatever. Do what you want," she huffed, and stomped off past them, out into the hall.

Vehan followed.

"Are we sure we need this faerie's help?" Aurelian hissed, close behind him. "She's worse than the people you hang around with at school."

Iron teeth will show you the way. But . . . only once the stars align will you receive the answers you seek.

Vehan didn't particularly want to team up with someone like the infamous Dark Star, especially when she'd been a waspish, obnoxious *child* through the better part of their first meeting. But what if this was the alignment the oracle had mentioned? What if "stars aligning" meant they needed Nausicaä? It was worth the shot. "You know who she reminds me of?" Vehan teased as they descended the steps back to the main floor. "Your younger brother."

"Absolutely not."

"Yup. Harlan. They have the same dry humor, the same attitude. Is that why you're weirdly growly with her? I say weirdly—I mean, growly with her in a way you reserve for only Harlan. That enviable bond of sibling rivalry? Normally, you just ignore the people who irritate you. I should know—you ignore *me* a lot."

He hadn't meant to say that, but luckily, Aurelian took it in stride.

"And I'm going to go back to doing that now."

"Yeah, I'm sure you will, but deep down inside, you know you sort of like me. I let you win at Marvin Party."

"First of all, it's *Mario* Party."

"No, that doesn't sound right—GAH!"

They rounded the bend at the bottom of the staircase, nearly colliding with Nausicaä. Vehan issued a cry of surprise, but Aurelian's quick reflexes caught him before he could trip down the last step. "Good news!" Nausicaä explained. "Nikos says Arlo went straight through back to Toronto, so that's one concern down. Bad news: I still don't trust her to keep out of trouble. So, I'm going to go check on her. If you want to follow and try your luck again, I'm not going to stop you, but maybe cool it on the guilt-tripping this time around? Also, it's definitely Mario Party."

She turned on the heels of her boots and made for the front door. Aurelian glowered, not at all pleased to have her defending him, very much how he acted any time his younger brother set aside their bickering to do the same. Shaking his head to hide his grin, Vehan continued after Nausicaä, but paused when a knocking stopped her as well.

"Uh . . . you expecting someone, Nikos?"

Vehan frowned, looking between Nausicaä's tight expression and the even deeper frown on Nikos Chorley's face. "What's wrong?"

"Nothing yet," Nikos replied, too easily to be believed. "Just that you can't knock on that door from the street—the only way in here is through the Hiraeth, and anything that needs to do so *there* is something that isn't generally welcome."

Vehan knew very little about the space they called the Hiraeth. His private tutors and schoolteachers taught it to him as an abstract, more of a state of mind than any real place—a space inside oneself where, if sufficiently calm and focused, one could tap into great power. When Lord Lekan had led them through it, he'd been beside himself with curiosity, but Aurelian hadn't liked it at all. He'd been quite adamant about not lingering. Where it made Vehan and Lord Lekan both relaxed and strangely light-headed, it seemed to rub Aurelian like a boar-bristle brush.

The knocking sounded again, a short refrain of five raps.

Nausicaä threw open the door, earning a collection of startled shouts from everyone in the room. The gumiho in the lounge leaped to their feet. Nikos armed himself quickly with an iron bat that had been propped against the counter, where the pixie who manned it had ducked down behind.

But there was no one at the door.

It opened into the Hiraeth, and the forest stretched on, but there was no sign of anyone or anything that could be responsible for the knocking.

"*Tch*—dull." Nausicaä pulled the door closed. The moment she did, the knocking resumed, five additional raps. "All right, well, sorry Nikos, you have fun with your haunted-ass forest. I have other things to be doing right now."

She opened the door, turning the handle in the opposite direction she'd done previously, but once again when it opened, it was out into the Hiraeth, not Toronto as she'd obviously intended.

And once again, there was no one there.

"*Something* has to be there," said Nikos, stepping forward with his bat to peer outside. "The door won't open to the street if there's something trying to get in from the Hiraeth."

"Oh my gods, it's probably the shitty changelings trying to mess with us. . . . Listen here, you ugly forest brats!" Nausicaä stepped outside. Vehan inched toward the threshold, peering out after her. "Be careful," Aurelian warned, though he, too, pressed closer for a better look.

Vehan watched from the doorstep as Nausicaä stomped through the patch of forest surrounding the hideout, shouting a lengthy string of impressive insults at various possible culprits. There was no sign of anything out there listening. A part of Vehan hoped it was a changeling toying with them, because those faeries were so elusive, the others at school had started a competition to see who could be the first to find one and bring back photographic evidence of the encounter. Of course, Vehan rarely had his phone on him, but Aurelian always had his.

He was just about to ask him for it when something in the distance caught his eye.

"What's that over there . . ." He pointed at the shadowy figure lurking by a far-off tree. Their edges were blurry, as though out of focus. He didn't expect it to help anything to narrow his eyes into a squint, and it didn't at all, but there was very clearly something out there. "Do you see it?"

"No? I don't see anything." Aurelian shifted, peering a little harder into the distance. His eyesight was much better. He should have been able to see the figure in much more clarity. "There's nothing there. Are you sure—Vehan!"

Vehan pushed past him, stepping out into the Hiraeth. That warm and slightly heady feeling of before swept over him as soon as he entered the forest, but this time around he was prepared for it. It affected him less, and though he did still feel a little sedate, the calm that settled in his chest allowed for a certain sharpening of focus. There *was* something in the trees, he could see it better now—a black-cloaked something with a mask around their neck, a bulbous nose, batlike ears, and lilac-tinted skin.

That something grinned. Its iron incisors gleamed as though winking at Vehan.

"It's the goblin—Pincer! Aurelian, he's here!"

As soon as he named him, Pincer fled. Unwilling to risk losing him a second time, Vehan took off after him, ignoring Aurelian's plea for him to wait and Nausicaä's vocal opinion on his poor intelligence.

The Hiraeth made him feel invincible.

His magic crackled raw and ready at his fingertips, more powerful than he'd ever felt it before. His breakneck pace should have left his muscles burning and lungs aching for air, but the faster he ran, the deeper he breathed, the more of the forest's magic he drew into his body and the less he felt the toll of exertion.

Whoops of ugly laughter sounded off around him.

"Vay the fae! Vay the fae," those whoops of laughter also cheered.

Vehan nearly collided with a tree when his head whipped to the side, and saw that he wasn't alone. There was more than just Pincer—he'd replenished his crew. Even more goblins closed in behind Vehan, dropping from the trees and slithering out from the brush. In glimpses he caught sight of something that looked like a gas mask on each of their faces. Was this a scare tactic? Did they just think it made them look more frightening, or was there something about this forest they knew better than Vehan not to inhale? He couldn't think, not with the goblins yipping and yelling and hissing taunts, so close they could practically nip at his heels.

"Vay the fae!"

"Princeling brat!"

"We'll get you just like you got our brothers!"

Vehan pushed himself a little faster.

The tables had turned. He felt foolish—this whole thing had been a trap, and now Vehan was separated from the group, hurtling through unfamiliar territory, pursued by the very thing he'd moments ago been chasing. He broke into a clearing—and tripped over his feet when a pocket of earth deflated in exhale beneath him. With his hands outstretched he tumbled to the ground, gasping for air and coughing it back up, dizzy and shaking and close to retching.

All at once he felt what such a brutal pace had cost him.

He rubbed at his chest, willing his heart to unclench. His eyes streamed. His head throbbed. He needed to get up, to keep running, to get away, but his body weighed him down like lead and he could barely move.

"Come on, Vehan. Get up," he scolded. "Get up, you don't have time for this!"

He pushed himself up off the ground and shakily rose to standing.

One step.

Two.

His panic receded. His breathing evened out. Curious, how this glade had fallen deathly still and silent. Had he somehow lost his goblin tail? Had he fallen into their trap? He paused and looked around.

There was nothing, no sign of life apart from him. The only peals of "Vay the fae" were hollow echoes in his ears. The canopy melted down around him. Mottled green and porcelain blue swirled together, slow as dye bleeding out in water. Looking up at it made Vehan's head hurt, so he dropped his gaze. The carpet of flowers beneath him seemed to be melting too. Gone were the bluebells scattered about everywhere else. *These* were flowers large as saucers, so bright a red and yellow and blue and orange and green and purple, it was laughable that he should ever have applied these names to anything else of those colors.

A light breeze sent their petals dancing in a kaleidoscope of color, plucked from their stems and tossed to the air. It was beautiful, marvelous, magic better than anything he could ever summon. They wove together and rode the curls of breeze like waves, bursting apart in a firework display above his head, and fluttering back to the ground.

Some of the petals took on shapes. Vehan watched them knit together and gasped in awe when they leaped to life as tigers and snakes and elephants and lions. The clearing became a human circus—his mother had taken him to one when he'd been a child, and he'd made himself sick on the cotton candy and caramel apples and whirling rides the clever humans pieced together, but what he'd liked best was the animal parade.

Laughing, he stuck out his hand. One of the tigers stalked closer, and he so badly wanted to pet it. Perhaps it would let him? Nothing could harm him here, after all—it was a circus; this was all part of the show.

"You *stupid* boy."

The ringmaster had arrived!

Tall and slim and oddly long-limbed, his body warped this way and that as he walked the field toward him, as though a reflection in bent glass. Vehan knew him. He *knew* he knew him. How did he know him? He couldn't remember. The long, gunmetal-gray hair, freezing-bright green eyes, and starlight-shimmery skin were all familiar, but of course, Vehan would have seen him on the advertisements for this show.

"You mortals are an absolute *pestilence.*"

Vehan laughed. The ringmaster's irritation was hilarious.

"Promises . . . promises . . . I loathe that I made such *promises* where you're concerned. *Keep him safe*—if only I'd known how much work that would entail."

As he made his way toward Vehan, the animals he commanded turned to greet him. They threw themselves in his path, leaping with ferocious snarls and thunderous roars, claws outstretched and deadly mouths flung wide. A thread of concern wove its way into the moment, but the ringmaster was a professional. With a swipe of his gleaming silver hand, the animals burst apart into showers of petals each before they could land their blow.

It was dizzying. It was spectacular. Vehan cried out in awe and laughed as one after the other, every petal animal was dashed to vibrant pieces. One had turned on Vehan—the tiger he'd wanted to pet—but just as it sprang at his face, it exploded as well, and petals rained down around him, sticking to his hair and skin and clothes.

The ringmaster gripped his jaw in the hand that wasn't dripping silver. "Open," he spat.

Vehan complied.

He had no reason not to.

The ringmaster shoved a stick of wood between his teeth, and Vehan groaned—it was rowan tree bark, a different sort of poison used to break faerie enchantments—but that hand held him tight by the jaw and forced him to continue biting down.

Slowly, the world began to right itself, draining of vibrancy, reassembling into solid shape. Vehan couldn't see much past the person in front of him, but in slivers he could make out splashes of vibrant blue across a field of death-gray flowers, their petals hanging limp as ashy shells.

"What are you doing here?"

Vehan could only stare around his bit of bark.

It was a painstaking process, but his mind eventually clawed its way completely from the fog that had settled over it. His body trembled, muscles in a spasm as his system worked through whatever drug those ashlike flowers had released into the air. Their pollen smeared sooty streaks across his hands and arms and clothes, but when he bent his focus to a close examination of the substance, he realized it wasn't only this.

"This is the *Hiraeth*. This isn't a playground for princes. Come."

The mysterious faerie gave him a rough shake; Vehan spit out the rowan wood.

The splashes of blue . . . It was on him as well, in his hair, on his face . . . warm and tacky and—"Blood," Vehan murmured thickly. The blue was faerie blood. There was *so much of it*. He looked past his savior, whose long, cold fingers of his bare hand were brushing at his shirt and swiping through his hair with little care, dislodging residual ash. The curious splashes of blue took on cruel violence now that Vehan realized what it was. It sprayed the field and pooled in steadily darkening puddles around crumpled, motionless bodies of the masked goblins he'd been fleeing.

Another ambush.

Those gas masks must have protected the goblins from the flowers' pollen.

He would have died, drugged and laughing, a smile on his face and none the wiser.

"I feel sick."

"I imagine you do."

His savior turned him forcibly about-face and marched him from the field. Vehan's steps were coltish—he tripped over his own feet multiple times, but the person behind him hauled him upright as though he weighed no more than a sack of flour. "I know you . . . ," Vehan slurred. "You were in the desert. You saved Aurelian and me from those creatures. You've saved me again . . . why?"

He tried to crane his head around and peek at his savior's face when no response was forthcoming, but the ice he met there was so cold and unamused that he flinched and looked away.

Back through the forest his mysterious faerie drove him.

The wood Vehan had bitten helped to detoxify his system with surprising swiftness, but it still left him feeling wrung out and weak, and aching all over.

"Vehan!"

The sound of Aurelian's voice brought a stinging to Vehan's eyes. He shook himself free of his savior's hold as soon as he spotted his retainer through the trees. "Over here!" he called, and no sooner did he speak than Aurelian was there in front of him, patting him down, wiping blood from his face and turning him this way and that, checking Vehan for injury.

"I'm okay," Vehan assured him.

"You look very much *not*." Anxiety weighed on Aurelian's brow, his eyes aglow with concern. It was so much like how Aurelian *should* be acting if everything between them was normal that Vehan felt his stinging eyes turn watery. "What happened? Why are you covered in soot and blood? Who is . . ." He trailed off, noticing at last who it was who'd delivered Vehan. "You."

Aurelian growled.

The faerie growled back. Quicker than a viper's strike his claw-tipped hand snagged on the front of Aurelian's shirt and reeled him in too close to those sharp bared teeth for Vehan's comfort.

"Let him go!" Vehan hollered with a force that stirred his nausea. Sparks danced angrily at the tips of his fingers, a threat to match his tone.

"Lethe?"

The faerie looked up. Nausicaä had caught up with them at last, strolling onto the scene with cautiousness that seemed at odds with her personality. She halted once the mysterious faerie met her gaze and raised her hands, a placating gesture of surrender. A heartbeat passed, then another. The faerie released Aurelian, the cloth of his shirt slicing apart in fine shreds as it slipped through his claws. "This is the second time I've had to rescue this mortal boy. First with the cava, today from a Sleeping Hollow . . . Parenthood is such a taxing profession, I don't know why anyone does it. Look, I'm actually *molting*." He extracted a hair off his cloak with distaste and flicked it in Nausicaä's direction.

Vehan blanched.

A Sleeping Hollow? Was that what that field had been? He knew of the place from storybooks he'd read in secret, snuck out of a section in their library restricted to Maturity and older. Sleeping Hollows were cursed grounds. They were sites that had known magic so dark and terrible that it left an indelible impression on the earth, and no amount of time could heal it over. The flowers that grew in its soil . . . Their ashen petals were what went into making Faerie Dust.

He watched Aurelian examine his hands before lowering them with something close to difficulty and wiping them off on his pants.

"Okay, so, there were a lot of words in that sentence that concern me," Nausicaä replied. "Question the first—"

"Collect your belongings and *go*," said the faerie—Lethe, Nausicaä called him. His tone had now grown as frosty as his stare, and slightly bored. "I was in the middle of something, you know. It's difficult to enjoy one's leisure time with children running around." He shuddered.

"Okay, but seriously, Lethe, what the fuck do you mean by 'cava'?"

"What's a cava?" Vehan asked. This term he *didn't* know. "Is that what those things were in the desert?"

Nausicaä looked at him strangely. "You said there was a facility in the desert. You didn't say anything about cava."

"Maybe because I don't know what that is!"

"I'm leaving," Lethe announced. "Please take your shrieking parasites elsewhere, cousin, before I decide I care that the High King has issued a very public warrant for your arrest."

Turning a glower on his twice savior, Vehan stood his ground. He was tired of having answers dangled in front of him like sweets, only to be snatched away by people who thought he shouldn't have them. If he was the only one who was going to take this situation seriously, he deserved to know what they did. "Here's an idea: I don't want to be here either. I'd like to not have to deal with any of this. I'd like to be at home, catching up on all my homework that's been piling up while I chase after scraps of a murder investigation. But I'm not, because I'm the heir to my Court. Because it's my responsibility to keep my people safe, and since no one else seems bothered to help, it falls to me to sort this out. The only reason I needed saving from that Hollow was because I saw the goblins we'd encountered in the desert, and maybe if you deigned to tell us what you know, I could save *you* from any further inexplicable involvement in my life."

Lethe stared down the length of his nose at him, expression at once mild and murderous.

"Please don't kill him," Nausicaä pleaded, so sincerely Vehan turned to her in shock.

"The goblins from the desert . . . the ones that led to our first meeting, you mean?"

Turning back to Lethe, Vehan nodded. "I saw one of them, Pincer, just outside the curiosity shop. I tried to apprehend him, but as you saw, he wasn't alone. It was an ambush. He led me straight into that Sleeping Hollow and probably meant to kill me, although how he even knew we were going to be at Nikos's shop to begin with—"

"The goblins led you there on *purpose?*"

There was a lightness to Lethe's tone that was somehow even more frightening than his snarl. His antifreeze eyes were bright with all the thoughts he kept to himself. Vehan shrugged, wary of whatever point lay at the end of this questioning. "Seems like."

"If there's anything duller-minded than a human, it's a goblin. They squabble and fight over territory, killing each other for pitiful scraps—they don't hunt fae down in packs, princeling."

"Well, today they did. I was *there*. I saw it with my own two eyes—before that Sleeping Hollow started playing tricks on them. You saw them. You *killed* them."

"I'm to spell it out for you? Fine. They lack the sophistication required to lure weak away from their groups to pick them off one by one, is what I mean. Someone else was behind this assault. The question is why, and were you the intended target, pretty Vehan, or mere distraction for your friends?" Lethe looked to each of them in turn, considering them like parts of an equation he was trying to solve.

"Shit!"

Nausicaä burst so suddenly into a cloud of black smoke that Vehan yelped. The smoke compressed itself down to nothing, and just like that, she was gone.

"What in the . . . how . . . *what?*"

"Lose track of one of your flock, Your Highness?"

Vehan recovered from one shock only to fall once more to the next. He ignored Lethe's taunt and turned to Aurelian, eyes grown wide. "You don't think they've gone after Arlo, too, do you?"

"Excuse me. Arlo?" Lethe laughed, a brittle sound that creaked wool and set Vehan's teeth on edge. "You couldn't possibly mean Arlo Jarsdel, could you? You couldn't, because no one could be that *foolish*."

What?

Vehan stared at him. "Yes? Arlo Jarsdel. She was with us but left to get some air. We were trying to get back to her before all this happened. How do you know her?"

Lethe's laugh morphed into a snarl as he became instantly incensed. "*Do not touch her*—a simple instruction! That worm, that jealous, pathetic worm, I'll gut him." What Lethe meant by this—why he should be so concerned about Arlo to begin with—was something Vehan couldn't even start to guess at, but the starlight in the faerie's face had drained down to the same ashen gray as the flowers in the Sleeping Hollow, and though their interactions had been brief up to this point, never before had Vehan seen him look so livid. "Get out of my way."

Vehan scrambled, only just managing to escape the temper that propelled Lethe forward.

The forest floor rose and fell, swelling on a breath—in the same span of time it took it to deflate, Lethe was gone.

Vehan had . . . so many questions. "One problem at a time." To Aurelian he said, "Let's go," and with no further hesitation, the pair of them tore back to the waiting shop.

CHAPTER 23

Arlo

~⚬~

S HE'D BEEN HOPING TO catch her breath in the forest—the Hiraeth had been soothing—but when Arlo fled past Nikos and the others in the Assistance's lobby and wrenched the door back open, it was directly back into Toronto she'd stepped.

This was fine. There was air out here, too.

Dropping her tote, Arlo crouched and stuck her head between her knees. How long she stayed like this she couldn't say, but she gulped the air as though she'd been drowning and tried to reorganize her whirlwind thoughts.

Vehan was right.

She *should* lend her help, even if all she could do was (somehow) get them through that sealed door. Surely the High King would forgive her use of alchemy if it meant the end of all these murders—if it meant keeping the prince of Seelie Summer from winding up in the news as well—and really, would it draw any more unwanted attention to herself than she'd already done so far, to follow Vehan to this mysterious facility?

But she was *scared*.

Cassandra's death was still fresh in her mind, and she didn't want to end up the same, another body on the news, reduced to a number, dismissed by the Courts in death just as she'd been in life—a human problem.

So yes, she was scared, and she was *tired*.

Most of her family regarded her as a nuisance. The ones who didn't treated her like she was delicate glass, fragile, incapable of doing anything for herself—even Celadon, whom she loved so *much* and who loved her so much in return, kept her too close sometimes. There were times she felt like some storybook princess held away from the world in a tower, forever only watching and never truly a part of anything. Nausicaä, Vehan, even Aurelian . . . They didn't know not to count on her. They didn't know that asking her to be a part of this team was actually condemning it to failure, that any time she tried to leave that tower, disaster followed.

She should tell them no, save both them and herself from another disappointment.

She should, but a not-insignificant part of Arlo didn't want to. A part of her whispered *what if*, the same as it had done in her Weighing, the same as it had done to chase her into the Faerie Ring and this entire plot to begin with—*what if* this time was different?

The minutes creeped by.

Arlo lifted her head from between her knees and scrubbed at her face, wiping away the tears she'd finally allowed herself to shed. She had to head home. It had grown late—she was cutting it close to her curfew, her hour was almost up—but this hadn't been nearly enough time to make such an important decision. She couldn't just leave, she'd have to go back in and tell the prince *something*, but what could she say? "What am I supposed to do here?" she wondered aloud.

Maybe they'd give her the night to think this over—that was reasonable, wasn't it? They couldn't expect her to sign on to this ridiculous, high-risk scheme of theirs without a little time for consideration; the least they could do was give her a few more hours.

There was no harm in asking. If not, she'd simply have to tell them no and be done with it. Turning back to the curiosity shop, she pulled the door open but found it wasn't at all the lobby she'd left. It was, for all intents and purposes, an exact replica, but gone were the faerie and fae adults. A human boy stood just as frozen as Arlo, caught by her sudden appearance, holding a broom in his hands. Scrawny, boar-black hair a wild mess of loose curls around his head, brown eyes wide in shock—he looked no older than Elyas.

"Uh . . . hello?" came his tentative greeting. "I'm sorry, we're actually closed . . ."

"Yeah, um, where did . . . is Nausicaä still upstairs?" Arlo spluttered.

"Who?"

"Nausicaä?"

The boy shook his head, confused.

"Uh, what about Nikos? Where did he go?"

The boy's heavy brow was knitted together in deeper concern. "My father isn't here today. Hey, are you okay? Do you . . . need help or something?"

She'd entered the wrong shop. This wasn't the Assistance, this was the human front of Chorley's Curiosities.

"Crap," she moaned, and backed out of the shop. Slamming the door closed, she tried again, but when it opened a second time, it was still the boy with his broom staring back at her, possibly contemplating calling the police.

She slammed the door again. No matter how she clawed at the hinges where it had previously opened, and knocked on that side of the wood, she couldn't get back to her friends.

"All right, well . . . I guess I'll just wait?" There wasn't anything else she could do. She had her phone, but she didn't have anyone's number to make that useful. If she waited out here long enough, someone would come looking for her, wouldn't they? She'd give them the rest of the hour she could spare before she really had to leave.

Brushing her hair away from her face, she turned back to stare unseeingly off down the street at the flood of vehicles and all the people with somewhere else to be, and leaned against the shop front's window.

Minutes ticked by.

No one came for her.

Time had run out, according to the clock on her phone, and the street started to grow congested with people venturing out for dinner. She should just go—if Vehan wanted her to change her mind, Nausicaä was apparently all too capable of finding her in this city.

With a sigh, she reached for her phone, intending to do what Nausicaä had suggested earlier and fire off a text to her mother. She'd tell her that work had run a little long and she was heading home now. Maybe her mother would buy it, maybe she wouldn't—she had to try, though. But just as she unlocked her phone . . .

"Help!"

Arlo paused.

She could have sworn she'd heard something—a child's voice calling out. It had been too faint, and Arlo had been too distracted to really tell. She waited and listened, looking around, but nothing seemed out of place. Nothing, she determined—her mind had been playing tricks on her. She carried on.

"Help me, somebody, *please!*"

That was no trick. There was someone in genuine trouble nearby. She whirled around, replacing her phone in her pocket—that cry had come from the alley between the souvlaki shop and a realtor's office, she was sure of it—but no one else seemed to notice. No one else on the sidewalk had stopped or turned their head toward the sound. They certainly noticed *her*, pale and wide-eyed in shock, staring off after something they couldn't hear, but continued by, giving her as wide a berth as they could manage.

"Crap." It would have to be her. She couldn't ignore this, couldn't just leave, and she couldn't get back to the others. "Crap, okay." One foot stepped in front of the other, bringing her in something of a daze to the alley, but it was just that—an alley, a narrow stretch of brick and a couple massive bins for trash, overstuffed black bags piled all around. Grime streaked the pavement and brick of the surrounding buildings, but between them, nothing.

There was no child here in danger. There was no one calling for help. In fact, there was hardly any life at all—hardly any *sound*, as though the alley wasn't just an alley in the least but a crevice carved from magic.

Arlo stared.

She could feel her heart pounding against her ribs, and so much adrenaline pumped through her that she felt light-headed and numb. This, she determined, was the reason why she stepped off the sidewalk and into an alley steeped in so much *wrongness*.

One step.

Two.

Arlo shivered and stopped in her tracks.

This quiet isn't natural, her brain warned. It could be magic, enforcing this silence; it could just be the press of the brick around her, the porous stone swallowing up the sounds of city life. She had to keep calm. Drawing a breath to fortify her nerves, Arlo peered deeper into the alley's depths.

"Hello?" she called. "Is anyone there?"

No response. She sighed and turned around, *relieved* that it had been nothing. The sound had been the result of the considerable stress she'd been under these past few weeks—when she got home tonight, she was going to take a bubble bath and binge-watch *She-Ra and the Princesses of Power* on Netflix until she fell asleep.

But then . . .

"Pretty petal."

Arlo felt her heart freeze. She knew that voice—recognized it instantly, along with the barely-there scent of brine and rot—and she didn't want to turn around. At the same time, she couldn't prevent herself from doing so.

The Reaper.

Magic it was, then—a glamour, and a powerful one at that, to be thrown over something outside oneself, more powerful than something this creature could manage, so it couldn't be working alone. Someone had to be helping it . . . but who?

She didn't have time to ponder the question.

Skeletal tall and looming over Arlo—no longer distorted, as it had been at the Faerie Ring—the Reaper stood well over eight feet and was sliver slim. Half its skull was missing, a hollow shell without any evidence of eyes or a brain, but it didn't need eyes to get around. It could scent the air just fine through the holes that were all that was left of its nose and *taste* the fear it inspired with its gaping mouth crammed full of jagged teeth.

It was nothing but knobbly bone and decayed flesh little better than graying tarp stretched taut across its emaciated frame. Every child in the magical community had grown up on the whispers of what this sort of faerie could do with its ancient, festering magic and elongated fingers, used to pry and break apart bone so it could suck the very marrow from its innards.

Reapers consumed.

It was all they did.

Like vultures, they were drawn to dark magic, to death and decay, and were legendarily difficult to kill.

Thalo Viridian-Verdell had won the position she now commanded by walking into the High King's throne room and dropping a Reaper's head at his feet. No one—not even the misogynistic members of the Courts who *hated* having a woman and mother as the leader of their army—had been able to deny after that that she was the one for the job.

Thalo Viridian-Verdell would stand a chance against the creature behind Arlo.

Her daughter could hardly stand at all.

"Pretty little Spring flower," the Reaper continued, its rasping voice like bitter wind scraping through a broken window. *"At last."* It leaned in to scent the air around her, and Arlo gasped, stumbling backward, covering her nose with her hands to try to block out the Reaper's putrid stench.

"Leaving so soon? I've been looking everywhere for you."

For *her*?

Arlo's mind reeled. Half of her was still keyed up with the adrenaline that had brought her here, while the other half was petrified by the surety of her impending death.

This was it.

She'd played the hero, and just as she'd predicted, she'd drawn too much attention. The Reaper was here for her; she was going to die—horribly, *painfully*. Reapers enjoyed their meals best when they were alive to scream and struggle, and dismemberment wasn't exactly gentle.

Matching each of Arlo's trembling steps toward the street with a long and easy stride, the Reaper prowled after her. "How many times you've slipped through my grasp . . . How many times I got the wrong mark . . . You mortals, you're all the same to me, but my Master was most displeased. He'll be happy tonight. Come here, little flower, let me *taste* you." The Reaper moaned in anticipation of doing so, but just as the tips of its fingers brushed Arlo's hair, she unfroze—and bolted.

Back out into the street she plunged, speeding away as fast as her legs could carry her. The Reaper followed—crap, she hadn't thought this through! Heedless of the very human world around it, it plowed out into the street as well, knocking pedestrians aside, crashing into bikes and telephone poles and cars that were lined against the curb.

The humans couldn't see it—it had kept some of its glamour, then, but they could certainly hear when it snarled, and the folk that were scattered among them screamed.

Arlo pushed herself harder. She'd never be able to outrun a Reaper; how she'd even managed to keep ahead of it this long meant she most likely had the city itself to thank. Reapers were fast, but the city was full of obstacles, and these creatures weren't used to navigating such spaces. The sound of something blowing through brick, of windows shattering and even more screaming and something heavy enough to send a ripple through the earth, made Arlo's head whip around—sure enough, the Reaper had misjudged a hurdle and crashed into a building beside it. It fell to the ground and *bellowed* its fury.

Sirens flared in the distance.

The Reaper swiped at the people who unwittingly got in its way as it clawed itself back to its feet.

Arlo pushed harder—the Reaper was after *her*, so she had to lead it away from the Danforth to someplace not so packed with potential casualties.

Something large sailed overhead. Arlo could hear it groan through the motion, watched as its shadow enveloped her. Overwhelmed by its size, she skidded to a halt just in time to narrowly miss being crushed by what dropped directly in front of her from the sky.

The Reaper had thrown a *car*.

There was no time to let herself panic over such a close shave or pat herself down like she wanted to make sure she'd actually survived. She bolted across the street, weaving deftly through the traffic that had screeched to a halt in awe over what must have looked like a Mazda picking *itself* off the ground. Wind-snap quick, she slipped among the mob of people running for safety and made for another alley, hoping it would lead to something slightly less congested.

But just on the cusp, her shoe caught her opposite heel—she tripped. Pitching forward, she dove for the cracked and crumbling pavement, her palms outstretched to catch her fall.

"Are you *kidding* me?"

There, barely inches from her splayed hands, was the not-troll's gods-damned *die*. It sat there, innocuous, face up on *four*, all polished jade and gleaming gold numbers and one hundred percent useless; she'd already discovered that in her last encounter with the monster closing in behind her.

"You can't outrun me, petal child."

The Reaper had finally untangled itself from its fall. It made its approach, picking its way across the street, batting aside the vehicles it passed. Fear rose like bile in Arlo's throat, and she gagged, but there was *no time for this*.

"I hate you," she seethed at the die she snatched up, and with strength that was purely adrenaline, she heaved herself to her feet.

People had gathered at the opposite end of the alley, drawn by their curiosity. With all the roaring and the shaking and the many other sounds of chaos, Arlo didn't blame them, but how long did she have until the Reaper turned its frustration on innocent people?

"Go back inside!" Arlo shouted as she tore through this gawking crowd. She tried to push them aside, and some of them scattered, but more only gravitated back to their places as though magnetized to the spot.

"Damn it," she cursed. She'd have to try a different tactic. "Hey!" She wheeled around, just as the Reaper knocked through the crowd too. "Hey, you . . . you stupid!" Oh, wow, she was going to have to get better at taunting in her next life, but the Reaper's attention swiveled from the humans it had started to consider, the humans that would be a much easier target than she'd proven to be. "You want me, you ugly piece of crap? Come get me!"

She ran.

The Reaper shrieked and pitched its toy aside, all too happy to engage in a bit of sport before it ate like any proper predator. It tore after Arlo.

Down another alley, out into another street, this one running through a residential neighborhood, where people were at least inside their homes and not in immediate danger. She pushed herself with everything she had, but behind her, the Reaper only gained momentum—it was toying with her, too, perhaps too curious to see how long she could keep this up to end it just yet, but there *would* be an end. When she came to yet another alley, tucked between two apartment buildings, her immediate reaction was to turn down it, to just keep this up until the Falchion arrived, or maybe the Wild Hunt . . . and only then did she realize her unfortunate mistake.

This alley had no exit on the opposite side, only a wooden fence blocking her in. Arlo was trapped.

"No more room, pretty flower."

Wildly out of breath, she squeezed her eyes closed. She took a moment to gather herself—this was it, this was her death. The fence was built too high to scale.

"Nowhere to run. I didn't think I'd have so much fun when they brought me here to collect their little would-be alchemists—when my Master instructed me to hunt you down as well. Are you ready to meet death, child of Spring?"

Arlo whirled around. "Why me?" The words flew out of her mouth before she could stop them, but they weren't a plea for life, as perhaps they should be. They were hot; they were angry; they were confused by what she could have possibly done to earn such a desperate desire to take her out. "Why are you out here specifically for *me*? What have I done that's so threatening to your *Master*?"

The Reaper laughed—a hollow sound rattling in its chest—and drew a few steps closer. *"What do I care? They offered to unleash me on your cities, permitted me to gorge my fill on failed stones. The darker the magic, the sweeter the flesh, like spice for your mortal delicacies—how could I say no? If my Master wants you gone as well, it's nothing to me. Another meal."*

"Well, hot damn."

Both Arlo and the Reaper shot their focus up to the top of the apartment building on Arlo's right.

"This keeps getting better and better! My princess *and* my Reaper, at long last. What's a girl to do with all this excitement?"

Relief coursed through her like a flood. Arlo had no idea if Nausicaä actually stood a chance against a Reaper, but she was here, and she didn't have to be able to best it—all she had to do was teleport them away. Arlo would live to see another day, where she was definitely no longer allowed to leave her mother's apartment ever again because Thalo was going to hear about this, there was no question about it, but the important thing was that she would *live*.

"So eager for death?" The Reaper sniffed the air. Unable to see Nausicaä, it apparently tried to reacquaint itself with the smell of her magic. *"I know you . . . what are you? Come down, little bird. Let me taste your fear."*

Nausicaä laughed, stepping off the ledge of the building; the pavement cracked beneath her feet where she landed. "Geez, and they call *me* dramatic."

A curious thing took place as Nausicaä spoke.

Darkness spilled from the center of her back between the blades of her shoulders. It unspooled in the air like smoke, seemingly endless, growing out behind her. For a moment, Arlo thought this was a cue for their escape. It seemed like the exact same smoke that had teleported them here. She took a step forward, hand outstretched to grab hold of Nausicaä's arm, but there was something different about this substance, giving her pause.

That unspooling darkness took on shape.

The indistinguishable mass, like a blot of ink spilling from its well, began to sift apart and grow. Flaring out on either side of her, it formed itself like massive, shadowy rags-like-wings.

Arlo retracted a step to make room for this spreading darkness. When a loud *crack* and patter of crumbling brick on the cement drew her attention to the wall, she realized her mistake—these rags of shadows *were* wings, and they were sprouting bones, the talons tipping their skeletal structure strong enough to pierce through stone. Soon, the frame of Nausicaä's wings took up more space than the narrow alley was able to give, and more brick began to crack and crumble to the ground all around them. Arlo could only watch in awe as the darkness itself became something else too.

Not quite leather, not quite feather, membranous black hung in shreds from ebony bone, and fluttered in some nonexistent breeze like strips of shredded silk. It smoldered, the way fire did when only recently extinguished, heat still pouring in waves from winding veins that glowed like embers.

Nausicaä herself seemed larger. Unchanged, at least from what Arlo could see of her back. But there was a blurriness around her too, like a negative image in a poorly taken photo—a hint of something greater and far more terrible than the hauntingly beautiful blonde looming between the eclipsing height of her wings.

This glimpse of Nausicaä as she'd once been—her former, Furious glory—was more than enough for Arlo to know that in this moment, the one she should fear the most was the person standing between her and painful, bone-crunching death. And yet . . . Arlo was the least afraid she'd ever been in her life.

In fact, something inside her felt almost . . . enthralled, so profoundly it stole her breath.

The Reaper certainly didn't look pleased—far from it. What was left of its face seemed to crumble, realizations of its own finally clicking into place. Whatever memory it had of Furies and Nausicaä, Arlo was willing to bet none of them were pleasant.

"Erinys," the Reaper rasped, bending itself into a grotesque parody of a bow. *"Forgive me, I didn't know that it was you."*

"Don't worry, sometimes I forget I'm me too." Nausicaä took a step forward, the talons of her wings scoring fissures in the walls. The Reaper fell fully prostrate on the ground, and Arlo marveled at the behavior.

"I beg you, allow this lowly creature its retreat. Do not condemn me to the Pool—I will leave the city. I won't come back. I do not wish to be Destroyed."

A Reaper, begging for its life. Despite everything, the miserable way it spoke strummed a chord of pity in Arlo's heart. "What's the Pool?" she asked.

"The Starfire Pool," Nausicaä replied in a way that made Arlo regret asking; her tone was so tight around contempt, it was a wonder Nausicaä could speak at all. "The pit where Immortals go to be Destroyed, for whatever reason . . . and where those who break the fundamental Laws are brought to die." She continued forward until she stood directly in front of the Reaper, arms folded across her chest. "Get up, I wouldn't send you there even if it was still my job to do that. You might be a creep, but you haven't done anything to warrant Destruction—eating people isn't dark magic, it's just rude."

The Reaper hesitated, as though it could hardly believe its luck. Then it lifted its head. *"You will let me go?"*

Arlo recovered from her awe at last. "Nausicaä, we can't just let it go. It's been killing ironborn; we need to bring it to the High King. We need to—"

"Yeah, is that why you're all the way out here?" Nausicaä turned around, hands falling to her hips. Her face was set with a sternness that took Arlo aback. "Were you going to arrest this asshole too and march him back to the palace like you were going to do with me? Listen, I'm all kinds of proud of the bravery it took to do that, but next time, do me a favor and let someone know before you take off after murderous plot-points. I'm sort of responsible for you right now. Starting a war with the Courts might be my retirement plan, but I'd rather not do it over your dead body."

"I'm sorry." Arlo sighed at the reprimand—it figured that she could be too sheltered and too independent all the same. "I tried to get back to you! But I couldn't get through to the right shop, and besides, what if . . . what if the Hunt is on its way? They're bound to notice a Reaper just blew apart a chunk of the Danforth."

Nausicaä snorted, something in the statement amusing.

"*I swear to you, I won't return to any city space,*" said the Reaper, even more distressed after Arlo's mention of the Hunt. "*Let me go, do not hand me over to the Hunt. I have information! I will trade that for my life.*"

Arlo pursed her lips. Shooting a glance at Nausicaä, she crouched her way under the smoking, fluttering barrier of those wings to get a little closer. "You said someone sent you here to kill me."

"Oh, okay, so that stuff with the goblins really *was* a distraction. Cool. Cool."

Arlo shot another look at Nausicaä, unsure of what she meant, but decided to save that line of questioning for later. She turned back to the Reaper. "You said someone wanted you to clean up after them—clean up what, the ironborn your Master's been experimenting on?"

It was vaguely disconcerting to be considered by something with a hollow head and no visible eyes. Arlo didn't think she'd forget the sight anytime soon.

"I was tasked to hunt down the would-be alchemists whose hearts had failed the stone they carried. I have no idea what their connection was to my Master. I never asked."

"Who *is* your Master, then? Can you at least tell us that?"

If she could just get a name, they wouldn't have to investigate Vehan's questionable facility. Arlo wouldn't have to get any more involved. This could all be over, and she wouldn't have to worry any longer about someone wanting her *dead*, or why. As much as her great-uncle wished to ignore all of this, he couldn't ignore an actual culprit—the adults would have to do their jobs, and Arlo could go back to whatever remained of the child she wished she was still, who only knew death as a concept and fear as a thing cured by a hug.

"I don't know."

And Arlo's hope wilted, much like the expression on her face. "You . . . you don't know?"

The Reaper shook its head. *"I do not. My Master and the one he answers to . . . Neither ever gave me their names, though I've met them both. I know that they're both male. That one is like you, ironborn. The other I could not scent. Could not taste. I only knew that they were there when they spoke. He calls my Master his hero."*

"So really," Nausicaä interrupted, "you don't know anything. That isn't much of a trade. And now I'm kind of pissed, so I'm thinking maybe I'll Destroy you after all."

"No, wait! Please, I can tell you where to find them! I can tell you what the scentless one is. I don't know their names, but the one my Master serves, I know what he serves, I know his ilk—please, promise me freedom and I'll tell you."

Nausicaä walked forward, coming up to Arlo's side. As she moved, her wings retracted. The negative space around her receded. The smoldering shadows were extinguished, and Nausicaä's mask of mortality slipped back into place. She shared a look with Arlo, the lethal lines of her face etched in continued severity, before turning the steel of her gaze back on the Reaper. "You'll tell me now, or I'll end you right here."

"The scentless one, he's with the H—nngh.*"*

Whatever the Reaper had been about to say was cut off by a groan.

The ground around them darkened, a plum-black stain pooling outward and eating away at the pavement on which the Reaper knelt. Arlo leaped away, helped by Nausicaä's yank to the back of her shirt. Together they shuffled out of the path of this mysterious, corrosive puddle of what looked to Arlo like the same shadowy substance from which Nausicaä's wings had sprouted.

"What's happening?" Arlo panicked.

"My old job," said Nausicaä, astonished. "But . . . why?"

Nausicaä's old job . . . Did she mean . . . Were *Furies* the ones behind whatever was happening right now?

"Wait!" Nausicaä shouted over the Reaper's renewed shrieking. It was being swallowed by the pool, consumed by the very ground beneath it, sinking down into the depths of someplace Arlo had a feeling she would never wish to go herself. "Wait! What were you going to say? The scentless one, who is he? Tell me!"

The Reaper couldn't respond. Its cries grew strangled, that darkness crawling up around its body, wrapping serpent-tight, binding the creature to its fate. It sank, and in mere, eternal seconds, it was going . . . going . . . gone.

The pool withdrew. The darkness reeled itself in and shrank to a drop, which the ground absorbed. Arlo and Nausicaä were left with nothing but a ringing silence.

"Shit."

Arlo's gaze snapped away from the spot where the Reaper had once been and sought out Nausicaä. She wanted to say something, to ask why Nausicaä looked so distressed when it was *her* the Reaper had named as a target. She wanted to know what would happen to it, where it was going, what all of this meant, but instead, when she opened her mouth . . .

"*What* did I tell you?"

Arlo jerked around. Somehow, a girl not much older than her had come between them and the back of the alley. Had she been there all along? Like the Reaper, had she been hidden under unusually strong glamour, biding her time, waiting for just the right moment to reveal herself? She was taller, larger than life almost, yet human in appearance. The long cascade of her black-ink hair, the angular features, the purple dress that clung like paint to her skin, none of it was technically out of the ordinary except for the fact that something about this girl was *different*—otherworldly. Her complexion was the gray of bitterly cold water, and nothing about her fit here, like a poorly edited image. The very air around her glistened—distorted, as though warped by a thin veneer of ice.

And her eyes cut just as sharp and steely as Nausicaä's.

She knew who this was without needing to be told—another Fury. Arlo shrank a step back.

Nausicaä rounded instantly on this intruder. "Not a whole hell of a lot, Meg. Hence why I'm still here. Why did you do that? Why did you sentence that Reaper to Destruction? So it killed a bunch of people, big flipping deal—it didn't use magic to do that, so it wasn't an immortal concern. You aren't supposed to touch it!"

The intruder—Meg—laughed. Her head dipped slightly back, the slender, pale column of her throat bared to Nausicaä, the sound reminded Arlo of an echo trapped in a bottomless pit, and made this Meg more frightening to her than the Reaper had been; she inched a bit closer to Nausicaä.

"Are you giving me a lecture about *rules*? How rich." The Fury, Meg, stepped forward, those gray eyes flashing. "I don't have to explain myself, not to you—you, whom I specifically ordered to stay out of this. What do you hope to accomplish, I wonder, in ignoring that? In running around after things that no longer concern you." Her gaze shifted to Arlo, looked her up and looked her down. "You can't possibly think you could earn your way back."

356

Nausicaä narrowed her eyes. "Piss off, I wouldn't come back if you begged me."

"Who would even?" Meg took another step toward them. "Beg for someone like you—I'd laugh if the very idea wasn't so pathetically *you*."

Not one to pass on a challenge—at least, from what Arlo had so far gathered on her new friend—Nausicaä crowded Meg right back. "Oh, you want to talk about things that are pathetic, do you? Whatever it did to piss you off, *how* long to catch up to one little Reaper? Big bad Megaera, so much better than everyone else, when that thing's been here for *days*."

"It was never a target until now," Megaera replied stiffly.

Something about the way she glanced at Arlo made her curious about what that meant. Was it that the Reaper had finally made itself enough of a nuisance to warrant Fury intervention, or that it had gone after something specific today . . . something the immortals wouldn't be all that happy about it harming?

Before she could ask what that could be, Nausicaä growled out, "*Why?* Don't get me wrong, I don't want back in your stupid little tree house club, I just want to know what's going on. Tell me *something* and maybe I'll leave it alone like you want!"

"Like I want?" Meg had surged forward. She seemed to grow larger in her anger, the aura of her magic easy now to detect, the way it flooded the alley—cool and salty, like glacial sea air. "You know what *I* want? It should have been you. It should have been you! *You* should have been the one to die, not Tisiphone. If the gods let me pick which sister to lose, *I would have picked—*"

Arlo moved without thinking.

Her nerves were still caught up in shock and adrenaline.

Megaera's words had been the most ghastly thing she'd ever heard anyone say to someone else—someone who, by the sound of things, was supposed to be family—and this was even in comparison to the one time High Prince Serulian had pulled her aside one memorable palace visit to tell her she'd ruined her mother's life by being born.

Nausicaä stood there as though stricken.

These were the things that made Arlo stride right up to Megaera and slap her in the face.

Only once the deed was done and Megaera's face had snapped to the side did Arlo realize she had, in fact, done it. But she wasn't sorry—she was deeply afraid she'd just survived a Reaper to be gutted by a Fury, judging by the look of pure astonishment on the face that now turned back to her, but she wasn't sorry. "Apologize!" she ordered. "That was an awful thing to say to your own sister. You can't mean that—tell her you're sorry!"

Nausicaä stared.

Megaera did too.

Arlo held her ground, slightly wishing it would open up and swallow her the way it had done for the Reaper, but even more slightly worried it would do exactly that. But for all Megaera bristled and drew herself imposingly, impossibly taller, she said nothing. She did nothing—nothing but turn and sweep out an arm, and leathery, glossy-black wings burst from her back. They wrapped her up quick as it took Arlo to blink, and she was gone.

The painful, indefinable emotion that Arlo occasionally saw in Nausicaä's gaze was bright and just as nameless as ever when she looked up at her, and then—like every other time Arlo caught it—quickly shuttered away. "You just slapped a Fury in the face."

"Yeah . . ." Arlo released a shaky breath, looking down at her palm. It stung—she'd slapped a Fury in the face, and *hard*.

"Come on," Nausicaä added gently as she threaded her arm through Arlo's. "That's enough excitement for one day, I think. Let's go find our straggling Summer fae and get you back for that curfew of yours."

CHAPTER 24

Arlo

～✦～

THE DARKNESS THAT HAD brought Arlo first to the Danforth spat all four of them out in the shadowy corner of the Indigo bookstore's courtyard, a few blocks down from the Palace of Spring.

The busy intersection of Bay and Bloor—not only one of the wealthiest shopping districts in the city, but home to several tourist attractions like the Royal Ontario Museum—meant there was plenty around to distract from their sudden reappearance. In the early stages of dusk, every lofty building donned a robe of steadily darkening, molten orange and royal plum, as though ceremony for the prince's return. The thousands of pale lights from cars, signs, streetlamps, and office spaces gleamed like its adorning jewels.

"Here we are. Right back into enemy territory. My thrill seeking knows no bounds," Nausicaä announced in a monotone sort of way. Vehan and Aurelian stumbled away from her, the prince falling to his knees to vomit on the ground. "Lovely."

"What just happened," Aurelian rasped, looking a little ill himself.

"I have a feeling you'd actually understand the scientific explanation, but I don't. Suffice it to know you just experienced your first teleportation. Hooray!"

Aurelian's glower was far from amused. "Please explain how that's possible. Only the Wild Hunt possesses the ability for teleportation, and even they have rules to govern its use in this realm. They're restricted from teleporting outside of night or into any building, yet you did this in daylight hours."

Nausicaä shrugged.

"Are you a member of the Wild Hunt?"

"They wish!" She laughed.

"What a terrible way to get around," Vehan muttered, peeling himself off the ground.

Arlo, meanwhile, had fared much better this time around. She wasn't certain she'd ever get used to this method of travel entirely, but it satisfied her to note that all she felt now was vaguely disoriented.

"How does this teleportation thing work?" the prince added. "Can you teleport inside buildings, too? Can you go someplace you haven't been before?"

Nausicaä considered her answer with a thoughtful tap to her chin. "Yes to both, but also no. I can technically pop up anywhere, but it's crazy hard to do that when you don't know what you're knitting yourself back together out of. It's a lot easier to get around these days, of course, because all I really need is a picture of the place I'm going, and the internet is all too happy to help with that. Google Street View was the best thing humans ever came up with."

"Interesting," said Vehan, then turned back to Arlo. "Arlo? Will you at least think about my request?"

Arlo had relayed to Vehan and Aurelian how she'd come upon the Reaper and everything she and Nausicaä had learned from their brief exchange with it. Nausicaä remained unusually subdued throughout the conversation, and Arlo thought it best to leave out any mention of Furies in the recap.

They'd wisely refrained from pressing Arlo any further, but here, apparently, on the cusp of parting ways, Vehan couldn't let her go without one last appeal. "All we need is for you to open that door. All I need is an ounce of the bravery it took you to lead a Reaper away from innocent people. You care. I know you do. No one would do what you did tonight if they didn't care about the lives of others. Please help us, Arlo. Please help *me*—I don't want to lose my life to this any more than you do."

Arlo looked Vehan in the eyes as he spoke.

She'd never seen anyone with a gaze that blue, and it was full of such intensity—such determination to do this incredibly dangerous thing, no matter the cost. No matter that he himself was still more or less a child and that the ones who should be rallying others to their cause, people like the High King, were content to bury their heads in the sand and let it continue.

But ignoring this problem wasn't going to make it go away.

If no one but a teenage boy and his bodyguard were going to try to do anything about it—if the world had somehow fallen to the shoulders of a child prince to keep it spinning—Vehan was going to do everything he could to meet that challenge, and win.

Arlo could read all of that in his steady gaze. It was the way he watched her back, as though he could see a hint of this in her himself, that made her look away.

Without quite knowing why, or what she was hoping to find, she glanced up at Nausicaä. She was met with a moment's complete inscrutability. Then, all those sharp lines and hints of haunting truth took on a softness that was quite unlike her. "It's your choice," she said. "I mean, if you go, I *guess* I'll go with you, if you want. Someone needs to keep you from getting yourself killed. If nothing else, the prince will owe me big for it, and the debt of a future king might come in handy one day. But you have to make up your own mind here. The number one law of the universe is choice, after all—bad things happen to the people who take that option away from you."

It was Arlo's choice.

She would have to be the one to decide the shape her future was going to take.

She didn't want to be a hero, she didn't want to die, but would her life really be worth living if it meant never taking part in things, regardless of the risk?

She thought of Nikos, putting his life and his magic on the line to help others who'd most likely never know.

"I'll think about it," she heard herself say.

Vehan nodded eagerly, a private smile touching the corners of his mouth. "Of course. Our plans can wait a few more days. I'll give you my number, would that be all right? That way you can reach me even when I return home."

Arlo agreed. Everyone exchanged their numbers, including Nausicaä (the folk might not have liked how much technology had become a part of their lives, but goodness if they didn't like their phones as much as humans did), and they parted ways. Arlo watched Vehan and Aurelian join the throng of people on the sidewalk, then disappear around the corner, her heart heavy and head full of thoughts. She slipped her hand back into Nausicaä's—the spark of their contact almost comforting now—and together the pair winked out of existence once again.

When they reappeared, it was on the cusp of yet another alley, this one right across the street from Arlo's apartment building.

"Thank you," she said.

Nausicaä nodded.

She eyed Arlo carefully but said nothing about what she thought. The silence between them wasn't exactly awkward, but Arlo found herself yet again wanting to say something to fill it. "So . . . are you really going to help them, then?"

Nausicaä nodded again. "Yeah, figure it couldn't hurt to let it look like I'm just trying to keep the heir to a Seelie throne alive. And he's right. I *am* interested. I mean, whoever's behind this? They're a level too dark for even my tastes, thanks. And I don't much care for them painting a target on your back, while we're on the subject. But they're creating philosopher's stones, and that's . . . that's something." She dropped a wink before retreating a step into the alley, away from Arlo, intent perhaps on whisking away.

"I'm sorry," Arlo blurted out before Nausicaä could make her departure. For some tight and fluttering reason in her chest, she wasn't quite ready to part ways yet.

Nausicaä paused to stare. "What for?"

"For what that girl—your sister? Megaera? I'm sorry for what she said to you. That Hunter, back in the throne room? Eris, I think you called him. He said you were kicked out of the Immortal Realm, right?"

Once again, a silent nod was all her question received.

"I'm sorry. For whatever happened that got you banished. I don't really know what you and your sister were talking about, but . . . what made you break the law and . . . and kill those people way back . . . no one just snaps for no reason. Something really bad must have happened to you, and I'm just . . . sorry for that, and . . . well, are you okay?"

The staring made Arlo uncomfortable.

Rosy heat bled into her face.

Nausicaä stood petrified under such sincerity, and they definitely weren't close enough to be sharing this kind of moment anyhow. Arlo got it. She understood. Hiking the bag she'd reclaimed from Vehan farther up her shoulder, she gave an awkward little wave farewell. "I mean, of course you aren't, it's been a long day. Just . . . I wanted you to know that I'm sorry. It doesn't change anything, but . . . yeah. Okay, anyhow, I'll see you around, maybe? Try not to get into too much trouble in the meantime?"

At last, whatever spell Nausicaä was under broke. She snorted. "You're weird, you know that? I mean, you kicked a lot of ass back there with that Reaper. I've known full-grown, puffed-up fae who wouldn't have been able to even look that thing in the face like you did, and let me tell you, I'm going to treasure always the look on Megaera's face when you slapped her. Seriously. Whatever part of the heart cockles are, you've totally warmed them. You're . . . you're something else, Arlo Jarsdel. But you're also weird as fuck."

Arlo couldn't really disagree. Her whole life, she'd felt like an outsider in every space she tried to occupy. *Weird.* Somehow, it didn't hurt to hear it now, the way Nausicaä said the term.

"But thanks, I guess. I'm fine. It's in the past. I hardly even think about it anymore," she continued gruffly, and Arlo didn't need a life-time of knowing her to be able to read the complete lie those words had been.

"You're one of those people who's all tough and prickly but actu-ally very sweet, aren't you," she teased in an attempt to make light of the situation and avoid mentioning what they both knew—that Nausicaä was nowhere close to fine, and what Megaera said was only the tip of that iceberg.

"Nah, I'm just as prickly on the inside as I am on the out. Like a cactus wrapped up in more cactus."

Arlo laughed. "Okay, well, thank you, cactus, for rescuing me once again. If I don't . . . I mean, I really won't be much help to you guys besides the whole door-opening thing, if I can even manage that, so if I don't change my mind and don't come with you, please know that I still appreciate your help to *me*."

"*Tch*—if you're going to be all maudlin at me, I'm leaving. It's no big deal. I just . . . well, that little girl in the café . . . figure I owed her one. Wasn't able to help *her*, so . . . but I'm not a good person! Stop looking at me like that! This whole thing has been a completely selfish attempt to assuage my own guilt and nothing more!"

Arlo had no idea how she was looking at Nausicaä, whose eyes had blown a little wider and tan face was starting to tinge blue in her apparent discomfort. Whatever showed on Arlo's face, she felt her chest constrict again. Unable to comprehend why it should make her so sad to catch this glimpse of hurt and panic under Nausicaä's bra-vado, she laughed. "Sure thing. Not a good person. The darkest star in the heavens—got it."

"I so enjoy when you get sassy with me." Nausicaä winked, razor amusement displacing her previous discomfort to curl the corners of her mouth.

Shaking her head, Arlo threw herself forward. This time, she couldn't really chalk her action up to anything other than the desire to just do it—to wrap her arms around Nausicaä's middle with no more purpose than to give her a hug, as though they were friends, as though they were *close*. "Good night, Nos."

". . . What?"

Arlo pulled back, confused.

It took her a moment to mentally scroll back through their conversation and pick out what Nausicaä was stuck on now, and winced when she realized what she'd said—how familiar she'd treated someone easily centuries older than she, and quite a bit more important, too. "Sorry, it just slipped out," she explained, and amended, "Nausicaä."

More silence.

Nausicaä hadn't hugged her back, just stood there like a statue, as if in the so many years she'd been alive, and despite her many titles, no one had ever given her either an embrace or a friendly nickname . . . or perhaps more accurately, as if it had been too many years since anyone dared to try.

When it was apparent her apology would receive no reply, Arlo jerked a nod farewell and spun quickly on her heels. She would take her leave before her social awkwardness could cause any more damage. "Sorry!" she called one last time over her shoulder. "See you around!"

She fled, leaving Nausicaä in the alley, and darted up the street to the crosswalk that would take her home. Her mother wouldn't be home for a few more hours yet, and with a brief text fired off to let her know she'd arrived home from a shift that ran a little late, she was finally left alone with her thoughts for the first time since she'd stepped outside Chorley's Curiosities for air.

Trudging to her bedroom, she shucked off her torn and debris-stained clothes and collapsed on her bed. Lying atop her duvet, she watched the sunset pour in through the glass doors of her private balcony and bathe her ceiling in orange and pink and porcelain shades of blue.

It had been less than two weeks since she'd turned eighteen and witnessed death in the Good Vibes Only café.

365

So much had happened in so short a period of time. So much in Arlo's life had changed. So much was going to keep happening until someone put a stop to it. Vehan . . . Aurelian . . . Nausicaä . . . These were the sorts of people who became heroes in the stories she read. The bold. The brave. The talented. The ones who were able to look death in the face and, despite their fear, hold on to their resolve a moment longer than anyone else.

I've known full-grown, puffed-up fae who wouldn't have been able to even look that thing in the face like you did.

You're something else, Arlo Jarsdel.

Arlo sighed—groaned, when she remembered how awkward she'd been in the alley, and wished she could go back and edit herself to come across a little more "cool."

But Nausicaä had been proud of her tonight. She'd never exactly treated Arlo like a delicate, incapable flower, but tonight had been the first time in their acquaintance she'd looked at—and spoken to—Arlo like an equal.

Like a *friend*.

Maybe the problem wasn't that Arlo didn't have what it took to be a hero. Maybe the problem was that she was once again letting herself get so keyed up by all the things she wasn't that she couldn't see the things she already was—resourceful and brave and, perhaps most importantly, not in this alone.

Maybe, if she could focus on those things instead, when all was said and done in Vehan's mysterious facility, she might come out the other side of this able to see herself in some way Nausicaä's equal too.

CHAPTER 25

Nausicaä

———⤜⤛———

GOOD NIGHT, NOS.

Nausicaä chucked a stone at the slumbering fountain below.

Casa Loma after hours was much preferable to its daylight schedule of operation, where the gorgeous gothic mansion tucked away in midtown Toronto was open to the public. As a tourist attraction and popular wedding venue, it was well maintained. The castle-gray brick, white and gold trimmed windows, and spires dipped in burnt sienna were kept in as near-pristine condition as could be managed, but it was the garden Nausicaä liked best. With its spring-green lawn, artfully arranged flowerbeds, and sprawling fountain of crystal-blue water, its loveliness was careful, austere perfection—a mask distracting from the towering oaks and creeping brush that fenced it in; the wild, clawing at its seams.

Good night, Nos.

Good night, Alec.

She chucked another stone at the moon's reflection in the water and watched the ripples expand.

It had been too long since she'd received a nickname through any amount of fondness. Tisiphone called her many things—clever things, silly things, sweet things, angry things—and she hadn't been the first. She certainly hadn't been the last, either, but nothing anyone had ever called her had caught her breath the way Arlo's "Good night, Nos" had done in its timid sincerity.

Damn it, she'd put too much work into closing herself off from things like this, into building walls to keep out others and their familiarity. Arlo's little "Are you okay?" and "Good night, Nos," that deities-damned hug, things no one had given her in *too long*, none of it should have struck her the way it did, and yet . . . "This isn't what I want," she growled.

"I'm afraid you'll have to be more specific."

"Eris!" Finally. She'd been starting to wonder how many stones it would take to draw the attention she sought. Nausicaä turned around to beam at the four who stood behind her. "I was starting to think you weren't actually bad at your job, you just didn't care."

She knew the High King wanted her brought in just as she knew the Wild Hunt would have no problem doing so if they actually put their minds to it. Nausicaä was clever, and she could teleport with much less restriction than the Hunt, who could only go where night brought them, thanks to all the rules the Courts had heaped on their presence here. Still, she hadn't exactly been hiding. She hadn't even left Toronto. And the positions the four Wild Hunters occupied granted them special abilities—Eris, as the leader, would only have to take hold of her to temporarily nullify every bit of power she possessed.

That she hadn't so much as run into any of them yet was one of the many things confusing her of late; it was time for some answers.

"Is that why you've summoned us? Eager for punishment, are you?" Eris stepped forward. His midnight cloak fluttered around his legs, hood lowered to reveal bronze-black and silver-freckled skin that glittered in certain angles like the heavens to which they rightfully belonged. Black hair with amber highlights . . . unnerving eyes the arsenic shade of white . . . strong both in features and build, he was just as Nausicaä remembered him. "You're a fool. Fortunately for you, so is the High King. After your story at the palace I'd rather have you around for anything that happens, but don't think to press my magnanimity."

"See, I always knew you liked me."

"I did, once."

The disappointment peeking through Eris's terse tone was another blow Nausicaä hadn't expected to feel, but did. The Wild Hunt and the Furies—their relationship had always been tumultuous at best, thanks to the lifelong competition between their units, but Nausicaä had been quite close to Eris and his cadre. Close to the point that he'd made her a cloak exactly like the ones all Hunters wore, that *only* they could wear. Exquisite things, those cloaks, capable of so much—more than mortals knew about—including allowing Nausicaä to alter her appearance to the exact likeness of Eris in order to sneak where she wasn't meant to be and secure the Fire that had led to her fall. More than a hundred years later, he still hadn't forgiven her for betraying the friendship between them, for the rules he himself had bent or over-looked in the course of that, for permission he'd given her to take a life not otherwise meant to be taken—just the one, not the ten additional others she'd discovered to be just as despicable as their leader—and the trouble he'd landed in for it when she'd rebelled. Out of everyone she'd lost since Tisiphone, it was him she missed the worst. "What do you want, Nausicaä?"

To say sorry.

For you to say you understand.

To go back to the way we used to be before I realized how terrible everything was.

Nausicaä opened her mouth, but none of the words she wanted to speak would come.

"Are you only going to talk to Eris, then? Not a single hello for me?"

She breathed a laugh. The tension eased. Vesper glided forward, lowering xis hood as well. Long and lean, golden and starlight shim-mery, with shocked-yellow eyes and ivy-green hair and adamantine silver in place of bone for teeth, xe was much like xis companions—beautiful in a disturbingly wraithlike way. Xe was also the young-est, claimed by immortality at barely sixteen years of age, and clearly much less angry with her than the others.

"*Hello*, Vesper. Needy as always, I see." She opened her arms, huffing when Vesper lunged a little too quickly for the embrace. Yue joined in—stronger, only a little shorter than Vesper and slightly older, with liquid-black hair, a pearly, fawn-brown complexion, and eyes brighter than violet poison. The adamantine weapons he'd been gifted were the twin daggers at his sides, which he could throw with unparalleled accuracy.

The amount she also missed these two welled up so fiercely and so suddenly that Nausicaä felt her eyes begin to sting. "Hi, Lethe," she said much more coldly to the fourth and final member of the Hunt.

Lethe sneered. His disdain wasn't new to her, and at the moment it was sour as his antifreeze gaze—he seemed even more irritable than usual, as good a reason as any to leave him alone.

"Enough. Vesper, Yue, remember yourselves."

"Aw, come on, Eris," Vesper whined. "It's been *years* since the gang was all together!"

Yue, never one for words where action would suffice, nodded fervently.

A sharp look was all it took to remind the two of their place; as Eris was their leader of the group, his word was law among them. If he ordered them to do something, they had to comply. Vesper and Yue dropped away, falling back in line beside Lethe, who busied himself with picking something out of his teeth with one of his deadly claws.

When all was as it should be, Eris repeated, "Why have you called us here tonight, Nausicaä? I won't ask you again."

"*Tch*—fine. Spoilsport."

She slid from the stone railing and onto her feet. Coming up to Eris, she planted herself in front of him and glared up into his stoic face. "I want answers."

"Specify."

"I want to know everything you know about these ironborn deaths and the people apparently disappearing off the street in some sort of black-market trade. I want to know what you know about philosopher's stones. I was so close to getting an actual damn name from that Reaper—the one I assume Lethe had you report to the Furies for punishment?"

Nausicaä could hazard a guess as to why, felt sure enough to bet on the fact that the Reaper had been wiped from the board because it had gone directly after the one mortal they wanted to keep safe. Arlo . . . but how did Lethe fit into that? Lethe didn't do anything for anyone unless it served a purpose he benefited from . . .

And Lethe's glare was absolutely frigid now—perhaps he was angrier than usual merely because of the extra work Nausicaä would have preferred he hadn't undertaken.

"He mentioned something about cava," she continued, jerking her head in his direction. "That's deep-waters bad shit, Eris. Why aren't more immortals involved in this? Why aren't the Furies acting on *that*? Why isn't the High King doing anything?"

Eris sighed. Frustration flickered across his expression. "My hands are tied, Nausicaä. Whatever I could tell you, the High King has forbidden. Whatever Lethe has told you, he shouldn't have."

"Then I challenge you."

At last, she'd surprised him into genuine emotion. Eris gaped at her, white eyes wide. "I . . . what?"

"I challenge you. Pick your game. If you win, I'll leave you alone. If *I* win, you have to tell me what you know. Anyone who beats the Hunt at a challenge earns a favor from them—that law is greater than the one that guards your tongue."

"Yes, and anyone who loses to us is taken to the Hiraeth, turned into a beast, and Hunted down for sport."

Nausicaä shot a finger at him. "Hence why I'd be leaving you alone. Come on, Eris. Fight me."

There was silence for a moment, in which all that happened was a battle of wills. Eris stared her down harder than ever before, but Nausicaä matched his severity with cold determination.

"Eris," Lethe practically moaned. There was such longing in his expression that Nausicaä actually shivered to see it. "Eris, I know

we have our differences. I know you're none too happy with my less-than-enthusiastic performance of late. But I *beg* you, let me take this challenge? Let me have this game. I promise, you'll see remarkable improvement in my service, if you do."

Silence resumed.

Eris turned his stare on Lethe.

Whatever the unrest in their ranks, Nausicaä wasn't surprised. Lethe was oldest of them all—older than her, by far. As rumor went, he was the very first Hunter that Cosmin had ever made. By all rights, he should hold the rank Eris commanded, except . . . he didn't want it. Hunters (for there were many) had once been living folk of remarkable ability, plucked from death and made immortal, employed as Cosmin's ferrymen for souls. Only the best of the lot, Cosmin's favorites, were given one of the four illustrious positions in the Wild Hunt, allowed to walk the Mortal Realm again as though once more alive—positions one could usurp only in a different sort of challenge. In life, they'd been hunters as well, of all sorts. Lethe had been a legend . . . but he'd also been cruel.

Time hadn't soothed that vicious streak in him at all—in fact, it only made it worse, and left him wildly unstable. He wasn't leader of the Hunt because he didn't want the responsibility—the shackle, as he put it—but Nausicaä didn't envy how difficult he was to manage, how hard a time Eris had always had of keeping him in line.

She might actually be screwed if Eris let Lethe take this challenge.

Damn it—she should have set better terms.

"No."

"*Whew—*" Nausicaä laughed before she could stop herself, breathy with relief. Both Eris and Lethe flicked a glance her way. "I mean, oh no! How sad."

"Eris—" Lethe started.

"The answer is no."

Rage contorted Lethe's face, so briefly one might have missed it if they'd blinked. He looked as though he might do what he wanted anyhow—as was his custom—but instead just opened his mouth to argue further. Eris held up a hand. "I will not reward your poor behavior. You take off without permission, Father only knows to where, and shirk responsibilities. When your performance improves, so will my favor. Vesper—I leave this to you."

Vesper—a kindness of sorts. She wouldn't let herself read too much into this, wouldn't let herself hinge too much hope on this action that Eris's anger was softening, but Nausicaä had already proven her ability to beat Vesper at a number of their games. Her odds of winning against xem were at least better than they would be against Lethe, even if Vesper wouldn't hold back by any means. This was a proper challenge—xe couldn't.

"Heck yeah!" Vesper cried, pumping a fist in the air. "It's on now, Alec. Just wait, I have the best—" Xe winced, and tossed her an apologetic look. "I'm sorry. I mean, Nausicaä."

Lethe, meanwhile, fumed. Eris stalked back to Yue, and it was clear he meant for Lethe to follow, but he took his time before doing so to ensure Nausicaä knew just how livid he was that Eris had prevented whatever form of torture he'd been looking forward to. She threw him a shrug.

"Come on, Nausicaä, come on! I have the best idea, let's go!" Vesper darted forward, taking her by the hand. The night descended. It spilled down around them as though the sky were a basin filled with ink, and something had tipped it over.

She hated this form of travel. The night was cool and vaguely slick. It wasn't wet, but it felt as though she was getting close and personal with sludge, and when it enveloped her completely, it filled her with a sense of being buried alive.

That sludge spat her out again on the roof of one of the city's buildings. Eris, Yue, and Lethe were gone. Only she and Vesper remained, and xe watched her now with barely restrained glee, the late-night breeze tossing xis hair around xis vulpine face.

"Okay, kid. What do you have for me?"

"How about a game of fetch?"

Nausicaä rolled her eyes to hide a swell of fondness. *Fetch*, they called it—running off into the world, Hunting down the deadliest creature they could find, and bringing back a trophy for proof of their encounter. Depending on the players, that trophy was often the creature's head, but Vesper had a kinder soul. Xe preferred to stick to bits that wouldn't be sorely missed by their owners. "Usual rules?"

Vesper nodded. "Sunrise is the limit. We meet back here. Ready to get your ass handed to you, Kraken?" Xe grinned, showing off all xis pointy metal teeth. However much fondness between them, xe was still a Hunter—xis entire immortal purpose was to win at things like this. Nausicaä didn't hold it against xem.

In fact, her answer was a grin of her own.

When Vesper whisked xemself off once more, Nausicaä remained where she was. She already had what she needed to win, gathered from the Hiraeth just hours ago, in fact, on the off-chance it would be useful. And hours later, when Vesper returned, it proved to be extremely so. She dropped that single hair on the rooftop next to the dragon scale xe threw at her feet, and Vesper groaned, defeated. Xe dropped to hug xis knees in a spectacular pout—"No fair, how did you even get that?"

"It doesn't matter—I win. Lethe out-monsters your dragon. Now tell me what you know about what's going on with the ironborn."

Xe sighed.

CHAPTER 26

Aurelian

〜⌒〜

THERE WERE SO MANY things people whispered about Riadne Lysterne.

Ambitious, they called her—from childhood her sight had been set on obtaining the Bone Crown. She'd trained for it, studied for it, lived and breathed and bled for it, pushed herself to perfection in everything she did and was satisfied with nothing less.

Intelligent, they called her too—the top of every class, the victor of every sparring match. She'd insisted on inclusion in her mother the queen's council meetings at such a young age that they'd doubted she'd be able to do much more than listen and were astounded to discover instead a keen mind for politics and strategy.

Beautiful . . . strong . . . talented . . . These were the things folk were careful to say the loudest about the Seelie Queen of Summer, because the *other* words they used to describe her . . .

Do you know why I brought you here, Aurelian?

The office where Aurelian stood was a place no one wished to be invited. It was, for the most part, completely ordinary, almost cheerful, a moderate-size room of off-gray carpet and butter-yellow walls. There was a large bay window to his right, a slate stone fireplace behind him by the door, and a solid oak desk so pale it could almost pass for white, flanked by four pure gold bookcases, two on either side. By this alone it was actually quite boring—not the sort of space one imagined for a queen, and not the sort of space one would ever assume a palace's every inhabitant could fear more than a dungeon.

It was the columbarium built into the wall between these gleaming units—directly behind the queen's desk—that served as the only visible hint of horror this room symbolized. Dozens of compact niches, set into another slab of nearly black slate; no inscription marked its purpose or revealed what those numerous slots contained. No inscription was necessary. It was Aurelian's imagination that he could hear the last, frantic beats of the hearts entombed in that wall—the hearts the queen took from those who crossed her; the hearts of people who, like Aurelian, had perhaps known a little too much about their beloved Queen of Light, but unlike Aurelian, hadn't been wise enough to bite their tongue.

Do you know why I brought you here, Aurelian? I'll give you a hint—it had nothing to do with your parents. Oh, I wanted them here, as a means for control, but do you know why I wanted you?

There was absolute silence.

No one spoke until the queen did first.

Aurelian continued to stand. He stared at the niches. He was so tired—it was late, and he'd had a long day. He'd only just returned from Toronto when Isolte, one of Riadne's retainers, had fetched him from his room and sent him to Riadne's office with tears in her eyes as though this would be the last time they'd ever behold him.

It wouldn't be.

He was far too useful a pawn still for Riadne to make him a trophy just yet. He stood and he stared and he waited, and willed his heart not to race in his chest, because he might not yet be for this mausoleum, but he wouldn't be called *here* unless Riadne was angry with him.

"Well?"

Aurelian tore his gaze from the wall. Riadne sat behind her desk, hadn't looked up from the report she so leisurely perused as though they had all the time in the world for this talk—and they did. She could keep him standing here for days if she wanted. Aurelian shifted, uneasy. "We . . . spoke with the High King, Your Majesty. Thank you for arranging that. His Highness was very happy you took his concerns seriously."

"Am I the sort of person who doesn't take their own son seriously, Aurelian?"

"No, Your Majesty."

Another tick of silence passed, followed by another.

How close you've become with my Vehan.

"You spoke with Azurean. How did it go?"

She still didn't look up at him. Aurelian honestly couldn't say if he preferred that. "He assured His Highness he was doing everything in his power to resolve this situation—" The queen snorted. Aurelian didn't dare make comment on it. "He thanked him for his concern and invited us to dinner with him and his family, which was why we were so late in coming back. I wouldn't say His Highness is appeased, but—"

He's really quite taken with you.

He takes to anyone who shows him attention.

Once again he was interrupted, this time by a knock at the door. The queen bid them entrance, and Aurelian's heart sped faster to see. "Ah, Zale. Good."

Do you know why I brought you here? Go on, take a guess.

Zale, the mer who'd been in Riadne's employment for ten years now, a member of her royal guard and Vehan's personal trainer. The merfolk could trade their fins for legs for fins again any time they pleased, but most didn't please. Most didn't like to keep away from their watery homes for long, if at all. They couldn't—the lengths that Zale went to ensure he didn't dry out here . . . Why he'd chosen to come to the palace of all places, Aurelian could venture a guess that he'd been lured the same way the queen had won his parents. But while Aurelian and Zale were friendly, it was Vehan who Zale was closer to. Aurelian didn't know much more than that about him.

Riadne looked up at last. She set down her report and leaned back in her chair, the severe structure of her face even sharper for the crackling displeasure in her eyes, all of it completely at odds with the serenity in her smile. "You let my son use the Egress without permission."

Zale stepped farther into the room, no longer in his ceremonial armor from earlier but a comfortable pair of brown cotton pants and a loose white sleep shirt. The navy cardigan he'd thrown over top only dressed it up barely, and it was clear by the mussed state of his green hair that this summons had pulled him from bed.

He met Aurelian's gaze in the briefest of glances before drawing himself to stiff attention at his side. "I did, Your Majesty."

"You let my son use the Egress to impose himself on the High King. Perhaps you didn't think it was your place to stop him? Excusable, because it's not. But you let him do this, and I've yet to receive your notice it was done."

Zale said nothing. Even he—so quick with words, so charming and personable, who used humor as deflection and whose wit often outpaced his common sense—knew not to press his luck right now. Not in this place. Not in the presence of those hearts lying cold as the stone that caged them.

Reaching across her desk, Riadne slipped a silver-handled letter opener free from its sheath and rose to standing. Aurelian swallowed, watched in apprehension as she made her approach, hands folded far too innocently behind her back for the glint of metal between their fingers. "Open your mouth," she said placidly, coming to a halt in front of Zale.

Color drained out of Zale's face, but he neither hesitated nor questioned the order. He opened his mouth, and Riadne made a show of peering inside. "You do still have a tongue in there. Urielle knows I've heard you use it enough—so fond of your voices, you merfolk are, but *you*, between your incessant chatter and songs . . . Sing something for me, Zale—after today, I'm worried you've forgotten how."

When Zale only stared, gray eyes grown large in trepidation, the fingers of Riadne's free hand snapped behind her back.

"Souls of Poets dead and gone, what Elysium have ye known, happy field or mossy cavern, choicer than the Mermaid Tavern?"

Aurelian bit his lip to contain a groan.

Whatever else the folk felt about humanity, they had always appreciated human creativity. This song, originally a poem set to music by the founder of the Mermaid Tavern for which the song had been named, was something most of them knew, but not because their schools spent an entire unit on the works of Romantic period human poets. "The Mermaid Tavern" jingle was almost as popular as the Goblin Market bar it advertised. Would Riadne be offended that this was what he'd chosen? Would she think he was making light of the situation?

"Keep singing," she said, lifting that free hand to pat his cheek. Her smile was too hollow for the fondness it pretended. "Aurelian." A step was all it took to plant her next in front of him.

"—*Have ye tippled drink more fine than mine host's Canary wine? Or are fruits of Paradise sweeter than those dainty pies of venison?—*"

"Yes, Your Majesty?"

Tell me, I want to hear you say it. I know you've figured it out. You're very good at playing this game, and I admit—I'm impressed. How long can you hold out? How long can all that fight in you last?

"Aurelian . . . such a clever boy. So willful. I know, despite your best efforts, that you love Vehan very much. I love him too. I would hate to see him come to harm . . . the sort he'd find in clandestine meetings with goblins and guns and the drugs I'm sure you're well aware that I know you used to partake in." He'd suspected, yes—there wasn't much the Seelie Queen of Summer didn't know about what went on in her Court, and that wasn't the worst of what she could use against him by far. Just as he knew she saw through his act with Vehan. So long as Vehan remained naive to it, it didn't matter. So long as he still had *time* . . .

More concerning at the moment was that she knew the bits Vehan hadn't told her about what had happened with Pincer. The turf war they'd found themselves embroiled in . . . the Faerie Dust they'd used as pretense for their meeting . . . Toronto was outside her web of control, but Aurelian didn't doubt she'd find out what else had happened there today. All she had to do was press *him* for the information, and he would yield. Riadne didn't need his true name to outmaneuver him.

"I don't anymore, I swear—"

"It doesn't matter."

"—*I have heard that on a day mine host's sign-board flew away*—"

"I don't really care."

"—*Nobody knew whither*—"

"All that's important is that you continue to do your job. That my son remains safe, and protected, and *alive*. You can manage that, can't you, Aurelian?"

Do you know why I brought you here?

"Yes, Your Majesty."

"Good. I would hate to have to punish your charming little family for your failings . . . would hate to have to appoint someone else to do your task. However tiresome I find your obstinacy, however much I wish you were just a *little* more obliging, Vehan is headstrong. He needs a retainer who can keep up with his excitable whims. Am I clear? Do you understand me?"

"Perfectly, Your Majesty."

Perfectly.

Riadne would replace him if she ever grew more than "tired" of this game they played, of the things he knew about her versus the things she held over him to keep him silent. His time would be up. She would replace him with someone who didn't care about Vehan nor Aurelian's family; she'd replace him with someone who would work *with* Riadne instead of against her to bend the prince to submission and mold him into a puppet for her absolute control.

Aurelian would be gone, and Vehan would break, and his parents, his younger brother . . . Those open niches in the wall would dwindle in number by three, he was sure of it.

"You are dismissed."

That Zale didn't deserve what the queen had in store for him in private, that he'd always been so good to Vehan, was the only reason Aurelian found the bravery to hesitate following such a firm command.

"Unless you'd like to stay for the show?"

Zale began a fresh refrain of, "*Souls of Poets dead and gone, what Elysium have ye known, happy field or mossy cavern, choicer than the Mermaid Tavern?*" because Riadne hadn't told him to stop singing yet, but his voice only grew stronger for what she'd just said.

He was a better soldier than Riadne deserved, braver than Aurelian by far.

"No, Your Majesty," he rasped, the words barely audible. "Thank you. I'll take my leave."

He exited the room.

He put as much distance between him and it as quickly as he could, but it wasn't enough. That song had grown louder, twisted in pain—jumbled, indecipherable, no longer words but a tune watered down by sobs and gagging, as Riadne made good on her unspoken threat to divest Zale of what she deemed useless to him: his tongue.

Do you know why I brought you here?

Down the halls—no one he passed said anything to him; there was nothing to say. "I'm sorry" or "Are you okay?" or "What's going on"—everyone was sorry, everyone knew what was going on, what *had* been going on for *years*, and *no one* was okay.

Up the floors—they were captives, dolls in a cruel child's playhouse, butterflies pinned under glass. Vehan knew. There was no way he couldn't. He was intelligent and observant like all children who grew up with parents whose fickle moods made them dangerous. Even if the queen went to terrifying lengths to keep him ignorant of the worst of it, to pretend at goodness and convince Vehan her "occasional heavy hand" was something he, too, would have to learn when he became king, because no one respected power that wasn't a little bit feared. Vehan was no less a prisoner in this household, and he knew the people who lived here with him were unhappy. Aurelian saw how hard he worked to mediate the nastier moments his mother couldn't help let slip in front of him, how hard he worked to "grow up," to ready himself for a throne his people longed for him to take before the queen figured out how to smother his light completely.

If Aurelian told him, it would all be over.

If Vehan found out how deep this truth really ran, there would be no more pretend. There was no doubt in Aurelian's mind that if Vehan knew just how horrible his mother actually was, he'd stand up to her. He'd try to stop her, maybe even dethrone her, because it was the right thing to do. They helped nothing by keeping this secret, and at the same time, were too afraid to speak it—to make it real and force the worst that would have to come before things could *maybe* get better.

"Move," he growled to the guards outside Vehan's door.

He hated it here. He hated this place. This wasn't his home, this wasn't his Court, these weren't his people. He hated politics and court intrigue and bored aristocrats who played nasty games with other people's lives like they were nothing more than hollow pieces in some elaborate chess game. He hated Vehan. He hated that everyone, including himself, was so wrapped up in keeping Vehan safe and happy and whole while meanwhile they were crumbling, dying, falling apart right beneath his nose.

But he loved him far more.

Vehan, who was too much like Riadne in all the *best* of ways; Vehan, who'd shed his own inhibitions just as she'd shed hers, and the resulting conflict would be something the prince would never survive, and Aurelian was *tired*.

Do you know why I brought you here, Aurelian?

"Vehan!" He burst into the prince's room, riled up and shaking, Zale's song an echo that wouldn't leave his ears. He had no idea what had brought him here, or what he wanted, or what he would say to Vehan except—the sound of retching broke his focus.

Aurelian's head snapped to the bathroom, and he moved without thinking to investigate.

There, on the white tiled floor, amidst a massive claw-foot tub, a waterfall shower, and pristine stark-white furnishings, was the prince curled over his toilet, vomiting up the meal he'd forced down back at the High King's table.

His black hair stood out like a glaring stain for all the cold, unfeeling lack of color around him—a pitiful figure, haphazardly dressed in gold pajamas. Aurelian felt his anger beginning to drain.

Silently he made for his side and sank to the floor, back pressed against the sink and head falling to join it. "You shouldn't have eaten so much with all that petal dust in your system."

Another retch—Vehan groaned. "I didn't want to be rude."

Aurelian laughed. The sound was weak and could just as easily have been a sob save for the fact that he didn't allow himself to cry over anything anymore. If he let the tears start, he had a feeling they wouldn't stop.

"I thought you'd gone to bed."

"I can sleep here."

Vehan spluttered a laugh of his own. It morphed into a groan, and more retching. The prince had managed to scrub all that petal dust off his skin, and thank whichever god decided to send them Lethe that he'd given Vehan that bit of rowan tree bark to lessen the pure, undiluted Faerie Dust to this, but Aurelian knew all too well how unpleasant it was to come down from this high. "Thank y-you." Vehan hiccupped.

His lips were dry and cracked, his glamour stripped away, the all-encompassing blue of his eyes were bloodshot sapphire dark as black, and tremors wracked a frame that in this moment looked impossibly fragile.

Vehan was so young.

Aurelian was young too.

"Thank you," he managed again, giving Aurelian a brighter smile than someone in his current position should be capable of. "It's selfish, I know, but I'm glad I'm not alone right now."

"Yeah," he replied. All the things he had to say, he was too tired for any of them. Drawing his knees up against his chest, he wrapped his arms around them and hugged them close, as though he could physically hold himself together, keep himself from flying apart in a thousand million pieces. It wasn't until Vehan's head dropped on his shoulder—the prince had now settled beside him, a towel softer than it really had the right to be flung across their laps like a blanket—that Aurelian realized that Vehan had fallen asleep. "Someone tried to make you into a vessel for a philosopher's stone, and I think your mother was somehow involved," he admitted to the silence. "I don't think you're selfish," he answered that lonely boy back in the Goblin Market. "I think you're wonderful, but I'm *scared*," he confessed.

It changed nothing.

He was running out of time.

He's really quite taken with you, my darling Vehan—but then, he loves so easily. He loved his father, too, and it devastated Vehan to lose him, but not quite enough. *It would devastate him to lose you, too—you, Aurelian, his last little friend. I've done my best to keep him lonely, to keep him starved for hope and affection, but the bond between you was instant. Rare. I couldn't pass up the chance, and you've figured it out. Please tell me you have? The* why *of it all.*

I brought you here to break him.

I brought you here to die.

And with you gone, oh, I suppose the only one he'll have to help him pick up the pieces of his fragile heart will be me, *won't it. And I assure you, it won't be useless* love *I'll use to rebuild him.*

Gathering up the prince, Aurelian deposited him back in bed. Fetched him a glass and some water for his bedside table. Left just as night became dawn. Went back to his room and lay on his bed and stayed there through every meal, every knock, until dawn became day became night again. Later, Vehan burst in with news that Zale had had "such a severe allergic reaction to something he ate yesterday that the palace physician had been forced to remove his tongue!" and a text message that lit up his prince as though he'd swallowed whole bolts of lightning.

And damn, Aurelian *loved* him.

Unfortunately, Vehan loved him too.

CHAPTER 27

Arlo

❧

ITIZENS OF THE COURTS of Folk. Free Folk of the Wild. Family. Friends—No doubt you've heard by now what took place last night in Toronto as well as this morning's address from the High King himself, which named a Reaper as culprit. According to our inimitable sovereign, this creature was also found guilty of the nine counts of slaughter of ironborn children—a crime that was, until now, carelessly attributed as the work of the Dark Star.

It has been declared that our Courts-wide emergency is finally over—it is not.

The Reaper may have played a part in this evil deed, but it did not act alone.

Too many questions have yet to be answered; too little information has been given to assuage our fears. The Courts have put to rest their vigilance, but we cannot *afford to do the same*. Until there is proper proof this shadow that looms over us is past, the Assistance begs you: look out for one another in the days to come. Keep each other safe. We must count on ourselves now. We must be strong where they are not—we must remember, we're all we've got."

Arlo hit replay.

We're all we've got—this tagline was everywhere. On Flitter, the Court's hottest social media platform. On Folk News, their largest news network. It had even spread past folk-privatized streaming and onto human sites like YouTube, where most of the comments were filled with things like *what the **** is this* and *is this some sort of movie promotion?*—but the views kept climbing higher and higher, and would continue to do so until the Courts managed to shut it down.

We're all we've got.

Arlo looked over at the die on her bedside table. It had been an eventful Sunday morning, beginning at the crack of dawn when Thalo had come into Arlo's room with a tray of bacon and pancakes smothered in maple syrup and an apology for how angry she'd been the day before. Arlo apologized for her comments too, but their reconciliation had been cut short by Thalo's need to head to the palace. Then had come the High King's address. Then had come the Assistance's rebuttal.

We're all we've got—she couldn't shake this.

They shouldn't be alone in this. *We're all we've got* was the reason things had gotten so bad. It had been what made Arlo venture into the Faerie Ring, why she'd risked both danger and the High King's punishment to at least try *something*, to help in any way she could to expedite the justice that the nine dead ironborn and the people who loved them deserved.

We're all we've got—it shouldn't be this way, and yet this was true now more than ever. Whatever the person behind these murders intended to do once they succeeded at making a stone, even more people were bound to die. The target would widen, spread beyond the ironborn community, maybe even the magical one too—and the only thing standing between them and this looming calamity were four teenagers, one of whom was hardly any use at all.

We're all we've got.

She lay in her bed, staring at her die, with the Assistance's entreaty playing in the background. Nausicaä had seemed so *sure* Arlo could help Prince Vehan break the seal he needed to get past. If only she could test this theory. They should have done so yesterday when they'd all been together, but Arlo had panicked, and the Reaper attack had prevented her from thinking clearly. Arlo wouldn't mind helping them get in if she felt just a little more confident she actually *could*— if she could scrounge up a sliver of genuine hope that she wouldn't disappoint. It really wasn't much they were asking her to do—just get them in. The High King didn't have to know it was alchemy that helped them do this. . . .

"Arlo!"

Arlo yelped in surprise. "Elyas!" She sat up in her bed, blinking at the boy who'd just burst into her room as though she'd been expecting him all along. "What are you doing here?"

Much like Celadon, Elyas liked to have his fun, but there was no smile on his face right now or glint of mischief in his bright jade eyes. Elyas frowned at her, and Arlo might have laughed at how much he looked like his uncle right now, except she was too busy trying to think back on what she'd done to make him angry. "Is everything okay?"

"Were you really at the Assistance last night?"

Caught like a deer in headlights, Arlo weighed her next move. "Did . . . Lord Lekan tell you that?"

"No," Elyas replied, breezing into the room for her bed. "He told Uncle Celadon. I just overheard them. Uncle Celadon isn't a very chill person, and also very loud when he's worked up, which he totally was about this news, so spill: Were you really there?"

"I . . . Are you going to tell Cel?"

"Probably." He dropped down beside her. "You know what he's like. I kind of snuck away since everyone's really distracted right now, but once he finds out—"

"You came by *yourself*? Elyas! That's so dangerous. You're eleven years old, and someone just posted a really controversial video condemning your grandfather for gross negligence. You—"

"Nope, you don't get to scold me, Miss Secret-Rebel-Operative."

Groaning, Arlo flopped back on her bed. She'd much prefer to be having this conversation with Celadon, but Elyas was a dog with a bone when he sensed a secret he didn't yet know. She'd have to tell him something. The problem was, once she opened her mouth to confirm that yes, she'd really been at the Assistance, other things began to pour out too. The Assistance turned into the resulting Reaper attack,

387

turned into her prior encounter with this creature, turned into what had happened at the Faerie Ring and the not-troll she'd met there.

"No one knows. Not Celadon or even Nausicaä. I sort of forgot about it when it was relevant, and any time I remembered, it never seemed important given everything else that was going on. But they gave me something, the not-troll. I don't really know what it is, but—"

Elyas held up his hand for a pause. "A strange faerie gave you something you 'don't really know what it is' and you *took it*? Arlo, that's, like, the first thing everyone learns not to do. Don't stick things into light sockets. Don't forget to look both ways before crossing the street. *Don't take gifts from strangers!* What if it was a geas? What if you owe this faerie troll person your soul now or something? What if—"

"It's just a die, look."

Arlo grabbed her die from the table and held it out between them. Elyas, with his flair for dramatics, cried out, "No, *ahhh*, don't touch me with your faerie curse!" and flinched away.

She rolled her eyes.

"Honestly, it's fine. I've touched it a bunch of times and nothing has happened. It doesn't do much of anything except follow me around. Like an item in a video game you can't drop from your inventory—I threw it at the Reaper once and when I got back home, it was here."

"Yes, because that sounds like safe and normal die behavior, no magic to see here at all." He plucked it out of her hand and shot off the bed.

Arlo scrambled after him. "What are you doing?"

Throwing open her balcony doors, Elyas went to her railing and proceeded to chuck it far as he could into the windy day.

"Elyas, *what are you doing?*" she cried, flying to his side.

Together they watched it fall back to the earth, wind tossing their hair around their faces. Elyas shrugged. "Testing. How long does it take it to come back?"

"I . . . don't actually know. I never paid attention all that closely."

"Hmm." Turning abruptly around, he strode back inside. Arlo stared after where the die had sunk out of sight a moment longer before turning to follow, but halted when she noticed Elyas had stopped in the middle of her room. "So, not long, then."

Arlo followed the direction of his stare. There, back on her bedside table, was her die.

"Cool . . ." Elyas hesitated. "But what's the point?"

"Who knows?" she sighed. "I only tried to use it that one time, but like I said, it didn't do anything." The not-troll had been whole worlds of unhelpful when giving her this twenty-sided mystery. Perhaps it didn't do anything useful at all. Perhaps Arlo shouldn't have been in such a hurry to get away. Perhaps she should have stuck around to ask them a few more questions so that she'd have an actual clue as to what to do with their present, or as Elyas had pointed out, to check if there were any strings attached in the using. "No, wait, the not-troll—they did tell me something . . ."

The die . . . The not-troll had told her all about the paths that Fate had laid out for her, and others, too, which would take her in different directions. Only now was she realizing she'd gone with the path her mysterious companion had wanted her on—the one that crossed with Nausicaä's—but the die, they'd told her something about that, as well . . .

"They said something about needing to roll it. All I've done so far is throw it, so maybe I should try that instead?"

"Yeah, okay, but this is all you. If you die, can I have your PlayStation? Father still won't let me get one, and I'll *never* beat Uncle Cel's trophy count at this rate."

"Sure thing, El." Crossing the room to her table, she picked the die back up. "Okay, I'm doing it." Closing her hands around it, she gave the die a shake in her palms.

"Wait, what, *here*? Arlo, this is your bedroom. What if something—" Arlo released the die. "Oh my gods, okay sure, just go ahead and do it then."

The die rolled, not far, and when it came to a stop, Elyas rushed forward to see what it had landed on. "Four," he observed.

Four. Again. Just like the other times she noticed what number it landed on.

"Did it do anything?" Elyas asked, looking back up at her. "Do you feel any different?"

"No . . ." She felt perfectly fine, in fact. Glancing around, nothing about their surroundings seemed any different from a moment ago either. Rolling the die had done nothing—so it really was useless after all. For some reason, this realization made Arlo sad, as though she'd been looking forward to there being some greater purpose behind this enigma, but it was useless, a disappointment, just like her.

Figured.

"Hmm." Elyas picked up the die and examined it in his palm. A few moments passed. "I have an idea. Come on, let's go up to the roof."

"What? Why, what's up there?"

"Just trust me."

"I'm in my pajamas!"

"So *change*, you diva, and *come on*."

Success Tower's rooftop garden was a well-manicured common space with seats for lounging and pockets of flowers to soften the city's steel. The northern view overlooked an ever-changing cityscape; the south presented a dazzling view of the sprawling Lake Ontario. No one was up here at the moment. Dense cloud cover blocked out the sun, making for a slightly chillier day, and coupled with the strength of the wind, it wasn't the best of conditions for relaxing outdoors.

Standing in the middle of the landing, Elyas opposite her, Arlo had no idea what he'd planned for her to try but hoped it wouldn't take them long. She'd misjudged the temperature. In her pink sweatpants and pastel-yellow tank top, her arms were already growing cold—she should have grabbed a sweater.

Elyas didn't seem bothered at all, but then again, he'd at least come in a pale green windbreaker, and there was always a bit of color in his cheeks, rosy for his glamour but blue underneath.

"Okay," he announced. "So here's what I'm thinking. Maybe this works like Dungeons and Dragons."

"I'm sorry, what?"

Dungeons & Dragons was a game, Arlo knew, and one played with multiple dice. One of those dice was an icosahedron—twenty-sided, exactly like the one she currently held. She'd never actually played the game herself, though, and had only the barest idea of what its rules were.

Thankfully, Elyas seemed to know them better. He waved his free hand at her in barely contained excitement, thoroughly over the fact that this could be dangerous and deadly, and now fully immersed in his curiosity. "You need an objective."

Arlo continued to stare at him.

Elyas sighed. "In Dungeons and Dragons, when you do certain things, the Dungeon Master will stop you to roll for a skill check and charisma and stuff. Maybe that's how your die works. Maybe you have to declare an action and *then* give it a roll to see how successful that action will be."

"Have you actually played this game before? I've never heard you talk about it."

"No. Well, sort of? I mean, I want to. I bought the starter kit . . . listened to some podcasts . . . I made up my own campaign and everything, but so far only Uncle Cel said he'd join, and this type of game works best when there's more than one player."

"Well, how come you haven't asked me?"

Elyas shrugged. He had a way of acting perfectly unaffected by things that would bother others, which he no doubt learned from many of his family members. To someone like Arlo, who'd been close to him his entire life, he had tells that betrayed what he really felt. "You've been busy lately. A bit stressed out over school and the hearing, and then all this stuff with that girl who died, Cassandra—I didn't want to bother you."

"Okay, well, after we're finished with what Prince Vehan has planned, we'll play your campaign, all right? Me *and* Cel. And I'll make the prince play too, and his friend Aurelian. And Nausicaä—she'd probably get the biggest kick out of this. But a whole team, yeah? Soon as we're done."

Elyas smiled, but it was the glow beneath his skin that gave his happiness away. "Deal. But hey, we're sort of playing right now—or we would be, if you'd stop stalling. Listen. It's really windy out today."

Arlo didn't feel this needed confirming, given the gust that had just blown his white-sand bangs into his eyes, but she nodded anyhow.

"What's the element UnSeelie Spring fae control?"

"Wind . . ."

It wasn't only UnSeelie Spring fae who could control this element. Fae born to parents of mixed heritage could inherit one, or both, or neither of their parents' elements, so it was possible for a fae living in Seelie Winter to have power over wind as well. But it was wind that UnSeelie Spring prized as "proper" inheritance the same way Seelie Spring prized their manipulation of nature, UnSeelie Autumn their command of the earth, and Seelie Winter water. In UnSeelie Spring, those with the strongest wind-controlling abilities were always held up as ideal, notable idols of their culture.

"And what's the one thing we've been trying to coax out of you forever? The one thing that would force the Fae High Council to grant you fae status?"

Arlo felt what little heat there was in her face cool into pale dread. She finally realized where this was going. "Elyas, no. You're not suggesting what I think you're suggesting. You can't really be saying I should ask the die to . . . what, make my magic stronger?"

"Not make it stronger, no—I'm willing to bet it's actually strong enough. What I'm suggesting is that you should ask the die to give your magic a boost past whatever's holding it back."

He tossed the die to her, expression far too serious for the absurdity he'd just spoken. Arlo caught it on instinct.

"Arlo. You just told me you *outran a Reaper*. Yeah, it was definitely slowed down by its surroundings, but it's a *Reaper*. Slowed down or not, an ordinary person—an ordinary *fae*—shouldn't be able to escape it like you did. Enhanced speed . . . that's a windborn Gift. You've got it in you, I know you do! What if this die could help draw out your magic properly?"

Impossible.

It couldn't be that simple.

After years of tears and stress and anxiety, of pushing and pushing and pushing herself to be better, and hopelessness when she wasn't. After a lifetime of magic that just wouldn't come, it couldn't be this easy. It couldn't be that all she had to do was roll some die like playing a game and this monumental problem would be solved.

But *what if* . . .

"What should I do?" she heard herself ask—quiet, as though speaking this question too loudly would scare away any chance of this working out.

"There's a lot of wind here today. Ask the die to help you make it stop. Just say: I make the wind in the city stop."

Again, without her permission, she felt her hand close over the die. Her eyes fell shut. "Okay . . . I make the wind in the city stop," she declared in a voice that was bolder, if still a little shaky.

Like a train chugging to a halt on its track, the world seemed to give a violent lurch around her and stutter to a halt.

The panicked beating of Arlo's heart was deafening in her ears, swelling to a crescendo in the sudden and complete absence of all other sound. Opening her eyes, she gasped when she realized the world had halted quite literally.

The world had turned an alarming shade of stony gray.

Everything around her had frozen. The birds in the air, the traffic in the street down below. Nothing moved an inch, time suspending them in place like bugs trapped in amber, where no one seemed to notice beyond the limit of this zone, which seemed to be a few hundred feet, as up above the clouds still streaked by. From what Arlo could tell, the cars and people down below carried on as though nothing was amiss. Maybe much like when they encountered a glamour, their minds were glossing over what they saw with what *should* be right.

Inside this frozen space, only Arlo was left mobile. Elyas had frozen too, fixed to the roof like a statue.

"Holy *crap!*" she cried, breathless in her mixture of wonder, alarm, and terror.

Had she actually done it? Had she failed to be specific enough, and in trying to stop the wind had actually stopped more? Was this reversible or permanent?

"*Please* don't be permanent." She could feel her panic kick up several notches.

Like Arlo, the die had retained its color: vibrant jade that seemed even brighter in this new and dreary world, and gold lettering, glittering almost cheekily up at her. "Stupid!" she cursed, both at herself and the die, and folded her hand back around the offending object. Lifting it over her head, her immediate reaction was to pitch it away, but her gaze caught on something else—a shimmering glint of emerald green above her head, which, when Arlo actually looked, turned out to be a number.

The number *17* to be precise, and it hovered in midair directly over her head.

Arlo stared.

"What the . . ."

And it was then she realized there were words as well, burning bright as polished gold, written on the very air. She took a step back to read them.

To her left was: *Escape Time Stop*.

To her right, and slightly grayed out, was the singular word: *Assist*.

To the front, she saw the word: *Roll*.

"Holy crap," Arlo repeated, because it needed saying twice. The not-troll in the nightclub had given Arlo a magical die, and Elyas had been right on the mark with how to use it. "Well, that was lucky. . . ."

The rapid beating of her heart began to slow out of its panic, but adrenaline kept it pounding firmly in her chest. She might actually be able to do this! On a whim, she uttered, "Roll," and the writing shattered into glittering dust, wiping itself out of the air.

The world remained frozen.

Waiting.

Arlo eyed the number above her once more and bit her lip. Shaking the die in her hand, she knelt to roll it on the ground.

18, the die proclaimed when it stopped a couple feet away.

Did that mean she'd cleared her objective, or did she have to roll seventeen exactly to make this work?

The world gave a clunk, then shuddered, then threaded itself back into gear. The train picked up speed on its track once again, and all of a sudden, the world burst back into fully saturated life.

A shudder passed through her then too, warm and tingling and *joyous*, like unfolding legs that had fallen numb and feeling the blood rush back through them.

The number above her was gone, and everything was back to normal as though it had never been otherwise. But that wasn't what made Arlo's eyes grow wide, her breath catch in her chest, and her throat close around a deluge of emotion—*hopeawefearbewilderment*.

Elyas blinked. Unaware that anything had happened since she'd called out her move, he opened his mouth, but before he could ask whatever he'd been about to say, nothing came. He blinked a few more times.

Together they stood on the rooftop and *gaped* at the sudden stillness around them, no hint of even a breeze as far as they could see.

Arlo had done it.

"Arlo," Elyas breathed, and he beamed. "Arlo, you did it."

They stood there for twenty minutes, just to make sure it had actually stopped.

"Make it start back up again!"

She didn't know how—she'd never been trained for this—but when she asked the die for help and once again cleared a much lower number, there was once again that tingling of magic, and the wind had picked up once more as though it had never faltered.

"Oh my gods, Arlo—do you know what this means?"

She did.

It meant she wasn't useless after all.

If this die could make her magic stronger, if it could help her succeed in something she'd been struggling with her entire life, how much harder would it be to get it to help her succeed at other things? Things like helping a prince break into a questionable facility guarded by alchemy?

This die . . . It meant there was actual hope that she could be something other than a disappointment.

"I have to send a text!" she cried, and fled back inside. Once back in her room, she snatched her phone from the bed and fired off a message:

Group Message
To: Vehan, Aurelian, Nausicaä

Arlo: I'll do it. I'll help you

Nausicaä: ▢=[]:::::> FIIIINE I will too

Vehan: Yes! Perfect—thank you! Okay, here's what we're going to do . . .

Hero sat on the floor of his office, slumped against the wall. The shelves that lined the room like ribs, the instruments and books they supported, the overhead strips of lighting, his desk—everything was gutted, twisted up, broken, hanging by wires the way veins held on to eyes pried from their sockets, or strewn like a spill of organs.

Nothing had been spared Lethe's wrath, not even Hero. His body was sore for the abuse he'd survived, his face split by a score of bleeding lines—four that streaked from his eye to his mouth and one that curled over his jaw where Lethe had grabbed him by his claws and *screamed* at him.

I should kill you for this.

You're nothing to me.

They're closing in on you, Hero. The prince, his friend, my cousin, Arlo—and I'm going to let them. I'm going to let them find you here, destroy everything you've built, reduce you to the pathetic waste you've always been. I told you to leave her be, but you couldn't—*why couldn't you do this* one simple thing?

We're through.

These wounds wouldn't heal over easily. Such was the nature of the claws Lethe wore; the damage they inflicted ran *deep* and could never be fully erased. But Hero had his stone—he carried it always. The magic it could help him perform should be just enough to stop the bleeding, and there was no doubt in his mind Lethe knew this.

We're through.

They weren't.

Lethe had destroyed his office, but he'd spared Hero's life. He'd been angrier than Hero had ever seen him, but he'd left him with *everything*, his stone included, when he could have easily taken it all.

"We're not through . . . You're hoping I'll redeem myself, aren't you."

Arlo was coming.

Lethe's warning was enough to know that Lethe hoped she'd leave as she'd come—alive.

Hero watched as droplets of blood soaked into his pants, growing a stain that spread wider and wider. They weren't through. Lethe had raged, but Hero hadn't expected otherwise should he catch wind of this plot before Hero could see it through. Lethe thought he needed Arlo—until Hero succeeded in proving he didn't—so of course he was going to be upset, of course he wouldn't understand what Hero was doing was all for *him*.

A book lay at his feet—his journal, one of many casualties to Lethe's raw ire. Gingerly he bent forward and dragged it back toward him. His journal was where he kept his ideas, the arrays he played with in the attempt to create something new and push his magic to further heights.

Arlo was coming.

She would *not* leave alive.

But his Reaper was gone, and he'd have to accomplish this goal by himself, and maybe he had better means to do so, anyhow, than a creature whose legend had clearly been nothing but hype. Incompetent . . . witless . . . clumsy . . . Hero flipped through pages until he landed at last on what he'd been looking for. The array drawn there was something he'd been working on for months now. It had proven difficult, much more so than originally anticipated. He knew he had the right formula, but something was missing, something he'd failed time and again to get *right*. In frustration he'd set it aside, but something in him whispered now *what if* . . .

What if this was the push he needed?

What if, now that he no longer had other tools to fall back on, he'd have no choice but to figure this out? What if all he'd been missing was proper conviction?

I'm going to let them find you here—good. Let Arlo come to him. Let her fall into his clutches, out of sight, trapped below the earth where no one would ever find her. Killing this girl would allow Lethe to see *him* for what he was, what he could be to him and every other immortal too focused on the *wrong person*. Killing her would remove her as an obstacle, but if he could somehow absorb what made her special on top of this . . . if he could add every bit of whatever measly talent she had to his own . . .

"But I can't risk you popping in on me again," he muttered, and flipped the page.

The array on its back had been difficult to craft as well, but he'd perfected it long ago. He just hadn't been given cause to use it until now. Lethe had always been welcome wherever he wanted to go. But Hero was out of strikes. He knew that Lethe wouldn't abide another attempt on Arlo's life. He'd kill Hero, the friendship between them be damned. Hero had to protect himself until he was ready to reveal his hand—had to cancel out what allowed Lethe to teleport into this laboratory.

Hauling himself to his feet, Hero tucked his book under his arm and made for a door that was now just a gaping hole in the wall.

Arlo was coming.

This would all be over soon.

Hero had much to do as fast as he could to prepare for her reception.

CHAPTER 28

Arlo

❧

I T'S SO *HOT* HERE," Arlo complained, leaning back against the ice
machine and fanning her face with a hand.

Before their plan could be set in motion later that night and
Nausicaä could come and smuggle Arlo out of her apartment, they'd
been forced to wait for Thalo to come home from work, see all was
as it should be, and fall asleep. Standing now outside Love's Travel
Stop, a sizable gas station on the edge of Las Vegas with nothing to do
but watch the numbers on her phone creep toward nine o'clock, she
found this nighttime heat was almost unbearable.

Back home, summer temperatures often spiked into 90—sometimes
even 100—degree weather much heavier and more humid than this, but
Arlo vastly preferred the cooler temperatures; she wasn't ready to face any
of that yet.

"Precious flower," Nausicaä cooed beside her, a disconcerting
imitation of the Reaper and falsely sympathetic to Arlo's discomfort.
"Shouldn't be much longer now, but you're welcome to go back inside
and buy more snacks?"

Arlo had probably blown her entire life savings on slushies tonight.
At the moment, she was so full of sugar and *blue* that she didn't think
she could stomach another drink. Besides, the store clerks had started
eyeing her numerous visits with suspicion. Shaking her head, Arlo
darted another look at her phone, and the message she'd been contemplating how to answer for the last half hour.

Elyas: Arrrrlloooooo. Hi. It's Cel. I know it's late. Back home. In
Toronto. Where you're supposed to be. Where I'm sure you are still,

because Elyas was DEFINITELY just making things up to distract me from the chocolate cake he'd been trying to sneak up to his room earlier when he told me this HILARIOUS story about you and the Seelie Summer prince joining forces to investigate the ironborn murders. Just as I'm sure Snapchat's location finder is lying to me when it says you're currently in Nevada. Right?

She regretted the bare minimum of her plans she'd told Elyas, but the more she weighed the pros and cons, the more she realized it might actually be wise to let someone not in her current company know what she was up to in case things took a turn for the worse.

Arlo: Please don't be mad.

Elyas: Mad? Why would I be mad? You're at home with Thalo, safely in your bed. Snapchat is just glitching out—Elyas will say anything for chocolate cake. You don't even know Prince Vehan, so of course you wouldn't be running around Nevada with him in the middle of the night. What's there to be mad about?

Arlo: Your sarcasm has been noted btw. But as you know, I met Vehan after work on Sat and it turns out he knows a lot about what's going on with the murders. He's in danger too, Cel. He needs my help and I want to give it. I'll explain everything tomorrow. I'm sorry. I would have told you sooner except I didn't want you getting into even more trouble too if we got caught and Nausicaä is with me! I'll be fine! And now at least you know where I am if I'm not back by breakfast tomorrow so . . . :D

Elyas: Arlo

Elyas: Cyan

Elyas: Jarsdel

She really didn't have it in her to deal with Celadon's anxieties right now, not on top of her own. Apart from his unending string of texts still lighting up her phone, there was nothing new from anyone else, nothing since Aurelian's terse reply that they would *be there in ten*, exactly ten minutes ago.

"Hey," called an unfamiliar voice. Arlo looked up from her phone to find an older man in a blue shirt and faded jeans, paused at the threshold of the Travel Stop. He eyed the two of them with a hopeful interest that made Arlo want to recoil. "You girls lookin' for some work?"

Work?

Nausicaä stepped forward.

Something about the way she peeled away from the wall made the man rethink his "offer," because Arlo could pinpoint the exact moment his leer turned into wary regret. "The sort of 'work' I tend toward doesn't end well for people like you," she threatened, stalking up to Arlo's side. Her voice was a husky drawl that dropped a shiver down Arlo's spine with all the chill of melting ice.

The man flinched away, undoubtedly because of the wraithlike truth glinting through Nausicaä's glamour. "Bitch," he muttered before hurrying into the store.

Arlo sighed dramatically. "We're going to be abducted and murdered before we can even start our investigation."

"Oh, look!" Nausicaä exclaimed. Her sharp features lifted in exaggerated but no less relieved delight as she pointed off into the distance. Soon enough, Arlo saw the headlights of a black Mercedes SUV pulling off the highway too, and onto the Apex that led to their truck stop. "Ten dollars says that's them."

"If it's not, I'm going home."

"Hey, I'm not a taxi service, so unless you plan on *walking* . . ."

"Very clearly someone will pick me up along the way," Arlo sniffed.

Nausicaä scoffed. "Abducted and murdered, remember?"

"I'm this close to preferring that to baking alive in the desert. I can't believe people actually *live* here—is it like this all year round? It must be death."

The SUV turned into the parking lot. Nausicaä stepped up to the curb as the car pulled into the space in front of her. The tinted windows made it difficult to see clearly through the glass, but when Arlo joined Nausicaä at her side, she could finally make out Vehan's enthusiastic grin behind the wheel; Aurelian's bland expression marked him severely indifferent to their existence.

"I feel like Aurelian doesn't like me," Arlo mused aloud.

Nausicaä snorted again. "I feel like Aurelian doesn't like most people, so I wouldn't take that to heart. Maybe if you were a handsome, black-haired, blue-eyed prince of the Seelie Summer Court . . ."

"Well, that's a narrow and specific list of requirements I'll never meet. Also—what *is* going on there? There was a really weird tension between those two back at the Assistance."

"Who knows?" Nausicaä shrugged. Then, with a laugh, she swung an arm around Arlo's shoulders to tug her against her side. The feel of all that hard muscle shocked a brief short-circuiting through Arlo's brain. "What's important is that *I* like you plenty, Red."

"Hooray," Arlo deadpanned, and heaved the too-heavy arm off her shoulders to escape the weird warmth it sent fluttering through her. She made for the SUV's backseat door, and as soon as she threw it open, a much-welcomed wave of chilled air rushed out to greet her.

"Took you long enough," she grumbled, throwing her travel bag and phone onto the seat and climbing in.

"Sorry, we had trouble getting away from the palace. I'm more or less convinced my mother knows exactly what we're getting up to tonight," Vehan apologized, smiling way too easily for the gravity of what he'd just said, as though it was perfectly fine the Head of Seelie Summer knew they were up to severe law breaking right inside her Court.

Arlo groaned.

"All right," Vehan announced once Nausicaä had joined them as well. "Everyone in? Are we ready to get on our way?"

"All in. Let's roll out, Prince Charmless."

"Let's do this," Arlo agreed, and to herself, added, "before I lose my nerve altogether."

If anyone heard her, no one said a word.

The SUV pulled out of the station and back onto the highway, continuing its journey northwest toward the middle-of-nowhere solar field that was their destination. The ten-minute drive passed in silence, but lack of conversation didn't make it feel any longer. In fact, time seemed to pass in a blur of dusk-drenched rocky earth and browning pockets of vegetation. The sky was almost fully dark now, nothing but ghostly embers guttering on the horizon to keep the day alive. With Vegas so near, the light pollution glowing in the air around the city meant it was nowhere near as dark as night *should* be, but Arlo rarely saw as many stars in the sky as she did now.

Absorbed as she was in those countless, glittering specks—and the worries blooming under the dagger-points of their cold light—it seemed to take the group no time at all to arrive at their destination.

The SUV pulled off to the side of the road and slowed to a stop. Vehan killed the headlights along with the engine, plunging them even deeper into the night. "We'll have to walk from here," he explained, turning to face Arlo and Nausicaä over the middle console.

This Arlo already knew.

They'd been instructed to dress appropriately, in the darkest clothing possible, so that they could sneak around unseen. For Arlo, this meant donning her dark red Blundstones, black jeggings, and matching black top. It was almost identical to what Nausicaä wore, save that most of *her* attire was leather, and none of it was really outside of what she wore on a daily basis.

White and gold being the official colors of the Seelie Summer Court, Arlo doubted either Vehan or Aurelian had ever worn so much black in their lives, though, especially when that color was one of their rivals', the UnSeelie Court of Winter.

Vehan's eyes appeared even more electric against his cotton shirt and fitted pants, black as his charcoal hair, and the pale warmth in his skin was diminished. He looked vaguely vampiric, his fine but sturdy features even more sharply cut into his face.

Dressed identically to the prince, Aurelian's lean body seemed even longer, and every movement now reminded Arlo strongly of a feline on the prowl.

A sidhe prince, a lesidhe guard, an ironborn girl, and a former Fury—they seemed less like a serious investigative team and more like the lead-in to some terrible joke.

Vehan came around the car to join Aurelian and Arlo, with Nausicaä in tow. "So, like I said," he began, waving everyone closer. "There's a bunch of solar panels a few yards out from here, and by those panels is a door in the ground. Pincer disappeared through it, so we figure there has to be *something* down there—something to do with where and why all these people are being taken, and, I suspect, the philosopher's stone experimentations as well. Whatever it is . . ."

"That's what we're here to find out," Nausicaä finished gleefully.

Nodding, Vehan continued. "Exactly. Which means this is a surveillance mission only, all right? We don't know what's down there. We go in, we survey, we come back out. We all have phones, so take any pictures that you can, and the moment we have something that'll finally make the High King *listen*, we leave. Nausicaä?"

Nausicaä snapped to attention.

"You'll be able to get us out from within the facility, correct?"

"Yup. Right back here to the car like *that*." She snapped her fingers, and a fraction of the tension in Vehan's shoulders eased. "I'd be able to get us in, too, if I knew what it looked like, but hey, where's the fun in that?"

Arlo was slower to shed her own tension. "What if we don't find anything? What if this is just another Faerie Ring or something? What if someone finds us first?"

"We'll have to play it by ear," was Vehan's grim reply. "Unfortunately, we won't know whether we're right or wrong about this place until we've had a look inside."

Aurelian turned to Arlo. "The way your friend struts around, I assume she has *some* form of combat training—"

"Remind me to kick your ass when this is over so I can give you a physical demonstration."

Ignoring this outburst (although his expression did fall a fraction flatter), Aurelian continued, "I assume you have none."

"In my defense," Arlo reminded him, "I did tell you guys I'd be extremely useless in this investigation."

Aurelian shook his head. "That's not what I meant. I didn't ask to single you out. I just think it may be best if Vehan took the lead and I took up the rear. I figure you'd feel most comfortable with Nausicaä as your immediate protection over myself."

"And *I* would feel more comfortable if you took lead with your fuck-off pretty princeling," Nausicaä cut in. "I don't know you at all. For all I *do* know, you could be working with our mysterious, murderous alchemist to capture Arlo and turn her into their next torture victim. Nah-uh. I take rear."

"Why are you this difficult? All this talk about trust, but of everyone here it's *you* who has the least of *mine*," Aurelian snapped, temper flaring.

"Well, you can damn well trust I'll punt you into the freaking sun if you start this fight you're clearly after, fae boy. Why are *you* this difficult?"

"Fight *I'm* after? *Me?*" Aurelian took a step forward, crowding Nausicaä's space, about three lifetimes braver than Arlo would ever be to do so. "*I'm* not the one who keeps threatening violence every time someone says something you don't—"

"Come on, you two, this isn't helping anything," Vehan warned, fixed in place, looking quite shocked by the quick escalation of this argument.

"Finish the sentence," Nausicaä hissed, ignoring Vehan to surge forward and crowd Aurelian in return. "Give me a reason. I'll—"

"Oh, wow, can you stop?" Arlo shouted, inserting herself between them. She glared first at Aurelian, then at Nausicaä, and flicked them each in turn on the chest. "Focus! Most of us don't actually know anyone here all that well. Let's stop pointing fingers and finding reasons to argue and just . . . get this done, okay? *Before* sunrise?" Before Celadon arrived with the cavalry.

"Agreed," said Vehan, looking between his friend and Nausicaä, his unease still distinctly visible. He cleared his throat. "We won't accomplish anything by assuming the worst of our allies."

"*Allies,*" Nausicaä scoffed. "I should have done this on my own."

"You're welcome to leave at any time," said Aurelian.

"*I'm* leaving," Arlo huffed, storming away from the group in the direction of the solar field.

"And *I'm* taking rear," Nausicaä snapped at Aurelian.

Aurelian hissed back at her—a genuine, catlike threat of irritation—but the matter was settled. Vehan took the lead with his friend stalking along behind. When Arlo felt a presence at her back, she slowed her stride to fall in sync with Nausicaä. "Do you really think we can't trust them?"

"Nah, they're cool. The lesidhe aren't the only ones who are good at reading auras. There's just something about Aurelian that pisses me off—and apparently the feeling's mutual. Also . . ."

Arlo looked over her shoulder to see if there was a reason for Nausicaä's sudden silence, and only then did she spot the private amusement curling her wide mouth. "Yes?"

"Well, if one of us assholes is going to play your stunningly attractive defender, like hell I'm going to let it be fucking Thranduil over there."

Arlo laughed despite herself. "I think out of the two of you, you're the one most like Thranduil."

"You're right. He's nowhere near fabulous enough. He can be my slightly inferior but equally arrogant son, Legolas."

"I'll let you be the one to tell him the good news."

They continued on, conversation falling away. Their trek diverged from the dirt road they'd taken to this point and snaked into the rocky desert. With so many more immediate dangers to worry about now, like the possibility of poisonous wildlife, it was harder to focus on what they hurtled toward.

Eventually, they came to a wire fence marking out the solar field's massive perimeter. Its panels seemed to stretch on forever. Aurelian strode forward and threaded his fingers through the fence, giving a sharp yank. The metal groaned and tore in two with laughable ease, splitting down the middle like torn paper. With strength like that, it was good he was on *their* side.

They filtered through and carried on toward the closest of four towering spotlights. Erected in the corners of the solar field, they bathed the panels in bright white light.

Vehan raised a hand in the air and curled his fingers into a fist, signaling for the group to halt. He turned to face them, placing a finger to his lips, then pointed to the pocket of light they were closest to breeching.

He shook his head—cut a hand across his throat—then just as silently pointed off to Arlo's left, along the edge of the spotlight's reach to the shadows that curled around the far corner.

Keep out of the light, Arlo assumed Vehan intended them to infer.

Nausicaä stepped back to allow her by, then followed behind. The two of them crept through the dark after Vehan and Aurelian, both fae moving with such long and graceful strides that Arlo felt a bit like a bull elephant trudging along behind.

A few inches shy of rounding the panel's corner, Vehan stopped the group again.

"There," he whispered, turning to face them. He spoke so softly that Arlo had to strain her ears to hear him. "The door is just ahead."

Moving up behind Aurelian, she peered around his shoulder and down the meandering length of the panels. She couldn't see anything but dark glass and gleaming metal, but then again, the prince had mentioned the door was in the ground.

"So how do we get in?" Nausicaä asked, her voice pitched in a matching hush.

"It opened just fine for Pincer, but for us . . . it's protected by more than just an alchemic seal. Between our talents, I think we can get through just fine, but it'll take some work."

"Awesome," Nausicaä breathed. "A proper infiltration." She seemed genuinely pleased when she broke ranks to sneak around them. Picking her way through the dark shallows, she made for the middle of the panel field, where the pools of light were weakest. Aurelian followed close behind, as though they were contestants on some survival show, competing to see who could solve this puzzle first.

"They're very . . . odd together," said Vehan, watching the pair settle into a somewhat stiff huddle. "I don't know Nausicaä at all, but Aurelian's not usually like this with people. He's more of the strong and silent 'this isn't worth my time' type when strangers irritate him. It's a bit how he acts with his brother, but . . ."

Arlo considered the observation, thinking back on what she knew of Nausicaä's behavior. She had no idea how siblings were supposed to act. The bond between her and Celadon served as the closest thing she had for comparison, and they got on extremely well.

But of course, they had their share of arguments, too.

"Some people just clash, I guess." Arlo shrugged. "I don't really know Nausicaä all that well, either, but I think there's . . . a lot of hurt inside her. Underneath all that swagger. She isn't as good at hiding it as she thinks."

"Aurelian, too," Vehan replied after a heavily weighted moment.

His voice was so quiet Arlo suspected the words were more for himself than her. She didn't really understand them, regardless. In lieu of reply, she nudged his shoulder and smiled when his gaze slid over to her, then jerked her head in the direction of their friends. "We'll just have to keep an eye on them. Come on, before they forget we're here and storm the castle without us."

Together, they picked their way over to the rest of their group.

". . . a guard into consideration. It's why Vehan and I couldn't get very far in our previous attempt at investigation. What they sent after us . . . I have no idea what they were, but their numbers were great enough to be a problem for two lone fae."

Aurelian was deep in explanation when Arlo slipped around them to plant herself at Nausicaä's side. Vehan took the opposite flank. "I have an idea to get us through the spotlights, but there's no telling whether it will work or whether it will trip some other alarm," he said.

As Vehan spoke, he lifted his hand. Flexing his fingers, he curled them into a fist. As they folded, the air around them hummed. It crackled around Vehan—sparking, even—and for a brief moment, the light from the powerful spotlights began to dim.

It was nothing but a demonstration of what he intended, but it left Arlo wildly impressed regardless. Celadon occasionally toyed with the breeze, and her mother had sometimes performed little tricks for Arlo's amusement as a child, but it wasn't often she got to see a fae flex their powers on any grander scale.

As heir to the throne, Vehan was expected to have a control of the electricity his people commanded that was among the best of those he'd one day rule. It thrilled the part of Arlo that still found magic so exciting to be able to see him put it into action.

"*Tch,*" Nausicaä scoffed. "Show-off." But as this showing off might work in their favor, she didn't seem too unhappy about the display. "All right, we turn off the lights and maybe that works, so we take a closer look at that door?"

Aurelian nodded.

Vehan grinned.

Arlo yelped a little too loudly for their current situation. The die in her back pocket had grown suddenly hot, enough to remind her of its presence. Fishing it out and ignoring the curious glances shot her way, she inspected it closely. It was perfectly cool in her hand, but the golden numbers glowed molten now, hot as Aurelian's eyes.

And somehow . . . almost instinctually . . . she knew what it wanted her to do.

"Is that another die?" Nausicaä asked, eyeing Arlo's hand suspiciously. "Because points for persistence and all, but the last one didn't work all that great back at the Faerie Ring, and I'm thinking we should find you a better weapon of choice."

Ah.

Arlo hadn't told anyone yet about her die—at least no one apart from Elyas. She couldn't exactly explain her desire to keep it a secret until she proved to herself it could actually help her. That what had happened on the roof hadn't been a fluke. She hadn't wanted to jinx her luck.

Closing her fingers around the die, she closed her eyes as well. Under her breath, she whispered firmly, "We use Vehan's magic to turn off the spotlights," and the moment she finished speaking, the world chugged to a halt exactly as it had done before; when she opened her eyes again, everything was still and gray.

"Arlo, what the actual fuck just happened?"

Not everything, apparently.

Arlo very nearly dropped the die in her surprise. She yelped, and whipped her head to the side to find Nausicaä, in full color and perfectly mobile, looking around in genuine shock. "Yo!" she loudly exclaimed. "Did you just *stop time*?"

Arlo met the mixture of surprise and amazement with stunned incomprehension. "Uh . . . yeah? I think so? But . . . how . . . ?"

A bit of razor glee unwound in Nausicaä's smile. She waved Arlo off. "I'm immortal. I don't have any time for you to stop. But never mind that—holy forking shirt, Red, you said you weren't useful! Where did you get a time-stopping di—*oh* my gods." Something had occurred to her then. Arlo could see it click into place behind her eyes. Nausicaä's wire grin split full and violent across her face. "Made a friend, I see. When this is all over, you and I need to have a little chat. Meanwhile . . ." She pointed straight ahead, redirecting

Arlo's attention to the golden words printed on the air. "Time is only stopped in the pocket around you—it's carrying on just fine outside its limit, so I'd hurry up and choose your play."

Her options were the same as before.

She could choose to roll, or choose to escape, but this time, it was *Assist* that caught her attention, glowing brighter than anything else around it. *Roll* was now grayed out of availability, but that made sense—it wasn't she who'd douse the lights, even if she had to do the rolling. Vehan would be the one performing the magic; all Arlo could do was assist him with the luck of pulling it off.

"Assist," she declared.

The words shattered. Glittering dust broke apart to weave itself back together again, in the golden shape of the number twelve.

Nausicaä whistled. "Difficulty level: moderate. Guess you gotta roll a twelve or higher to pull this off. This is exciting!"

Relaxing her hold on the die, Arlo shook it in her palm and released it. It rolled away from them and landed . . . on the number eighteen.

"Ha!" Nausicaä cackled, supremely amused. Arlo released the breath she'd held, relieved. Reaching forward, she reclaimed her die and the world threaded back into gear. Life returned to their partners, and Vehan, who'd noticed nothing in his momentary pause, turned to Arlo. "Is everything all right?"

Nausicaä turned a wide and lazy grin on the prince. "Just swell. Bring down the house, Charmless." When Vehan shrugged and raised his hand back into the air, she shot Arlo a wink.

That hand closed into a fist once more.

The night began to hum.

The harder he squeezed, the louder that humming grew. The air took on a bitter taste, a lot like touching one's tongue to the end of a live battery, and the hairs on the backs of Arlo's arms and neck stood straight up.

Sparks crackled.

Zipping through the air like white-hot fissures in the dark, they shot straight for Vehan's fingers. His skin absorbed the electric current like a sponge in water, and as the night began to dim, the prince began to glow brighter. It was almost as though someone had cranked his internal radiance, and when the spotlights faded down to almost nothing, his hand flew open wide to release the current he'd leached from them.

The surge of power quickly overwhelmed the grid the lights were on. The bulbs grew bright as day, and Arlo flinched away from the glare. Then . . . four loud and shattering *pops* perforated that glow, and the light was no more.

Night swept across the desert, darker than before.

A groaning rent the air, accompanied by a heavy clunk that Arlo could feel shuddering through the earth beneath them. Several of the undoubtedly expensive solar panels cracked in the process. Nausicaä flung a protective arm out to steady her before she could topple over, but in moments, the chaos settled. In its wake, the silence was deafening.

"Wow, good job, Vehan. You broke the murder factory."

Sheepishly, Vehan scratched the back of his neck. "Sorry. I may have overdone it. I was only trying to turn off the lights."

Quietly, in Arlo's ear, Nausicaä added, "Nice play," and Arlo had to duck her head to hide her sudden flare of pride and the way it warmed her face.

Aurelian stood so abruptly that the conversation died, all eyes on him while he stared at the field of panels.

"Psst." Nausicaä tugged on one of the legs of his pants. "What do your fae eyes see, Legolas?"

Paying no attention to Nausicaä, he lifted a hand to point at the panels and warned, "We're about to have company."

Lesidhe senses were twice as sharp as that of their sidhe counterparts. No one argued with his observation.

"Guess we knocked a little too loudly," Nausicaä sighed. Rising to stand, she swiped a hand through the air, and on the downswing of her stroke, the black katana she'd summoned in the Faerie Ring reappeared in her grasp. With it sheathed, she held it out as a bar between Arlo and whatever greeting they were about to receive.

Arlo, who'd risen to her feet now too, clutched her die close to her chest. With a flick of her eyes, she met Nausicaä's gaze and nodded—hopefully she looked a little less terrified than she felt.

"Time to see what we're up against, I suppose," Vehan added, a soft sigh ghosting over hard determination. He also swung his hand through the air. Apparently, he'd kept some of the charge he'd collected from the spotlights, because a beam of light shot from his palm, forging itself into a humming, electric sword.

"Here," said Aurelian. He held something out to Arlo, and when her attention snapped to the object, she realized it was a dagger. Long and glinting sharp, it was better than the nothing she had currently for her defense. "Take this."

"Um, but what will you use?"

"Lesidhe have no need for weapons to defend themselves. We aren't allowed them, besides. I didn't bring this for me."

Tilting her head in consideration of this offer—it surprised her he'd been so thoughtful when all along he'd held himself so removed—Arlo accepted the dagger. "Thank you."

Aurelian nodded.

There was no time to spare for further contemplation of his behavior. The commotion he'd picked up on had finally grown loud enough for Arlo to hear as well. A pneumatic hiss opened the door in the ground, and out of this space poured an infantry of indistinguishable, humanoid shapes to complete the RPG her life had suddenly become.

CHAPTER 29

Arlo

~~~

YOU'RE ON DEFENSE!" NAUSICAÄ clipped at Aurelian.

He nodded and dropped back to place himself as a shield in front of Arlo.

"Ready?" Vehan asked, a flick of his wrist stirring angry sparks from his electric weapon like a rattled hive of wasps.

Lifting her fist into the air, Nausicaä angled a deadly grin at the prince. "Highest body count wins?"

Vehan formed a fist of his own and knocked it against hers. "If by highest body count you mean highest number of people incapacitated but still very much alive, then yes."

"Wow, so *boring* . . ."

"Yeah, no, please don't kill anybody," Arlo tried to warn, the comment drowned by a loud and throaty roar she shouldn't have been surprised to identify as Nausicaä's, but was regardless. Mildly horrified—but mostly amazed—she watched both prince and Fury spring into action.

It was understandable that Aurelian and Vehan had found it difficult to determine what had chased them away from the panels the first time they'd attempted this infiltration. In the dark, their attackers were little better than faceless shadows vaguely resembling men, if much taller and broader and a bit misshapen.

Few folk shared a natural likeness to humans, but all could bend their glamours to appear as one. They could be up against anything, and without much light for them to see by, it was hard to assess the situation.

"It's a little dark!" Arlo heard Vehan shout above the clang of metal striking metal, and the enraged buzzing of an electric blade landing numerous blows against steel.

"Oh well, time out, guys, the prince has to find his *flashlight*. You know, I'm not the one who turned the friggin' lights off to begin with!"

"I'm just saying—*urgh*—I'm just saying this could be easier and that I have no idea if I'm attacking friend or foe here."

"Here's a hint: if you stab me, I'll fucking kill you."

"Surprisingly enough, that isn't helpful!"

"Oh my gods." Arlo rubbed the space between her brows and sighed. Then, dropping her hand, she reached into her back pocket and traded her die for her cell phone. One thing to be said about modern technology was that the flashlights on phones were actually fairly bright. Never before had she been so thankful for this as she was now. Tapping the app, she illuminated their battleground.

It wasn't much, but when Aurelian added light from his own phone, it made for a brilliant combination. Vehan's wish was granted, and Arlo immediately regretted her hand in this.

"Uh . . ."

The prince faltered.

Caught off guard by the sudden revelation of what they were fighting, his legs were swept out from underneath him, landing him roughly on the flat of his back.

"Vehan!" Aurelian cried, starting forward. Equally concerned over the prince's predicament, Arlo followed.

Thankfully, Nausicaä was less affected by their opponents' identities.

Walking monstrosities of metal and flesh, the armor the creatures wore appeared to be melted right into their skin—skin that had clearly been harvested from multiple sources and sewn together, forging a grotesque parody of a human being. Their dull, bulbous eyes and slack and sunken faces showed no sign of thought or life within. They were shells, possessed no magical aura, and judging by the automatism of their movements, it was possible they were wholly unaware of who they were, where they were, and what they were doing.

The sight of them alone was enough to excite a crawling under Arlo's skin, while Nausicaä's revulsion expressed itself in a singular, eloquent, "*Urgh.*"

She'd seen much worse, apparently, and Vehan's urgent need for assistance took precedence over her affection for theatrical displays.

From what Arlo could tell, there were only about ten of the swarming creatures. The lack of blood from the ones their side had managed to "incapacitate" meant Nausicaä had refrained from dealing the death she'd threatened, but their opponents held no such qualms about taking lives.

The way they lunged and slashed with their own daggers, glinting in the flashlights' glow, was too violent for any other intent. It was possible that Nausicaä had been toying with them at first, but somewhere between realization of what they were fighting and noticing Vehan on the ground, a switch in her had flipped.

This time, there was no roar to herald her assault.

Most of the creatures had shifted their focus to the sudden vulnerability—the winded prince, scrambling to reclaim both footing and sword—but the one Nausicaä had been locked with in battle remained behind.

Lifting a leg, Nausicaä aimed a powerful blow to its chest. In one smooth, simultaneous motion, she took hold of the cover still wrapped around her katana's blade, and in less than a second, a lethal *shiiink* unsheathed her weapon. Following her blade, a perfect arch of ruby red curled through the air like ribbon.

The creature dropped to the ground.

Arlo gasped, frozen in place, but Nausicaä spared none of her focus for the dead *thing* she'd left behind.

Following her blade's momentum, she swung on her heels so quickly and so artfully that Arlo wondered if she'd been born with that sword in her hands, and had dedicated the entirety of her very long life to learning its use.

A short spin brought her close enough to the creature nearest Vehan (preparing a strike of its own) to land a powerful blow. Controlled by her immortal strength, the blade cut vertically through armor, flesh, and bone alike—straight through the creature's heart and spine and out the opposite side.

It slid apart in halves, falling like a marionette cut of its strings.

"Trying to steal all the attention for yourself, huh?" Nausicaä shook her head. When she tossed aside the sheath she held, it burst into smoke the moment it hit the ground and freed a hand for Nausicaä to haul Vehan back to his feet.

Aurelian rushed forward. "Vehan—"

"I gave you *one* job, Legolas!" Nausicaä snapped, sparing a glare for Aurelian's approach, Arlo hot on his trail—Arlo, whom he was supposed to be keeping out of harm's way until Vehan's immediate danger made them both forget themselves. "Get back there and take her with y—"

"Guys, watch out!" Arlo interrupted, skidding to a halt behind Aurelian and waving her dagger at the five other creatures still very much alive and pressing in around them.

One made a stab at Nausicaä, but the strike was caught before it could land—this time by Vehan. A flare of angry buzzing filled the air as his electric sword rose to bear the brunt of the weight the creature threw behind his blade. Whirling back around, Nausicaä rejoined him in battle.

She and the prince made short work of the remaining creatures. Vehan was very obviously comfortable with his blade, but next to Nausicaä, whose every step and flick of wrist turned concise movements into the most beautiful dance Arlo had ever witnessed, he looked no more skilled with his weapon than he would have when first learning to use it.

Content that Vehan was no longer in danger and able to handle his own once more, Aurelian ushered Arlo away from the fight.

"What *are* they?" she asked. Her attention swiveled between the graceful sway of Nausicaä's body and the corpses left in her wake. "Why aren't any of them attacking you and me?"

Aurelian shook his head. "I don't know. But whatever they are, they don't seem to have much awareness . . . They don't seem to feel much pain, either."

Together, they watched a creature fall to the ground, no sound or twitch to betray what it felt; one moment alive, and abruptly the next: a motionless heap on the earth.

"They bleed *red*," Arlo observed.

When the last of them fell, the silence that usurped the clang of metal was louder than any other noise this evening had known. It rang for the several minutes it took the group to knit back together, Arlo and Aurelian shuffling forward while Vehan and Nausicaä fell back.

"Cava," said Nausicaä, after a moment longer of no one else knowing what to say. "Remember back in the Hiraeth, Your Highness?" She looked pointedly at Vehan. "*Those* are cava. Artificial humans with no souls, killed and given life again by one hell of a dark array . . . That's why I didn't really care about killing them. They're just . . . hollow shells. There's nothing about them that's *anything* anymore."

"*Necromancy,*" Vehan spat.

Aurelian had doused his phone's flashlight, but Arlo kept hers lit, angled at the ground to keep from blinding them. Though the resulting shadows warped their features, she was able still to see the absolute disgust on the prince's face.

Nausicaä shook her head. "Well, yes, but that's still alchemy, believe it or not—alchemy at its worst . . . or best, I guess, depending on which side of the argument you fall. Alchemy at its most powerful, for sure."

"This is bigger than you're allowing us to understand," Aurelian said.

Arlo looked at Nausicaä. When she trained her steely gaze on Arlo in return, Arlo repeated the question she'd asked back at Assistance

Headquarters. "What else does a philosopher's stone do besides turn things to gold and grant eternal life?"

"Stones," Nausicaä corrected.

"What?"

"Stones. Plural. There's more than one. In fact, according to my hard-won source of information, there are seven, and each has its own little party favor for the fool smart enough to make one."

Confusion weighing darkly on his brow, Vehan frowned at Nausicaä. "In your own time, of course, but it certainly would be lovely if you would condescend to share some of what you suspect we're up against. *Before* we hurtle off after our deaths, preferably?"

Nausicaä's glare began to sharpen into the lethal edge of the blade still in her hand. In the interest of keeping things civil between them—Nausicaä's temper had been a live wire all night—Arlo decided to intervene before another argument did first. "So, what do they do, then?"

"Well," said Nausicaä, happily turning her attention back to Arlo. "One turns shit to gold, and another does grant immortality. But there's also one that allows you complete control over any heart you wish to possess, and one that will grant you tireless endurance. Another will grant you beauty, and another freedom from the need for mortal sustenance, and then last but certainly not least, command over the Infernal forces such as Furies and demons and all the big bad scaleys locked away in the Lower Deep. Because the stones? They're not just lumps of magical rock."

"Yes, we know that already," Vehan reminded her. "They're hearts."

"No. They're not. Well, yeah, they're that, but that's just because, much like the ironborn required to grow them, the stones are also vessels. Those hearts are the only way these spirits can physically enter the world."

"Spirits?" Aurelian echoed, raising a brow.

"The Sins."

Silence stretched among them again, Nausicaä's response a little too casual for what she'd just said.

"When you say 'sins,'" Arlo ventured, "do you mean . . . ?"

"Greed. Pride. Lust. Sloth. Envy. Gluttony. Wrath. Yeah—the Sins. They aren't just behaviors in people—they're actual entities, negative energies as old as the freaking Titans. They used to have bodies, so the legend goes, but stones are the only way they possess a corporeal form now. One stone for each, and each has its own special power specifically designed to entice stupid mortals into summoning them into the world—'cause they can influence it still just fine, but apparently they blew their chance of causing direct chaos way before I was born. The last time I was privy to such knowledge, the Sins were all squared away in the depths of the Immortal Realm. The challenge I had to win just to learn a bit more . . ." She trailed off, a look overcoming her that was strangely human to Arlo—almost genuinely *worried*.

Vehan's brow joined Aurelian's in incredulity—Nausicaä had yet to actually tell them who she was—but they contained the questions leaping in their eyes to allow her speech to continue.

"There's a big long legend tied to why the Sins are imprisoned, and now isn't the time for that story," Nausicaä explained, shaking herself out of whatever thought had momentarily consumed her. "But it's Bad News Bears if some asshole manages to bring 'em all back up here, is all I can say."

Holding up a hand, Vehan, it appeared, could restrain himself no longer. "So, what is a cava exactly, and what do they have to do with any of this?"

"Well, cava is the plural of the term. The word *you're* looking for—the singular—is cavum. And like I said, they're artificial beings: dolls made out of bits of real people, and I think we just found out what the murder factory is doing with all those humans they've been collecting, hmm? It also takes a fuck-ton of magic to bring a doll to life. That someone's gone ahead and made a small *army* of them means the likelihood we're up against someone who's already succeeded in making a stone is a whole one hundred percent." She shook her head, dropping her gaze to the dead cava strewn around. "I'd snap your picture here and go back to the car—the Courts can't ignore this. It baffles me that my sisters have. You can end your investigation here, but I'm not done with this place now that it's gone and made itself so interesting. Those cava came from somewhere, and that array on your chest, Vehan? Someone tried to make the gods-damned prince of Seelie Summer into a philosopher's stone—probably didn't know at the time that this would only work on ironborn, sure, but that was ballsy as fuck, and I have to say that I'm kind of impressed they gave it a whirl at all."

Arlo watched as Vehan squared his jaw. "I'm staying," he declared firmly. "We came all this way, and if what you said is true, this is so much worse than Aurelian and I previously thought. If there's someone inside who can explain what's happening here . . . how I came to have this array . . . I can't risk letting them get away in the time it would take for the Courts to act on the proof of a picture. I'm staying. Our deal still stands, though, Arlo—all you need to do for us is deactivate the seal on the door, and you can go home. You don't have to come with us."

"Oh no. I'm coming," Arlo replied, with more resolution than she felt. The escalation of this plot terrified her, but almost to a degree that she couldn't fully comprehend why it should scare her off. She'd already decided she'd do this, and her die hadn't failed her yet. She could help them do more than just get in, and by the sound of things, they would need as much of that help as they could get.

We're all we've got.

Besides, Nausicaä could simply spirit them away, if things became too intense. "If I can break open that door, I'm coming with you. I want to know what's going on too."

To Nausicaä, Aurelian added quite sternly, "You're not lending this aid in an attempt to steal one of these stones for yourself, are you?"

Arlo's heart gave an odd sort of lurch.

Command of some immortal army, tireless endurance, control over *people* . . . with things like that at her disposal, the chaos Nausicaä seemed to be after would be all too easily accomplished. And if she could coax an alchemist into working with her to make other stones—an alchemist just like Arlo, whom Nausicaä had been unusually invested in where very few others had ever cared before . . .

"*Tch*." Nausicaä flicked her wrist, and her katana evaporated in pitch-black smoke. "I have serious issues, and boy do I like setting shit on fire, but I'm not a psychopath. Also, I'm far too creative to copy someone else's evil scheme. Also, *also*, I'm competitive as fuck—like hell I'm going to let someone else's temper tantrum upstage mine, so before you ask: *yes*, I am actually going to try to put a stop to this bullshit. If you are too, then I guess that makes us allies."

She held a hand out to Vehan, and Arlo breathed a quiet sigh of relief.

Hesitating only briefly, Vehan thrust his hand into hers, and their pact was sealed. "You have my unwavering support, Nausicaä . . . ?"

"Kraken."

He wavered. "Are . . . are you serious? What, were all the other surnames taken?"

"I can snap your neck in, like, less than a second. I think you should let me call myself whatever I want."

"Fair enough."

They shook, and Vehan dropped his hand. Nausicaä turned to Aurelian. "If this is going to work, I need you to know one thing."

Aurelian said nothing, but his golden eyes watched her intently.

"There's a noticeable bit of friction between us."

Aurelian continued to stare.

"I will have your back, regardless."

Still, Aurelian looked on, saying nothing.

"I will have your *prince's* back, regardless."

Finally, a reaction—a muscle leaped in his tightening jaw.

"But if you ever leave Arlo unguarded like that again in the moments I'm trusting you to have *her* back, the Seven Sins and the ruin they serve will be the least of your concerns. Got it?"

He nodded, a flicker of contrition in his face before his composure resettled on cool indifference.

"Wonderful. All right, we should get moving before whoever's down there sends another wave along."

Nausicaä was right. They didn't have time for this Q and A. The door the cava had poured from had closed back up behind them, thanks to the seal on its surface, and now it was only Arlo who could unlock it for them.

She made to follow her friends, who'd already started for the door, but a hand at her elbow made her pause. "I'm sorry," said Aurelian softly when she turned to gauge what he wanted. "About before . . . about leaving you unguarded . . ."

Arlo shook her head. "He's your friend, right?"

In the gloom still illuminated by Arlo's phone, she saw that the question made Aurelian uncomfortable. "He's my prince, and as his retainer, it's my duty to protect him."

The statement sounded too rehearsed for it to be the whole truth, but Arlo wouldn't press the matter. "Then don't be sorry."

The questioning tilt of his head told Arlo he didn't understand. "Don't be sorry for wanting to protect the people important to you," she explained. "Isn't that what all this is about, anyhow? Protecting people? Besides, don't listen to Nausicaä. We've known each other for like . . . two weeks? Enough time for me to know she blows pretty hot in certain moods . . . not enough time to warrant raging revenge if I bite it in this mission."

It was Aurelian's turn to shake his head. "Nausicaä doesn't strike me as a person with many friends. She'd be upset to lose you, trust me."

"I guess," she replied, not all that convinced. "But still, don't worry. I'm not upset, we're good."

"Good." Aurelian nodded, then strode past her. Arlo followed after him, careful to keep her eyes from examining too closely the faces of the cava as she picked her way through their heap. Coming up between Aurelian and Nausicaä, she peered down at the door they stood huddled around. True to Vehan's word, an array had been stamped into the surface of the metal—a simple circle, but drawn within was a diamond shape with the same strange symbol hovering above each of its points like a compass, all four connected by intricate strings of complicated equations.

"So . . . uh . . . what do I do here?" Arlo asked, angling her phone for a better look. "I don't actually know how to do alchemy—it's forbidden, remember? We're not even really supposed to *talk* about it, and this is only the second array I've ever seen in my life after the one on Vehan's chest."

"Take a look at these symbols," said Nausicaä, reaching to tap the one above the northern point. "Do you know what that is?"

Everyone peered down at the array. Vehan and Aurelian gave a silent shake of their heads, but Arlo . . . "Iron?" she said after a moment, in a barely-there voice to match the barely-there memory that suddenly flashed through her mind.

An impossible memory, thinned by time, mired in fog too thick to see through.

But she could still hear . . .

Her father's voice—*and this is iron, do you see the strength in its strokes?*

"And you thought you'd be useless." Nausicaä beamed. Arlo startled. The memory dissipated like steam. "That *is* the magical symbol for iron. All physical substances are made of matter, and all matter is made of particles. Those particles all have their symbols, yes? Well, magic has given them symbols too. When you piece them all together, balance the science with that magic and imbue these equations with enough power, you can actually hijack that physical substance. You can bend it to whatever you can invent for it to do—within reason. I'm not an alchemist either, so I can't really get too much into it, but that's the basics. It gets complicated, and scary in the wrong hands, but if you were allowed to study this in school still, Arlo, they'd start you off real easy. They'd start you off with shit like iron."

"Okaaay . . . but what am I supposed to do with this information?"

Pulling her hands away from the array, Nausicaä raised them into the air. "Nope. Sorry. That's all I've got." She turned to Arlo. "Listen. Activating another alchemist's array is a pretty fucking advanced skill, but I'm willing to bet it'll be a cinch for you to similarly *de*activate this thing. You've got it in you. I wasn't lying."

"If you say so, but how to do that?"

Nausicaä shrugged.

Sighing deeply, Arlo examined the array a little closer. "I mean, have we tried physically damaging it? Like, breaking it up or something to disrupt the flow of magic?" She had no idea what she was talking about, but it sounded like their easiest solution. Whatever random clip of conversation she'd overheard to help her recognize that iron symbol—where had it even come from, she wondered, and why did it wear her very human father's voice—was conveniently silent now.

Summoning her katana once more, Nausicaä dispelled this theory by dragging the tip of her blade against the iron. The array sliced apart, but in moments, the magic that formed it sealed it back together, good as new.

"Hmm." Arlo eased herself to her knees. Placing her dagger on the ground beside her, she reached out to trace one of the iron symbols— it warmed under her touch. She had no idea how to bend this particular skill to deactivate arrays any more than she knew how to activate them. All she knew was that Nausicaä's magic seemed to give her own a boost. "If we could somehow unbalance these equations, shouldn't that mean it would stop working?" she mused aloud.

Nausicaä crouched down beside her. "What are you thinking?"

"Give me a second."

Keeping her hand on the array, Arlo closed her eyes. The symbols seemed to burn in her mind, standing out against the darkness. She could see them clearly, but something was missing—the warmth she could feel under her fingers was absent from the replica she pictured. "Nausicaä," she called, her eyes still closed. "Can you maybe do that thing you did before? With your magic? To jump-start mine?"

Wordlessly, Nausicaä complied. A bit of iron-and-woodsmoke magic unspooled from its hiding place and leaped all too enthusiastically for Arlo. It must have learned in the short span of their acquaintance how to interact with her a little more gently, because unlike all the other times before, it didn't so much stab her as it did thread itself piercingly together with her own aura. The surge of additional power was exactly what she needed to make the array in her mind burst into glowing warmth.

A tinge of bluish-white light pressed against the black of her closed eyes. "I'm going to try dissolving one of the symbols," she told them. She couldn't explain why, but her gut instinct told her this was the right thing to do, and for some reason, this warmth under her hand felt familiar. Focusing hard as she could, she channeled all her magic into erasing the symbol at the northern point of her imagined array.

Under her hand, the one on the door grew hot.

"Shnazzy," Nausicaä complimented, blowing out her cheeks. "See? You're a freaking natural at this."

Withdrawing her hand, Arlo opened her eyes. She retrieved her dagger, rose to her feet, and watched in awe with everyone else as the heat drove the symbol at the northern point of the real array to crack apart—and this time, remain broken.

"We should really, *really* find you an actual mentor, forbidden magic be damned." Nausicaä raised a foot and slammed it down on the door so hard that it dented inward. She repeated the action, and the iron door snapped away from its hinges to clatter down into the newly opened metal stairwell waiting for them in the depths below. "Well, there it is. Our dark descent. Ready to wreak some havoc?"

"*Investigate*," Vehan corrected firmly, taking out his phone to snap a picture of the cava behind them and the hole in the ground through which they were about to enter. "This is an investigation, first and foremost. I'd like to avoid as much conflict as possible here. Impressive as you are, engaging in any further battles with our current numbers isn't wise. We just want to find out what's going on before our elusive alchemist gets the chance to cover their tracks again."

"Sure, but what I said sounded cooler, so we're going with that, okay?"

Frowning, Vehan once again sparked with irritation. "You don't take anything seriously, do you."

For a moment, there was no response.

Then, Arlo watched as hard consideration turned to tired gravity. Never before had she seen Nausicaä look so old.

"One hundred and sixteen years ago, eleven people learned the answer to that question, Vehan Lysterne. What you all know as the Bermuda Triangle became a Sleeping Hollow. I already have a therapist, thank you very much. I even turn up for my appointments once in a while. But if you'd rather go back to my place and chat some more about this around some ice cream, please just say so now. Otherwise, let's just be thankful this century is turning out to be a high point in my depression and get on with this mission, all right?"

At an apparent loss for what to say, Vehan held Nausicaä's gaze a little longer. He settled on a curt nod. "Just try not to get us killed."

"Try not to make it so appealing," she quipped, her humor instantly recovered. Dropping a wink at the prince, she concluded the matter by jumping down into the stairwell.

CHAPTER 30

Nausicaä

T HE STAIRS LED INTO a dim hallway, nothing more exciting than a monochromatic stretch of tile, aluminum plating, and eerily glowing emergency lights that trailed down the center of the ceiling. Nausicaä had been in enough laboratories over the years, for various reasons, to recognize this cold and clinical atmosphere for what it was in a simple glance around.

"Kinda quiet," she mused. Her voice echoed loudly in the bare, enclosed space. "You know, you didn't have to knock out *all* the lighting with your little party trick, Charmless."

Vehan scowled at her. "I told you, that wasn't my intention. And, for all we know, it could always be this dark down here."

"Uh-huh. Yeah, because 'turn off all the lights' is the first thing they teach you about workplace safety. Rich people." She rolled her eyes. "You going to turn them back on for us anytime soon?"

Vehan muttered under his breath but nonetheless complied with her suggestion. He flexed his hand, open and closed and open again. Nothing happened. His expression, ghostly in this muted lighting, grew more annoyed by the second. "Well, I would, but something's not right down here. I can't bend electricity the way I usually do. It's like there's an interference."

"I'm concerned about the lack of activity," said Aurelian. "I don't hear any nearby movement."

At his side, Arlo lifted her phone above her head. She was close enough for Nausicaä to glimpse the string of messages from her no-doubt-irate cousin, culminating in I'm giving you one more hour and if I don't hear from you, I'm telling Father where you are. She swiped away his panic with a huff when she next lowered her phone, and said, "Uh . . . guys? Does anyone else have service? Because I have nothing."

Nausicaä pulled out her phone now too—bright teal and obnoxiously large, it was the latest in a very long line of broken, fried, and drowned iPhones; given her track record, the odds of this one surviving much longer were slim. Everyone else followed suit to lift their phones as well, at varying angles, as though this would help them catch a better signal. "Wonderful," she sighed. Turning her phone on Arlo, she snapped a picture.

"Hey!"

"A little dark," Nausicaä concluded. "But the camera still works fine, at least. Boo, I was hoping to see what Pokémon I could catch down here on Go." She looked up into Arlo's frown and smiled widely. "Well, what do we say? Do you three still want to chase after answers with me even if we can't call out?"

"Can you still teleport us to safety if it becomes necessary?" Vehan hedged.

"Yeah, yeah, don't worry. We're not *all* useless here." Nausicaä waved off his concern. It would take a hell of a lot more interference than whatever blocked their cellular reception to put her teleportation out of commission. "All right, so we poke around until we find someone to harass for answers?"

"But we stay as a group," Vehan added. "Nobody wanders off on their own. I don't trust any of what's going on right now."

It was highly unlikely Aurelian would stray too far from Vehan's side, given his pattern of behavior. Arlo seemed to know full well she had about one trick and jack-all else to use to protect herself should she encounter any difficulty on her own. So far, Vehan showed an annoying commitment to keeping the group together. It was her, Nausicaä suspected, that the warning was meant for; of the four of them, she was the most likely to abandon at least two in their team should they start to slow her down.

"Yes, sir!" She shot him an exaggerated salute. "So are we going now or what?"

Arlo raised her dagger into the air.

"Yes, Arlo?" Nausicaä graciously permitted.

"So . . . if in our poking around we happen across a bathroom . . ."

Vehan turned to stare at her, mildly incredulous. Nausicaä, meanwhile, could hardly contain her laughter. "Okay, folks, if we come across anyone, make sure to also ask for directions to the nearest bathroom on top of whether they've been murdering children to make philosopher's stones and kidnapping people and why."

"You were at a rest station for nearly an *hour* before we came to get you," Vehan pointed out, bewildered.

"It was hot . . . I had a lot of slushies . . ."

The prince rounded on Nausicaä. "Why did you allow her to consume so much liquid?"

"Um, I'm not the boss of her?" she sneered. "She can make whatever poor decision she likes."

"This isn't a field trip to a *chocolate* factory."

"Indeed it isn't, Veruca Salt. But it's a big place in the middle of nowhere. There's going to be a bathroom, and we can investigate along the way. Come on, Arlo—if video games have taught me anything, it's that there's a treasure chest around here with a map inside. We'll find what you seek, beautiful maiden." Latching on to Arlo's arm, she pulled her out from the center of the group and started off down the hall.

It was surprisingly easy to find the laboratory's facilities.

Unfortunately, this was just about their only success.

Everything was on lockdown, thanks to the magic Vehan and Arlo worked on the place, which meant every door they'd come across had to be forced open. Nausicaä stopped the party multiple times to allow herself to take a peek inside random rooms and found that the ones that weren't devoted to storage for supplies (for everything from guns to blades to medical equipment and tools) were break rooms outfitted with plush sofas and well-stocked but out-of-order vending machines.

"This is weird," she announced, rocking one such machine in the third break room they'd found to force it to dispense its candy. "I feel like we're infiltrating someone's very fancy clubhouse. M&M?"

She offered her hard-won bag to Arlo first, then the others after she declined.

"Are you seriously going to eat that?" Vehan inquired, eyeing the yellow bag with suspicion when it was thrust in his direction.

"After listening to you nag me to stop making so much noise for so long? Yes."

Vehan rolled his eyes. "Has no one taught you to be wary of taking candy from strangers?"

"Strangers?" Nausicaä wrinkled her nose in mock offense. "We're not strangers. Vending machines and I go way back."

"There corridors are endless," Aurelian interrupted, taking a seat beside Arlo on the sofa. "We've been walking for almost an hour and haven't found anything besides lounges and storerooms. There's no hint of an elevator or a second stairwell. Maybe it's time to consider we were wrong and that there really isn't anything here besides what we've already discovered outside?"

Popping a handful of M&M's into her mouth, Nausicaä chewed and considered the suggestion. "We haven't checked all the rooms yet," she reminded him. There had to be *something* here they were missing; no one put all of this in the middle of the desert just because they were bored.

"Is there a way we can use this, maybe?"

The room focused in on Arlo and the object in her hand.

"That depends. What is it?" Vehan asked, stepping closer for a better view. "What does it do?"

Arlo shook her head. "I don't really know. It works a bit like Dungeons and Dragons, though . . . at least, from what Elyas has told me." Judging by the blank expression on Vehan's face, Nausicaä figured he had no idea what that was. She laughed, though, to hear this rare gift likened to a tool from a tabletop role-play game; no doubt the one who'd given it to her would find this amusing as well. "Basically, it's a magical die," Arlo continued. "I tell it what I want to do, and if I roll a high enough number, we . . . succeed in doing it. I got it from someone in the Faerie Ring. They looked like a troll, but I don't think that's what they really were."

"If that's the genuine article, they definitely weren't a troll," Nausicaä confirmed, popping another candy. If what Arlo said was true, that troll was exactly who she'd thought they were back outside where she first learned Arlo possessed this power. "I mean, I didn't see them myself, but if they gave you that die, then they were most likely Luck. Chance. Fortune. Whatever you will—they go by many names and many faces. The important thing is that you met a freaking *Titan*, Arlo. They gave you that die, and if you really have no idea what it does, then it sounds like you're still in the new-car trial period." She grinned around her candy. "A bonus for us. No one tries to hook someone on a gimmick's flaws. Luck's going to play this nice and sweet for you—pull out all the stops to give you what you want—so that you'll choose to keep this power once they come to demand your answer. What you choose to do is up to you, but *meanwhile* . . ."

She approached Arlo, leaning in and curling her fingers back around the die to close her hand. "You save that for when we're in a pinch. Trial periods have limited usage, and I wouldn't want yours to be used up on trivial things."

"Okay, but this means . . . what, exactly? A *god* gave Arlo something that makes her abnormally lucky?" Vehan asked. "I mean, I'm sorry, but that's ridiculous. There's a strict pact between us and the gods, keeping them out of our business. Why would one turn up in the Faerie Ring?"

"Titan," Nausicaä corrected. "Luck isn't a deity, they're a bit higher up than that—and while we're on the subject, also genderfluid. Their pronouns are 'they' and 'them,' and like many of the immortals who are genderqueer and nonbinary, don't use 'god'—it's too male a term. On a whole, we all just use 'deity' instead. But anyhow, to answer your question: yes, a deity gave this die to Arlo, and no, it doesn't exactly make her extra *lucky*." She sighed. Over a century here and still it surprised her to realize how much the mortals didn't know about the people they'd once worshipped. "Listen, it's not really my place to explain the deities and their tricks, and I don't know all the details here, besides. I've only ever met one Hollow Star before, and they—"

"What's a Hollow Star, exactly?" Arlo blurted.

Nausicaä didn't blame this particular bit of ignorance. Even among the immortals, Hollow Stars were a mystery. Most only knew of them from sparse whispers, as Luck was strangely protective of their carefully chosen pawns and knew how dangerous immortal interest in them could be—and Arlo already had plenty of immortal interest to begin with. "An Otherworld term, I suppose," she explained. "It's what Cosmin calls the children his partner adopts and the term caught on. I guess it isn't well-known down here, either, but basically a Hollow Star is what *you* would be, Arlo, if you choose to continue to use that die when Luck pays you a second visit. A Hollow Star is someone who takes their destiny away from Fate—away from the stars that serve her—and into their own hands. Amazingly easy, that trade. All it takes is the mortal's consent and boom, Fate hands you over. Luck becomes your patron immortal, and honestly, of the lot, they've always been one of my favorites—not that we're on very good terms, me and the many deities."

"How do you know all of this?" Vehan cried, suddenly quite exasperated. "This stuff about deities and philosopher's stones and Titans—how do you know any of it? Who *are* you?"

For a moment, Nausicaä seriously considered not answering. Vehan wasn't awful. Of all the fae she'd encountered in her time, he was certainly one of the kinder, and she could tell his heart was in the right place and all, but . . . well, if there was one face she'd never forget, it was that of the man who drove Tisiphone to her death—of

Heulfryn . . . with his bright, clever eyes and ample charms and raven-black hair, so very much like the young prince's here. Aurelian was growly with her, she was growly right back at him, but *Vehan* . . . just looking at him set her on edge. Her dislike was a little more personal, however unfair that might be. "I used to be a Fury," she divulged at last in the spirit of sportsmanship, not because she actually wanted to. "Once upon a time. Then I went ahead and broke a few fundamental laws, killed some people I wasn't supposed to touch, and was cast out of the Infernal Court. Stripped of my name and the best of my powers. Tethered to the Mortal Realm for fuck-off eternity. Now I'm no one. Blotted off the family tree. A 'Dark Star.'"

Of all the nicknames she'd received, she liked that one the best. Even better was the way it made the folk shiver when they said it, as though it were some kind of curse—though at the moment, Vehan and Aurelian were less afraid and more visibly shocked.

"Yup, that's right. I'm an immortal. At the moment, I'm on your side. So long as Arlo's with us, Luck is too. You really couldn't have asked for a better team than this, Prince Vehan, so I ask you, honestly, has that answer made a difference? Are you going to stop questioning me at every turn now that you know who I am?"

Vehan snorted, eyeing her warily. "No, probably not."

"Exactly."

Aurelian cocked his head as though considering Nausicaä anew. "I'd always believed Furies were a myth. And, I'm sorry, but ugly as well."

The statement rankled her—ugly, yes, of course that's how mortals had seen her—but rather than snap at him, she beamed. "Ha! You think I'm pretty."

"I think you're not unattractive. There's a difference."

"Oh, wow, easy on the love confessions, Aurelian. I'm flattered, really, but I'm afraid—as I'm lesbian—you're not exactly my type."

"I'm afraid, as I'm gay, you're really not mine, either."

"Good, so now that that's settled. Maybe we can move on and save stupid questions about people's pasts for later?"

"I only asked them in the first place because in order for us to work as a team," Vehan replied a touch hotly, "it's important that we're all at least reading from the same book, if not the same page."

"Wow, that was really profound. Truly inspired. It's almost like you've spent your entire life operating under the belief that you're entitled to get anything you want simply because you want it, *Your Sidhe Fae Highness.*"

"Guys . . ."

"Oh! That's rich, coming from *you*. Strutting around with your inflated ego, doing whatever you like because the world is dispensable and the only interests Nausicaä Kraken serves are her own."

"Guys, probably shut up now?"

"I don't have an entire Court and a personal bodyguard to wipe my ass for me, so yeah, I *am* going to serve my own—"

"Guys," Arlo hissed, leaping up from the sofa and grabbing both Vehan and Nausicaä by the arm. "Shut *up*—Aurelian hears something."

Glowering at Nausicaä, Vehan shook himself free of Arlo's hold and moved off to where his friend had wandered from the couch during their argument.

Nausicaä watched him go, frowning.

"You okay?" Arlo asked.

Transferring a much softer look to Arlo, she nodded.

In her current mood, Nausicaä knew her admittedly frightening features had to be standing out sharper than they usually did. When anger and bitterness swelled too close to the surface, her carefully woven beauty had a tendency to turn skeletal.

How close to expiration was the mask behind which Nausicaä hid her darker, festering emotions? What would happen when it could no longer contain them? It scared her to think she could break even further than her current shattered state—to entertain the possibility that something worse lurked behind it, waiting to consume whatever had been left after her fall.

Arlo, though . . . the way she stared up at Nausicaä, Arlo didn't seem afraid at all of whatever monstrosity she saw.

Stupid girl.

Why had no one taught her to keep away from deadly things?

"What's going on?" Nausicaä asked to break the tension and lead her thoughts to safer ground.

Arlo merely shook her head and pointed to the open doorway. Aurelian and Vehan stood in a motionless huddle off to the side, peering out into the hall and listening intently. Extracting herself from Arlo and throwing her candy aside, Nausicaä moved to join the fae by the door.

Vehan shifted to make room for her, admitting her close, however stiffly.

A moment trickled into a minute, which trickled into two. Nausicaä saw nothing.

"Well?" Arlo whispered.

"There," Vehan breathed after a long moment. A small gesture of his hand pointed to something in the distance, and Nausicaä craned to peer around him.

"A cavum!" Finally, a bit of action. "Guess all the banging around attracted some attention after all. You're welcome."

"Should we follow it and see where it's heading?" Aurelian asked over this jibe.

As fun as it was to flex her fighting prowess with the dead-eyed creatures they'd fought outside, Nausicaä hoped there was something more than cutting down cava in store for them tonight. This *thing* walking around . . . It had to have come from somewhere; chances were it had somewhere to go as well.

Following it was their best option.

She nodded. Arlo, looking several shades paler than usual, nodded her agreement too. Quieter than they'd managed all evening, the four trickled out of the break room and back into the hall, creeping after the cavum as close to the creature as they dared and as far back from it as they could keep while holding it still in their sights.

They were probably being watched on cameras.

Occasionally, Nausicaä spared a glance for the ceiling, and the corners where those sorts of things were kept. There was nothing there, but that didn't necessarily mean they weren't being watched. For all that this facility gave off the appearance of human command, there was magic working behind its scenes—she could feel it. If they really were dealing with someone using this space for alchemic experimentation, there were dozens of ways that someone could be tracking their progress without human technology.

Nothing she could do about that, at the moment.

On they crept after this grotesque guide. There were several moments when Nausicaä had to wonder whether the cavum was deaf or simply leading them to some undisclosed place—a trap, perhaps—expecting them to follow. Personally, she hoped it was the latter.

They rounded another bend, sneaking out into a hallway they'd visited already. Nausicaä recognized it by the fact that it led nowhere—a dead end, boasting nothing but supply closets.

The creature hobbled on.

It made its way to the end of the hall and the wall that closed it off, and she was now firmly convinced their end goal was a trap. Whatever that was supposed to be, they wouldn't find out until it was sprung. Most likely, something might try to rush them from behind. This must have occurred to the prince as well, because he dropped back even farther in line to take up the rear, much to Aurelian's apparent dissatisfaction.

He glared at the prince, but there was no time to debate the matter.

Having taken command of their progress, Nausicaä lifted a hand in the air and curled it into a fist, bringing the group to a halt.

The creature had stopped as well.

It stood now, staring fixedly at the white concrete wall as though whatever had wound it into action had finally run its course.

"This is really starting to freak me out," Arlo whispered, latching on to the back of Nausicaä's tank top. The hall they'd left behind was quiet. By the confused shake of Aurelian's head, even he could detect nothing closing in on their ranks.

"Maybe we should just ask it what it's doing?" Nausicaä whispered back.

"Oh yeah, great idea—hello there, how are you, I know your friends just tried to kill us, but would you mind terribly explaining what—"

"Sure, that'll work," Nausicaä agreed, bulldozing over Arlo's sarcasm with perfect sincerity. In a louder voice, she said to the creature, "Hello there! How are you? I know—"

Her words were cut short, but not by Arlo's frantic tugging, or the hiss from Aurelian, or the reach-around swat from Vehan.

The creature didn't seem to hear them at all—or if it did, continued to ignore them. Instead, it watched as something in the wall gave two soft chirps, and a small light tucked up against the ceiling flicked to green-glowing life.

The wall opened up like a yawning mouth, parting horizontally at the middle and retracting into the ceiling and floor. Bright fluorescent lighting spilled from the growing gap.

"Uh . . . ," said Nausicaä. She abandoned all pretense of whispering, and when the creature continued to pay them no notice, she took a step away from the wall. "Well, shit."

Arlo had followed, still clutching the back of her tank top, careful to keep close as she peered along with Nausicaä into this sudden, fully-powered extension of the hallway.

The cavum didn't go far.

A few feet of tile paved the way to the unmistakable gleam of an elevator door. The creature hobbled toward it and turned to face them as soon as it reached the far end of the hall.

Anticipating some attack, Nausicaä threw out an arm to usher Arlo behind her. Vehan and Aurelian rushed forward now too, the prince attempting to draw on the current thrumming through the facility and flick a beam of light off the palm of his hand; once again, his efforts to arm himself were thwarted—a tiny, small fraction concerning, in Nausicaä's opinion.

"Damn!" he swore, gritting his teeth.

The creature made no move for them, though.

It stood by the door of the elevator like it was standing at attention, eyes trained sightlessly forward, waiting for them to approach so it could admit them through to the next part of this apparent tour.

"At last," Nausicaä drawled. This little display wouldn't unnerve her, if that was the intention here. She cocked her head to slant her skeptic shade down the hall. "The quality service I paid for."

"Apologies," said a man's voice from all around them. Smooth and light in pitch, the voice was weirdly familiar to Nausicaä, and it rang more than a little smug. *"After all that violence outside, it was hard to find a willing replacement to play your guide."*

Nausicaä snorted. Cava didn't have the will to volunteer for much of anything. Sliding her gaze away from the creature, she frowned up at the ceiling. "God?"

"Not quite," the mysterious voice chuckled. *"Though I have to say, I'm on my way to becoming something better."*

"The sad thing is, I bet you believe that too."

"And so will you, by the end of tonight. But come!" The elevator at the end of the hall slid open with a soft whir. *"I expect you have some questions, to come all the way out here. I'd be happy to give you their answers."*

Nausicaä dropped her gaze back to the group. "So, this is ominous. Probably dangerous. Definitely inadvisable for three teenage fae. I'm down, but I'm immortal. It would take more than what this realm could collectively throw to kill me. Again, you guys don't have to come along. You have enough evidence as is."

"But not my answers," Vehan reminded her grimly.

"I say we do it."

Everyone turned to Aurelian. He had out his phone, snapping a picture of the scene before them, but paused when he realized the intensity of the attention on him. "We've come this far. If you can teleport us out whenever we choose, Nausicaä, the personal risk in undertaking this tour is still rather low," he explained with a twitch of a shrug. "I say we do it."

Nausicaä looked to Arlo.

Of everyone present, she was the most vulnerable and the only one Nausicaä actually cared about coming to harm. But Arlo shook her head and, in a move of surprising boldness, threaded her arm through Nausicaä's. With soft but genuine conviction, she said, "Like Vehan said, right? We've come this far, I'm not letting you leave me behind now."

Swallowing down a swell of fierce emotion, Nausicaä tugged her even closer to her side. *"Weird,"* she whispered, harking back again to their alleyway conversation.

Arlo laughed gently. "Yeah, but so are you," she whispered back. With her head turned to keep this bit of play between them, it was a little impossible for Nausicaä to stare at anything but the smile tugging at the bow of Arlo's mouth.

"Yeah," she swallowed. "Definitely." Clearing her throat, Nausicaä gave herself a little shake. In a much louder voice, and to the group as a whole, she said, "All right, well, our disembodied host seems to have been expecting us anyhow. Might as well play along while things are still interesting."

"How, though, were we expected . . . ," Vehan wondered, watching Aurelian lower his phone. "We were careful to keep this quiet. Besides the two of you, only my mother and the High King were told we had suspicions about this place."

"Questions to ask along the way, I guess," Nausicaä placated, beginning forward with Arlo fast on her arm.

They boarded the elevator.

"We better at least get a portal gun out of this," Nausicaä groused when Vehan and Aurelian joined them and the doors snapped closed in their faces.

Without even a stir for warning, they plummeted.

CHAPTER 31

Arlo

❧

I N SECONDS, IT CAME to an abrupt stop.

Arlo pitched forward.

"Speedy!" Nausicaä exclaimed, catching her deftly around the middle.

There were better adjectives Arlo could think of to describe their method of arrival, but when the elevator doors sprang open, what was revealed distracted her from sharing them. The hall that waited to receive them was different from what they'd snuck through on the floor above. Here, aluminum plating replaced the tile completely, paving the way from their elevator to the identical doors at the opposite end. Much softer fluorescent lighting loomed overhead, and the floor had been inlaid with equally pale floodlights. Instead of the concrete they were used to, the walls on either side of them were enormous sheets of glass—windows, Arlo realized; she wasn't sure she wanted to know what they overlooked.

"Welcome to Aurum Industries." The voice had returned, spewing out of invisible speakers. *"My name is Hieronymus Aurum, founder of this humble facility—most here call me Doctor, but you, dear guests, may call me Hero. If you'd kindly make your way to the end of the hall, it would delight me to guide your tour."*

Arlo frowned at his callous levity. It surprised her that Nausicaä, whose entire persona seemed built on these very foundations, did much the same. "'Hero,' huh?" she said, sharing a glance with Arlo. "Looks like we've just found our dearly departed Reaper's 'Master.' *Tch*. How dare he make me excited for this stupid tour like I'm waiting to get on a ride at Disney World. Now I'm just going to be disappointed the whole time."

Shaking her head, Arlo stepped out of the elevator and into the hall.

"Oh my *gods*," she gasped. Her brain switched to autopilot and propelled her toward the sheet of glass to her left.

This hall was a bridge, and both sides looked out over the same horrible view: a hangar, so large it could serve as a stadium, and along the walls were hundreds of cells that stood like vertical coffins.

Every single one contained a slumbering cavum.

A central device sat beneath them, extending multiple mechanical arms to pluck the cava from their chambers and set them—still asleep—on a conveyor belt at the far left side of the room.

Nausicaä joined Arlo's scandalized inspection of the view outside the glass. Clicking her tongue, she fished out her phone from her pocket and snapped a shot of the scene. Vehan and Aurelian took to the opposite side of the bridge, and judging by their matching gasps, were no less revolted by what they saw.

"Our tour begins with the breathtaking view of what we call the distribution station. Aurum prides itself in its achievement as the first to perfect the creation of cava—the artificial soldiers you see down below. Living, breathing beings that require no rest, no battery, no charge to keep them going; they feel neither pain nor fear, possess no individual will to hinder their efficiency, and are stronger and faster than even the fae. They are, if I say so myself, the perfect—"

"Yeah, yeah," Nausicaä interrupted, peeling herself away from the glass and replacing her phone in her pocket. "We get it. You're disgusting. You can shut up now."

Arlo looked away.

"Those are *people*," she choked out, the stinging heat in her eyes spreading to her heart. Her anger began to boil. "Those are people you're experimenting on down there!"

So many people—were they all abducted and trafficked by those goblins Vehan had mentioned? Did the world truly care so little about what happened to the poor and homeless that the hundreds it would take to "furnish" all these cava could all go missing without even a mention in the news?

"Hero" replied with a chuckle. *Yes and no. They* were *people, my dear. Many different people. Now they're something better."*

"You have an incredibly skewed view of what constitutes 'better,'" Vehan scathed. He, too, pulled away from the glass and stalked to Arlo's side. A moment later, Aurelian joined him, and Arlo only just caught the tail end of him fiddling with something on his phone before he slid it back in his pocket.

"Such upstanding morals! But narrow-minded. It's not your fault—you're only children, after all . . ."

"Tch," Nausicaä scoffed. "Children you're apparently afraid to say this to in person."

"Oh, don't worry, there's plenty of time for that later. For now, we must hurry along! I have other things to show you first."

Another mechanical whir opened the door at the opposite end of the bridge, but instead of a second elevator, it led into another room.

Arlo felt queasy. She didn't want to see whatever it was their host had planned to show them. She didn't want to see how these cava were made—as she suspected they were going to find out—and whether or not there were worse atrocities waiting farther within. She didn't want to see proof that it was possible for someone to treat another living being so horrendously, because just like her witnessing the death of Cassandra, proof would make this *real*.

Hundreds of people, all of them harvested from right under their noses . . . Their deaths would be made real with a single step over that threshold, and Arlo didn't think she could handle that.

A squeeze to her shoulder alerted Arlo that Nausicaä's hand was there. When she turned to look, she saw genuine concern, out of place in the former Fury's expression. "You okay? You're pretty pale."

Arlo opened her mouth to speak, but dread poured like tar over the words she wanted to say, and it took a moment to unstick them.

"I just . . . look at them all down there. All those people . . . this place. It's . . ."

"A lot," Nausicaä supplied, and Arlo nodded. "Do you want to leave? We *can*, Arlo. Maybe we even should."

Oh, they definitely "should." Someone other than a group comprised of teenagers "should" be the ones to deal with this. This entire investigation "should" have fallen to the adults. All the victims of this psychopath's experimentations "should" still be alive. Arlo "should" be stronger, given that she knew this wasn't going to be easy, and yet . . . no matter how many "should"s she added together, none of them mattered.

They were deep in a boss-level dungeon well above what they could handle, and they definitely, absolutely, one hundred percent *should* leave.

"*Well . . . ,*" said their host, inserting himself into the conversation at last. A note of delight played under his tone. "*You can try to leave, but I'm afraid to say you won't be going very far.*"

The elevator snapped closed behind them. As soon as it did, the green light situated over the doors flicked to glaring red.

Arlo's dread grew even thicker.

"*See, I can't just let you go running off now that you're finally here, Arlo Jarsdel. As irritated as I was that my Reaper failed to dispose of you—the* trouble *I've been in for that attempt on your life—this is, I've decided, the better approach. You see, if I deal with you myself, not only will that remove you as my last and largest obstacle, but I'll finally learn what it is that makes you so intriguing to my benefactor, when no one in your wretched Court seems to care for you at all.*"

"Nope—don't like that! That's our fucking cue to energize," Nausicaä announced with a great deal of false cheer, clapping her hands together. "Gather round, class—field trip is over. It's time to leave."

"You watch *Star Trek?*"

"Aurelian, this is *not the time!*"

"Wait."

Everyone turned to Arlo and stared.

I'm giving you one more hour, and if I don't hear from you, I'm telling Father where you are.

Hieronymus was right, most of the Eight Courts couldn't care less about Arlo Ironborn Jarsdel—but Celadon cared a great deal, and if there was one thing she'd learned about her cousin over the years, it was that Celadon never made an idle promise.

This was a lot.

This terrified Arlo right down to her core.

An absolute stranger wanted her dead—her, specifically, having never met him once in her life or done him any wrong (at least, to her knowledge).

None of this should be up to her and her companions to make right, but they were the only ones here. It was unfair, completely, but if they could keep Hieronymus talking long enough for the High King to arrive, he wouldn't be able to escape them as he might if they left now. This entire nightmare could be over as soon as tonight, and Arlo's desire for that apparently outweighed her desire to flee herself.

She'd made up her mind to stick out this investigation, and she wasn't going to turn back now.

Still pale, still more than a little nauseated, but quickly regaining control of her panic, Arlo looked to Nausicaä. She had a plan, but how did she convey this without alerting their listening host?

"Hang on, Nausicaä." She reached into her back pocket and extracted her phone. "This is sick and twisted and all kinds of wrong." She pulled open her message history, tapped on the text from Celadon, and angled it for all to see but any possible cameras. "But I don't think we should leave just yet."

Nausicaä cocked her head, glancing over the message. With a twitch of a grin, she flashed her thumbs-up. Aurelian and Vehan shared a look between them, but whatever they made of what they'd read, they nodded deference to her lead, and that was good enough. If Hieronymus could see them, he didn't make comment—if he'd been able to read the text on her phone through whatever means he used to watch them, he didn't react to it at all.

"All right, Cave Johnson," Nausicaä said. "I guess you have your captive audience. But mind your manners or you'll go back to playing by yourself, got it?"

"Perfectly."

Drawing closer to Arlo's side, Nausicaä added under her breath, "This is all very Gryffindor of you, but remember—any time you need, we can teleport to safety. Don't push yourself too hard, okay?"

"Okay." Arlo nodded, grateful for the support. "I'm fine for now, though. Just . . . got in a bit of a spiral. We need to keep Hieronymus distracted—and it couldn't hurt to find the control panel those elevators are connected to for when our backup arrives."

"I think we can manage that." Nausicaä waggled her brows.

"Good. Thank you, seriously. But Plan B is definitely teleporting out of here. I hate this place—I hate what this man has done to all those people." She looked back out through the window at the cava.

Silently, Nausicaä slipped her hand into Arlo's, a warm fizzle shocking up her arm. It redirected Arlo's focus, first in amazement down at their interwoven fingers, then back to Nausicaä's face. She looked like she wanted to say something but couldn't. Her expression was the rawest Arlo had ever seen it—a mixture of grief running deeper than the darkest pit of any ocean, and *guilt* so strong it painted that sadness pale in comparison. And why Nausicaä should be feeling either of these things right now, Arlo didn't know. It grieved her, too, to see.

"We're ending this tonight," Nausicaä promised.

Arlo nodded. "Yeah. Well, no time like the present, I guess. Let's get this over with." She glanced at Aurelian and Vehan, and the matching looks of resolve on their faces. Hoping her plan wouldn't get them all killed, she took charge of the group's procession and led them into the next room—a brightly lit, circular chamber contained by yet more glass.

And a panel of controls.

Various monitors hugged the perimeter, most of them keeping track of different areas in the facility. Beyond these, outside this hub, the conveyor belt from the previous room continued to bear the cava onward.

"Boo, disappointing. It's like he wasn't even trying to make this difficult for us," Nausicaä complained. Arlo had to agree that this seemed a little too easy.

As the door they'd entered through slid closed and locked, the one at the opposite side slid open, much as it had done in the previous room. Hieronymus's voice returned.

"The control tower. From here, our production line is maintained and overseen by highly trained and dedicated staff. It's also where our final product receives one last assessment."

Dropping Nausicaä's hand, Arlo stepped toward the controls. She searched for a switch or button that might open the elevator behind them on the off chance it could really be that straightforward. Finally, she had to admit the flaw in her plan—were any of them particularly skilled with computers? Maybe she'd have to use her die after all.

"Go ahead."

Startled, Arlo turned around. Aurelian had slipped up beside her while she'd been deep in thought. His head was bent in consideration of the panels, a serious frown tugging at his mouth. "I'll see what I can do about opening the elevators, if you can buy the time."

"Are . . . are you sure? Do you know what to do with all *this*?" She gestured at the panel.

Aurelian, already engrossed in his thoughts, said nothing. Arlo decided not to question a good thing further. Relieved, she added quietly, "Okay, well, thank you. We'll buy you time."

"Are you okay on your own?" Vehan asked in a whisper, coming up behind them. "I wouldn't feel right letting Arlo go ahead of us when I'm the reason she's here." He took something from Aurelian's back pocket stealthily enough that Arlo could only see the action, not what he stole. Aurelian stiffened, feeling Vehan do so, and looked up from the panel to snap his head to the prince.

Arlo didn't miss the flash of anxiety in his expression, but he seemed less concerned about whatever Vehan had taken and more about what he'd said.

"No, I'd rather you stay with me, Vehan. Your mother wouldn't—"

"Relax," Nausicaä called, already across the room. "We'll look after your prince. He'll be fine. I'm immortal, remember? Extremely badass. Nothing touches any of you without my say-so."

Arlo was struck with the impression that if Aurelian *were* the cat he often resembled, his ears would be flat against his head right now with the way he glared at Nausicaä. "Considering how antagonistic you've been toward us, I'm not exactly comforted by that."

"Maybe we could *all* just stay here?" Arlo suggested, the sudden tension in the room thick enough to make her hesitate.

"We'll be *fine*, Aurelian," Vehan reassured, overriding Arlo's comment. Rolling his eyes, he clapped his friend on the shoulder, then made his way to where Nausicaä waited. "Just do your magical computer thing and we'll take care of the rest."

Aurelian muttered something even Arlo—standing right beside him—couldn't hear. She bit her lip, eyeing his profile, displeasure obvious on his face. "We won't let anything happen to him, I promise. It's only the elevator that seems to be on lockdown—if things look like trouble, we'll come right back."

The sharp nod she eventually received was all the reply she was going to get from him, she concluded. Aurelian spun back around, resuming his inspection of the panel, his frown etched a little deeper than before. With a sigh, Arlo left him to his business and rejoined the rest of the group so they could carry on into the next room.

"And here we have what I like to call the armory," Hero continued amiably.

They entered another walkway, sandwiched between more windows.

The conveyor belt continued on. It carried the already outfitted cava through this third chamber without pause and off into the next. It was a much bigger room than the one the control tower overlooked, with massive machines dotted along the assembly line. There were yet more mechanical arms, these ones inactive, and most likely the tools by which the cava's "armor" was affixed.

Besides the machines and bins of materials scattered around, there was nothing else inside this new chamber, and still no sign of a single employee—no one manning the arms or anything else, and no one to guide the cava along their way.

Arlo could understand if maybe "Aurum Industries" simply kept to daylight hours of operation—it was pretty late in the evening, after all—but then why leave the conveyor belt running if all was closed for the night?

"As the name suggests, this is where we take our soldiers and spruce them up with a little titanium plating. Of course, as you've already learned firsthand, titanium is far from indestructible. I'm pleased to report a tremendous improvement with the metal we've recently managed to synthesize to take its place."

Vehan tugged on Arlo's arm. Wordlessly, he pulled a phone out of his pocket, just enough to show her the screen—still no service, but the app currently in use was recording this entire exchange, no reception or internet required.

It was Aurelian's phone; Arlo remembered it from earlier. Now at least she knew what he'd been fiddling with before and what Vehan had stolen from him.

Vehan pressed his finger to his lips to signal keeping this information between them. In case they *were* being watched, Arlo kept her approval to a minute nod. With no further exchange than this, they made to follow Nausicaä, already striding for the end of this stretch of hall.

"What are you getting out of this?" Arlo wondered aloud, hoping to draw even more from their host now that she knew about the recording. "What does any of this have to do with creating philosopher's stones?"

If they couldn't get their elevator open, they'd at least escape with the answers they'd come for.

"Getting *out of this?*" Hieronymus tittered another laugh. *"Nothing, exactly, but far more than your precious young brain could comprehend, should I waste the time to explain. Suffice it to say, the price of experimentation on this level is quite steep. I've gone some time without the recognition I deserve. All of that will change once I dispose of you—as soon as my beautiful creations hit both human and folk markets, and entire Courts and countries make their bid for my support where once they denied me theirs."* He paused on that last, scathing note to dwell on its rancid pettiness, but composed himself quickly to continue. *"As for what this has to do with the philosopher's stone project . . . I'm sorry, but once again the answer is: nothing and everything. You'll just have to wait and see, dear Arlo."*

They crossed into the next room, but what greeted them was a sight that threatened to shatter Arlo's resolve to see this investigation through.

"Ah—my workshop."

It needed no explanation.

As nothing was in operation at the moment, there was no live demonstration for them to bear witness to. Arlo thanked every deity she could name for this, because the suspended horror on the other side of this hallway's glass was terrible enough without a live show. She wouldn't be able to close her eyes ever again without seeing this scene of surgical tables and the sinister tools required for human tanning.

The conveyor belt ran through here, too, yet still it had somewhere else to go, disappearing through another hole at the end of the room. Arlo didn't know if she could stomach another escalation of this depravity—she was already practically hanging off Vehan, the pair of them stricken in place by what they couldn't look away from.

"Humble though this rudimentary lab appears, great results have been achieved inside these walls. Such scientific advancement with so little funding, so very few tools . . . To think how I began and what I soon shall grow to be . . . It makes me sentimental just to give it words."

"It should make you fucking sick," Nausicaä condemned, speaking up at last. She had been unnervingly silent, taking in sights and betraying nothing of what they made her think and feel. "I mean, this is actually pointless. Cutting all these people up just to sew them back together? I'm all for crazy random shit, but there's something genuinely wrong with you. Cava don't require *mutilation* to be created."

"Perhaps." Hieronymus's glee had turned slick as oil. *"Honestly, though, there's very little that's pointless in my methods. I mean, really, if I sent my creations back into the world looking as they came to me, some of them would eventually be recognized. I'd be in trouble, more than I am now, don't you think? Besides, people are far happier to get the ugly things they want if they don't have to be reminded of where they came from."*

"Right." Nausicaä spared another glance for the torture chamber around them. "Seriously, I think you should come out now. We're done with this tour. Come out, or we're leaving, and we'll come back with a lot more than just the High King and his Hunters—I still have a few friends of my own who'd just *love* to put you in your place."

Another peal of delighted laughter rang out above their heads. *"No, no . . . Haven't you realized this yet? I'm afraid you won't be leaving."*

"You think so, yeah? Well, I'm sorry to tell you that I'm not your run-of-the-mill faerie, you evil little shit."

"Oh, I know you're not. I know exactly who you are, Alecto. I know you, and Vehan Lysterne, and Aurelian Bessel, and the star of this little show tonight, the fair Lady Arlo. I've been preparing for this, you see— hoping for it. I have such plans in store."

Dread welled up once more in Arlo's throat, heavy on the back of her tongue.

"You know who we are?" Vehan's brow was knitted together.

"Yes. Some of you I've known for quite a while, too."

"You're after something," Arlo interrupted. "You don't just want me dead. You would have sent something else to do that for you, if that was the case. You said you wanted me *here*—why? Enough with the games and just *tell* us!"

"Intelligent little thing, aren't you." It didn't sound like a compliment, the way their host said this. *"Honestly, I would have preferred my Reaper kill you and have done with it, yes, but you're right. I can make use of you here. There's another experiment I wouldn't mind running, and you're just the girl for the test."*

The way Nausicaä's face drained of color was deeply concerning to Arlo. She had no idea what Hieronymus was hiding behind his veil of insinuation and threats, but judging by Nausicaä's expression, the ex-Fury knew something she didn't. Vehan didn't look any easier about the proceedings. Arlo . . . she just wanted answers. She just needed to buy a little more time. "I don't get it," she snapped. "I'm not an alchemist. I have no idea what you're up to and no way of stopping it, even if I did. I'm nothing special, I'm no one, and I don't see—"

This time, when the doctor laughed, it was the coldest and cruelest he'd sounded all evening. *"And because you don't 'get it' is exactly why that power of yours is wasted. You have no idea why I'd see you as a threat? Why I want you gone? Arlo Jarsdel—yes, you absolutely are no one. Unfortunately, others don't agree."*

"Arlo," Nausicaä rasped in a way that suggested something very unpleasing had occurred to her. "Vehan, come here, please. I think I've figured out his game, and we really need to leave."

"Oh no. No, no, no, you won't be going anywhere. Figured it out, have you? Well, you're a bit too late. With Arlo's powers added to mine, and the wealth now at my disposal, I can turn my sights on things much greater than these tin-plated puppets and underground laboratories."

Arlo's powers *added* to his?

"Arlo—shit, we *really* need to leave. Holy shit, don't . . . just don't touch *anything* and come here!"

"Yeah, Arlo, I'm sorry—it was stupid to come here. This is bad, we need to go. I should never have made you do this." Vehan linked his arm back through hers, reaching to take Nausicaä's hand.

"No, I don't get it, I *don't get it!*" She tore out of the prince's grasp, glaring up at the ceiling. A little more time—just a little more time and this could all be over. "Do you think I'll join up with you? Is that what you're after? Are you going to try to persuade me to help you kidnap innocent people and turn ironborn into stones? Because I'll *never*—"

"*Share my fame and genius with the likes of you? Naive child, I don't want your help, I want your alchemy, plain and simple. Thanks to my genius, I've finally mastered the means to take it from you, and once I do, my benefactor will no longer idolize you over me. They'll lend me their full support, and I will be the one they trip over themselves to keep from harm. Meanwhile, you'll find a few of my security measures rely on something other than the power grid you overloaded to get here, so Nausicaä, you won't be magicking anyone out of this particular mess.*"

Nausicaä lunged for Arlo, taking hold of her arm so suddenly that Arlo didn't have time to flinch away.

But nothing happened.

Arlo's brows furrowed as Nausicaä's face fell. "What's wrong?" Arlo hedged, already fearing the answer.

"I can't teleport," Nausicaä gasped. She looked to be trying quite hard, and there was actual fear now in her eyes, growing with every failed attempt at whisking them away. "It's not working! What did you *do*?" she snarled, tearing her gaze away from Arlo's face to glare up at the ceiling now too.

"*You know, before I did this, I truly was nothing. A brilliant man—a genius—but woefully unskilled in the only thing that mattered in the eyes of your precious Courts. To them, I was a shame to the name of magic, and so, they stripped me of it altogether.*

"*They took my memories, too, but my anger remained. The heart does not forget as the mind so easily does. When my glorious benefactor returned my knowledge to me, I was reborn with such determination.*"

"You created a stone," Arlo concluded, bewildered. "You created a stone and did all of this . . . because of a grudge against the Fae High Council?"

"*I am a genius, my dear, but not the sort to manage that. I created a philosopher's stone, yes, but only under my benefactor's patient guidance,*" *and what I do here is not against the High Council, though I hope my creations bring them the destruction they deserve. No . . . the cava are purely for the money. My genius is quite expensive, see? Wealth is what legacies are built on, and legacies are what make a man great—not the magic you and your kind so covet.* Magic," he spat. *"May the High King and his sycophantic Courts choke on their beloved crutch. Magic will not save them from what is coming, I assure you."*

"So." Nausicaä looked to be edging toward manic—Arlo doubted she'd ever gone without the use of her powers altogether in all the years of her very long life, and didn't seem to enjoy the experience of it now. "Your sin is Greed."

"Sin? Wanting to survive is a sin, is it? To live life with respect and dignity and comfort . . . no, that isn't a sin—it's only thought of as such by those already in possession of these things. Wealth is what drives this world, after all. Wealth, not magic, and without it, you are nothing. You have nothing. *After what the Courts did to me—how low they cast me in rejecting me from their society—I swore to myself I would never be nothing again."*

"You've done all of this for petty revenge and *money?*" Vehan sounded half-ill merely saying the words. "All these people, all this time and effort and risk, you did it all for your own—"

"Enough," Nausicaä roared. She crossed to the still-closed door at the end of the hall and kicked it hard enough to dent the steel. "Open up. I know you're in here somewhere, and if you don't open this door, I'll fucking break through it myself and *drag* you out of there. You think you know who you're dealing with? You think you're prepared for *me?* Why don't we test that theory, huh? Open this *deities-damned door!*"

She kicked it again, and the dent caved deeper, groaning under the assault.

It wouldn't take her long to make good on the threat she'd delivered.

"Nausicaä!" Arlo warned, taking a step toward her. Just as she did, the door slid open and revealed the innards of one last elevator, much like the one that had brought them here.

"A splendid idea! You're a little too attached to my true target, anyhow—wouldn't want you getting in the way when I begin the process of transferring power. Why don't we run a different sort of testing? I have the perfect venue for your demise too. One I think you'll quite enjoy, my furious little ball of fire."

Snarling, Nausicaä stormed inside the waiting elevator. "I'd tell you I'll carve those words into your tombstone, if I was going to leave enough of you to fill a grave."

She turned, and in doing so, Arlo caught the unbridled fury hollowing out her face. A skeletal promise of death warped her razor-sharp features and powerful strength, lending a vulturelike edge to her appearance that completely disfigured her traditional beauty.

This was the closest Arlo had ever seen Nausicaä come to matching what Arlo's imagination conjured of what lurked beneath the Fury's many masks. It was the closest Nausicaä had come in Arlo's presence to letting the anger inside her truly take over.

Suddenly, it was imperative to Arlo that she be inside that elevator too. Despite the fact that it played directly into the doctor's hands to bring herself to him, Arlo had to follow her friend. She had to push aside her own anger and fears to take charge of this situation, because Nausicaä was *afraid*. She was clearly caught in a dangerous spiral, and if Arlo allowed her to go on alone in this state, she might even get hurt.

Darting forward with a speed she'd never before managed, it only took her moments to reach Nausicaä's side. If she'd let Vehan's shout of surprise delay her even a second, she wouldn't have made it—but made it she did.

Arlo cleared the elevator doors just as they snapped closed behind her.

Their group severed into two, leaving Vehan and Aurelian behind. Nausicaä stared, bewildered.

"We're a team," Arlo panted, bending to catch her breath and will her heart to slow its frantic pace. She glanced up. "We're doing this together, okay?"

Nausicaä swallowed. Her furious edge had softened a fraction, but she seemed stuck between her pale, avian wrath and the haunting beauty of her usual false arrogance. She also seemed to be searching for something to say, but that was stuck as well. Smiling, Arlo straightened and took a step closer to her.

"A dark and hollow star," Arlo said, holding up her fist in the narrow space between them. Something burned in her chest she'd never before felt . . . though it was possible her heart was just trying to commit a mutiny for that sudden burst of exercise. "I'm not going to let you face this alone."

She began to regret her words when she noticed the steel in Nausicaä's gaze turn glassy. "I'm sorry . . . ," Arlo hurried to tack on. "I mean, I just feel like we—"

Her apology was interrupted.

It took a moment for her brain to comprehend this pause—to realize it wasn't that Arlo's mouth had stopped moving because she'd run out of words but because Nausicaä's lips had pressed against her own.

A kiss.

She stood, unmoving, held in place by her surprise. She'd never kissed anyone before—not in any way that mattered—and here she was, with Nausicaä full and sudden and fierce against her, a burst of wild flame, and the only thing Arlo could think was: *oh*.

"Oh, shit," Nausicaä gasped, peeling away. "I'm sorry, I didn't mean to do that. I mean, I *did*, but—" Her voice was low as ever, and rasping still, though with far different emotion than the anger inspired by their mysterious host. Whatever she'd been about to say, it, too, was interrupted, but not by anything as pleasant as a kiss in return—Arlo was still too stunned to speak, let alone take that initiative.

No, much like their initial ride, the elevator gave no warning before it *plunged*, so quickly that Arlo rocked forward and fell into Nausicaä, who caught her and wound her arms tight around Arlo's torso, anchoring Arlo against her.

Red and blond hair tossed around their heads like a flurry of fire and sand.

The rapid descent filled Arlo with a curious weightlessness. Her heart was a war-drum beat in her throat. When the elevator finally stopped, she felt numb and hypersensitive—light-headed and leaden—all at the same time, but she squared her jaw and stepped back from Nausicaä. Once again, she squeezed the hilt of her dagger to draw on its strength.

"Hey, Arlo?"

"Yeah?"

"Remember when I told you to use that die of yours sparingly?"

Nodding, Arlo reached into her back pocket and extracted the object in question. The numbers glowed golden hot, as they'd been for quite a while now, simply waiting for her to call on Luck to lend them aid.

"Get ready to use the absolute crap out of that thing."

CHAPTER 32

Arlo

~~~~~~~~

"WELCOME!"

Arlo and Nausicaä exited the elevator.

The moment they did, the doors sealed shut behind them, and the light that marked its operational status flipped over to red. They were trapped. There was nowhere for them to go but forward.

Drawing a breath, Arlo willed herself to remain calm. She could contemplate the moment she'd just shared with Nausicaä later. Aurelian was (hopefully) close to hijacking the system that separated them. Celadon knew where they were. Arlo's plan had brought them this far; she could think up something to bring them back—she just needed to keep her cool and approach this new problem with a level head.

Side by side, they pressed into the room.

There was quite a lot of space for the little that comprised this section of the factory, illuminated by countless floodlights marking out its wide-flung limits and a scatter of spotlights overhead.

A slender man stood at its center, his hair pulled back in a short tail behind his head. Stationed in front of motionless, fully armored, and much sleeker cava than the ones they'd seen so far, he might have cut an impressive image in the bespoke pinstripe suit he wore, but Arlo wasn't in the mood to be impressed.

Something else contended for that honor, besides.

Her attention snagged on something at the far left side of the room—a gargantuan, gaping hole built into the floor, sectioned off by a railing. An incinerator, Arlo realized, but its bowels glowed so hotly it could just as easily have been some pit to hell. As the conveyor belt ran to its final destination high above their heads, cavum after cavum dropped into its open, waiting maw.

"Starbucks guy?"

Arlo's head whipped back to the man at the room's center. Now that Nausicaä mentioned it, the man *did* look familiar.

"It *is* Starbucks guy! Wow, dude, you fucking *suck*."

"I did tell you you'd regret your rudeness. I'm so glad you've decided to volunteer yourself for this experiment—and look! You've even brought along Miss Jarsdel. *Goodness*, but you've made my job a little too easy tonight." The man walked forward at a leisurely pace, his hands clasped behind his back. A grin quirked the corner of his mouth as he spoke—yes, Arlo recognized him now, however new his scars were, like a score of nails across his face. The disdain in his eyes was exactly the same as it had been on their first meeting. "You've almost taken the fun out of this, if you ask me—*almost*, but not quite."

Nausicaä's lip curled over her teeth in a soundless snarl, and in her hand, her katana assembled. "How long have you been after Arlo?"

Hieronymus—for this could be no other—paused but otherwise chose to ignore Nausicaä's outburst. Judging by his titter of laughter, he felt wholly unthreatened by her blade.

"You'll notice I left you access to the little hoard of knives I'm told you keep, my dear Alecto. I was tempted to take that from you too, because adamantine armor is quite costly to create—in more ways than one. But my latest model of cava need testing. What better way to do that than to pit them against another legend?" His eyes fell to Nausicaä's weapon, a greedy glint of longing in his eyes. "Starglass—a metal forged of stardust and the goddess Urielle's Fire. The same Fire that gave birth to *you*, if I'm not mistaken? One of the rare few Furies they've ever dared to make from that violent, uncontrollable element. Both you and that metal . . . You're simply *priceless*."

"You made a better batch of cava, so now you're going to destroy the old ones?" Arlo asked, slightly confused and more than a little aghast.

"A pity, yes, like I said—but no one pays good money for outdated models, and I'm afraid the wrong people would take notice if I carted too many of my creations to the new facility that this meeting of ours necessitates."

"Guess what," Nausicaä snapped. "The wrong people noticed."

She lunged.

Her patience whittled to its end, she sliced through the air with inhuman speed, ripping the sheath off her blade and tossing it aside. She made for their host, and in the span of time it took Arlo to blink, threw every ounce of her weight and wrath into the piecing blow she aimed at his gut.

The katana *shattered*.

Whether because of the force behind Nausicaä's blow or whatever it was that protected Hieronymus from her blade, it shattered right down to the hilt. Tiny shards rained down on the ground between them, tinkling softly.

Arlo watched the scene, hardly believing her horror could grow any more profound.

"But there are many uses for stardust, did you know?" Hieronymus hadn't even flinched.

"That's not possible . . . ," Arlo heard Nausicaä murmur, astonishment warping into denial. "No, that's not possible. Only the Wild Hunt has—"

She cut herself off.

She retracted a step . . . then two.

Nausicaä had arrived at some conclusion, Arlo gathered, and by the increasing glee in Hieronymus's grin, he noticed this as well—and she was right. "Only the Wild Hunt has permission to wear the stars as a shield," Arlo heard her accuse in a particularly stony tone. "What did you say was the name of your benefactor again?"

That grin growing into a sneer, Hero darted a bare hand out to wrap around Nausicaä's wrist. Before she could react, he tugged her closer. "I'll tell you what: win against my army, and I'll tell you everything you want to know."

Nausicaä cried out, and the sound snapped Arlo from her wary observation. She started forward, but Nausicaä had already torn herself free. She stumbled away from the doctor, and Arlo rushed to catch her before she could fall.

"What the . . . ," Arlo gasped when she noticed what had startled her friend so badly—Nausicaä's wrist, half her arm, and almost all of her hand were now leafed in perfectly polished gold.

"The stone?"

Their host was very clearly obsessed with wealth, among other things. If he'd managed to create a stone, it wasn't a stretch to assume this Midas touch of his was a "reward" of that achievement.

"As much wealth as anyone could want, right at your fingertips? Looks like Greed to me. Definitely one stone down." Nausicaä nodded grimly. "I was right—the stones glow colors corresponding to different Sins. Gold for Greed, red for . . . who knows, but we need to stop this before another stone is made and that color changes again."

With Arlo's help, she righted herself once more. Whipping her gold-leafed hand out to the side, she summoned up a different blade. A cutlass, this one—long and elegantly curved, the hilt was an intricate dance of metal loops that curled to make slots for her fingers. "I *liked* my katana, you dick. Do you have any idea how much of a bitch it's going to be to replace that?"

"Let me save you the trouble, then, hmm?" Hieronymus replied, throwing his own arms wide. "What need will you have for Starglass blades when your wretched immortal soul is finally put to rest?"

The adamant-plated cava stirred to life at last.

The smooth precision of their movement alarmed Arlo. Their metal casing couldn't have been all that light, and given what Arlo already knew of their predecessors' ungainly, jarring gait, she hadn't expected these newer models to arm themselves so easily with the weapons equipped on their backs. And yet they did just that, darting around their master as though gliding on ice.

"Arlo, get back!" Nausicaä ordered, hunkering down into another lunge. "Did you see the floor?"

She hadn't, but looking now, Arlo wondered how she could have missed the two arrays. Large enough to stand in, there was one on either side of where Hieronymus had been when they entered this room.

Arlo didn't need telling not to put a foot inside those rings— especially not when she knew what this man wanted from her.

"Worry not," Hero said over the commotion. He moved casually to the side to preside over this *test* like some ancient Roman emperor attending a gladiator match. "My cava obey my orders. My magic is what gives them purpose. Until they dispose of you, it's only you they're after, Nausicaä."

The battle commenced. Arlo backed away; she'd never seen anything quite like this.

Nausicaä moved under and over blows that were backed with so much power they dented the floor when they missed their mark. She was careful to keep from flourishing or leaping around more than necessary, but when she did, it was with such silent grace that once again Arlo found herself entranced. Every movement seemed more like a professional ballet than a high-stakes battle to the death.

And the blows Nausicaä delivered in return were just as deadly.

Her blade clashed loudly with the cava's plating, making sparks fly, the strikes singing out like screams in the cavernous room.

She held her own, but didn't seem to be causing much damage, and the battle started to look like a contest of who could outlast the other. Nausicaä was more than good, she was *brilliant*, but there had to be twice as many cava as there'd been outside this facility when she'd had Vehan at her side to help.

But Vehan wasn't here.

All Nausicaä had was Arlo, and Arlo was damned if she didn't try her hardest to assist.

Assist!

463

Arlo looked down at her die.

She had to *assist* Nausicaä, but how in the world could she do that? In order to get the die to work, she had to have some plan of action. Looking wildly around, she found nothing to jolt her inspiration.

"Could really use your help right now," she sang anxiously under her breath. It would be wonderful if Luck could take pity on her inexperience and point her in the right direction.

Almost as soon as the thought occurred, the world slowed down and stuttered to a halt. It fell to shades of gray, and in the air were scrawled her golden options. Everything had frozen—the battle, the doctor, the conveyor belt, and the cava plummeting to their fiery deaths.

"*Uuurrrgghhhh,*" Nausicaä groaned, doubling over to catch her breath, using her cutlass for support. "I may or may not be a high enough level for this boss battle. Let's go back to the previous save point and farm some EXP."

Well, there was an idea.

After all, the world was frozen—no one would be able to stop them from getting back in the elevator and leaving. "Can we just . . . go?"

"*You* might be able to—I mean, if your escape didn't rely on a locked-down elevator. As for me, I'm actually pretty stuck here. Magic is all about rules and whatnot—taking this show on the road qualifies as altering the natural flow of time, and as an immortal, if I want to keep what few perks I have left, that's one rule I truly can't break."

"All right, then . . . fine. I . . . guess I'll roll for an assist, then? Maybe . . . maybe an assist in . . . Aurelian figuring out the controls and getting us the heck out of here?"

"That would be super-duper, Arlo."

At the mention of the word, *Assist* glowed even brighter until the golden writing burst into glittering dust and reformed itself into the number twelve.

She rolled the die and watched it land on twelve exactly.

"Thank fuck," Nausicaä exclaimed in relief, and when Arlo moved to collect the only weapon she could properly wield (the knife she still clutched like a talisman would have been more helpful to her if she'd ever learned how to use one), Nausicaä fell to her ready position once more.

The battle resumed.

Hero still looked on from the sidelines, eyes glittering with something a lot like triumph.

Arlo scurried farther out of the way. A well-aimed kick sent Nausicaä tumbling in her direction, bringing the fight a little too close for comfort.

"Customer complaint: maybe next time we can roll to assist the girl fighting the horde of zombies," Nausicaä groaned. Heaving herself to her feet, she was only barely in time to block the cleaving blow aimed at her head.

"I'm sorry!" Arlo panicked. Maybe she needed a more detailed plan of action when rolling for an assist? "I'm sorry—maybe I can do that, too?"

"I wouldn't be upset if you tried!" Nausicaä hollered as she aimed an angry blow at her attacker's head.

Trembling, Arlo lifted her die for inspection. The numbers were dull, and no matter how many times she squeezed her hand around it, the world continued to unravel at its usual pace. Even when she tried suggesting minor actions, the die remained unresponsive. "It's not working! It's too soon, I think. I can't roll again! Maybe we just have to give it a minute or something?"

"Yeah, okay, sure! Sounds cool, I'll just keep doing my thing over here. No worries, everything's fine, this is *fun*."

There was a kernel of truth in that blatant sarcasm—Nausicaä *was* having fun.

She might prefer the battle to be a little easier, but every time Arlo caught a glimpse of her face, it was sapphire-flushed and full of burning focus, and her eyes glinted with dark, delighted fire.

Arlo looked back down at her die as though vigil might encourage it to recharge faster.

One minute became two.

An ear-piercing shriek echoed around the room, startling Arlo into dropping the dagger Aurelian had given her. She covered her ears and attempted to block out some of the sound while tracking it to its source. It didn't take long to find; the conveyor belt, she noticed, moved now three times the speed of before, and judging by the crunch and grind of gears within, the steady stream of cava pouring off its end had become too much for the incinerator to handle.

A frown twisted itself across Hieronymus's face. The adamantine cava were undeterred from their task, and Nausicaä continued to fend them off, but the man who controlled them no longer paid attention. "It seems that little vermin have started nibbling at my wires. That prince and his friend . . . I should have locked down every room. Never mind, this only makes my job easier. The quicker those cava are disposed of, the better."

Aurelian . . . Was he the one responsible for speeding up the conveyor belt? Is this what her assist had won her? Glancing once more at the pile of cava clogging the incinerator, Arlo found her idea at last.

"Nausicaä, keep the cava busy!" she called.

"Oh, okay," Nausicaä huffed. "Out of curiosity, what was I doing before this particular instruction?"

Arlo ignored the sarcasm. Lowering her hand, she checked her die again and found its color had returned—whatever assistance she'd lent to the universe was finally paid, and she was able to call on Luck once more.

"We just need a distraction to buy us time until Aurelian opens the doors and the High King arrives," she muttered under her breath. "We can do this!"

"Who are you talking to?" Hieronymus snapped, his attention back on Arlo. He started for her, and Arlo shuffled to keep as much space between them as possible. "What's that in your hand? Show it to me!"

The adamantine cava only gained momentum the longer this fight wore on. Though Nausicaä didn't seem to be slowing down either, all it would take for this battle to turn for the worse was a single one of those deadly blows hitting their mark.

Nausicaä was right. They were seriously under-leveled for this fight. Arlo had to act now before this could escalate any further—before their murderous host could activate one of those arrays and end it all.

"The cava clog the incinerator and break it down!" Arlo shouted.

Time chugged to a stop. Everything but Arlo and Nausicaä froze.

"You've lost me," Nausicaä panted. Relaxing her sword back at her side, she worked a bit of stiffness from her arm. "Why are we clogging the incinerator?"

"We're going to cause a distraction. The conveyor belt going faster? That has to be Aurelian making progress with the controls. If we can keep this going a little longer, when the High King arrives, he and the Falchion will have no problem getting down here to us," she explained as she examined the golden options in the air.

"And we're one hundred percent certain that your handsome fae prince is sending help to our rescue?"

"Yes. When Celadon says he's going to do something, he does it."

Escape glowed bright as ever.

Assist was dulled out of selection.

"Roll," said Arlo.

The options burst apart and scattered. They filtered through the air to seek out different parts of the room, where they reassembled themselves into numbers.

Apparently, Arlo had more than one option for creating her distraction.

A bit of dust shifted into the number ten, gleaming gold directly above the doctor's head.

The dust that had run over to the incinerator fashioned itself into a glittering green three.

Directly above the cava that Nausicaä had been fighting, glaring scarlet formed into the number eighteen. Nausicaä looked perversely pleased by this, as though it were some sort of honor that whatever was going to happen with the cava she fought had been ranked the hardest to achieve on the scale of their luck.

"What do I have to do here?" Arlo wondered aloud. "Do I have to choose which distraction I want, or just roll and hope to clear all three?"

Nausicaä shrugged.

Deciding to let her instincts guide her—they hadn't steered her wrong yet—Arlo rolled the die and hoped to clear at least the incinerator and complete the final stage of her plan.

"Nineteen!" Nausicaä crowed. "Ha—hope it's something good."

Arlo darted forward to gather her die. Time lurched back into gear. Just as Hieronymus whipped to the side, even more confused than before as to how Arlo was suddenly in a whole new location, another loud and awful noise rent the air.

The ground began to tremble, upsetting the balance of nearly all the remodeled cava, who clattered to the floor in a tangled heap—judging by how sturdy and skilled they were in movement, this was no doubt owed to her successful roll and explained why that particular result had been so high a bar.

One distraction down.

Across the way, the incinerator shrieked. It worked even harder to force the cava into its molten bowels, until, with a tremendous *bang,* its glowing depths were extinguished, and thick black smoke began to spew from its choking mouth.

Two distractions down.

"What's going on?" Hieronymus fumed. *"You."* He snarled, rounding back on Arlo. *"You* did this. How? What did you do? Is this the power that makes you so much better than everyone else?" He seethed a moment longer, and Arlo used his momentary tantrum to skitter farther away. It didn't take him long to collect his composure, though. After a deep inhale to steady himself, he added, "It doesn't matter. It doesn't matter! I'm going to take your alchemy from you no matter what you do."

He reached into the inner breast pocket of his jacket, his eyes taking on a dangerous, golden sheen.

"*Don't touch her*, he says. *Arlo Jarsdel isn't to be harmed*. Well, your protector isn't here now. I'll take your power and make it mine, and whatever fate has in store for you, it can give to *me* instead. You spoiled fae brats—*leeches* of society. It cost me *everything* to see my dreams come to fruition. You think that you can come in here and take that away from me with *magic*?"

His madness was clear in the laughter that punctuated his speech.

Arlo could only watch, fixed in place by a spike of her panic.

Who was this "he" he mentioned? She remembered the Reaper talking about a second master. The Scentless One? Someone else had been giving orders, and from the sound of things, this "scentless" being and their murderer were at odds in their objectives.

Hieronymus pulled back his hand and revealed what he'd extracted from his jacket—a smooth and vaguely misshapen stone, as perfectly gold as the leafing on Nausicaä's arm.

"You think your pathetic, fledgling magic will stop me? You think you're a better alchemist than I am?"

He laughed again.

"Magic can't defeat me—not now. Not now that I have my philosopher's stone! Your parlor tricks are nothing against the might of my achievements, and I'll only achieve more. I'll take you out, and once I do, my genius will *finally* earn the respect it deserves. I'll be—*ah!*"

His rant had been abruptly concluded by the sudden collision of a cavum, hurled directly at him through the air—Nausicaä capitalizing on the cava's tangled confusion. She growled across the room, "Oh my gods, shut *up*! Some of us are trying to enjoy a fight here."

As he lost his grip on the stone, it skittered out of the doctor's hand and rolled toward the array closest to Arlo, farther from the flurry of

swords and cava where Nausicaä was at last gaining the upper hand—
and there, that had to be their third distraction, because it was almost
as though time had stopped without the need of Arlo's die, as both
she and Hieronymus were so absorbed in watching the stone roll, and
roll, and roll to the center of the array, then rock to a stop.

"THE STONE!" Hieronymus shrieked at the cava. "GET THE
STONE! LEAVE THE FURY AND GET THE STONE!"

Arlo shot forward before her feet could remember her paralyzing
fear.

Hieronymus scrambled, clawing himself upright. He lurched
across the floor in an attempt to reach the stone before Arlo, but it
was useless. Across the way, his adamantine army lunged to obey their
new orders.

Arlo ran.

She ignored the way her heart hammered in her chest.

She ignored the hulking metal bodies hurling for her from the
other side of the room, death glinting off their blades in the light bent
by the rising plumes of smoke.

She ignored their host's hysterical shouts, and the string of
Nausicaä's profanities, simultaneously urging Arlo to keep running
while also trying to reclaim the cava's focus.

Arlo ran straight into the array, and when the stone was at last
within her grasp, she dove.

"NO!" Hieronymus screamed.

"ARL—*oh*!" Nausicaä gasped.

Arlo heaved herself to her feet.

The cava had caught up to her at last, and it was all she could do
to narrowly avoid the ground-splitting swing of a very large and very
heavy blade.

"YOU FOOLS! DON'T KILL HER YET!"

Wildly, Arlo chanced a glance at Nausicaä, a panic thrumming in
her veins that had nothing to do with her own dire situation. What
she saw made her blood run colder than it had all evening.

There stood Nausicaä, clutching her lower abdomen.

Nausicaä stumbled, retreating from Hieronymus, who'd risen from the floor to take advantage of Nausicaä's own distraction—her urgent flight to Arlo's aid—and ram a blade into her side. A dagger, now dripping sapphire blood.

Arlo's dagger . . . the one she'd dropped just moments ago.

"NOS!" she cried. Both die and stone in hand, she plunged into the swarm of cava. Deftly—impossibly—she darted between their lethal blades. They reached for her, for the stone they'd been tasked with retrieving, but like a curl of breeze, she slipped between their fingers, crouching, weaving, snaking her way toward Nausicaä.

Arlo knocked solidly into Hieronymus with all her weight and fury. He toppled once more, but Arlo didn't linger. She carried on. "Nos! Nos, are you okay? Are you all right? *Nos!*" She dropped both objects in her hands to catch Nausicaä where she fell just outside the ring of the opposite array, and eased her to the ground.

Arlo shook so violently she could barely shift Nausicaä into her lap and apply pressure over her wound. She could hardly see the blood at first with all the black Nausicaä wore, not until it trickled over Arlo's fingers; not until she felt it soak through her leggings, warm and wet and terrifying, and pool on the floor.

"Hey," Nausicaä replied, her husky voice shot through with cracks of humor. The weakness in it was so unlike her that it sounded like someone else's voice entirely. "We should have a talk with Aurelian. Ask him . . . ask him where he got a blade that can injure a freaking Fury so badly."

Arlo felt a little light-headed, seeing all this sapphire blood. "You'll be okay. You'll be okay, you won't die, you won't—"

"*Tch*, no. It's just a flesh wound. Hurts like a bitch, though, and I'm probably going to slip into a damn healing trance any second now to get the bleeding to stop. A terrible defense mechanism, really. Here I am, about to pass out in the middle of . . ." She shook her head. Pushing against Arlo, she tried to haul herself upright. "Can't trance yet. Can't . . . leave you alone to fight this, damn it! Pull yourself together, Nausicaä!"

"Nos—*don't*! You're hurt, don't move!"

"How touching."

Arlo's head snapped to the side and she curled herself protectively over her fallen friend. Hieronymus stalked toward them, back on his feet and strolling at a leisurely pace. His grin dripped curdled triumph.

"*Friendship*. It's funny, the things they tell you wealth can't buy. They're wrong, of course—everything has its price, and when you're the richest man in the world, even loyalty is for sale."

"Get fucked," Nausicaä spat. She groaned and shook her head again, fighting the pull of this trance she'd mentioned. Arlo tightened her hold around her, tucking her even closer. "I hope that loyalty stabs you right in your nicely dressed back."

"You won't be around to see it, if it does," Hieronymus sneered. "After all the trouble you've put me through, though, I think I'll let you watch as I drain your little friend here of her alchemy first. Unfortunately, she won't survive the process—the other test subjects didn't—but you've already watched one person you love die, haven't you, Alecto? I've heard the stories. What do you say to running another experiment, hmm? Care to find out if it hurts just as much when you lose your precious Arlo, too?"

He raised his hand, stepping even closer. His army assembled around him.

"I'll . . . fucking . . . destroy you," Nausicaä snarled through her fading consciousness. "You touch her . . . and I'll destroy you. Just like I . . . destroyed the last . . . who was that stupid."

Arlo stared at the symbols on the ground beside them and sorted through the doctor's words.

"Arlo," Nausicaä rasped, weaker than before. She seemed determined to keep her focus long enough to slip something into Arlo's hand.

Tearing her gaze from the array and the mass of cava regrouping behind the doctor, Arlo sought out Nausicaä's face. Icy pale, Nausicaä held her gaze a moment longer. Then, at last, her eyes closed and she fell still. A fresh shock of panic began to steal through Arlo's system, but it was then she realized what Nausicaä had slipped her.

The die.

All at once, Arlo saw what she had to do.

"You know what?" she heard herself say as she raised her gaze back to the doctor. At the same time, almost of its own accord, she turned the hand supporting Nausicaä's back to touch her fingers to the rim of the array beside them. "You're actually really stupid."

Hieronymus faltered. "I beg your pardon?"

"These arrays on the ground . . . They transfer and drain powers?"

"Yes," he snapped, forgetting himself, stepping even closer so he could tower over Arlo. He didn't notice the foot he touched just barely to the ring—but Arlo did. "It took me quite some time to master the art of bending magic itself to my will, but nothing is impossible with the right amount of intelligence and motivation."

Arlo snorted.

"Like I said—stupid."

She closed her eyes. It was really quite simple. As easy as it had been to picture the array that sealed this factory's entrance, the one below her drew itself crystal clear in her mind. By imagining its symbols dissolving, she could deactivate an array. . . . What would she have to do if she wanted to try and *reverse* one?

You invert the symbols.

Another memory, wrapped in fog, conveyed in her father's gentle voice.

This time, with Nausicaä in her lap, vulnerable and depending on Arlo to get them out of this situation, Arlo was able to draw on her alchemy without assistance.

The array in her mind warmed to glowing life almost without prodding.

She had no idea where her knowledge of this magic was coming from. Her father wasn't ironborn, and he'd certainly never practiced alchemy. . . . Wherever she'd picked this up, the memory must be scrambled with another, distorted by time and too many other things laid on top of it. But where could she have possibly overheard any of this?

Invert the symbols—she wouldn't question it, not now, not when she was so *sure* of herself and what she had to do to stop Hieronymus Aurum from *winning*.

"This whole time you've been after my alchemy, but you never stopped to consider what other gifts I have." The symbols in her mind began to turn like a dial. As they did, the ones on the floor began to rotate too.

"What are you doing?" Hieronymus gasped, looking down at his array. "What's going on, what is this? My array! You can't possibly—"

"I'm no alchemist."

She opened her eyes.

"Not like you. I'm something better. Something a little less tangled up in *rules*."

Hieronymus screamed, rigid where he stood. Whether it was shock or pain that rooted him in place, Arlo began to feel it—the trickle of power. It came to her slowly. She didn't want to kill him, didn't want to draw too fiercely on the link that seemed to have formed between them—a link she could almost see, like a pulsing, glowing blue thread—but she had to weaken him, had to prevent him from using this against them, and as she did, she could feel something in her begin to tremble.

Too much! some instinct in her screamed. *Too much, you're not ready!*

The tower everyone kept her in, Arlo felt it begin to quake. As though it was built on crumbling rock, she felt every shift of its foundations, every tremor that threatened to collapse that tower in on itself and drag her down into yawning nothingness. She removed her hand from the array, her eyes on Hieronymus, her focus on breathing and keeping as still as possible as the trembling subsided . . . as it finally stopped.

The array on the floor dimmed back down to chalk.

"*What* did you just do?" Hieronymus rasped. Somehow, he seemed even deadlier for the magic he'd just lost. "What did you just *do to me?*"

Their time was up.

The array couldn't hurt Arlo now, but the cava still could.

The die in her hand was cool to the touch, but she knew what she had to do to get it to help them—what price she had to pay, what role she had to assume to move past the limitations of her trial period. She remembered now the other part of what Luck had told her back in the Faerie Ring, what she had to say and do if she needed Luck's assistance.

She couldn't put it off any longer; she had to make a choice, had to save herself and Nausicaä from their would-be tomb by any means possible, and if agreeing to what Luck had offered was the only way, that choice was clear.

"HELP US!" she shouted.

Lifting the hand concealing her die, she tossed it aside and released it to the room. Loud enough to make her voice echo, she at last said exactly what Luck had wanted from the start. "I WANT TO MAKE THE DEAL—I'LL BE YOUR HOLLOW STAR IF YOU HELP US!"

Laughter overlapped her echoing cry.

The die rolled away.

It rolled, and rolled, and far out of Arlo's reach, it landed on the number four.

"Help you?" Hieronymus mocked. "Oh, I will, and it will only take a moment, though I'm afraid to say it will hurt quite a lot."

He raised his hand. "You think you're oh-so-clever, child? You think you've rendered me powerless? You might have broken my array, but do you think I won't just *kill* you here anyway?" He snapped his fingers. Arlo threw herself into a protective shield over Nausicaä, however useless the action would be against the doctor's intentions.

She could almost hear the squelch of a blade puncturing her organs, but despite her imagination, nothing happened.

When one moment stretched into two and they remained unharmed, Arlo lifted her head and dared herself to see what was taking the doctor and his army so long . . . and found the cava frozen.

Not by time.

Not by Arlo's die.

Hieronymus stood there, still as death, his fevered glee usurped once more by shock as he stared down at his chest—where he'd been speared straight through by something that looked a lot like a hand, blood and shreds of flesh dripping from its claw-tipped fingers.

Arlo gasped when that hand closed into a fist and yanked itself back through this gruesome cavity, and Hieronymus—dead—crumpled to the floor.

It was then she noticed, through the burning scent of smoke and overheated machinery, a cool aura, sickly sweet, like that of rotting flowers.

CHAPTER 33

Aurelian

~⊰⊱~

AURELIAN HAD BEEN ALL of eight when his parents allowed him his first computer. An HP laptop—large and bulky by the standards of what he currently owned—was far from the sort of thing most lesidhe children begged their parents to get them for their birthdays, but he'd won them over in the end.

It was the most expensive present they'd ever bought him, back then. He cringed to think now how hard it must have been to scrape together the money when they'd had so little at the time—when he and his younger brother, Harlan, had attended human elementary school, and his parents had run a modest business, selling baked goods from their tiny home.

This control tower—with its panel of buttons and switches and blacked-out lights arranged around the most impressive computer Aurelian had ever seen—was slightly more complex than that laptop of long ago.

It was, however, conveniently protected by no more security than a simple password. Aurelian had taught himself ages ago how to hack past such things, and while his mother was going to light him up one side and down the other when she found out what he'd been up to tonight, one good thing to come out of this adventure was that he'd at least be able to finally tell her his "unfaelike fascinations" weren't as much a waste of time as she and so many others believed.

"We have a problem."

Aurelian turned his head without taking his eyes off the computer's monitor. He'd know Vehan no matter what—his aura was a gentle fizz against Aurelian's own, like carbonated water, gingery and citrus-tart on the back of his tongue.

"Just one?" Aurelian said dryly.

Vehan drew closer. The warmth he radiated as a Seelie prince of Summer spilled down Aurelian's back, but he didn't have time for the way that made his muscles tense.

"Funny. Hilarious," Vehan deadpanned. "Meanwhile, Nausicaä can't teleport, and she and Arlo just disappeared down another elevator, and I'm fairly certain Hieronymus Aurum is about to kill them both. This is . . . this is actually terrible. This is not at all what I'd hoped would happen in coming here. Aurelian, we *need* to get these elevators working—we have to get them out of there. I can't have the High Prince's favorite person in the whole world dying because of a stupid plan *I* concocted."

"Oh, well, if we *need* to, I guess I'll actually put some effort into this."

He couldn't help it.

Vehan was a source—of irritation, of confusion, of fear, of frustration and late-night musings and embarrassing dreams he would *not* allow himself to think about in conscious hours. And the stress of their current situation only compounded these things.

"Please tell me you're joking."

"Of course I am."

"Well, stop."

Vehan peeled away. Aurelian felt his shoulders relax a fraction. "Don't touch anything," he warned, because leave it to Vehan to somehow find a way to seal them down here for good—the fae in general weren't all that capable when it came to modern human technology, even the bits they actually liked. But Vehan seemed almost determined to win a medal for how terrible he was with it.

"So, have you almost got it, then, or . . . ?" Vehan returned to peer over his shoulder, undoubtedly lost as to what he saw on the screen.

478

It was Aurelian's turn to sigh. "Oddly enough, no. For some reason, I'm a bit distracted—*there.*"

They were in.

"You did it!" Vehan crowed.

Aurelian leaned closer to the screen. Restoring power to the panel was his first priority. After that, he had to assume it was trial and error until they found what controlled the elevators. A few minutes of tinkering, and his mission was successful. The lights on the panel clicked on one by one, blinking as their system booted back to humming life. Satisfied that all was going well, he examined their many options.

"This would be easier if things were labeled," Vehan mused unhelpfully. He reached across the way, directly in front of Aurelian's vision. "What about that one there?"

"Vehan, stop! I said don't touch anything."

A curious sensation flooded Aurelian then, not unlike what he'd felt earlier outside this facility. The air around them shivered, and he could almost swear he detected the faintest skip in time, like a glitch, as Vehan reached for the console.

It passed just as quickly as it came and left no evidence it had been anything more than his imagination.

"I wasn't going to touch it," Vehan cried. "I was just pointing!" He snatched back his hand, completely unaware that anything had been amiss. The slight downturn of his mouth betrayed his sulking, but the pout was quickly replaced by terror—as Vehan's hand had brushed a dial on its way back.

An ominous creak of gears split through the facility's otherwise silence. Out beyond the control tower, the conveyor belt of cava churned at three times its original speed.

"Well, okay," said Vehan, relaxing a fraction. "Not the *worst*-case scenario, then. We can just turn it back . . . down."

Aurelian could feel his blood pressure rising. "You broke it, didn't you."

"I did not, I barely even touched it! It's locked in place—*you* give it a try, great and powerful computer genius."

Brushing the prince aside, Aurelian did just that, but just as Vehan had said, it wouldn't budge. What was the point of a dial that only turned one way? Had Vehan actually broken it, or was there some separate dial for turning down the speed?

"I guess we're looking for *two* things now . . . ," Vehan muttered, apparently wondering the same.

Aurelian sighed again. "The elevator is still our priority. Maybe there's an operator's manual around here somewhere. Do *not* touch *any*—"

"I, Vehan Soliel Lysterne, Crown Prince of the Seelie Court of Summer, command you to *not* finish that sentence."

Aurelian pursed his lips, eyeing the prince through no small amount of distrust. "Don't touch anything," he warned, regardless of Vehan's command, and disappeared beneath the panel.

There was a kick to the heel of his boot. "Ass," Vehan hissed. Concealed by his current position, Aurelian allowed himself a muted trace of a smirk.

"Tsk, tsk, tsk."

The sensation that flooded through him now was also familiar, but unlike the last, Aurelian knew this one immediately as dread. He shot back up from his inspection, catching the back of his head on the panel in his haste. How had he missed it—that writhing against his skin, like maggots in a decomposing, bloated carcass? How had he missed it—that foul taste on the back of his tongue, like rancid flowers and battery acid, making him want to gag? How had he missed the mold-black aura eating at his periphery? Because all these things he'd encountered before, the first time right outside this very facility. Sure enough, when Aurelian wheeled around, it was Lethe he found, which didn't make sense at all given the glaring red lights above the elevators still marking them locked and the uniform this mysterious being wore.

"You're . . . a Hunter."

It was the first thing he could manage to say.

There he was, the being that had found them in the desert days ago. There he was, the being they'd encountered in the Hiraeth. Lethe was just as terrible to behold as ever . . . but this time, overtop his glinting silver trimmings and tight black tunic was a glimmering cloak of midnight, infamously known as the garb of the Wild Hunt.

"How did you get in here?" Vehan asked in equal awe. "The elevators . . . The Hunt isn't supposed to be able to teleport inside buildings."

Lethe tilted his head, bemused in a way that only increased Aurelian's discomfort with this situation. Waist-long gunmetal hair spilled down one side of his body in a wild mess of knots and braids and what Aurelian suspected were woven bits of the Hiraeth. He peered at Vehan not unlike a spider in its web, waiting for the first bit of struggle to signal its next meal.

Lethe may have saved them twice before, but there was no doubt in Aurelian's mind that his appearance now meant nothing good.

"His Highness asked you a question," he heard himself say faintly.

Heaving a sigh, Lethe stretched long arms up into the air and languidly folded them behind his head. "I heard it. I just don't care for foolish questions. Obviously, I came to be here through magic stronger than someone's underestimation, and a certain disregard for rules—much like yourselves, by the look of things. Alchemy. *Mmm.*" He paused to exaggerate a shiver. "Having fun?"

"We're trapped in a secret underground laboratory that's kidnapping humans and targeting ironborn for alchemical experimentation—so no, we're not having *fun,*" Vehan spat, and his vehemence was hot enough that Aurelian took a protective step closer to him. "What are you doing here? Are you in on this too?"

"This?" Lethe glanced around. "On and off, but on the whole? No." His grin grew wider, revealing his teeth. There were dozens, sharp as serrated blades, and yet more deadly was the silver glinting at the tips of his left-hand fingers—his scythe. Every Hunter had one, as the legend went. Though the model varied on the user, each Hunter wore an adamantine weapon forged in the fire of dying stars, which allowed them to harvest souls from mortal flesh. Now that Aurelian knew him for what he was, he was even more horrified how close those bits of metal had come to the prince too many times before. "Sorry, this isn't exactly my taste. The death that stains this place is *delicious*, to be sure, but . . . no. This was merely a curiosity I enjoyed checking in on."

"Enjoyed?" Vehan cried, aghast. "You 'enjoy' that so many innocent people have died? I don't understand, you're supposed to be *good*."

Aurelian noticed Vehan's hand flex between them. Perhaps it was lucky that his command of electricity was temporarily disabled. If he attacked, there wasn't much Aurelian could do to protect him from a Hunter.

"Good?" Lethe pulled an expression of deep disgust. "Don't be revolting. I'm immortal, little faeling prince—I have no use for your pathetic notions of 'evil' and '*good*.'" He dropped his hands back to his sides, and with them fell his humor. "Now, step away from those controls before you break something."

Vehan crossed his arms. "Absolutely not."

Aurelian added his agreement by stationing himself between Vehan and the Hunter. They were no match for Lethe. The entirety of Seelie Summer would be no match for Lethe, if stories about Hunters were to be believed, but Aurelian had his duty; they couldn't get out—he couldn't whisk Vehan away to safety, as was always his top priority—but he could make certain Vehan wouldn't come to harm before he did. "Stay back," he growled, low in his throat.

"If you don't get out of my way, lesidhe brat, you won't be leaving here alive."

He bared his lethal teeth, antifreeze eyes flashing. Aurelian was under no delusion that an eighteen-year-old lesidhe fae could ever intimidate an immortal deity of death, but he took a step forward, regardless, and bared his teeth as well.

"Are you going to challenge me?" Lethe laughed, that creaking sound that made the hairs on the backs of Aurelian's arms stand on end, and twirled his adamant-capped fingers. "Come on, then."

Challenging a Hunter was beyond foolish, but what other option did Aurelian have? He had to get these elevators working. He had to get Vehan and Arlo and Nausicaä to safety. If Lethe wasn't going to let him do this, he would have to play the distraction and hope that Vehan could do it instead.

"Your Highness?"

Vehan's expression turned even more severe. "How many times do I have to tell you to call me Vehan, and no. I know what you're thinking, and *no*. I'm the one with more experience fighting. I'm—"

"Skilled with a sword, but you don't have that right now, do you?"

"*Aurelian*—"

"*Vehan*. Start pressing buttons."

Aurelian darted forward.

It was very true, Vehan was far more skilled with a weapon than Aurelian would ever be, but one advantage he had over the prince was speed. Lethe skittered away in a blink, his cackle of glee chasing him across the room; Aurelian was quick to follow.

A swipe of the air with those metal claws—Aurelian ducked it easily.

A feign to the left and a boot to his right—Aurelian deflected the blow.

Lethe was angry beneath his mask of boredom. There was no other explanation for why he'd toy with him this way. At any moment, the Hunter could end Aurelian's life with a swiftness even he couldn't dodge; at any moment, he could decide these playful jabs no longer suited his mood and fell Aurelian in the time it took him to shape his laugh.

Behind them, Vehan pressed buttons.

He flipped switches.

He turned dials.

Lights flared brighter, then much too dim; the air from the vents blasted arctic cold air, then hot as a furnace; one of whatever he'd pressed set off an alarm similar to what had nearly deafened them on their first visit to this facility. The sound made him wince, and Lethe took that opening to throw so hard a punch to Aurelian's chest that he fell to the floor, gasping.

"Aurelian!"

"Keep . . . pressing . . . buttons," he wheezed, attempting to get to his feet.

"No . . ." Lethe pressed a boot to his lower back, his tone once more coolly amused. "No, I think I *like* you on your hands and knees." He applied pressure, forcing Aurelian to brace himself on his arms so as not to be flattened against the metal floor.

"Maybe if you took your position a little more seriously, it wouldn't have come to this," Lethe continued to taunt. "Maybe if you weren't so wrapped up in your pity and pointless deceptions and fear of death, you wouldn't be this useless."

"What . . . would you . . . even know about that," he gritted out.

"What, indeed." He dropped another laugh, dipping over Aurelian so close he could feel his breath against his ear. "You know, you remind me of someone. She, too, spent too much time in pointless emotions. It made her dull. Made her *weak*. Doused her fire . . . Perhaps we should see if you can do a little better?"

One moment, Aurelian's arms were about to give way under Lethe's surprising weight. The next . . . Lethe was gone. With a speed almost as though he'd vanished from the air, Lethe flew from Aurelian, and before Aurelian could push himself to standing, a gasp that would haunt him for many nights to come told him exactly where Lethe had gone.

"Darling Vehan—such a pretty little thing you are. What do you think, Your Highness—in the spirit of where we are, should we run a little test?"

"Julean—no, *don't touch him!*"

484

Lethe's grin split so wide across his face it looked like it might break. Aurelian barely noticed. He barely noticed it was Vehan's true name out of his mouth, the one the prince had chosen on Maturity and had given to *no one* but Aurelian, not even his own mother. He didn't notice he spoke it like a plea to Vehan himself to just stay alive. As Aurelian tore to his feet and flung himself at Lethe, the only thing he *could* notice were those damned claws at his prince's throat.

The trade-off was effortless.

In a singular motion Lethe threw Vehan aside and grabbed for him, and using Aurelian's momentum against him, slammed him— face-first and *hard*—into the panel of controls. There was no time to think, no time for retaliation: Lethe scored a singular claw down the back of his neck, and it burned right down to the bone.

He screamed.

"The time for indecision is over, Aurelian Bessel. The geas that compels my protection of your prince is almost spent. You'll need all your strength for what's to come. Get better at staying alive."

Lethe reached a hand over Aurelian's head. It wasn't until he vanished properly this time—the light dimming black only long enough to swallow him—that Aurelian realized he'd been spared.

It wasn't until he lifted his head that he realized the Hunter had pressed a button.

It wasn't until Vehan rushed to his side and helped him off the panel, distressed and close to tears as he checked Aurelian over for injury, that Aurelian realized what that button had done.

"Vehan," he croaked. "Look."

He pointed through the open door, back down the hall, at the elevator that had brought them here—and at the light above it, no longer red but green.

CHAPTER 34

Arlo

ARLO COULD ONLY STARE.

"Well, that was . . . *disappointing.*"

At first, she could have sworn the darkness had spoken.

In this dimly lit and smoky room, it was hard to make out much in the shadows, let alone the imposing figured swathed in midnight robes.

Not robes, Arlo realized.

The figure lifted a foot to nudge Hieronymus out of his path. As he strode forward, the floodlights caught the fluttering ends of his cloak and glinted off the fabric as though it were spun from diamonds—or perhaps, more accurately, the stars.

"All the wealth his avarice could want, and still the greed outgrew the man."

Arlo didn't recognize this voice. It was just as light and rotted sweet as the scent of his magic, and as smooth and cool as water pooled in the depths of some forgotten cave. Every word made Arlo want to shiver.

She didn't recognize the voice, but she recognized the figure, and now she knew exactly who that aura near Good Vibes Only had belonged to. When he knelt before her in a crouch and looked her, grinning, in the eye, she knew who it was that had come to her rescue. She'd forgotten about them until now—those antifreeze eyes that had watched her so closely in the High King's throne room.

The Wild Hunt was here, and for the very first time she was staring a Hunter in the face.

The moment transfixed her.

"My deepest apologies, Arlo," he said with an almost impossible amount of sincerity to his featherlight tone. "I specifically told him to leave you alone. Look at what it got him."

The Hunter reached out, brushing the backs of his long, cool fingers against the edge of Arlo's jaw.

He was oddly arresting. Beautiful as a corpse made up for its funeral. Arlo wasn't surprised.

At this proximity she could see beneath his hood, and much like with Nausicaä, there was a lethal edge to his features—a vulture sharpness that could have made them twins. Toning down the full potential of his horror was a soft and coyly curling mouth, wide eyes framed by heavy lashes, and cheekbones thrown like daggers toward the hidden tips of his ears.

"He had very strict orders, but I'm not surprised." The Hunter sighed and rose to his feet. He had a way of speaking—a dull but flourishing lilt in his tone—that made everything he said sound like a well-rehearsed bit of musical theater that his heart was no longer into delivering. "He was a miserable creature when I found him—so *whiny*. It was all I could do to give him the means to see how this Icarus would fly. To see how far he'd go with this little project of his."

"You . . . the *Wild Hunt* is the one behind this?"

The Wild Hunt was pledged and bound to the one who wore the Bone Crown. They couldn't act on their own, which meant . . . "High King Azurean, too?"

"That buffoon? Heavens, no. Your crumbling defender isn't pulling the strings in this operation—and neither is the Wild Hunt, for that matter."

"But you—"

"Are growing quite bored with our endless servitude to *peace*. We used to strike fear into mortal hearts. We used to be *warriors*. My siblings have forgotten, but *I* haven't. The Wild Hunt was a herald of destruction, once upon a time—we, the Four Horsemen of legend.

487

Now we're little better than your janitors. Eris might be content to play by our divine father's rules, but *me*?"

He shook his head.

"Worry not, dearest Arlo. Hieronymus thought he could outsmart the luck that gives you favor, thought he could outsmart *me*, and now he's paid his price. You've discovered who's behind the Reaper attacks and put an end to his vulgar experiments. You may rest easy now knowing no one else will have to die to further his success." He rose. "Your part in this is over for now. If you'll excuse me, though, I really must be going." He made to leave but then paused. Turning back to Arlo, he slapped his hand lightly against his hooded head. "I almost forgot, I'll be taking that with me."

With a snap of his fingers, the golden philosopher's stone appeared in his hand.

"Why are you doing this?" Arlo half cried, her patience severely frayed. "You kidnapped people, used them for cruel experiments, and you're using ironborn for stones—*why*?"

"Me? No, in the long run, I'm merely a cog in the works, just like you. Just like *him*." He frowned down at Hieronymus, splayed on the floor.

"You're not just like me." Arlo narrowed her eyes into a glare and bared her teeth in vehement rejection of the very idea. "We're not the same. Tell me! Just give me a name—who's doing this?"

The Hunter cocked his head, and for one eternal minute stared silently back at her. "What would you do, I wonder, if I gave you what you wanted?" Retracing his steps to her, the Hunter dropped back into his crouch. His green eyes searched her face, looking for something. Arlo leaned away, this Hunter's deathly beauty no longer curious to her but repulsive.

Judging by his frown, this reaction didn't go unnoticed.

He lifted the hand not clutching the golden stone and brushed the tips of his fingers over the space between Arlo's collarbone and breast. "A hero . . . a Hollow Star . . . There are other things that you could be too, but you're not ready. Not yet."

"Don't touch me," Arlo hissed, flinching farther away from his hand and the unpleasant shudder that rippled through her at the contact.

The Hunter bowed his head, his compliance immediate. "As you command."

As suddenly as he'd knelt, the Hunter rose. Arlo watched him go, relieved but more confused than ever.

"A reward for your bravery this evening—call it a consolation prize." The Hunter stooped, retrieved something from Hero's body, and tossed it back to Arlo. "Catch!"

Something small sailed at her head, arching through the air and refracting light in glints of gold. Arlo pitched herself forward to catch it.

She peered down at the object and saw it was a ring.

A simple band of gold, stamped with a sigil of a black serpent winding around a series of golden orbs. It was vaguely familiar, but at the moment, Arlo couldn't place how she knew it.

"I look forward to our next meeting, Arlo Jarsdel. Ta for now."

As she tore her gaze away from the ring, Arlo snapped her head back up to the Hunter, but he was already gone. At last, she and Nausicaä—an unconscious and not-at-all surprisingly heavy weight in Arlo's arms—were alone.

Hieronymus lay lifeless in a pool of blood. The armored cava, without the magic they needed to fuel their operation, presided over his death like monuments to the atrocities they'd suffered at his hands.

Arlo was . . . overwhelmed.

All at once, it came rushing in what she'd done . . . what she'd followed Nausicaä into, and what she only barely managed to survive—what she *wouldn't* have survived without Nausicaä, Arlo's mysterious alchemic talent, and the luck she'd carried here in her pocket.

They'd won, somehow without managing to win anything, because for all the answers they'd found this evening, so many more questions rose to take their place. Right now, in the raw wake of everything, Arlo could process none of it.

The lurch of gears thundered in the room, stealing Arlo from her downward spiral.

Lifting her gaze, she saw that the light above the elevator door was green again.

Equally unable to process this, either, she simply watched as the doors slid open a moment later and a crowd of people poured forth.

"Arlo!"

Was that her *mother's* voice she heard?

"Arlo!"

"Arlo!"

The cacophony of her name shouted over and over by so many different voices threatened to tip the scales of her fragile state, but it was the sudden, fierce embrace that started up her tears, followed by another closing in on the opposite side.

"Arlo, oh gods, baby, you're *safe*. Thank Cosmin, I was so worried!"

"Arlo . . ."

"Mom?" Arlo sniffed, the name coming out in a hiccup. "C-Cel?"

Both Celadon and her mother eased back, clearly struggling to maintain the tremulous confidence in their gentle smiles—but then Celadon spotted Nausicaä unconscious and bleeding. "Arlo . . . what *happened*?"

The sob choked out of her before she could stop it, and Arlo flung her arms around her mother and cousin once again. She was so relieved to see them and, goodness, the High King had finally arrived.

There was Vehan, too, and Aurelian . . . three of the Wild Hunt, the High Queen, Reseda . . . and someone else who, through her tears, Arlo didn't recognize at first—tall and morning fair and beautiful as carved ice. When she drew close enough, Arlo could just make out the same charcoal hair and electric blue eyes as Vehan.

Riadne Lysterne, Arlo realized. Queen of the Seelie Court of Summer.

Vehan and Aurelian had managed to get the elevator doors working, and Celadon had made good on his promise, just as Arlo believed he would.

"It's okay," Celadon breathed. "It's okay now, we've got you. I'm sorry, Arlo, I should have come sooner. I should have come the moment I found out about this . . ."

"I'm sorry too, Arlo," Vehan added, pausing just a few steps away and looking on in horror. "This was a tremendously stupid plan."

"That it was," the Queen of Seelie Summer replied to her son, her voice as smooth as unblemished stone. "Vehan, we'll talk about your involvement in this later. Miss Jarsdel?" She turned her attention on Arlo, and it was enough of a shock to have such an important figure outside of her family address her at all, that Arlo's hysterics abated entirely. When Queen Riadne bent herself into a sweeping bow, Arlo very nearly forgot how to breathe. "It is my deepest regret that my own blood has caused you such misfortune tonight. You have my apologies."

Arlo stared.

"Come on." Thalo bustled, ignoring Queen Riadne. When Celadon shifted Nausicaä into his arms and began inspection of her injuries, Aurelian rushed forward to lend his aid as well. Arlo's mother guided Arlo to her feet. "Can you stand? Are you injured?"

"No," said Arlo, her voice strangely light. "I'm okay. But Nos . . ."

"Let Celadon take care of your friend. Come on, baby, let's get you home."

Arlo couldn't remember ever wanting anything more in her life than to do exactly that.

CHAPTER 35

Arlo

T HE SUN WAS JUST beginning to peek over the horizon out the window, but with everything that had gone down that night, Arlo hadn't been able to sleep. Instead, she kept vigil, sliding a chair up to Nausicaä's bedside and resting her head on her folded arms, watching over her friend's recovery.

The fight had taken more from Nausicaä than she'd let on.

To expedite her healing, they'd needed Aurelian's unique talents. Lesidhe were the only fae capable of using their magic to heal others—the sidhe fae could only heal themselves. Now her injury was nothing more than a giant, ugly bruise, but Nausicaä had yet to awaken.

That was okay.

Nausicaä deserved to rest for as long as she needed.

If it hadn't been for her, none of them would have survived their ill-planned mission. Thanks to Aurelian's audio recording of the entire "tour" of the facility, Nausicaä had been exonerated from the suspected crimes against her.

Brought back to the medical wing of the Tower, she was given the full extent of preferential treatment to ensure her perfect recovery. It had taken many reassurances on Arlo's part, but eventually Celadon and Thalo had left the two alone.

Not fully alone, as it turned out.

"You forgot something."

Arlo's head whipped to the side. She regarded the person who'd spoken—the being at the foot of the bed, their hair a flaming fan of shamrock green, their face beset with cosmic black eyes, their every angle cut as sharply as the facets of a diamond. She'd never seen them before, not like this, but she knew them at a glance. There was no mistaking who it was in their dress of emerald gossamer and silk-like-melted-steel, their every limb dripping golden jewelry, and their olive-green chest exposed in the deeply low cut of their attire, tattooed with the very same runelike pattern she'd seen on the not-troll in the Faerie Ring.

The horns were different. Before they'd been short, but now they stretched—glittering, volcanic black—proudly from the being's temples, curving back and to a blunted point at their fine-boned chin.

On the bed, they set Arlo's die—the one she'd forgotten in the pits of the cavum factory.

"I thought immortals couldn't enter the Mortal Realm," Arlo blurted. "How are you here?"

"You are the blood of one who forged this rule. I'm here because you invited me. But never mind that; plenty of time for intricacies later. Did you have fun on your little adventure?"

Arlo looked at the die, then up at Luck's suspicious passivity. *"No,"* she bit out. Nothing they'd done that evening could ever constitute "fun."

"Good. I'd have taken that away from you if that was all you intended to use it for."

Her indignation flaring, Arlo balled the blankets into her fists. "You know, you could have *told* me what that die did. How to use it. We were almost killed down there because of you."

"Because of me?" Luck shook their head. "You *won* because of me. You're a very clever girl, Arlo Jarsdel, and I was testing that. From here on out, that die won't be so easy to wield. There are rules, and I had to see if you have what it takes to think on your feet and face down a situation you never in your wildest dreams could hope to survive on your own. I told you, didn't I? Something is coming. Something big. Something that requires the sort of nerve you only find in heroes, without the stagnation of their short-lived roles. I want to make sure you're ready."

"Why *me*?" Arlo sighed.

It didn't make sense.

What was it about Arlo that attracted all this attention from people who had no reason to notice a too-human child? There was nothing at all special about Arlo. . . . Sure, her alchemy might be a little further along than what was normal, but you could find people like her by the dozen. All they'd require was a bit of training. "Ready for what? And what *is* it, exactly, you want me to do?"

"Would you like to find out?"

A private grin drew across Luck's face, some knowledge tucked away in the corners of that smile that Arlo couldn't read. They were baiting her—daring her to take their offer. All she had to do was pick up the die and agree to their terms, and whatever it was that was going on, Arlo would have a place in it. "What will you do if I don't?"

"Nothing." The deity shrugged. "I'm only offering this help if you want it. The choice is yours. If you don't want to follow your friends into this battle at all, that choice is yours as well. You don't have to do anything you don't want to do, Arlo Jarsdel."

Arlo looked back at Nausicaä.

Her gaze wandered to the soft gleam of gold that gilded Nausicaä's right hand from the fingertips to mid-forearm—a thin layer only, but no magic they'd tried had been able to wash it off. Arlo suspected Nausicaä would be amused by it more than anything else.

She'd be less amused by other things. There was no way she wouldn't chase down what she was going to learn upon waking, for starters. A Hunter had his hand in this, and she didn't need any more motivation to hurtle after death than she'd already exhibited. Nausicaä wouldn't let a betrayal this grand go ignored or unpunished—of that, Arlo had no doubt.

The part of Nausicaä that was still a Fury was reflected in the shards of her past.

And the two of them, they were . . . something.

Arlo thought on the kiss they'd shared just that night. She had no idea what it meant, what she herself *wanted* it to mean, but she knew with absolute certainty that Nausicaä was important to her.

They were a team, if nothing else, and just as Arlo wouldn't have made it out of that factory without Nausicaä, she was starting to realize Nausicaä wouldn't have fared too well without *her*. Nausicaä would need the luck that had saved them both now more than ever if what this deity—Titan?—told Arlo was true.

A dark and hollow star.

Arlo didn't understand it yet—this compulsion inside her to *look* at Nausicaä in a way she'd never looked at anyone else, and come away breathless. What she did understand was that wherever Nausicaä went, she was going to follow.

Taking a breath for courage, Arlo stretched her hand to pick the die up off the bed.

"All right, Dungeon Master—I accept. Read me the rules."

Riadne

O F ALL THE IMPROVEMENTS she'd made to the palace since her coronation, Riadne felt particular fondness for her columbarium. It amused her, the fear its mere existence aroused, the dread that drained the color out of those she summoned before it. It comforted her, the reminder it served that *she* was the one in control now, that in one of those niches was the heart of her mother, a torment never again able to touch her. It inspired her, the knowledge that soon Azurean's heart would join her collection too.

Above all else, it kept her safe. Few could even manage to look at it, let alone get close enough to examine its contents to discover that one of these slots was in fact a lever, that the columbarium was in fact a door, and that on the other side was a heart of a different sort—the other half of her office, where she kept many things she didn't want the world to learn just yet.

Not until their planned reveal on the Solstice.

"Why did you let him live so long?"

Sealed away in this private space, Riadne traced a finger on the glass of a handsome mahogany cabinet around an object placed on a shelf within. Its appearance was much too innocuous for what she knew it to be—obsidian black, more like a lump of coal than a heart; Pride, the very first stone she'd acquired; the stone Azurean had long been guarding; the stone that wasn't truly hers yet, and neither was the longevity it bestowed, not until its previous possessor died; the stone Lethe had switched for a fake and brought her years ago when all of this first began.

She turned around. "Hieronymus Aurum—you let him live much

too long. He'd created his stone—why didn't you just kill him then and have done with it?" Mockery tugged at the corner of her mouth. "Don't tell me it was sentiment. Don't tell me you actually *cared* for that pawn?"

Lethe glared at her from her desk, where he sat with his legs stretched out on its surface. He was pretty as a rose strung up to dry, something once beautiful, forever trapped in the space between his last breath of life and the rot of death. Her sometimes lover—never friend. They were oil and tar, barely getting along, but Riadne needed him. Lethe needed her. "I let him live because I let him live. I don't have to explain myself to *you*. Catch."

He threw her the stone he'd been tossing between his hands, solid gold and polished to a point that Riadne could see herself reflected in its misshapen facets.

Pride . . . The stones had an order they had to be created in. Pride had to be summoned first, and luckily for her, someone had already done the work required to create its vessel. Greed had been next in line. Two down, five more stones to go—five more alchemists to sacrifice to their cause. Once a stone was made, it could be used by anyone, ironborn or not, but to be created . . .

"I hope you aren't as attached to the others," she warned, opening the cabinet to place this new acquisition beside its kin. She closed it once more and turned back around. "The stones won't answer to anyone else until its current possessor dies. I trust you won't let sentiment betray me, Lethe. You started this; you're the one who came to me looking for the means to secure your freedom. If you let me fall, if you let this fail, I'll bring you right down with me—you, and the girl you're protecting."

Baring his teeth in a silent hiss, Lethe rose from her desk. "I wonder who you think you're talking to right now." He poured across the room toward her, seeming to grow larger with every step, filling the room in his temper. "That you would dare to make such a threat against *me*."

He came to a stop, looming over her. Riadne scoffed a laugh and rose a hand to splay it on his chest. "So testy today." She patted the muscle beneath her palm, then slid around him. "I'll give you some time to mourn your broken toy. Get over him quickly. It'll soon be time for our next in line to make their big debut, and I need you to make sure they're ready."

She made for the door. She had other things to do right now than coddle a pouting immortal—a son to debrief, a meeting to prepare for, and the Solstice growing ever closer.

"Good luck."

Riadne paused. "Excuse me?" she asked over her shoulder.

Lethe was a sudden presence at her back, an oppressive shadow that filled her with a wriggling *wrongness*, his magic like worms against her skin. But Riadne was a queen—she made no visible reaction to this display of dominance, however much she wanted to flinch away. "Good luck. You'll need it if you think the likes of *you* could ever 'bring me down.'" She tensed when she felt his lips press against the back of her neck, and Lethe creaked a laugh. His shadow fell away slower than it had enveloped her. "You forget who I am. There's a reason why the Lord of Death himself went out of his way to restrain me."

She whipped around—two could play at cruelty, and cruelty was something Riadne had always been better at than others. But Lethe was already gone.

It didn't matter.

He could underestimate her all he wanted—her wall was filled with the hearts of people who'd done the same. "You can keep your luck," she spat at the empty room. "You forget who *I* am. You forget who I will *be*, once this is over."

Once this was over, once all her players were gathered and all seven stones were hers, once Riadne sat not only as High Queen but greatest of even immortals, she would take much enjoyment in reminding him. She'd turn the freedom he craved into yet another shackle, and bring him to heel with tenfold the degradation he inflicted on her any chance he got. Lethe would plead for her mercy. Lethe would apologize. Like all the others before him who thought they were better than her, Lethe would beg and tremble and cry, and none of it would spare him from the ruin he so deserved.

She didn't need fortune for any of that—to the ones who were foolish enough to hinge their success on such nonsense, she wished *them* good luck.

ACKNOWLEDGMENTS

The path to publication isn't one you walk alone. There are so many people I have to thank for making this book possible, for standing with me through this journey and offering their love and time and support, which in itself leaves me awed and immensely grateful.

To begin, I'd like to thank my family—my mother for teaching me the strength and perseverance necessary to get this done; my father for the video games and bedtime stories that fueled my imagination; my brother and sister, for being the very first friends in my life, my most precious people, both of whom I couldn't be more proud; to my grand-parents, for the gifts of magic and loving family; my stepparents, Steve and Chrystal, for all their enthusiastic support; my aunts and uncles and cousins and stepsiblings, who've all been so enthusiastic about this whole thing; and Diane Larsen, for all the Disney vacations. You have all been invaluable, and I love you each with all my heart.

I've been beyond fortunate to have not one but two brilliant agents behind me and *A Dark and Hollow Star*, and I don't think I'll ever be able to properly express how much it means that both of them saw something worth fighting for in this story. Thank you, Lindsay Mealing, the first of my champions, for our time together and for giving me the tools I needed to take my first steps as an author. Thank you, Mandy Hubbard, for enthusiastically taking up the reins. Thank you, thank you, thank you for loving my girls as fiercely as you do and bringing such passion and determination and belief to this partnership.

Sarah McCabe—you are an absolute FORCE. Thank you for being the editor this story needed. Thank you for seeing this story as worthwhile, for taking that chance, for being the part that *A Dark and Hollow Star* was missing to make it beautiful and whole, and for putting so much patience and energy into getting it there. Thank you for the sheer delight it's been to work with you. Thank you for loving Nos in all her messy, dramatic glory.

Special thanks to the amazing Simon Pulse and McElderry teams—

everyone who's worked on this in any way, including Mara Anastas, Liesa Abrams, Chriscynethia Floyd, Justin Chanda, Karen Wojtyla, Anne Zafian, Laura Eckes, Katherine Devendorf, Rebecca Vitkus, Sara Berko, Jen Strada, Lauren Hoffman, Caitlin Sweeny, Alissa Nigro, Anna Jarzab, Emily Ritter, Savannah Breckenridge, Christina Pecorale and the rest of the sales team, Michelle Leo and her education/library team, Nicole Russo, Mackenzie Croft, Jenny Lu, and Alison Velea. Additional thanks to Christophe Young for your absolutely breathtaking cover art.

For all the ups and downs of publishing, the happiness and tears, celebratory dinners and sad-cake, I wouldn't trade a moment of it, and part of the reason is because it's led me to meeting such wonderful people in the writing community, like Priyanka Taslim, Kat Enright, Natalie Summers, Sadie Blach, Maria Hossain, Zabé Ellor, Erin Grammar, Dan Rogland, Brittany Evans, Jennifer Yen, Adrienne Tooley, the 21ders debut group, the whole of the Toronto Writing Crew, and so many others too numerous to name here, but know that you are all so deeply appreciated.

Thank you to every sensitivity and beta reader who's ever given me even a moment of their time.

Thank you to Kade, for being my rock and supporting the whole heck out of me and my dream, even though it's taken up a great deal of our very limited spare time together.

Thank you to Debbie Belair and my coworkers at the Wine Rack for being there through this entire wild ride; to *Final Fantasy XV* and *Breath of the Wild*, which I played obsessively while writing this; to my cat, Zack, for presiding over this entire process and only occasionally sitting on the computer while I tried to work; to all the queer authors whose books came before this one, as well as the ones that will come after—you are the reason I found the courage to do this.

Jeryn Daly, Colleen Johnston, Abi Alton, Shana VanDusen, Laura Feetham, Jee Hewson, and Jessica Flath—I couldn't have done any of this without any of you. Thank you, for everything. I find it impossible to put into words just how much it's meant to me having you all in my corner, cheering me on; there's family you're born with, and then there's the one you choose—you will always be the heart and soul of everything I do.

To Julianna Will. What do I say? "Thank you" doesn't begin to cover what you deserve for the hours and days you poured into critique/beta reading every version of this story, the phone calls and e-mails and messages, the pep talks and the celebrations at every stage of this game, for all the things you've done to help me turn this dream of mine into a reality, and most importantly, all the adventures we've gone on together that led to this one. You are a rare, true light in this world. I'm forever and always honored to call you my friend.

And lastly, but certainly not least, a very large thank-you to *you*, the reader. Once upon a time books were the only space in which I felt heard and seen and safe. I am grateful to you for giving me the chance to pass that favor on.

ABOUT THE AUTHOR

Ashley Shuttleworth is a young-adult fantasy author with a degree in English literature and a slight obsession with *The Legend of Zelda*, *Kingdom Hearts*, and *Final Fantasy*. They currently live in Ontario, Canada, with their cat named Zack and a growing collection of cosplay swords.